PENGU

Trai
the
Heart

Paisley Hope is an avid lover of romance, a mother, a wife and a writer. Growing up in Canada, she wrote and dreamed of one day being able to create a place, a world where readers could immerse themselves, a place they wished was real, a place they saw themselves when they envisioned it. She loves her family time, gardening, baking, yoga and a good cab sav.

@ @authorpaisleyhope

Also by Paisley Hope

Holding the Reins

Training the Heart

SILVER PINES

BOOK TWO

PAISLEY HOPE

PENGUIN BOOKS

PENGUIN BOOKS

UK | USA | Canada | Ireland | Australia
India | New Zealand | South Africa

Penguin Books is part of the Penguin Random House group of companies
whose addresses can be found at global.penguinrandomhouse.com

Published in Penguin Books 2024
001

Book Design by Cathryn Carter – Format by CC

Typeset in 10.92/14.11pt Fanwood by Jouve (UK), Milton Keynes
Printed and bound in Great Britain by Clays Ltd, Elcograf S.p.A.

The authorised representative in the EEA is Penguin Random House Ireland,
Morrison Chambers, 32 Nassau Street, Dublin D02 YH68

A CIP catalogue record for this book is available from the British Library

ISBN: 978–1–804–95374–7

www.greenpenguin.co.uk

MIX
Paper | Supporting
responsible forestry
FSC
www.fsc.org   FSC® C018179

Penguin Random House is committed to a
sustainable future for our business, our readers
and our planet. This book is made from Forest
Stewardship Council® certified paper.

A Note from the Author

For Kentucky Derby race training, the purchasing of a yearling, the road to the derby and racehorse training in general consults were used, but please understand this book is a work of fiction and terms, events and the road to Wade & Ivy's Kentucky Derby may not be an exact replica of anyone else's. Remember: Fiction is supposed to be fun and events may be changed to meet the storyline.

Warnings:
Open door sexual content (a lot)
The impression of fertility struggles—discussion of
Past emotional abuse—discussion of
Past alcoholism—discussions of
Breath/rough play/anal sex/dirty talk (a lot)

To those searching for their grumpy, loyal, protective cowboy who will tattoo "mine" on his hand just so it looks pretty wrapped around your throat, don't give up, babe.
Your Wade Ashby is out there.

GLOSSARY

Yearling—A horse between the ages of one and two

Breezing—A horse's fastest pace

Juvenile—A horse between the ages of two and three

Qualifier—A prep race for a horse before races that count toward
          their points

Handily—When a horse does work without help

Turn Out—The action of letting a horse wind down

Switch Leads—When a horse changes its front foot

ALEXA . . . PLAY
Wade & Ivy's
LOVE STORY

https://open.spotify.com/playlist/1UQsaNVH6fgsuQ59UylIrJ?si=a643082d82df4fc5

1. *Stone's Throw*—The Red Clay Strays
2. *Coming Home*—Leon Bridges
3. *The Devil Wears a Suit and Tie*—Colter Wall
4. *Like a Wrecking Ball*—Eric Church
5. *Spotless* (feat. The Lumineers)—Zach Bryan
6. *Sand In My Boots*—Morgan Wallen
7. *I Feel a Sin Comin' On*—Pistol Annies
8. *Heart Like a Truck*—Lainey Wilson
9. *In Your Love*—Tyler Childers
10. *Bells of Every Chapel* (feat. Billy Strings)—Sierra Ferrell
11. *Son of a Bitch*—Jessie Murph
12. *forefathers – Stripped Back*—Liam St. John
13. *Porch Light*—Josh Meloy
14. *If I Had a Lover*—Dylan Gossett
15. *Worst Way*—Riley Green

PROLOGUE
Wade

July

"In my defense, it was the *longest* slow burn in history. I just lost track of time, and then there was a detour on the way here . . ."

I shuffle down the front steps of the big house, while this small, animated woman just rambles on beside me, trying to explain in way too much fucking detail the reason why she's late for her interview with me.

I stare out to the field wondering what the fuck she's talking about and what the fuck a *slow burn* is.

She continues laying out the entire damn plot as I breathe in the late morning Kentucky mountain air, knowing somehow that I'm going to regret asking this but fuck, I just need her to get to the goddamn point.

"Explain," I say.

"Explain? A slow burn? Or how the book made me late?" She doesn't even give me room to answer if I wanted to. "Slow burn is . . . you know, the part that leads up to . . . the spicy side of the book . . ."

Spicy?

She waits all of one millisecond for me to speak, and when I don't, she continues. "Anyway, the main character I liked the best, he had just kissed her, finally . . . because the other man she was with, he had just finished, they were roommates—"

I stop and spin around, startling her as I look down at her with a face that I'm sure asks her what on earth she's talking about.

She blinks and looks up at me, realizing she definitely has gone off the goddamn rails here. But for some reason she *still* keeps talking. "Well, what I mean is, he was about to get his own turn with her and . . ." She trails off for less than one second, looking down at her boots, then starts again. "Anywho . . . I'm here now, so I can find out later which one of them—"

Nope.

"Just . . . Jesus Christ . . . Do you understand what it means to be professional? At all?" I ask, stopping her from finishing that sentence because I somehow think that discussing her book—that sounds a hell of a lot like some kind of porn—might be considered sexual harassment, although at this moment, I think I might be the one being violated.

Her mouth pops open but she doesn't speak. I take that as my cue to continue walking.

"I'm sorry for being late, and for wasting your time, Mr. Ashby," she says in a much more professional tone, as if I'm giving up on her before the interview even starts. Which, until right this second, I was.

I grit my molars. Something about the way she says my name all defeated like that brings me down a peg. Maybe my family is right. Judging by how nervous this woman sounds right now, maybe I was too abrupt with her when she showed up for her interview all of six minutes late. I just didn't have the patience. All I want is to get through this goddamn day and take a breather after a long-as-fuck morning with my lawyers and my ex, Janelle.

I stop my long stride again, ready to turn and face this little spitfire, to tell her we'll start the interview over on a much more professional level. Before I can even speak, I realize she's moving too fast and she's not looking up so she doesn't even notice I've stopped until she plows right into me and stumbles backward in the grass.

"Fuck, shit. Fuck . . . I'm sorry," she offers as I grip her elbows easily in my hands to steady her.

"Look, Miss . . ." I let her elbows go as she regains her balance, trying hard not to notice how pretty her violet blue eyes are when she looks up into mine.

"Spencer." She says it as if it would be beyond rude that I'd forget her name. The one she just repeated when she met my family less than five minutes ago.

Okay, maybe it is, even for me.

"Right. Miss Spencer, I'm gonna cut the bullshit right now." I turn and start to walk again, and she keeps up as I approach my office doors and plow by two ranch hands that physically stop their work to check the woman out keeping pace beside me. I shake my head at them as we pass because they're all a bunch of fucking hornballs on my ranch.

"I'm not looking for somebody inexperienced here," I say. "Even though it's only temporary, I need an experienced trainer to take Sam's place."

I push through my office doors and she follows me. As I walk around the back of my desk, she stands on the other side, in her worn-in jeans, perfectly fitted black t-shirt and matching black cowboy boots, arms folded under her perky tits, holding them up like a little shelf. My eyes meet hers and I realize something I said pissed her right off.

"Oh, I get it, you're one of *those?* You think just because I'm young and a woman that I'm inexperienced?"

I take my hat off and toss it on my desk. *Fuck me, I'm the furthest thing from one of those. This bratty little—*

3

"I can see I'm wasting my time expecting better of you," she challenges.

I lean forward, placing my palms on my desk, speaking low so she realizes I'm done entertaining her attitude, and fuck, I'm the one in charge here—not her.

"It has nothing to do with you being a woman. Some of the most respected trainers in the industry are women. Hell, the trainer you're here to replace now, is a woman."

Something in her eyes softens and looks almost sheepish, as she drops her arms to her sides.

"Oh, I just assumed with the name Sam—"

"Samantha," I cut her off. "Assumptions most always get you nowhere," I add gruffly.

I rake my hand through my hair and sit down, leaning back in my chair. She's got a feisty attitude, I'll give her that, and she's probably the prettiest woman I've laid eyes on in, hell, a really long time. Alright, she's fucking breathtaking. I'm talking my-dick-stood-at-attention-the moment-she-tossed-her-long-raven-colored-hair-over-her-shoulder-as-her-boots-hit-the-dirt breathtaking.

Ivy Spencer. I look at her now and wonder how I could've forgotten her name.

She follows suit, relaxing a little as she sits down across from me. I take a breath before I continue. I wasn't intending for this interview to start off so intensely. I'm not actually an asshole. I just have so much going on all the damn time that I speak swiftly, and nine times out of ten, out of frustration just so I can move onto the next task.

"Look, if we're being honest here, you are young, you can't have more than what? Five years' experience?"

There's that defiant look again. Her heart-shaped face gives nothing away—high cheekbones, a slender straight nose, and plump pink lips, those features are all perfectly settled. It's her eyes. Her eyes are stormy and tell me she's fixing to put me in my place, and fast. If I wasn't so fucking exhausted today it might amuse me.

"Almost *fifteen,* actually. If you count all my intern hours, but even without that, I have a degree in Equine Studies from U of K, on a full scholarship, five years of training thoroughbreds at Bellingham Ranch . . ." She cocks a brow as if to ask, *impressed yet, Mr. Ashby?* "Three years at Nottingham Rehabilitation Center before that as a cooperative. Oh, and four summer internships with the American Quarter and Thoroughbred Association under Peter Sampson during high school and college." She mentions a well-known trainer that helped to train the 2015 Triple Crown winner.

Well, fuck.

"Hasn't anyone ever told you? Assumptions most always get you nowhere," she says. A coy little grin turns her pretty lips up, and something about it makes me want to do all sorts of things, most of which are highly inappropriate, to wipe that look right off her face.

I grunt and she seems to relax a little.

"Look, I'm good at what I do. I have a modern approach I'm guessing this ranch doesn't run with—one that might help you, especially if you're hoping to make another derby run at some point," she offers.

I look at her and wonder if she could possibly be the one to take over. Fifteen years? So she's been working with horses since she was . . . a kid? I shake my head, some compartment of my brain asking me why I'm so interested in her life story.

She stands up and motions to the door.

"You want to show me around this place while we talk or is this interview just going to be you sitting there judging me silently?"

My mouth falls slack for a brief moment at her sassy tone, then I get it together and return my hat to my head as I stand.

"Barns are this way," I huff out as I breeze by her.

Twenty minutes later, we're standing outside our large arena watching one of our trainers, Dusty, try to work with a nervous new colt. This colt is skittish, and just getting him to keep eyes and not spook has been a task.

Ivy stands watching, learning the horse's ways like she has a telepathic connection with him while I answer questions from three of my ranch hands. For some reason, all of a sudden they've decided they need to be working right where Ivy and I are. As if I don't know it's because she's the attraction of the hour.

One of my leads is chatting Ivy up like they're old friends. They laugh, and I instantly know this woman cannot work here. She's too distracting, too charming. These fuckers will never get anything done if she's here, and I'm all about productivity on my ranch. The last thing I need is one more thing to worry about on the daily.

"How's it going, Sarge?" Nash, my lifelong friend, claps me on the back, coming from breakfast at the big house with my mother and sister.

"Argh," I grunt out.

"That good?" he asks, chuckling. "You think maybe you're being too hard on her. Six minutes late? Really?"

"Maybe. Her resume is good." I give that much to him, watching as she grabs a training stick down from the tack wall and takes it upon herself to enter the corral.

Nash and I look at each other and then quickly go after her as she swings the gate open, making sure it's safe to enter.

"Mind if I try?" she asks Dusty boldly.

Dusty looks at her like, *who the fuck is this?* And then he smiles wide.

"Have at it, he's a stubborn bugger, won't let me assert any type of dominance with him."

She nods and takes her place in the ring in front of the feisty horse.

"You ever heard of the Parelli program?" she asks both Dusty and myself.

"Can't say I have," I say as I watch her take the leader rope from Dusty. She's a different person now than she was when she was all fired up in my office. This woman right here is calm, collected and perfectly at home around this antsy horse. She takes a moment to graze one hand down his nose and whispers something to him none of us can hear.

"It's the idea that horsemanship can be obtained naturally through communication, understanding and psychology, versus mechanics, fear and intimidation."

She takes the training stick and lets the string hanging off the bottom come up and rest over the horse's back before sliding it off gently. The horse spooks, but instead of her tightening up on his rope, Ivy simply raises a hand to him and then gives the horse more space.

"That's not the way we do it around here," I say to her as I lean up to the rail and watch her, because fuck, watching Ivy with this horse is almost mesmerizing.

"Why do you do it the old-fashioned way?" she queries.

To which I lamely reply, "Because that's the way it's always been done."

Ivy keeps moving, trading between trailing the string over the horse's back and swiping it in circles like a lasso in the dirt. Every time the horse spooks, she whispers something to him and then centers him by bringing the string back over his barrel, and fuck, after ten minutes of this continuously, he manages to keep his eyes on her and move with her for a solid thirty seconds, calmly rounding in a circle with her as she leads him.

"See, the way I've been trained is, you want to have a real partnership with your horse. That requires earning his trust and helping him to feel safe. And we can't do that with the old-fashioned, traditional training methods. What they do look for is

7

safety and security. And if they don't find that with us, they will never trust us. They will never become willing partners."

"Sounds like some kind of new age, hippy shit to me," I bark out, without thinking, as Nash nudges me in the ribs with his elbow. Clearly, what she's doing is working. I just don't like being wrong, or out of control. Both of which I am right now.

Ivy takes the horse around the pen a few more times, continuing her method, and when she's satisfied he's had enough she unhooks the leader and lets him loose. Walking up to me she pushes the training stick to my chest, looks up at me with those blue eyes and says, "Hey, you're the Chief around here, I'm just telling you what's worked for me is all. Just like working with people, you gotta build respect, not just expect it. Thanks for the opportunity, I'd love to help your family's ranch while Sam is away." She breezes between Nash and me and turns to look back over her shoulder. "That is if you don't *assume* I'm not up to the task." She smiles as she says it.

Nash leans into me and whispers, "Fuck, Sarge. I think you just met your match."

I cross my arms over my chest and watch her go, knowing full well not only is she going to be trouble, but fuck, she pretty much just hired herself.

CHAPTER ONE
Wade

October

"*Before my mind is ready, my body is. Chase grabs me by the back of my head, fisting my hair as his mouth devours mine.*"

"Christ almighty, do you do anything else?" I grunt as I fumble to turn down the volume on the stereo that isn't mine in the truck I don't own.

"*I want him on his knees. I want him to drown in my—*"

"You need help there, Chief?" Ivy giggles beside me as I finally grasp the right knob to turn down her audiobook so we can avoid listening to the narrator climax us all the way back to the ranch.

"I've got it," I bite out. I push two silky hair ties down on the shifter so I can pop Ivy's Silverado into reverse.

Not surprised I have to fight off these damn things to be able to do something as simple as drive. In the few short weeks Ivy has worked on my ranch, I'm pretty sure she's left one in every crevice of the silos office imaginable. It was day one, when she left one on my desk, then came looking for it later, that I learned hair elastics have a specific name when they're all soft and fluffy like this—*scrunchie*—and Ivy hoards them. All different shades, all different patterns, as if she may suddenly need thirty-two extra at a moment's notice. She has a tower of them on her desk, every color of the rainbow and then some. Bright and happy-looking twenty-four-seven—just like her.

In fact, everything about this woman is feminine and sun-shiny, including this truck of hers I've been roped into driving tonight. There's a piña colada air freshener hanging from the rearview and a mishmash of lip balms and hand creams in the cup holders. It's a goddamn beauty parlor on wheels.

Her crimson-painted lips curl into a devilish grin with my open disdain of her book choice.

"Drive a girl's truck and you have to live with the consequences." Ivy laughs. "You know I like my books." Her wide, almond-shaped eyes dance with mischief as she pulls *my* blazer tight over her red evening dress. I lost it to her when she said she was cold and Cole's sleazy cop buddy was about to offer his to her. I'm driving her home. It only makes sense she wears mine.

"Just another way for me to shake your nerves, boss . . . don't you know I do it on purpose?" She giggles as I shake my head at her.

I don't doubt she does. She's been throwing me off and test-ing my 'always in control, always have a plan' mantra since the first day I met her. But she was clearly the best choice as our temporary lead horse trainer. I'll admit she impressed me during her interview, and her mentor with the AQTA wouldn't shut up about her when I called him for a reference.

After working with her day in and day out over the last few weeks, I can see what he was raving about. Ivy is brilliant, with a knack for calming the horses and connecting with them like no one I've ever seen; she never loses her patience with any of them, from our feistiest colts to our slow-as-molasses old steeds.

But fuck, she gets under my skin. It's not her fault, it's mine, because I'm having a hard time ignoring that not only is she gorgeous, but the more I get to know her, the more I realize she's totally oblivious to her looks and her sassy, alluring charm. Which means she thinks nothing of it when every ranch hand I have bends over backward to get up early and deliver her coffee in the morning, or when they offer to take on some of her morning chores for her. These pricks have never shown up early for work a day in their lives, and all of a sudden, they're in the barn before the roosters rise and happy as fuck about it?

Ivy is thrilled they're all 'so nice', as she's told me on many occasions, which leads me to believe for how experienced she presents herself to be, she is a bit naive about the opposite sex.

This has me both keeping an eye out for her constantly and sobering myself up from getting caught staring at her too. I'm holding it together, but it's only been a few weeks and I'm pretty sure the balance of it has aged me ten years already.

I salute my younger brother Cole goodbye out my window as I pull out of our town pub's parking lot. He's standing in the doorway of the Horse and Barrel watching me go, grinning like a fool at me driving Ivy's truck off the lot.

I'm only her chauffeur because my sister CeCe and her girl crew adopted Ivy as one of their own tonight. Inviting her to celebrate CeCe's new engagement 'Not Angels'–style. Which basically means, drink way too much, and dance all night long on the Horse and Barrel dance floor. So here I am, leaving anyone behind us with a bumper sticker that says "*cowgirls just wanna have fun.*"

I look over at her smug grin, and I gather she thinks her book smut has embarrassed me.

"I'm sorry I made you blush at my romance novel," she hums as she pulls her hair down, not sounding sorry in the slightest. I watch in my periphery as it tumbles in waves around her shoulders.

"It takes more than a little *smut* to make me blush," I retort.

Ivy makes a wounded face at my words.

"It's a steamy romance book, not *smut*, and it was just getting to the good part when I got to the bar. I was looking forward to it for on the way home. I didn't expect you'd be driving me." She snickers, still not a hint of embarrassment in her tone.

It's not lost on me that not only does she read it any chance she gets, she also just drives around town listening to full-out porn on any given day and owns it. I'm all about a woman being confident in her own skin and enjoying sex and everything it has to offer, but because I'm my own worst enemy, I scoff at the term she used—*romance*—loud enough for her to swat at me.

She laughs, the cocky laugh of too many "Nash and CeCe are engaged so let's party" shots. "Well, we can't all be grumpy prudes, so excuse me for enjoying a good love story."

I'm just going to keep my mouth shut here. I'm the furthest thing from a prude she'll ever meet. In fact, I'm a firm believer that there should be no limits when it comes to sex. To hold back would be a waste in the one area of life you can let go—an escape.

So . . . grumpy? Sure. Prude? Not a fucking chance.

"Oh no you don't, don't even think you're staying quiet. Inquiring minds want to know, what's making you huff out all those judgy noises at me? Have you got something to say about my choice in literature?" Ivy challenges, then adds, "Cat got your tongue?"

I scrub my face with my free hand. I'm still not completely used to this smug little firecracker and the way she manages to get under my skin.

"Come on now, spill it," she says, cocking one eyebrow at me. I turn to her for a split second while I drive.

"The plot of this book has fucking nothing to do with love or romance," I deadpan, pointing to the dash.

"Yes, it does," Ivy argues defensively, feigning shock before she adds, "I mean, they both seem to love her in their own way."

They? Jesus fucking Christ.

"Alright, I'll bite. Let's start with this. What's it *called*?" I ask as we pass the Laurel Creek town sign and start cruising through the dark countryside.

"What's it called?" She repeats my question, taking her plush bottom lip between her teeth.

"That's right. This steamy romance you're hell-bent on defending, what's the title?" I look over at her, counting the seconds she sits in silence. "What's the matter?" I ask. "Smutty book name got your tongue?"

Ivy grimaces. "No . . . it's just, that's not a fair question because the title doesn't sound romantic."

Now I'm invested.

She looks down to check her nails, in the dark no less, as if they need her attention desperately.

"What's the name, Trouble?" I repeat.

Ivy sighs and stares out the window. "*Filthy Lords of Sin,*" she whispers, barely audible.

I nod. "My mistake. Sounds mighty romantic."

Ivy huffs out a breath but doesn't say one more word on the subject and keeps her eyes out the window.

I rest my fucking case.

I let her off the hook and get the radio working. Colter Wall croons to us as we drive. I settle into it. But the silence only lasts all of three minutes because this woman must talk cheerful chatter at all times.

"What a beautiful party for the sweetest couple. I know I've only been here a little while but I really like your family. They're all so nice."

"Yeah, they're all just swell," I say, sounding way more bitter than I intend, before I add, "Never thought I'd see Nash settle down."

My best friend of twenty years and soon-to-be brother-in-law—officially. It was a surprise to say the least, when I found out he was seeing CeCe in secret all summer. But after I had the chance to calm down and realize what his intentions were, I knew without a doubt that they were perfect for each other. Even if their constant kissing and hand-holding makes me want to toss up my last meal, I'm glad Nash and my baby sister are happy together, and maybe they'll actually break the Ashby curse that has always plagued the three of us when it comes to relationships.

"I just have one question, and stop me if it's too personal," Ivy queries.

Ah, fuck.

"Don't do personal," I bite out.

"You don't say?" Sarcasm lines her tone. "I promise it won't sting, I'm just curious." She takes my silence as the go-ahead. "I just don't get it, what's the real story behind your family then?"

I blink at her, not understanding.

"I mean, they're all so nice and welcoming and they seem like fairly happy people, so are you like, adopted, maybe grew up in a different household? The long-lost brother that still holds a grudge?"

I turn to look at her. Ivy's blue eyes dance with all the trouble that earned her that nickname. I feel my brow furrow as she laughs at her semi-funny joke for way longer than warranted.

"You know . . . your face does things other than scowl?" she muses as we pull down the driveway of Silver Pines, my family's ranch and training center. My home. My responsibility.

I pass my cabin on the old dirt road to get her home. Ivy has taken Blue Eyes, our fifth cabin, as her humble abode for her time here. It's the one closest to mine. She could have chosen any of the cabins that were empty but she chose Blue Eyes for two reasons that she prattled on about. One, because her eyes are blue, which in my opinion is kind of an understatement. They're so blue they're almost violet some days, the color of a cloudless winter sky . . . or whatever.

And her second self-proclaimed reason was because the Blue Eyes deck backs onto the north woods, and she says she likes her privacy.

Probably so she can sit out there and read her smutty books in peace.

"Home sweet home," she quips as she turns to me. "Well, thanks for driving me home, Captain Joyful, it was a fun night aside from the last fifteen minutes, of course."

The only response I give her is a huff as I hop out of the truck and walk around to her side. Ivy removes my suit jacket from her curvy frame and hands it to me as she climbs out.

"I'm not cold anymore, thanks," she says as I take it and trade with her, dropping her keys into her palm. Our size difference is a lot more noticeable when we're only a foot apart. She barely reaches past the top of my shoulder even in those shoes she's wearing. I wait, expecting her to go into her house, but instead, she mumbles something like *"not waiting one more second"* as she struggles to remove her black heels in the grass.

"Mmm . . . goddamn, that feels good." She groans a throaty sound that makes me swallow, *hard*. "I've been wanting to do that all night." She giggles innocently as the other heel comes off and a few more inches disappear from her height. She turns a smile up to me.

I look away from her to clear my head of the noises she's making while she mumbles how good the grass feels on her bare feet, something about grounding herself to the earth, while I gesture to her front door. She looks at it, then back to me with an *are you serious?* face.

"I think I'll make it in, boss; you can go home now. I mean, you can see my porch from your porch." She points at my cabin, only two hundred feet away.

I shake my head. "I'll go home once you're inside."

She tips her head back and laughs as she saunters up her front steps. "Okay, I'll humor you," Ivy calls over her shoulder. "But only because I've had a few drinks. I'm a big girl though, I can handle myself." She pats her purse and winks. "Bear spray."

Of course she has bear spray in her purse. The little spitfire probably wouldn't even need it, she'd probably bond with the bear and feed it from her back door.

"Night, Chief, see ya early," she singsongs. Her door closes and I'm left standing there shaking my head at the whirlwind that is Ivy Spencer.

I toss my coat over my forearm and walk the short distance to my own cabin, Bluegrass.

My cabin is the biggest on the property besides the big house itself. It's the boss's cabin, the only one with two bedrooms and two bathrooms, and I've finally got it the way I want it after being back here since my separation. I did most of the work myself to update the kitchen, with Cole's help.

I walk through the front entryway and flick the light on. I breathe in a sigh of peace. This is my place. Dark log cabin walls and weathered wood floors fill the open space. It still smells faintly like leather and tobacco from previous residents over the years. The little kitchen straight ahead has new walnut cabinets and stainless steel appliances.

There is a good-sized living room to the left, with a floor-to-ceiling cobblestone fireplace and windows that look out to the big house and barns in the distance. It's the perfect place to sit with a whiskey at the end of the day listening to my favorite vinyl. It's also the only place I don't have to worry about leading everyone, about the ranch, my mom living alone as she gets older, filling my dad's boots, Janelle, the future.

This is my space to just be Wade, whoever the fuck that is these days. No time for self-reflection when you have an entire ranch to run and next year's derby pressure breathing down your neck. I loosen my tie and toe my uncomfortable-as-fuck dress shoes off. I'm mentally going over tomorrow's workday as I feel something light hit my foot while I'm hanging up my suit coat.

I bend down and scoop it up to get a closer look. Ivy was wearing my coat for all of twenty goddamn minutes. I bring the soft fabric to my nose and breathe in Ivy's sweet, sugary-like scent. *Fuck me*, it's nice. I pop the black satin scrunchie in the basket on my fridge as I head for the shower.

Finders keepers.

CHAPTER TWO
Wade

NASH

Morning boys. @Sergeant, thanks for taking one for the team last night and driving Ivy home. I made sure your truck was locked when I left and I can come grab you to pick it up later.

NASH

Also, did she have fun? Rae won't stop talking about her.

She had too much fun because this family never seems to keep a professional boundary

COLE

@Nash Pay him no attention. He's just pissy because he had to sit two feet from her and pretend he didn't notice how she looked in that red dress.

She's my employee

NASH

Your employee? I said that once too. Something about thinking you shouldn't that makes you want to look at her even more?

COLE

Fuck. We've talked about this too many times. It has to stop.

NASH

Sorry, you two are my only friends 🙍

NASH

I didn't even see you two leave? I came back from my office and you were gone.

We looked for you but you and CeCe were MIA and we didn't want to know why

COLE

Again, not the image I need to add to my morning coffee, Jesus.

NASH

I plead the fifth and boys, thanks for being there. I can't fucking believe I'm engaged.

COLE

LOL the best part is, he has no idea

Fuck no he doesn't, not a clue.

NASH

The fuck are you two talking about?

COLE

Just brace yourself

NASH

Brace myself for what? A lifetime of happiness?

I smirk. I know exactly where Cole is going with this.

CeCe planning a wedding. Imagine what she's like at the office and times that by about a million

NASH

You're exaggerating. She'll be fine. Weddings are supposed to be fun.

COLE

Narrator: It was at that exact moment that he realized he was fucked.

NASH

Fuck me

Have a nice day bud

I slide my phone in my pocket and glance out the window. The sun is just clearing the top of Sugarland Mountain as I pop the lid onto my travel mug of coffee and start the walk from Bluegrass to the main barns. Normally, I'd drive so I have my truck on hand for the day, but since my truck is still sitting in the Horse and Barrel parking lot, I'm relying on two feet and my heartbeat this morning and I'm looking forward to the short walk to clear my head.

My mind wanders to my father, as it usually does. He's been gone just over ten months; sometimes it feels like an eternity, sometimes it feels like yesterday. That's just the way grief works, I suppose. Everything I do on this ranch, I do hoping it's what he would've done. We've finally made a good profit this summer. Our boarding stalls are full, we're running lessons and offering training again.

Last year was lackluster for us. He was so sick, I was dealing with my separation from Janelle and we just let things fall a bit by the wayside. Now, I feel like I've got my focus back, jumping right in, and I'm seriously considering doing what my mom and siblings want. Using Ivy's time here to help me find a one-year-old horse of our own, and start training it for next year's derby qualifiers. The whole process and road to a derby will take our ranch over a year and a half, and even then, we may not make it. The Kentucky Derby isn't the most lucrative financially, but it's the pinnacle, and following in my dad's footsteps by entering a prize thoroughbred seems inevitable.

We have the time and resources to do it finally, but we need to get on finding our competitor so we can start training right away. It's going to take everything I've got, all the help Ivy can offer me and a small fortune to do it, but with our financial situation looking up thanks to Nash's help and having a much better year all around, I think it's possible. I could take Ivy under my wing, give her the training experience and a little separation from my desperate little ranch hands that can't stop staring at her.

"Morning, boss." Ivy smiles as I cross into the barn. She looks so fresh faced and ready for the day. Her raven-colored hair is piled high on her head in a big messy bun, soft little wisps frame her face, which is free of makeup. She's wearing one of her many pairs of Levi's jeans that fit her ample curves like a second skin and a white, perfectly fitted and low-cut Eric Church tour t-shirt that her full breasts are seriously challenging the confines of.

Yeah, I know, she's my employee, but I am a man. And any man would have to be dead not to notice Ivy.

"You don't seem too worse for wear after all those margaritas," I observe.

"I brought her a coffee from the big house," Haden, my lead ranch hand, pipes up from a stall. Of course he did, and of course he's already here helping her when he should be leading a small team to muck out all the stalls. Would you look at that dedication?

"Heard she needed it after last night." He grins.

Ivy smiles a megawatt smile at him that makes me grit my molars. He's the last one I want bringing Ivy anything.

"Your family sure knows how to party," she states as she closes the stall she was working in.

"Hmmphh," I grumble.

Haden chuckles at my lack of words but Ivy doesn't bat an eye at my response. At this point she's just used to it.

"Oh, and I printed out the registration info for Nashville, and left it on your desk, if you're interested. It's on the twenty-seventh. Have you thought any more about it?" she asks.

Right, the annual Nashville breeding sale. Our best chance to buy a yearling.

"I have been thinking about it," I say, rubbing my jaw. "We need a jockey and a shit ton of time to train next winter and spring, plus I'd be forgoing a lot here to work on it."

Ivy nods, used to my indecisiveness on the matter. We've been going back and forth since before she officially came on board.

"I can help Ivy in any way you want, boss," Haden pipes up, ping-ponging between my face and Ivy's. "I can accompany her for any training exercises with the yearling, take on more chores here, whatever you guys need. I could even go to Nashville, Ivy could come too ... if you're too busy and you want her feedback?"

Ivy eyes him hopefully, then looks back to me. "It's a solution if you're worried," she offers.

Like fuck it is. Haden's been looking at her like she's dessert since she stepped onto this ranch, and although he's a good cowboy, the best I've got maybe, he's a proverbial manwhore. He's been with more Laurel Creek buckle bunnies than anyone in town, even Cole. And for that reason, the idea of him spending copious amounts of alone time with Ivy feels like a great big *fuck no* to me.

I clear my throat, an impulsive decision creeping in.

"No, I've already decided. Haden, I'll just need you to take on more responsibility for us to do this. To fill in for me when needed, be my eyes and ears here on the ranch as we go through the motions."

What am I doing?

I pull my cowboy hat off and run a hand through my hair as they both stare at me expectantly.

"I've already booked the hotel for us in Nashville," I lie. "We'll go look and see what we think."

"*We?*" Ivy asks, her eyebrows raised in anticipation. I look down at her and nod.

"Yes, you're our trainer right now and for the foreseeable future, so you'll come and have a say," I say lamely.

Ivy squeals and launches her pint-sized frame into mine, taking me by total surprise as she molds under the crook of my arm and locks her hands behind my waist.

"Fuck yes, Chief. I won't let you down. I'll train the shit out of that horse for you, he'll be racing like the wind by the spring," she says excitedly into my ear. Her voice is soft and husky. It's a recognizable voice that makes the little hairs on the back of my neck stand up, especially when she's this close to me, and you can tell she's not trying to make it sound sexy. It just *is*. Her hands on my back, her soft warm body pressed up against mine, coupled with that voice makes for the exact moment that my cock decides to wake up and see what's good.

Settle down, big fella, this is not your cue.

I detach her hands and step back. "Alright. Well, there's lots to sort out so I'll be in the office when you're wrapped up here. Come find me and we'll start planning."

She nods, the look on her face an apology for hugging me. "Sounds good," she says, back to professional.

Haden chuckles from his stall, and I have the sudden urge to cuff him upside the head, as I turn to walk into the silos office.

Time to look for some goddamn hotel rooms.

CHAPTER THREE
Ivy

I've never put much faith in people. It's not that I don't like people, I do. I just find it easier not to get too close to most of them, keep them at a distance. It's much easier for me to relate to animals, especially the horses I work with. People are fickle and will almost always let you down or leave, given the chance. Especially men. In my experience, most men are easy to read. The ones I've met or worked with over the years are one of two things: they're either afraid of me or doing their best to try to fuck me, both figuratively and literally. Most men don't take me seriously and they almost always think they know better than me. The equestrian world is full of these types of men, so I'm no stranger to getting a read on a man and learning where I stand with them real quick.

Until I met Wade Ashby. Wade is certainly not afraid of me, nor does he look at me like he wants to fuck me. Wade Ashby might be the only man I've ever met that is wearing a sort of scowl twenty-four-seven, but oddly enough, despite that, working with him comes easier than with any other man I've ever worked with, because Wade is something else entirely.

Strong, professional, smart as hell, respectful, and so fucking in control all the time it makes me wonder if there's ever a time or circumstance where he loses that control even for a minute. At first glance he appeared unassuming and kind of mysterious, like a sexy Henry Cavill—if Henry was 6'5", played the part of a horse rancher and wore a constant grimace.

Then he opened his mouth, and I learned pretty quickly that Wade Ashby was not going to be the 'get to know you better' type. I've been struggling to keep up with his two moods—grumpy and really fucking grumpy—since I arrived. How furrowed his brow is over those deep green eyes that stare through my soul when he looks at me tells me every morning what kind of day I'm in for. One thing is certain, they're almost always staring at me with a look of disapproval, because Wade is very set in his ways and likes to remind me every chance he gets that my more modern way of training isn't his style.

Since I've recently made a promise to myself not to let anyone fuck with me or my emotions ever again, I give his attitude right back to him most of the time, which oddly enough he seems to appreciate. Most days, Wade's mood is very predictable. But today? Today is the first day he really threw me for a loop and surprised me.

I don't know why Wade decided to firmly commit to finding Silver Pines a new racehorse, but I don't care either. I'm running with it. Twenty-nine years old and training a potential derby horse? Hells yes. It's a far cry from the Winding Eagles trailer park I left behind in Jellico, and it's my shot to make a real name for myself as a trainer.

I've been hoping since the day he hired me that my boss had a sense of adventure under that gruff exterior somewhere, but I wasn't holding out for it. Until now of course, because now he's taking me horse shopping in less than two weeks. I'm so excited I could scream it from the rooftops.

I continue my work with my newest horse buddy, Nutmeg, getting on the thinking side of his brain. I met this horse my first day here. He's come a long way and is Wade's seven-year-old niece Mabel's favorite riding horse. Which makes sense.

My father was a horse vet and he always thought that horses—all animals, really—have kindred spirits, and so far, Nutmeg seems a lot like Mabel, rambunctious and needing a lot of play time. I give him his wind down exercises as I feel my phone buzz in my pocket. I ignore it for a few minutes as I work, then I turn Nutmeg loose into the pen and pull my phone out.

CECE

> Thank you so much for playing guitar for us last night. I hope you had fun.

Have I mentioned—my cranky boss aside—I am in love with his family? They have made me feel so welcome, so of course I said yes when Nash asked me to strum CeCe's favorite Shania Twain song as he proposed last night. Everyone has been ultra-sweet aside from Wade, but I don't take it personally because he looks at *all* of us like it just annoys him to no end that he can't do absolutely everything on this ranch without help.

> It was my pleasure, I had a great time. The Not Angels know how to party.

CECE

> Yes, we do it well.

> I'm not sure how much fun your brother had though. He didn't seem too pleased to have to drive me home.

CECE

> He's never pleased, I just tell people it's part of his charm.

> Tell me about it, he even seems annoyed about making a potential derby run, which in my opinion is super exciting and a cause for some serious celebration. Does he even know the word celebrate?

CECE

> He's decided to make a derby run? For sure?

Shit. I type, then stop myself. Then type again.

> Well, we're going horse shopping so I think so? He didn't tell you?

CECE

> I must have missed that announcement. 😜

> I think I just shoved my foot in my mouth, so act surprised when he tells you?

CECE

> Your secret's safe with me. Whatever the reason, I'm glad he's thinking of going for it. We'll be cheering you on and we're willing to help any way we can.

> Thank you, for not saying anything, and your support.

CECE

> Of course. Us girls need to stick together.

For the second time today, Wade catches me off guard. Why wouldn't he have told his family if he's already booked us hotel rooms?

My phone buzzes again but this time it's not Wade's sister. It's my ex's sister.

27

CHELSEA

> I hate to bug you. Brad won't leave me alone about reaching out to you. I'm sorry to get in the middle and I miss you, I hope you're doing okay.

I sigh and put my phone back in my pocket. *Not today, Satan.*

It's three months since I left Bellingham Ranch and the devil himself, aka Brad. I used to respond to his sister Chelsea and his mother; I actually felt like their family for a time. I try not to be upset with them. I know how persuasive Brad can be when he wants something.

Now I spend my days mostly ignoring them all if they reach out. What I really need is a new cell phone and number. My phone is ancient but it's all I can afford with the financial obligations still weighing on my shoulders. I tried to block Brad's number in the beginning, but then he got creative, messaging from his family's phones or calling me from his ranch. I keep telling myself it will be short-lived. Brad doesn't do well alone. I've been hoping that he'll find someone new to attach himself to and leave me the hell alone. So far, he hasn't figured out where I am and I'm hoping he never does.

I go to fetch Nutmeg and start bringing him to his stall as I ask myself for the millionth time how I *ever* fell for Brad's manipulation. I not only fell for it, I dove right in, head first. He's the Prince of Bellingham Ranch, old money. The kind that seems highbrow on the outside but it's all really a disguise for what lurks underneath.

Although I didn't know it at the time, Brad is a narcissist through and through. One with a mean streak, a side I got heavily acquainted with over the last few years. I grew up like many other little girls, hearing the words "don't ever let a man treat you poorly." And "know your self-worth." I had a great dad who taught me to be strong and bold. But it was so calculating and happened so slowly that I didn't know the emotional hold Brad had on me until I was in it, deep in it. The more dependent I became on him and his ranch, the less he tried to hide his ways. He played on every insecurity I had and made me somehow believe he was the best chance I would ever have of stability and security.

Somewhere in those years with Brad, I lost my own version of myself—the version I was raised to be. Looking back, I believe now my dad was looking down on me and he helped me leave. When the man I'd known since I was a baby, my mentor at the American Quarter and Thoroughbred Association and one of my dad's best friends, told me about Silver Pines looking for a new trainer, something in me said, *This is your chance. Take it.*

It wasn't an easy road to get here, but I made it.

And now, as long as I can keep my new boss from combusting with pure, unfiltered irritation for the next few months, I have a home and a job I'm really loving, not to mention a great addition to my resume when it's my time to move on.

I pop the leader rope and halter on the front of Nutmeg's stall, close it up and breathe out a sigh, taking in the mountain beyond the barn. Brad Bellingham isn't ruining my mood today—no one is, because Ivy Grace Spencer is about to train a derby horse!

HADEN

Sarge is looking like he's going into overdrive waiting on you, he's pacing around on the phone and shit.

HADEN

Better hurry up and get in here before he changes his mind about looking for a new horse.

I grin.

> Maybe you should try giving him a hug, he sounds like he needs one.

HADEN

> I'd like to keep my arms

CHAPTER FOUR

Wade

"You could've just pissed around her ankles, Sarge. Might have been easier than committing to hundreds of thousands of dollars on a horse," Haden says smugly from my office doorway, his arms folded over his chest. I've known him since he was thirteen and sometimes it makes him a little mouthier than the other hands I have on staff. "We all know the ranch rules. She's off limits," Haden adds.

"For fuck sakes." I pull my hat off and throw it on my desk. "She has nothing to do with my decision," I grunt. I have zero patience for this, I've been calling Nashville hotels for reservations for an hour. Of course, the horse auction would be the same weekend as the Nashville Marathon so there's nothing available online. I'm hoping by phoning I may get lucky. So far, I'm coming up empty-handed for a trip I supposedly already booked. This is why I never do things without thinking them through.

"So, if she's got nothing to do with your decision, you won't have any issue with me taking her fine ass to dinner? Maybe a movie? Snuggle in the back row?" Haden grins.

I give him a look of warning. One he knows well by now.

"You're pushing your luck, and you already know my answer to that." He's taking her to dinner over my dead body. "You just said you knew the rule. The last thing I want to do is have to look for another new trainer when you pull your fuckboy routine on her," I add.

Haden chuckles and pulls his hat up to rub his forehead.

"Just getting a rise out of you, boss. But hey, congrats on the path to racing again. Your pa would be proud," he says seriously. "And I mean it, anything you need, I've got you."

I nod in response. As annoying as he is, I know he's got my back around here.

Ivy's husky voice echoes down the hallway. I hear her before I see her, singing a Sierra Ferrell song, and the sound isn't bad. Alright, it's actually really fucking good, as she breezes through her office door, which just so happens to be directly across from mine.

She catches both mine and Haden's attention through my glass window that looks into hers as she pulls a trademark scrunchie, cherry red this time, from her long thick hair. Masses of shiny waves tumble down around her shoulders like water lapping the shore. Haden audibly gulps. To make matters worse, she bends forward to reach into her bag for something and her cleavage makes a spellbinding appearance as her hair falls in front of her. For the second time today, my dick takes notice of her in the most inconvenient moment.

"Fuck," Haden whispers, pulling the word right out of my head. I backhand him in the shoulder for looking at her.

"Sorry, but shit, you had to go and find the hottest horse trainer on the planet and then tell us all she's off limits?"

"You got enough notches on your bedpost," I reiterate, watching in my periphery the way her breasts curve to her slender waist. I bet I could fit both my hands right around her while I—

"Maybe it's time you head to Lexington with Cole, meet

yourself a woman so you can follow your own rules," Haden snickers in a whisper, as he claps a firm hand on my shoulder.

I grunt, pissed that he noticed me looking at her when I'm supposed to be the example here.

"How are you making out, boss?" Ivy knocks on my door frame as she speaks, poking her head into my office and shutting Haden up instantly. He clears his throat and walks around the side of my desk.

"Have you had a chance to go through the auction registration yet?" She looks at her cell phone and approaches us, and from my full height I can see right down her shirt, which is not helping my dick to stand down. I avert my eyes, but fuck—tight, low-cut t-shirts and cleavage are a man's biggest weakness.

"I have an hour before the school tour gets here, if you need any help?" she asks.

I turn to Haden, who's wearing a shit-eating grin on his face that says he sees right through me.

"Sure, come on in." I nod toward the door while keeping my eyes on Haden's so he doesn't look down her shirt, because he fucking will. "Haden was just leaving anyway, got some mucking out to catch up on."

Almost an hour later, we've registered for the auction and have all our ducks in a row. We've also gone over the tempting year-old prospects or 'yearlings.' Derby horses have to be three years old, date specific, to race, which means we'll have over a full year of training and qualifying ahead of us when the horse is two.

I look up at Ivy from my notes and speak.

"There are a few horses I'm looking forward to seeing in

Nashville." *You know, the place we'll be sleeping in my truck if I don't manage to find us a hotel.*

Ivy is animated and full of hope as she talks about her plans and pulls up all the training research she's done that she'll have to execute over the next several months. It will be a full-time job for both of us, leaving Hornball Haden mostly in charge of Silver Pines with me as a consultant.

"This one's sire raced in the derby, and was mated with this dam," Ivy says, pointing a slender finger to names on the screen that mean absolutely nothing to me.

She looks up at me, her violet eyes expectant.

"You have no idea who these horses are, do you?" Ivy asks as I shake my head.

"Never was very good at homework," I say.

She rolls her eyes, and even that is something I can't seem to look away from as she continues. "This one's sire, Prince of Amarillo, came in fourth in the derby in '16, and his dam, Pearl of Night, raced in the Oaks two years ago," she says, mentioning another well-known race. "We'll have to get a small list of prospects together, but this is the one I really want to see." She points at my computer screen again. "Rustling Winds. He could win. Look at how beautiful he is. Look at his bloodlines." Her excitement is contagious as she rambles on. A spark of electricity trails up my spine unexpectedly, thinking about getting involved in racing again. I used to like it. Truth be told, I used to fucking love it. Those years with my dad, I remember feeling alive in the stands, watching with bated breath.

"These yearlings are strong and so well bred, I'm ready to train day and night. I'm determined."

"Well then, I suppose that's all we need," I bite out sarcastically.

"It actually is." Ivy cocks a brow at me. "One thing you may not know about me is when I want something, I get it."

The funny thing is, I don't really fucking doubt her. She just has an aura about her that says she's been through some shit and lived to tell the tale.

"We'll see how we do," I say as I stack up our documents into one neat pile and place them in a folder. I'm taking a big chance, planning something at the last minute like this. I just hope I don't live to regret it. My dad's voice rolls through my mind, telling me to loosen up a little and go with the flow more, just like he always used to.

"On a personal note, Wade, my dad and I used to watch the races together. He taught me to ride, taught me how to connect with the horses, taught me to train really before I was even grown, before he died." Her gaze is focused on a memory for a moment, then her baby blues snap back to mine. "To be a part of something like this has always been a dream, I've just never had the opportunity, so thank you for giving it to me." She places her delicate, warm hand on my forearm. I look down to where she's touching me for just a split second before she pulls away. It's nothing but a friendly pat, but her graze leaves its mark on my skin regardless.

"Sorry, what can I say? I've always been the touchy-feely type, boss. I can't help it, it's part of my makeup." Something about hearing how touchy-feely she is and how close she's sitting to me right now makes me set my jaw and look away from her.

Maybe Haden's right, a trip to Lexington with Cole might just be in order.

She smiles and brushes it off and starts talking because that is just what she does. "I'm really looking forward to the next few months. It's going to be great and amazing publicity for Silver Pines, if we qualify. A new challenge. You'll see." She looks over my shoulder, out toward our large round pen where the noon school tour is taking place and kids have started to gather.

Maybe it's her positive energy output, or the moment, or some combination of both, but for a split second, I almost feel myself grin as her energy and excitement connect with mine.

I can be spontaneous, and fuck, a new challenge might be just what I need.

"Fuck yes, you know what? Let's do this damn thing then," I say.

Ivy looks up at me and her mouth pops open for all of one second at my words, then she giggles as she stands. "That's the spirit, Chief," she says as she starts to gather her things at the same time Haden pops his head in to ask her a question.

My spontaneous mood is interrupted as I look down to my cell on my desk as it buzzes; it lights up with my mother's name.
Fuck.

> **BOSS LADY**
>
> You wanna tell me why I have to hear we're shopping for a derby horse from Haden Brooks?

Should've had that conversation with her first. She doesn't like to be left out and she'll remind me every chance she gets now for the next several weeks, I'm sure.

> You knew I was thinking about it. It's what y'all want isn't it?

> **BOSS LADY**
>
> It is. I just don't like hearing information second hand on my own ranch.

> **BOSS LADY**
>
> Invite Ivy tonight. You both can tell me all about it.

> I'm sure she has better things to do. I can fill you in.

BOSS LADY

> Fine, I'll ask her myself, she won't say no to me, we get on like chocolate and peanut butter.

I grimace and face the inevitable before I answer.

> Goddammit, Mama. I'll ask her since she's standing right here.

BOSS LADY

> Good. I'll see you both later then.

I can almost see my mother's satisfied grin from here. No one ever says no to her.

I huff out a breath and clear my throat. Time to stop my resident horse trainer that no one seems to be able to get enough of before she walks out the door with Haden.

"Ivy . . ."

She turns to face me expectantly.

"You have plans for dinner tonight? My mother has summoned us to talk derby with her."

Ivy's smile spreads across her face like there's nothing on earth she'd rather do.

"An Ashby dinner? Hells yes." Her eyes light up even more, as if that's possible. "Tell your mama I'll bring a pie." She hums as she heads down the hall, and fuck if I don't watch her perfect ass go before standing up and spying something cherry red on the corner of my desk.

Another goddamn scrunchie.

CHAPTER FIVE
Ivy

I think Wade Ashby has dimples when he smiles. Today is the first day I've ever seen the hint of them because it's the first day I've ever seen him kinda, sorta grin. And Lord have mercy, it's a sight. He's always striking-looking, but when anything other than a scowl takes over that man's face?

He's on a whole other level.

I want to see more of it. I'd like to dive in and make a home in that smile. The promise of that smile makes me think there was a time in his life where he might have given the best hugs. Like maybe once upon a time he was someone else.

I'm sure that smile is the very line between his Jekyll and Hyde.

What I don't get is why he doesn't use it more often. I get that everything on this ranch has rested on his shoulders since his dad's death, but aside from that and his recent divorce, I can't imagine what could have happened to make him *this* morose all the time.

At the end of the work day, I head to Spicer's Sweets on Laurel Creek's main drag to grab a lemon pie as a gift for my spirit animal Mama Jo. I would do anything this woman asked me to;

she is easily the coolest person I've ever met. Kind, tough-loving with all her kids, understanding, wise, and funny as all get-out.

She's the mama I used to know but there's just something more about her. She's the perfect cross between *don't even think about messing with me* and *come on in while I bake you some cookies.*

I smile to myself as I hop back into my truck to drive back to the ranch. It feels nice to have actual plans tonight, to be included. Leaving a relationship and the life you know, even if it isn't one you're happy in, can be lonely. I can feel myself slowly weaving into the threads of Silver Pines and I'm here for it. I should probably keep reminding myself it's only temporary but I'm more of a *let the universe guide you* type of woman, and this place is a joy I want to be in the moment with right now.

My cabin is quiet when I enter rather clumsily, juggling everything. I drop my purse onto the bench in the entryway and flick the light on with my elbow, only it doesn't come on. I run the standard drill of turning it on and off quickly two or three times to convince myself it really doesn't work, and then move through the small hallway to my kitchen at the back of the house. The time is dark on the stove, and when I open the fridge, it's clearly not running.

Shit.

What do I do in this house if the power goes out? I set my pie down on the old butcher block counter and tap my nails on it for a moment, looking out the front window toward the barns. The light is on over the doors there, and so is Wade's living room light across the path. So it's obviously just me. I fiddle with a few of the circuit breakers in the mechanical room but nothing happens.

I chew my bottom lip for all of ten seconds before I text Wade to see if he can help. I wait for him to answer but he doesn't. Five minutes later, my impatience takes over, and I toss my boots on and push through the front door, making the quick walk down the gravel road to Wade's cabin. I still have to shower and I refuse to be late for my first Ashby dinner.

It's a nice night for Kentucky in October, no breeze but a slight chill in the air. I shiver on the porch as I wait for Wade to answer my knock. His lights are on and his truck is here, back from the Horse and Barrel. I cross my arms over my chest to cover my nipples, which could cut glass right now in my t-shirt. I knock again. A little too hard maybe, because the old wooden door creaks open just slightly.

"Wade?" I call. "Sorry to bother you but I think something is up with my power."

I poke my head in and look around his clean and orderly cabin that is one hundred percent his personality. Tyler Childers plays through a set of vintage speakers on vinyl, and a half-empty glass of honey-colored whiskey sits on the counter. The cabin is warm and homey, there are throw blankets on the worn, chunky brown leather sofa and chair. That surprises me a little. I didn't picture Wade as the throw blanket type.

"Wade?" I call again, coming fully into the cabin. "Knock knock." I shouldn't be in here, but the door was open, so he has to be here somewhere—

Every thought in my mind floats into the air like bubbles rising in a glass of freshly poured prosecco when Wade walks into the living room, wrapped in nothing but a towel that hangs low on his narrow hips. His wavy hair is wet and disheveled, a few strands touching his forehead. He's freshly shaved and his wide jaw flexes as he crosses the room, droplets of water clinging to the broad, powerful shoulders that anchor his smooth, muscular arms and chest. It's a chest that doesn't disappoint, like it's chiseled from sun-kissed marble; a light dusting of hair trails down to a serious six-pack—hell, maybe even eight—and it leads my eyes like a lit runway to the deep V that disappears into his towel.

Even his calves are mammoth and strong as he turns to flip

the record. His entire back and part of his left shoulder is covered in colorless tattoos, a symphony of black and various shades of gray. I take inventory quickly of what I can make out. What look like tree branches stretch over the planes of his skin, some sort of tribal designs weaving through them, and his spine is etched in one single column of armored writing: *"All things share the same breath, the beast, the trees, the man."*

Holy shitballs. Ranching makes that kind of body? I should really speak. Say something, anything. But I don't. Instead, my eyes feast on my boss's sneaky-hot body for a full twenty seconds before he even notices I'm in the room.

"Jesus Christ, Ivy." He startles as he sees me, a moment frozen in time as we just stare at each other, but Wade gathers himself together almost instantly.

He moves toward me. Although you'd think he would be, he doesn't appear to be self-conscious in the slightest. I guess, why would he be with that body? That body makes me wish bath towels were the new official uniform of Silver Pines cowboys.

I swallow and pray my voice doesn't betray me as Wade pushes a hand through his wet hair, picking up and draining the glass of whiskey off the counter only an arm's length away from me, his eyes never leaving mine.

When he swallows his jaw flexes before he speaks. "There a reason you just barged into my house?"

My mouth pops open. *Speak, Ivy.*

"My power . . . cold . . . I have none," I fumble. "Pie."

Pie? Shoot me now.

I clear my throat as he looks at me like I have a second head.

"Have you already been to the big house? Mama Jo got you drinking?"

I shake my head. "Sorry, I was just . . . cold. I have no power, I texted to see if you could help, I got a pie."

Pretty sure I just gave him finger guns. I want to die now.

I avert my eyes from him.

"S-sorry to intrude." I'm a blubbering mess staring at this man from his foyer.

Wade's brow furrows. "Don't worry about it. It's my fault for leaving the door unlocked," he says with absolutely zero emotion.

Ouch.

"Give me five minutes and I'll be over." He sets his whiskey glass in the sink and nods to the back of the cabin.

I smile awkwardly and turn to leave, but my forehead stops me as it smacks into the still-open front door.

"Fucking shit," I curse, holding a hand to my throbbing brow bone. Maybe the floor could just open and swallow me whole? Even the fiery pits of hell would be better than the embarrassment of ogling my boss so hard that I just walked into a goddamn door. I've always been a bit of a klutz but this is just next-level.

Wade is beside me faster than I can fathom, gripping me as I hold my own head and force the dots from my vision.

"*Shit* is right, let me see," he says. The heat from his warm body and the fresh clean scent of leather, spice, and something else? Citrus? Rose? I cling to it as he inspects my head. A strong finger tilts my chin up and he looks into my eyes. My lady bits come alive with his touch and this proximity. "Just checking to see that you're not concussed," he says, looking at my injury.

His emerald eyes meet mine, making me feel sort of all tingly and jelly-like. I watch as they drift to my mouth. His throat bobs as he swallows.

Concussed? No.

Turned on? Check.

My jaw falls slack as his warm, large fingers press gently across my forehead until I wince when he hits the spot I smacked. "You might end up with a good bruise there but I think you're okay."

"Wouldn't be my first," I say nervously. *What the hell is wrong with me?*

His dark eyes assess me. "I don't really think you should go back to your place alone on account of you might take yourself out somehow on the way back, so just . . . sit," he says, gesturing to the living room.

I stand there for a beat too long and don't respond, because the muscles in his arms when he points across the room are just . . .

Wade's gaze finds mine.

"Ivy, sit," he commands.

I blink, then move to the spot on the couch he's pointing to. *Yes, sir.* Who am I to argue with bossy Wade Ashby?

He disappears for less than five minutes and returns in well-worn jeans, a long-sleeved black Henley that clings to every tempting inch of the body I forever can't unsee, and a black Tennessee Titans baseball hat he curves the brim on with both hands as he walks. He looks totally together and relaxed. The polar opposite of me.

He bends down when he makes his way over to me, smelling even better now with some sort of aftershave. Wade has the kind of scent you just want to lean into and inhale deep.

"Still alright? Don't feel nauseous or anything?" he asks, lightly skimming his fingers across my forehead again. "You don't have a goose egg, that's a good sign."

His eyes hold mine in place. The deep green gives way to little flecks of brown that are only noticeable when he's this close to me.

He blinks and it breaks my trance.

"Sorry about all this." I smile sheepishly as he stands and nods toward the door, his jaw tense again.

"I'll grab my tool bag from my truck on the way out. Let's go."

I do as he says, this time making sure to actually pull the door open before I decide to walk through it.

CHAPTER SIX
Ivy

"**O**n!" I yell from my kitchen to Wade at the back of the house as whatever he did just turned my power back on.

Simultaneous beeping commences as my house comes alive. All I can think of is getting this man out of here and collecting myself a little before I go to dinner.

"All set, then," he says as he enters the living room. "Something blew the breaker to your kitchen, and whatever you were doing back there, you must have shut the entire panel right down. The cabin is old, so try not to have too much plugged in and running at the same time."

"Thank you," I say. "I did have the washer and dryer running at lunch and a space heater, maybe I didn't notice before I came back to the barn that it went out. I didn't mean to . . . I mean, I'm sorry I barged into your house. I didn't expect you to not be decent," I say, trying to sound as professional as possible.

Wade raises an eyebrow as he packs his tools back up in his tool bag.

"I should expect it. I didn't nickname you Trouble for nothing, *Trouble*." He drops his gaze quickly but not before I see them.

The hint of dimples. Twice in one day.

"What's twice in one day?" he asks, his face already back to expressionless.

Fuck my life. I said that out loud?

"Twice in one day that I've done something stupid . . . I-I'm going for a shower, so I'll see you later," I say as I give him an awkward quick wave and dart down my hallway.

"Might want to check the water before you get in so you don't end up with another injury," Wade calls as he closes the door behind him and I disappear into my bathroom, properly mortified and wondering errantly if I have time to flick it to the image I now have mentally saved of my boss before I go to dinner with his whole family.

I'm not quite prepared for the scene unfolding in the big house when Jo's dad, Dean, opens the door to me just after six. The Ashbys' big burly golden retriever, Harley, nuzzles right up to me looking for cuddles the moment I come in. CeCe is sitting on the floor in front of the sofa in the living room looking beyond beautiful as always with Nash propped right beside her, hand on her knee while he watches hockey highlights on TV and sips bourbon. It's almost like he can't not be touching her. Mabel is behind CeCe on the couch styling her long blonde hair in different braids and clips, and a drawing is taped to the coffee table with writing in a man's untidy scrawl that says "*Able Mabel's Beauty Salon*."

Cole and Wade are in the kitchen in deep discussion as Jo bastes two mammoth-sized chickens freshly pulled from the oven.

Dean takes my coat with the most comforting smile and hangs it in the closet. I say thank you and smile at him then turn to the room.

"Hi, y'all," I say as I enter the open space.

Seven pairs of eyes turn and land on me before the quiet explodes with "Hi" and "Come on in."

"Lemon is my favorite," Jo says as she kisses me on the cheek. "Was Wy's favorite too, you've got good taste." I grin, happy she approves. Her long blonde hair smells like cinnamon. She's homey and comfortable. Everything my own mother isn't anymore but used to be and it tugs at my heart. "Wade, be a gentleman, pour this woman a drink," she quips as Wade's eyes lock on mine across the room.

His half-naked torso flashes through my mind, making the room suddenly feel just a little too warm. He's still wearing that black Titans hat but now it's backward, making him look even younger, more carefree and dangerously hot.

It's a look that's definitely working for me. His sleeves are pushed up and strong forearms ripple with muscle as he works to roll out biscuits. He nods and breaks my stare when he reaches for a towel to dust the flour off his big hands.

Jo takes my pie and sets it on the counter as Wade hands me a small crystal glass with a double shot in it when I arrive at the kitchen island.

I go to take a swallow but his hand darts out and ghosts over mine, stopping me. His touch sinks beneath my skin and almost makes me shudder with the quick contact. I berate myself when it happens. One glimpse of him in a towel and suddenly I'm a teenage girl with a crush?

"We drink with a salute," he says matter-of-factly. "So, you got a toast for us?" he challenges, leaning on his elbow looking up at me.

I draw a blank for a moment, then I smile sweetly.

Put me on the spot, deal with the repercussions.

"To bosses that forgive me for barging in on their half-naked asses, deliver me first aid and fulfill a sort of superhero fantasy by then fixing my power?" I offer.

Jo, Cole and Dean turn and look at me. I grin as Wade's cheeks turn a fine shade of pink, but he doesn't take his eyes off mine, always in control as he taps his glass on the counter and takes a drink. "Salut," he says.

"There's a story there and I'm invested. Did he fix your power half-naked?" Cole sits down and looks back and forth between us before adding, "Also, I'll put your first dollar in, but around here, if you cuss, Mabel takes your money."

I look out at the living room to see Mabel wearing an ear-to-ear grin, baring two missing front teeth as she's waving at me.

"Noted." I smile back.

"You were saying?" Cole asks about my story.

"Forgot to lock the door. She's clumsy and just walks into people's houses uninvited like she was born in a barn. No story," Wade deadpans.

Cole grins and pops a handful of peanuts into his mouth from a bowl on the island.

"Not surprised he was half-naked. Wade never wore clothes when he was young either."

"Just not self-conscious," Wade says, his eyes telling Cole to shut his trap, but it seems to fuel Cole.

"The moment we got in the door, he'd strip right down to his boxers." Cole chuckles.

"And his hand was always holding onto his no-no parts too," Mama Jo pipes up, giggling.

I raise my eyebrow and start laughing with them.

"Christ sakes," Wade protests, trying not to let his niece hear.

"Uncle Wade, that's another!" Mabel yells from the other room.

Wade doesn't miss a beat, stuffing a couple dollars into a tiny cowboy boot on the shelf beside the kitchen island, shaking his head, muttering something like "she has supersonic hearing."

"It's true. I don't even have any candid pictures of him until after he was ten, he was never wearing anything. That boy'd be outside in the yard in his bare feet and shorts, collecting bugs and making mud pies. At home in the wild," Jo says as she stands on her tippy toes and plants a smooch on his cheek. "He was a free spirit back then."

"Nothing like keeping things professional at an Ashby dinner," Wade grunts, and I smirk as I sip my bourbon. Damn, it's good bourbon.

Cole leans in and cracks a smile; he has the same dimples as Wade, only he doesn't seem to be afraid to use them. "Rumor has it he still keeps a hand on his no-no parts any chance he gets."

Wade cuffs the back of Cole's head, knocking his hat to his lap.

"He doesn't grip those reins harder with his right hand for nothing," Dean barks out from the den, earning a hearty laugh from Nash and Cole.

"Too far, Dad." Jo wrinkles her nose. "Sorry, honey," she says to me. I just smile and wave it off.

"I thought you wanted to talk about the derby, isn't that the whole reason we're doing this on a Tuesday?" Wade asks, trying desperately to change the subject.

"Yes, let's talk derby. Wade, mash those potatoes and dinner will be ready. Then we'll chat. And we're doing this on a Tuesday because it's the only chance we've got. I'm leaving with Sandy and Theresa to go to Wears Valley for our girls' week tomorrow," Jo reminds them all.

The guys all nod.

"Do I have to eat Dad's cooking *all week*?" Mabel asks from her makeshift salon, looking horrified.

Cole chuckles. "You're right, Mabes, how dare she leave us all to fend for ourselves for a week?"

"You know how to cook just fine, boy. You just don't do it unless you absolutely have to. I taught you just the same as I taught the rest of them."

"Don't be too hard on him, Mama, some people are just born with more talent in the kitchen," Wade says.

Cole makes a face at him as he pops more nuts into his mouth.

"But I have to agree, to close this kitchen down for almost a week? It's plain unacceptable. Two stars on Yelp from me," Wade bites out. He's looking way too serious for just making a rather witty little joke.

I giggle in response and his eyes flit to mine.

"Hush your mouth, both of you. At least Wade cooks. You know, it wouldn't hurt you to find a lady friend to bake your biscuits for you, Cole, since you won't do it yourself," Jo says.

"Even if she just let him look at her biscuits, it'd be a start," Dean hollers in.

Cole grunts something no one can hear.

Jo winks at me as she hands me the cutlery.

"Set the table, honey? We all earn our keep here; we don't believe in guests."

"Suits me perfectly." I nod and take the silverware from her and smirk all the way into the dining room.

Younger Wade sounds like he was a far cry from the serious, straight-laced bridge troll I'm working for now. I can't help but wonder if it's possible to catch a glimpse of him. I look back at him in the next room as he grimaces at something Cole says

Right now, it doesn't seem too possible but I've got time. I think I want to find out.

CHAPTER SEVEN
Wade

"So, we'll leave on the 26th and be back on the 28th," I say as we eat. I've just filled the family in on what we have to do in Nashville and the yearlings we're looking at.

"I'm in to help Haden and the boys as much as possible. I've been thinking about taking a step back from the bar a little if you need more help," Nash says as he takes his seat next to CeCe at the table.

I nod. "Much appreciated."

"It's our slow time anyhow, we've got this." Mama smiles at me, her eyes doing their crinkly-in-the-corner thing. "Your dad would be very proud of you taking another shot at this. Lots of memories."

"It's always been a dream of mine too," Ivy pipes up. "I'll try not to let y'all down. I'll do my best as Sam's stand-in."

Ivy's sitting directly across from me and she looks effortlessly pretty, especially after a couple shots of bourbon. She's wearing another pair of Levi's and a long-sleeved hunter green sweater that hangs off her shoulders, which are fucking stunning by the way. Her dark hair is in thick cascades down her back and half held up by some sort of a clip contraption that looks like a butterfly.

She must be giving her hundreds of scrunchies the night off. Thin silver earrings that look like strands of tinsel almost reach her shoulders, and maybe it's the bourbon talking but for an insane second I imagine taking one into my mouth, along with her earlobe, and then sweeping my tongue down her silky, biteable neck.

Fuck. Not cool. Employee. She's your employee.

I shift in my seat, averting my eyes from Ivy, choosing instead to watch Harley in the corner gnawing on his bone. I like the other view a million times better but at least this one isn't semi-bricking me up under the table.

"I'm sure you'll do very well, darlin'. It took Wyatt three seasons and two horses before he placed," Mama tells her.

"He seems like he was a great man, I wish I could've met him," Ivy says as all of us nod.

"So do we." CeCe smiles, squeezing her arm beside her. "He would've liked you straight away."

"Everything I've heard about him, it seems he was a lot like my dad," Ivy states.

"Terrible at tile rummy?" Cole asks with a grin.

"Always the one to eat the last cookie and put the box back in the cupboard?" Mama pipes up.

"Terrible at catching fish?" Nash adds while the table chuckles.

The air is too heavy. I don't talk about my dad too much at once. It's still too fresh. We all get together as a family still, do all the same things, but it never feels quite right. One of our crew is just gone and we'll never get that back. Some moments, the weight of that is fucking crushing. I feel the sudden need to drink more, swiping the bourbon off the table and filling my glass.

"Your daddy pass on?" Papa Dean asks her.

She nods. "Yes, when I was fourteen. He had an unexpected

heart attack. He was my very best friend." She grins as she says it, like a million memories fill her eyes.

"Well, we have that in common, my dad was mine too," CeCe tells her quietly. Nash squeezes CeCe's shoulder as she says it. I still can't believe how quickly he became the doting-husband type.

"What about your mama, is she still on the right side of the dirt?"

Mama drops her fork at Pop's words.

"Dad. That's not an acceptable way to ask that."

"It's fine." Ivy chuckles at my no-filter grandfather. "She's still on the right side of the dirt, sort of. She kind of became the child when my dad died, I became the parent. She drinks more than she should now, I help take care of her."

"That's not an easy task. Sorry to hear that. You have any siblings?" Cole asks as he takes a bite of his mashed potatoes.

"One younger sister, Cassie. She doesn't come around much, but our older neighbor, Mrs. Potter, she checks in on my mama for me every few days and makes sure she gets her groceries. She's always cared about her. I think she has a soft spot since she knows what it's like to lose a husband. She's a widow too." Ivy shrugs.

Something in her eyes makes me want to reach across the table and grab her hand. I find the will to stop myself.

"What was your dad's name?" I ask, without thinking or even understanding why. I never ask people personal questions.

"Bill . . . Billy," she says back to me softly, shrugging, her violet pools boring into mine.

"A toast." Pop holds his glass up, cutting the thick air around us. "I always say life is like toilet paper . . ."

"Jesus Christ," Cole snickers under his breath.

"You're either on a roll or you're taking shit from somebody. Better to be on a roll. To Ivy, for rising above the shit life has dealt her, to her lost dad Billy, and to Wy." He taps his glass on the table and we all follow, a smile playing on Ivy's lips.

"Well, that was maybe the most ridiculous and possibly the sweetest toast I've ever heard." Ivy giggles as she takes a drink.

"Shit, honey, you ain't heard nothing yet," Mama Jo says.

"You all owe me some money," Mabel says, pointing her fork at the swear boot.

"I think I like you all." Ivy giggles again.

"The feeling's mutual, dear," Mama says.

Pop stands with his empty plate in his hand. "Alright, who wants some pie? Wade, you want some of Ivy's pie?" he blurts.

I run a hand through my hair as most of my family snickers around the table.

This fucking family.

"All of you, get your heads out of the gutter. I just know he loves lemon," he adds, raising his hands in innocence.

Ivy locks eyes with me and chuckles openly at Pop. Goddammit, she's moved over to the dark side, and fuck, I hate that it looks good on her.

"She sure fits in with the fam." Cole nudges me with his elbow as we clean up. I look out to the dining room and see Ivy parked in front of the couch while Mabel goes to town on her hair. Her wide smile takes up her whole face while she chats with Mama and CeCe.

"Maybe she needs to come to some more dinners, poor girl doesn't seem to have a family," Nash adds. Of course he'd have a soft spot for that, since we became like his family when his parents died.

"This was supposed to be a business dinner, I gotta maintain a little professionalism," I grunt, and Nash smacks me with the dish towel he's holding.

"Loosen up. Fucking cranky old man," he whispers, looking into the next room to make sure Mabel doesn't hear him cuss.

I look back at him. "Just trying to keep some boundaries, which is a normal, healthy thing to do."

"You know what else is a normal and healthy thing to do?" Cole grins.

"Yeah I do, and trust me, I'm overdue, but I can't really meet anyone right now, seems I'll be doing all things training for the next few months."

As I watch Ivy, I realize I'm looking forward to more time with her than I should. I can't stop myself from wondering what happened with her family. Whatever it is, it hasn't made her unhappy. Ivy doesn't seem jaded like me; she seems kind, affectionate even, as she smiles up at Mabel. And she's so damn confident in herself, as much as I hate to admit it, it's sexy as hell.

She didn't even look away when she walked in on me in a towel. I take a swallow of bourbon as I think of what she could've seen walking right in like that. I often don't wear clothes around my own house; it was a total fluke I even had that towel on.

Maybe I should've left the room when I noticed her, instead of standing there half-naked, but I thought if I approached her, maybe she'd learn her lesson and leave in an uncomfortable huff, never to make that mistake again.

Instead, when she looked up at me, her eyes said *I think maybe I'd like to wear your hat sir, thank you very much,* and ever since I've been semi-hard thinking about the soft skin of her face under my fingers and her juicy fucking lips partly open, the perfect place for me to slide my—

"Earth to Sergeant," Cole says, calling me by my age-old nickname. "You're staring, bro."

"I am not," I say defensively.

Cole chuckles in response. *Fucking bourbon.*

"You should really come with me to Lexington, you need a night out," he says.

Lexington equals sex. Whenever Cole needs to get laid, he skips town for a night for one of his one-night stands—that way he doesn't risk messing with someone's sister or teacher from our lives. Small-town problems when you're a manwhore like Cole.

"Mabel is going to be with Ernie and Trudy on Saturday," he says, mentioning his ex-wife Gemma's parents. They are actually stable, kind people and they spend more time with Mabel than her own mother does. "If you need a night to get away, let loose, let me know. I always welcome a wingman." He grins as he says it.

"I'm not a fuckboy like you," I snark back.

"At least I'm not wound up like a goddamn jack-in-the-box waiting to pop. You need to get out of town for a night. Trust me, it will help with the way you're *not* staring," Cole retorts

Nash laughs quietly on his way by, sweeping the floor. "Ahh, don't be too hard on him. After all, he *is* going out of town. Nashville, right? Good thing you won't have any distractions there." He winks at me.

I glance at Ivy in the living room, hair now done up in several clips, joining Mama and CeCe playing Just Dance in her painted-on jeans. As she rolls her hips to the music and her hands raise up over her head, my mouth goes dry as a fucking bone. I let out a shaky breath before swallowing the last of my bourbon.

Nope, I definitely won't have any distractions with Ivy in Nashville in the adjoining hotel rooms I was able to find.

The only rooms in the entire fucking city.

No distractions there *whatsoever*.

CHAPTER EIGHT
Wade

"*I* realize you got a lot going on right now, but that doesn't mean you can just ignore me and my needs."

I pull my hat off and toss it on the ottoman, rubbing my forehead because I have the same fucking conversation almost every single night.

"I don't just have a lot going on right now, Janelle, I know you were sneaking around with Darryl Smith. Once I can't trust you, it's over."

Janelle crouches down in front of me, her long, bleach blonde hair falling over her shoulders. She pouts her bottom lip out at me and looks up at me with her blue eyes trying to entice me, but it doesn't work. I used to think I loved those eyes. Now, every time I look into them all I see is the reflection of another man.

I stand and push her hands away, willing my walls back up. I'm moving back to the ranch in three days; there's not any reason I have to put up with her shit anymore.

"Stop trying to pretend like you don't want me, Wade."

"I don't want you, Janelle, I used to want you. Now, I'm just fucking tired, I have the whole ranch on my shoulders, my dad's so fucking sick." And throwing up, and sleeping all day *every day, and he has sores on his skin from the chemo.* "I'm exhausted."

"You're always exhausted, but I'm your wife. For better or worse. It's high time you forgive me already and pay attention to me, like you used to. Why do you think I had to look elsewhere?"

Right, it's my fault she stepped out on me. The joke's on her if she thinks I'll ever trust her again, never mind forgive her.

I close my eyes and scrub my face with my hand, giving myself a second to keep my composure. I feel movement behind me. Two warm hands slide under the back of my t-shirt. I'm just about to protest until I hear it.

"Stop trying to pretend you don't want me, Wade." A soft, husky voice fills my ears, one that makes gooseflesh break out over the back of my neck. One that isn't Janelle's. I don't dare open my eyes. I want this voice in my ears. I smell her, sweet vanilla and sugar.

A groan rumbles from my chest as I spin around and her small hand cups my cock through my jeans.

My belt buckle comes undone and a palm is pressed to me, stroking me, lips press against mine. The taste is even better. I reach my hands around her waist as my mouth claims hers, her back is so warm under her tank.

"I knew you wanted me, Chief." Ivy pulls her face back from me, plump lips swollen, pupils blown out, chest heaving.

"Fuck yeah, I do," I mutter as I back her into the wall. I pull her small hand up to my lips, sucking every one of her fingers into my mouth before wrapping them back around my cock as she moans that throaty little sound I've been dying—

A clap of thunder causes my whole cabin to shake. My eyes fly open to the buzz of my phone and the storm. I realize my hand is firmly planted around my own cock and Ivy's scent is still in my nose.

Fuck.

I grab my buzzing phone off the bedside table.

Janelle. Like my dream was warning me she was trying to get to me. Another loud clap of thunder roars through the house as my phone starts again.

"It's midnight, Janelle." My voice is hoarse, and fuck, I'm so hard it hurts.

"Wade, the roof is leaking . . . the kitchen . . . there's water everywhere." Her voice is even more high-pitched than normal and loud as hell in my ears after the soft husky one she just woke me from.

"Son of a bitch. I'm coming."

I hang up, and toss my jeans on, willing my hard-on to go away as the idea of Ivy's hot warm body pressed against mine keeps flashing through my mind. I grab my keys and blast out the front door. This is the second time the roof has leaked in the last four months. She's definitely going to have to get that replaced. I'm basically like Janelle's glorified landlord at this point.

Soon enough, I can just ignore her, I remind myself. I'm counting down the fucking days until that house isn't mine anymore. Her bank financing is set to go through at the beginning of December. Until then, I have no choice, I have to help, only to ensure nothing gets ruined and it hinders the financing that is going to offer me the final severed tie from Janelle.

The drive from the ranch to my ex-wife in our ex-house takes ten minutes. As I drive, I try to sort out what the fuck that dream was. It felt too real, and fuck, I really liked it. It makes no sense to me. I've been around plenty of beautiful women in my life, there is no excuse for my rogue thoughts about Ivy. I tell myself it's just because it's been a while for me as I feel my cock start to inflate again at the thought of her pressed against me.

Goddammit. Cleaning the barn. The dentist. Cole's bare ass jumping into the creek, I repeat to myself as my cock instantly deflates. Cole's ass does it every time.

I sigh and prepare myself for battle as I pull into the driveway. Janelle has always been a force to be reckoned with. I should have known the first weeks we got married that it was destined to end up a dumpster fire. The girl I thought Janelle was disappeared right before my eyes the day the wedding was over and it wasn't all about her anymore. She was no longer a bride. She was only a wife—her words. But I went with it for a long time. Happy wife, happy life, right? Wrong. We were complete opposites and not in the good ways.

I like the outdoors, she does not, I wanted to stay in and she wanted to go out, I wanted kids and she never did. I really knew there was no hope for us when my dad got sick and she was out drinking and screwing townies instead of being there for me and my family. A couple months before my dad died, I made the choice to leave. I'd trusted her, and once I couldn't anymore the rest seemed pointless. It made sense for her to stay in the house when I knew I needed to be at the ranch all the time, and it didn't feel like my home anymore.

When our divorce came through at the end of the summer, I agreed to let her keep it. Now I'm so close to the house being hers I can taste it and it tastes like fucking freedom. I park my truck in her driveway and raise a hand to knock, but before I can the door swings open to Janelle all fired up, looking at me like it's taken me way too long to get here.

"I just don't know what to do, I put buckets under it. It's coming from the same place as before." No *hi, thanks for coming*. Just *get to work, soldier*.

"Probably the damn spot where the eaves trough runs off again," I grunt out. It's barely raining now so I decide the roof is safe. Even if I slip off it's a better fate than staying in the house listening to Janelle tell me all the excuses why she hasn't taken care of this.

"I think it's fixed, but only temporarily, Janelle. I told you in the summer it needs replacing. Did you call Jake to give you an estimate?" I ask thirty minutes later when I re-enter the house after adding more seal.

Janelle pouts.

"Been busy." *In other words, no.*

I frown at her.

"You can't neglect this shit. I can't be your first call when something goes wrong. We're not married anymore. You have to get used to it. I'm getting Jake here tomorrow, only because I can't sit around and hope it gets fixed. You have the money budgeted in to your refinancing?"

"Yes. Of course." She says it as if it would be crazy that she wouldn't, but I know better.

"Good. He'll be here when you're done work."

She stands and smirks, stalking toward me with a fuck-me look on her face. One I know well. One half the town knows well.

"I don't want to get used to it. I'll make it worth your while if you stay a little longer, like old times. You're looking damn good at one a.m., Wade." She reaches a hand up to my jaw and it actually repulses me. Even the faint scent of her Chanel N°5 turns my stomach.

I scoff, grabbing her wrist. "Not a fucking chance, Janelle. Those times are over." I sidestep her and grab my rain jacket, inspecting the bucket to be sure the leak has stopped one more time. "Empty the bucket and check it in the morning," I bite out.

I'm out the door so quickly that I barely hear her yell, "I didn't want to fuck you anyway, Wade Ashby."

CHAPTER NINE
Wade

When I get back into the silos office the next afternoon after a full day of phone meetings with our auction agent and a handful of suppliers, I'm ready for the day to be over. It's only 3:30, but after getting just a few hours of sleep and struggling to not give in to fisting my cock with Ivy's image in my brain, I'm wrecked.

There's a mug of strong black coffee on my desk.

"Saw you coming back. You look tired today, Chief," Ivy says as she gathers her things to go out and work with Haden and two horses. She's looking like a breath of fresh air in another pair of jeans and a flannel, tight and tucked in, her tattered cowboy hat over a long black braid that dances down her shoulder.

"Yeah . . . didn't sleep," I reply.

"That storm kept me up too." She smiles.

Yeah, the storm, that's what kept me up.

"Are you going to work with my horse?" Mabel asks from the silos door, making both Ivy and me turn to greet her in surprise.

"I am, and Cosmic too." Ivy smiles.

I look around for the adult that brought Mabel to us.

"Where's your—"

"Right here," Cole says, poking his head around the corner, dressed and ready for a shift as Laurel Creek's Deputy Sheriff.

"Gemma has to . . ." He looks down at Mabel then back to me. "Work. She couldn't pick her up from school. CeCe's on her way. Mabel's going to have dinner and sleep at their place tonight while I work, but she wanted to come to the barn to wait, if that's fine?"

"You can come with me," Ivy says, holding out a hand to Mabel.

Mabel's smile takes up her whole face and Cole breathes a sigh of relief,

"Thanks, guys. I-I wasn't expecting . . . I just can't miss a shift right now."

"It's fine, man. Mabes probably asked her mom to work so she could come hang with us and Nutmeg. Right, Mabes?" I ask, rustling her hair. She giggles in response and happily skips out of the barn with Ivy.

"She's not at work, I'm guessing?" I ask Cole when they're out of earshot.

"Fuck no, she just texted me an hour ago and said she went to Lexington with two of her friends and forgot she had to pick Mabel up today." He puts air quotes around *forgot*.

"You're a good dad. Fuck Gemma." I pat him on the shoulder. Cole's also a good cop and I know he's stretched thin right now. "We've got Mabes for you. Now go keep those streets clean." I grin, knowing his night will probably consist mostly of splitting up a few bar fights and watching *Breaking Bad* on the iPad he keeps in his sheriff's truck.

Laurel Creek is usually pretty quiet on a Wednesday night, or really any night.

"Fuck you," Cole says, sensing my sarcasm. "And thanks."

I nod and take a big gulp of my coffee before heading out to observe the training. But when I get into the barn, I can hear Ivy and Mabel talking from Nutmeg's row as they ready him, so I start unpacking a large order that must have just arrived and text some of the boys to come help me.

"When can I learn jumps with him?" Mabel asks.

"Well, he's not that kind of horse, but if you want to start learning that, I'm gonna bet we start that training in the summer when you're done with school. But it will maybe be Sam that does that with you or Dusty. That's their department."

I set my jaw involuntarily, surprised that I don't really like thinking about a time when Ivy isn't on the ranch.

"I think Sam won't come back," Mabel says.

"Why do you think that?"

"She has babies now."

Ivy laughs at Mabel's answer. "She does, but your Uncle Wade says she loves the horses and lots of mommies go to work after they have babies." A moment of silence passes. "Pass me the brush please, honey," Ivy says to Mabel.

"He likes to be brushed," Mabel says as she hands her the wide bristled tool. Mabel's little face is deep in thought from what I can see. "If she doesn't come back, will you stay?"

"Hmmm . . . well, that will be up to your nana and Uncle Wade."

"If you do stay, who will train the horses when you have babies? I like when you're here."

I smirk at Mabel's personal question. Kids have no filter.

I pull a box down from the pallet I'm unloading as I wait to hear Ivy's answer.

A long silence makes me lift my gaze and glance between the aisles at Ivy's face. Her eyes are distant. She forces her lips to turn into a grin.

"You don't have to worry about that with me, honey. The

horses are my babies." She tweaks Mabel's chin and Mabel seems satisfied, but I'm not.

As I watch the two of them lead Nutmeg and Cosmic out of the barn like two peas in a pod, I can't shake the same feeling I had before. Ivy Spencer's layers run deep, and that mystery isn't really helping me to push her from my mind. In fact, it's making me think about her even more. I have no clue how to get through the next few months and keep things professional, but at this point? It's going to take a fucking miracle.

Twenty minutes later, my phone buzzing in my pocket pulls me from deciding between putting away the feed delivery and watching Ivy and Mabel work with Cosmic. For the klutzy way she handles herself, Ivy's sure a natural when it comes to working with the horses as she takes her time to teach Mabel how to run through some basic groundwork.

Two texts wait for me when I pull my phone out. One from Janelle asking me if I can change the roofer appointment I made for her today, and the other from the roofer.

JAKE PARNELL

> I'm here Wade and Janelle isn't. Are you coming instead?

Fuck sakes, Janelle. I repeat the mantra, *the day my name is off this goddamn house can't come fast enough.* I type a quick *on my way* before I tuck my phone in my back pocket.

As I'm leaving the barn, heading over to tell Mabel she's going to have to come with me, I see CeCe pulling up the driveway.

Mabel skips over to give me a hug goodbye from where she was watching Ivy work. I approach Ivy—now mounted on Cosmic—and she trots over to me, guessing I want to talk. Fuck, she looks good up there. Her cowboy hat is letting just enough of the day's sun on her face to amplify her violet eyes. She looks at me expectantly as I just stand there dumbfounded, taking in how pretty she is.

"Boss?" she asks, the hint of a grin playing on her lips.

I blink and come back to the present from last night's dream, which is playing like a reel in my head.

"Uh . . . when those boys get here, get them to finish up what I was doing in stable four. Still two pallets to unload. I have to . . . take care of something."

Ivy nods. "That's why I'm here, Chief."

I turn quickly so I can avoid staring at the enticing way her body moves on the horse as she rides off.

I spend the next couple hours going over the roof job on my not-house with Jake and shooting the shit with him. We went to school together, so we always have lots to gab about. By the time we're done, we decide a drink and a burger is in order so we head to the Horse and Barrel and convince Cole to come meet us for dinner in the middle of his shift. Partway through the best burger in town, my phone is buzzing and lighting up on the table.

"Who's *Trouble?*" Jake asks, looking down at my phone as Nash slides into the booth with us.

Nash looks down at my lock screen and grins.

"Little late to be working, ain't it, Sarge?"

I give him a *shut the fuck up* look as he chuckles and then I check to see what Ivy is after.

TROUBLE

> I've been doing some research on the auctioneer that's running the show in Nashville. If we want a yearling at the best price I think maybe we could offer him a little convincing. Now hear me out . . .

The fuck? I watch as the bubbles appear, then disappear for a moment as I hear Nash say to Cole and Jake, "Must be a work emergency." *Dick.*

> **TROUBLE**
>
> Nothing too unprofessional, maybe flash a grin or undo a couple buttons in the front row during the auction and we could distract him enough to get Rustling Winds for under a million.

What the fuck is this woman talking about?

> There's not a chance you're doing any such thing to get a horse. We'll pay whatever we need to get the right yearling. And I don't think his wife would appreciate that.

> **TROUBLE**
>
> Oh no, Chief I didn't mean me, I meant you. And rumor has it his husband won't be there. 😌

I scrub my face with my hand as I stifle a grin.

Cole whispers to Nash, "Must be a funny work emergency?"

Jake pipes in, "What the fuck am I missing?"

I continue to ignore them. Maybe it's because I like seeing her name light up my phone but I can't stop myself from playing back.

> You trying to sell me out for a horse? I'm appalled.

> **TROUBLE**
>
> Just looking out for the ranch. Be open-minded, think about it. I don't condone doing anything wrong, just flirt a little. Harmless.

> I'm a respectable man, stop trying to pimp me out.

TROUBLE

> Yes sir.

I look up to find Nash sipping a bourbon and grinning at me like the cocky motherfucker he is.

"Got that work problem solved, Sarge?"

The rain is back as I hop into my truck over an hour later. I look out the windshield to see what kind of storm I'm dealing with. All I can think about is Janelle's roof holding up through it so I don't have to go back to her house tonight.

It's really coming down as I turn down the muddy drive to Silver Pines. The big house is eerie and dark with my mother gone. I'm just pulling into my own driveway when I see a shadow move on my porch behind the rail in my headlights.

I freeze then grab my full-size Maglite from the backseat; we've had coyotes and black bears in this area before and I'm not taking any chances. I stalk toward the front porch as the shadow moves again. Just as I'm about to go beast mode and start making all sorts of noise on the porch rail with the flashlight, I hear the tiniest, "Wade?"

I blink, then squint in the dark.

"What the—?"

I rush to flick the porch lantern on, only to find a damp and disheveled Ivy crumpled beside my front door in a wicker chair.

"I'm sorry . . . I just didn't know where else to go."

CHAPTER TEN
Ivy

"Jesus Christ . . . what happened?" Wade crouches down beside me, swiping my damp hair off my forehead.

"I was teaching Nutmeg to navigate in the rain."

"At ten o'clock at night?"

"Well no, I was out right after I talked to you. I couldn't unwind and I heard the rain. It's beneficial for them you know, to learn to navigate in it—oww." I wince as I try to move my ankle that I've already pulled out of my boot.

Wade moves down to it. "What did you do? Ivy, your ankle is swollen . . . I think I need to take you to the hospital to get it checked out."

"Hospital? No, no it's fine. I—fuck," I mutter as I try to grab hold of the wall to help me stand, but Wade is faster, gripping under my elbows.

"Uh-uh. Nope. We're going. Now," Wade commands in that voice that tells me not to argue.

"I don't—I don't have insurance. I'm trying to save . . ." *I'm still helping my mom with some of her bills since she spends her government money on booze.*

"Nonsense. It happened at work so the ranch will pay the

bill. Now whether you're done protesting or not, I'm going to get you to the truck."

I nod and lean back against the wall. Wade disappears for all of one minute and returns with a bottle of water, an ice pack, and a dry, warm coat. He gently pulls mine off that got wet while I hobbled here from the barn. Jo is gone and CeCe is at Nash's with Mabel. I'd assumed Wade would be home and was surprised to find he wasn't when I got back.

"Okay, let's go," he says, his voice gruff and rushed, as he hands me the ice pack and curls his powerful arms under my legs. I wrap my arms around his neck and settle into his warm, strong chest.

"It was so stupid. I didn't think to check the radar, it was such a nice, crisp night. I figured, why not?" I feel my cheeks heat just thinking about the reason I was all keyed up and having trouble getting to sleep. Him and the way he looked at me today before he left the ranch in a hurry. The way his eyes raked over my body for just a split second. Just long enough for me to notice and have it send goosebumps over my skin.

I look up at him for a moment. It's not so bad being in Wade's arms with his warm, fur-lined flannel coat around me. He sets me on the passenger seat of his truck. The scent of leather and spices with a hint of mint fills my senses. It's fresh and clean. It smells like Wade.

He hops into the driver's side, looks at me, and with a sort of huff, he speaks, "You should definitely bring your legs this way"—Wade gestures to the bench seat between us—"prop them up here, to keep it elevated." He turns the key, and the truck roars to life.

"Gravity will make it swell more if you don't," he adds.

I nod and pull my other boot off, then lift my legs to rest them across the front seat, doing a little dance of trying to place them so my feet don't touch Wade's muscular thigh. The ice slides off my ankle but he catches it, then gently lifts both my feet onto his lap and meets my gaze in the dark cab of his truck.

"*Elevated*," he repeats, holding the ice to my ankle.

I just nod in response, because when Wade's voice hits that deep octave I just have no words and there's no room to argue. We begin our drive, and my feet in his lap make me nervous so I start to tell him what happened.

"There was no thunder the whole ride. I saw the lightning as I was just getting back to the barn, but it was too late. I couldn't dismount fast enough, Cosmic spooked, and I just landed funny on my ankle trying to hurry to get off him. I don't know how I managed to get him secure but I did it and then . . . I started walking. It took me a while. Maybe a half hour to get back to the cabin. I figured you'd be home."

"I had to go to my ex's for something—you should've called me." His jaw sets and flexes. I can tell he's upset with me.

I huff out a breath in response and toss my damp hair into a bun on top of my head.

"I didn't bring my phone. Once I realized you weren't here, I was just taking a minute to rest on your porch and then I was going to go back to my cabin and try to sleep, see how it was in the morning. It was just careless all around. I'm really so sorry for all of this," I say, feeling so damn stupid and irresponsible.

The dark country cruises by us as I continue, looking out the front window.

"I like to ride in the rain. I used to do it with my dad, it was kind of our thing," I say, because I feel like him driving me to the hospital forty minutes away at ten at night seems like it may need a deeper explanation.

"Did you have your own ranch?" he asks right away.

I answer, grateful for the distraction. "No, but we had a small house on about ten acres. My dad bought my sister and I our own horses. He loved animals."

Wade's eyes are fixed out the window on the rainy countryside.

"I'm really sorry you lost him. That must have been so hard at that age," he says.

The lump in my throat grows and tears sting my eyes. I swallow down the urge to cry.

"It's been a long time since anyone has ever said that to me. Even when he died, I don't think I heard it much," I say quietly.

"Why not?" Wade asks, sounding even more frustrated than normal.

I look over at him to try to gage his mood, to see if this is his way of distracting me from the pain or if he's truly interested. It's impossible to tell so I take a deep breath and tell him a little bit of the story.

"After my dad died, my mom went off the rails, daily glasses of wine turned into bottles and eventually we just lost our family nest-egg. The horses, the land, the house, she couldn't pay for it. By the time I was sixteen, Winding Eagles trailer park became our home."

Wade is silent beside me as his jaw tenses while he stares out the windshield, focused on the rain.

"I went from grieving my best friend to becoming my mother's babysitter of sorts, I guess, my little sister's caregiver, and then eventually, both of their financial support. I worked two jobs after school until Cassie was old enough to start working and contribute. My mom worked odd jobs for a while. The depression she fought after my dad died just consumed her."

Something in Wade's face softens.

"My mother isn't a bad person. She has the biggest heart but my dad was the love of her life. It was like her will to live was lost. She fell into the darkest hole and just couldn't or wouldn't come out."

71

"I know that loss. My mom says a piece of her died with my father," Wade offers.

I nod in response.

"Some people are just stronger than others. Your mom is such a strong woman, I admire her," I say truthfully. "She didn't cower when her husband died, she took care of his family. I didn't know her before but it seems like maybe somehow she grew stronger."

"She has her moments but she is a tough cookie, I'll give her that. She's also kind of a control freak, she'd want to make sure us kids were all okay," Wade adds.

I giggle. "The apple doesn't fall far from the tree then, is what you're saying."

"I have no idea what you're talking about, I'm the most easy-going guy around." Wade says it so seriously it makes me grin. "You're not going to call me on my bullshit, Trouble?" he asks.

"I'll give you a break since you're driving me to the hospital." I smile, then add, "But only this once."

Wade nods, back to serious.

"Fair enough. So, what now?" He continues, "Is there a chance for your mom to get sober, maybe start fresh?"

I turn to look out the window. *I wish for that every day.*

"My mom's tried to sober up many times. Every time I hope this is the time she makes it, but so far it never has been. I'm still helping her out when she needs it, now that my sister has moved, I'm all my mom has."

Wade nods and changes the heavy subject. "How is it feeling?" he asks. "Is the ice helping at all?" He nods toward my foot in his lap.

"I think a little. I'm so sorry, Wade."

"Stop apologizing for your ankle, fuck. It was an accident," he says as he reaches down and gently squeezes my calf.

I can tell instantly that Wade doesn't reach out and touch

people often; his touch is cautious, but even with the pain I'm in, this touch resonates with me, it's oddly comforting. I look up at him and my eyes meet his in the dark for a fleeting moment. His hand is still resting on my leg.

"Are you hurt anywhere else?" he asks

"I don't think so, but we still have thirty minutes left in this drive," I say quietly, grinning to lighten the mood.

He shifts the ice on my ankle as I take a breath, feeling rewarded with the hint of a grin I see on his face. He squeezes my calf one more time before he lets go and returns his hand to the wheel.

"Yeah, you're more than a *little* accident-prone."

"Yes," I say honestly. "All my life. Tripping-*up*-the-stairs expert right here," I say, raising one hand.

"Well, maybe don't touch anything. Just keep your hands in your lap," he says.

I smile back at him and exaggerate folding my hands in my lap.

Must be a world record. For the third time in as many days, there are the hint of those dimples again.

CHAPTER ELEVEN
Wade

I couldn't tell you why I insisted on getting Ivy's life story on the drive here. I'm breaking my employer/employee barrier more and more every day with her. I also couldn't tell you why I sat right beside her for an hour while she waited to see a doctor, making uninteresting conversation about the *Ice Road Truckers* episodes that played in the waiting room. Or why I agreed to stay in the actual room with her while she saw the doctor. I didn't question it; I just did it. I stayed while the doctor pressed and prodded at her ankle, and now I'm waiting, right outside the room while they x-ray her.

I just need to know she's okay, because it happened at the ranch. The last thing I need is a workplace injury complaint—at least that's what I tell myself as I'm *still* sitting here.

"It's just a mild sprain. But you should stay off of it for a few days, maybe even a week, if you want it to heal as quickly as possible. Keep it elevated. Only really walk when you have to, and get some crutches for the first few days." The doctor gives his diagnosis and treatment as Ivy nods, listening intently.

"A light compression will help with support, and you can

start walking on it more as your pain allows. Take ibuprofen if you need to for pain." He looks between me and Ivy. "Do you have someone to help you get around?" he asks.

"I—I can't train effectively until it's healed anyway." She looks up at me with big blue eyes. "I could go stay with my mama, I suppose. Take a break and rest. Good thing it's my left foot, I could make the drive." *So she can look after her mother while she tries to heal? Don't think so.*

"It'll be me. I'm helping her. She lives on my ranch," I say without even thinking, as Ivy's eyes meet mine in question across the room.

Her mouth falls open to speak but the doctor beats her to it.

"Good," he says, seeming satisfied, giving Ivy pamphlets on healing time and R.I.C.E. treatment. He smiles a friendly smile at Ivy. "The more you take care of it in the first few days, the better it will be. If it gets worse or isn't healed up in a few weeks, come back and see us."

He exits the room before his last words have even left his mouth, already looking into the folder for his next case in the busy ER.

He isn't gone one second before Ivy turns her gaze to meet mine.

"Wade. How can you help? You can't come over every day for a *week*. I'll just go home to Jellico for a few days. You can pause my pay. This isn't your problem—" She's rambling, not unlike the first day I met her.

I sigh, putting my hand over hers in her lap, just to settle her. She's a sight right now, damp hair all pulled up, her sugar scent mixed with rain, her huge icy eyes looking up at me, all the while her small frame drowning in my winter coat.

Fucking hell. I'm about to make a colossal mistake but I just can't stop myself.

"You'll just stay with me at my cabin for the first few days," I say.

Her eyes grow as wide as saucers in her pretty face. "Wha—how?"

"It's the easiest way. I have two bedrooms. You'll even have your own bathroom. Just until you're on your feet of course, a week tops. I never even use that side of the house. There are crutches at the big house already from when CeCe was a teenager. They'll fit you just right, I'm sure. You can use those when you need . . . er . . . privacy, the facilities and what not."

Smooth, Wade.

The last thing I need is her in my space tempting me even more than she already does, but apparently I'm a sucker for punishment.

"I need you to be better, so it *has* to be this way. We have to be in Nashville in less than two weeks." Am I going overboard acting like she needs twenty-four-hour care for a sprained ankle? Probably, but no going back now.

She still doesn't speak and I wonder if I just crossed a line.

"You can't be on your own, and if we're being real, hobbling around your own place will probably just offer you another way to take yourself out," I bite out, using my dad's voice, the one none of us ever argued with.

Again, real smooth, Wade. Christ. What the fuck am I doing?

I stand quickly and scrub my face with my hand, ready to apologize for making her uncomfortable.

"Okay. I'm not going to argue with you," she says quietly.

Oh.

"I need the help, doctor's orders, and I want to be in top shape to go to Nashville and this stupid mistake was my fault so . . . okay, I'll stay with you." She blinks and then gives me a shy smile. "Roomie?" she adds.

The grateful, melty look on her face sucker punches me right in the chest.

"Okay," I say, nodding my head. I haven't thought this far ahead, so I move robotically, helping her into the wheelchair the hospital has provided to get her to my truck.

A million thoughts race through my head, the most prevalent one being . . . *I am entirely fucked.*

CHAPTER TWELVE
Wade

"I'll leave early, but I'll be back every day by noon to make sure you get lunch and then again by dinner. I'll let everyone know in the morning that you'll be away for the rest of the week. I'll handle everything you were supposed to do for the next few days. This is your space, I'm just down the hall but you shouldn't hear me on this side of the cabin," I say as I follow Ivy to the other side of the living area.

She's using the crutches we grabbed from the big house and they do fit her perfectly. The second bedroom and bathroom at the end of the short hallway are neutral, spacious and useless to me. In years past, other bosses have had kids that needed the space. For me, it was a space my mother could go to town on, testing out her hand at making it look like it belonged on some decorating show she watches.

"This is so pretty," Ivy says, sounding surprised and taking a glance out the window. "I'll do all the things this brochure says," she adds, holding up the pamphlet the doctor gave her. "I'll be out of your hair in no time, and I will be ready for next weekend. Even if I'm still on crutches." She smiles at me, a rueful smile.

"I'll show you the bathroom," I say, averting my eyes from hers like an awkward motherfucker. It's fairly large for a second bathroom, redone by Cole like the rest of the cabins a couple of years ago. The shower is spacious and has a comfortable shower bench built right in and a removable sprayer for her to use. The glass door will allow easy access. It really is the best place she can be this week.

Ivy's temporary room is all soft blues and creams in the bedding and curtains, with a wrought iron bed frame surrounding a comfortable bed. There's a tiny antique desk in front of the window looking out to Sugarland Mountain in the distance and our pastures, as well as a small dresser and matching antique ivory mirror, and a wingback chair complete with throw cushions and a fuzzy blanket strewn over the arm.

"This is perfect." She breathes out a sigh of what I can only guess is relief, then sits down in the chair in her room.

"If you need anything, just let me know—as much as possible, especially for the first day or two."

She places a hand on my forearm. "Thank you, Wade, I mean it. Thank you."

I nod and pull my arm away, looking to the living room like a nervous teenage fool.

"Let's get your things from your cabin in the morning. Right now, you need some pain meds and some sleep." It's after midnight, she must be wrecked, and I'm wrecked after being awake for almost twenty hours.

"Stay put, I'll be right back," I say to her.

She looks up at me with tired eyes. "I'm not going anywhere, but if you leave me here too long I might fall asleep right in this chair." She yawns as she finishes her sentence.

I make quick work of grabbing a few necessities. Some ibuprofen, a cold bottle of water, one of my t-shirts, a pair of my sweatpants that will be way too big for her but they'll be warm in my chilly old cabin, my brush, and a hairdryer I don't even think I've ever even plugged in let alone turned on.

When I return, she's sniffing quietly, looking out the window and crying, which is the last thing I am ever prepared to deal with. I hate when women cry.

"I just . . . haven't had anyone offer to take care of me for a long time . . . I don't know what else to say, it just hit me that you didn't hesitate," she says, keeping her gaze fixed out the window.

How long has it been since someone cared for her? Fucking hell.

"Well, around here we take care of each other."

She smiles through her tears as I bend down to look into her eyes. "You may be a slight pain in the ass right now, and way sappier than usual, but no burden on account of the ankle," I say, offering her the bandana from my back pocket to dry her tears, which she takes eagerly and nods.

She blows out a raspberry. "Nothing like a mushy sweet pep talk from Wade Ashby to make a girl feel better," she says.

At least her sass hasn't left her with her injury.

"Alright, the sappiness is over. Just get me to bed," she adds.

I say nothing else, ignoring that statement fully. I just wait awkwardly, turning on a lamp and closing her blinds as she dries her tears and pulls a brush through hair that's so thick it's still a bit damp as she pulls it from her scrunchie, then I help her into the bathroom so she can blow-dry it and get ready for bed.

Ivy leans on one crutch while drying as I grab her a washcloth and fresh toothbrush. She attempts to stand freely to do the back of her long hair then winces, settling back down on the crutch, muttering a few cuss words on the way as she can't get into the right position.

"It's fine, the rest will just dry while I sleep." She smiles at me.

I grunt, done watching her struggle, and then move toward her.

80

"Let me," I offer. "I have no idea what I'm doing but how hard can it be?" I shrug.

Ivy looks at me stunned for just a moment and then hands me the brush, an unsure look on her face. "Have at it, boss." She smirks.

It feels like a challenge. She swivels her body around and I flick the blow dryer on. I pull the brush through her silky strands while fanning the dryer back and forth until her hair resembles a sugar-scented sheet that hangs down her back. Even the tanned tone of my hands is stark in comparison to her hair's raven hues, and the urge I have to run my fingers through it and bring it to my face once it's fully dry almost completely consumes me.

Once I put the dryer and brush away, Ivy fluffs her hair around her shoulders and smiles up at me. Oblivious to how she looks.

Downright fucking stunning.

"Bet you've never done that before." She giggles.

"Fuck no, but I'm pretty fucking good at it if I do say so myself," I say back.

"It's impressive, my hair isn't even frizzy," she says, running a hand over it.

I clear my throat and throw out a practical excuse.

"Can't go to bed with wet hair, you'll catch a chill," I offer.

She nods. I say nothing more, handing her the clothes, and passing her the toiletries I fetched for her earlier.

"I'll give you some privacy and I'll get your pillows set up. I'll stay out here just in case you need anything I might have forgotten," I tell her.

I set her bed up the way the diagram in the pamphlet shows, stacking a pillow between the sheets for her foot, to keep it elevated, and then I wait. I hear the water running for a few minutes and then it's just silence. Ten minutes goes by where I internally argue with myself about knocking. My conscience wins and I'm just about to knock when I hear the door open,

I help her with it immediately. It's when I pull it fully open, when I actually see her—in my sweatpants, the bottoms rolled up on her small frame, swimming in my t-shirt which looks way too good on her—that my breath involuntarily catches in my throat.

"The sweatpants are so big I couldn't balance without the crutches long enough to pull them up and pull the drawstrings tight and tie them, they kept falling down," she says and then shrugs. "It took me a few tries."

I act as non-affected as possible by the idea of her pants, *my* pants, coming down around her ankles. Making my way over to her, I begin to help her move to the bed. It's when we're right beside it that she snags one of her crutches on the area rug and threatens to fall right over.

I catch her, with perfect timing but not before we tumble fully onto the bed. Ivy gasps as I cage her in below me so she isn't jostled. This one second feels like a hundred with my arms around her, looking down at her below me, so vulnerable, so soft. Her lips pop open as she stares up at me. It's this precise moment that my cock takes notice she's pressed beneath me.

I clear my throat and separate from her before she can feel it, pulling her up to sit.

"Told you, accident-prone." She smiles in apology.

"Fuck, you weren't kidding. Did that hurt you?"

"No, just feeling highly and completely awkward, other than that I'm good." She grins as the words come out honestly. "I just need some more practice with the crutches."

"You'll get used to them, but maybe don't move around much when I'm not here, don't need you taking out the other ankle," I say. It comes out sounding more annoyed than anything, but fuck, in my defense I'm trying to will my cock to stand down and right now that's not an easy task with her sitting there looking like a goddamn snack in my clothes.

Five minutes later, she's actually in the bed, ankle elevated, and covered.

I nod once. "You good?" I ask, trying to sound casual.

"Yes, very. This bed feels dreamy." She smiles. I don't tell her it's the same bed she has in her own cabin, I just shut her lamp off. She yawns, her mouth forming a perfect little O.

"You missed your calling, should've been a personal support worker," she says quietly. "Quick on the draw . . . good reflexes . . ." she says like she's counting off my qualities on her fingers.

I nod, trying to forget what it felt like to hover over her.

"Call if you need me," I say simply as I pull the door closed behind me.

"Night, Chief."

I make my way to the kitchen, and pour myself a stiff bourbon. I take a moment to breathe after all that. The last thing I expected when I woke up this morning was that Ivy would be sleeping down the hall from me tonight. I bring my drink to my lips, and as I do, I realize somewhere in the midst of all that brushing and hair drying, I ended up with another one of Ivy's scrunchies on my wrist. I shake my head and toss it in the basket, adding it to my growing collection.

Then, I get right to work.

CHAPTER THIRTEEN
Ivy

"So, what are you saying?" Brad looks at me from our kitchen table, cell phone still to his ear, cowboy hat on his knee. He was having an early lunch when I came through the door from my appointment. In truth, my appointment was over hours ago but I just drove aimlessly after that, registering. I sniff and take a tissue to the kitchen window. Looking out at the pastures I love so much, I try to absorb the news the doctor just unloaded on me today.

"Dr. Marshall says I will have a hard time because my uterus isn't exactly hospitable. My cervix seems like it may just be too short to carry a baby to term. He said I should go on good birth control, to regulate my periods better." I'm tired of crying. I've been crying all day, since I was told this news. "I thought you'd be happy," I say to Brad as he sits, quietly nodding.

"You know how I feel about kids. But I'm not happy you can't have kids, Ivy. Just more relieved it's not in the cards for me when it wasn't in my plan. And you should go on birth control. I've been telling you that for two years," he says.

I flinch at his words as reality smacks me in the chest for the *hundredth time. Always about what he feels, never about me, ever.*

"Brad, I haven't even processed this yet, and I never wanted to take birth control. You know how I feel about messing with the natural order of things. But for now, I will. I'd be scared to get pregnant if it's not possible for me to carry a child," *I say, feeling the tears welling up again, my body wishing, begging for him to come to me, wrap his arms around me and tell me it will all be okay. That he loves me enough anyway. That I'm still worth it.*

"I'm sorry," *I offer, looking for the common ground between us, knowing it's not my fault but still feeling the need to apologize.*

"Hey, it works out good that we're together. Another man might be heartbroken over this." *His comment isn't snide, but it still makes me feel worse all the same, and my heart shatters even more.*

Brad looks up at me, no emotion on his face, and he says nothing. Five minutes passes, me looking out the window with my tears, Brad still sitting on hold on the phone.

"Uh, I'm gonna go for a drive, clear my head. Is there anything you need?" *he asks.*

Affection? Understanding? Love? the voice in my head screams.

"No." *I sniff.* "I'll be fine."

"Okay . . . and don't worry, honey, I'm the kind of guy who sticks things out, okay? Even through things like this. See why we're meant to be?" *He smiles.* "This is a lot for you to deal with, we'll go out for dinner tonight. I feel like Mexican anyway, Shafer was just talking about that new place on Baxter Street . . ."

I block out the rest of his rambling. That's the last thing I feel like doing, but I nod anyway robotically.

". . . but I'll be back. I just need some time, fresh air," *he finishes awkwardly as he grips the front door handle. The only thing I got from anything he said was that it was a lot for me to handle. Not us. Me. Brad says nothing more as the person he's on hold for comes on the line. His face goes blank as he swings the door open.*

"Rick, I'm great, buddy, how are you?" He chuckles as the front door closes behind him like it's any other day. The moment I hear his truck fire up I let the tears consume me.

I open one eye, expecting to see my own cabin ceiling, then smother a tiny cry as I stretch. *Right, ankle, pain. Shit.*

The dreams of Brad not being there for me come a lot less now but they still come, and I wonder how I didn't see it when I was in the thick of it.

Can't go backward, only forward, Angel. My dad's age-old saying runs through my mind as mid-morning sunlight streams through the windows, little dust fragments floating in their beams as I gently try to move my foot. Miraculously, it doesn't feel quite as tight as it did when I fell asleep. It's still propped on the pillow Wade placed there for me; in fact, I don't think I even moved. I search for the clock, knowing my cell phone is still in my cabin, likely dead at this point.

Ten a.m. Good Lord. I just slept for almost nine straight hours. In Wade's cabin. My boss's cabin. The boss who tenderly blow-dried my hair last night and behaved like a perfect gentleman when I pulled him down on top of me in bed. The boss that didn't even bat an eye helping me even though it seems like making himself uncomfortable is the last thing he ever wants to do.

I sit up and stretch myself out. My ankle is still swollen but it definitely feels a little better than last night. When I get to the living area, I see the coffee table has been moved and a blanket is ready for me on the sofa, and my mouth falls open as I look to the kitchen in shock. Either Wade's gone overboard or a pack of yellow Post-it notes exploded. They are everywhere, in various places around the cabin.

The first note I see is on the very fancy-looking gas range stove and it says, *"Don't fuck with my stove until I teach you how it works or there will be hell to pay,"* in his angled, manly scrawl.

His coffee maker is ready with coffee to be brewed and Post-it instructions on which buttons to press depending on whether I like a light or dark roast. A mug sits beside it and my phone, which is plugged in and fully charged with two missed calls from *Brad 1* and *Brad 2*—Brad's ranch and house lines—beside a crockpot on the peninsula that is full of warm oatmeal, and a bowl, sugar, maple syrup and honey. The note in front of it reads, *"Didn't know what you'd like so here is everything."*

A tight feeling takes over my body. Knowing he made the effort to go get my phone for me, and that he was in my cabin, doesn't even bother me. I'm grateful he even thought about it. I'm not sure how to manage the feeling as I wonder briefly when he did this. After he left me at one a.m.? Did he not sleep all night?

I press the button for dark roast because I need something strong this morning. This whole situation is a little overwhelming. In the time my coffee takes to brew I make my way around the comfortable cabin. I probably shouldn't venture into Wade's side of the house but I can't help myself. I move slowly down the dark hall and peek into his bedroom. The door is wide open and the entire space smells like Wade straight out of the shower. There isn't much in here, just a massive king-size bed, maybe the biggest one I've ever seen. The walls are deep wood like the rest of the space, and his large rustic headboard takes center stage. The bed is perfectly made with solid navy bedding, and one dresser with a simple lamp sits against the far wall. I make my way over to it and take in the things sitting on top. A docking station for his phone, antler bookends around vintage copies of

The Great Gatsby, The Art of War, and a few others I don't recognize, a very old cowboy hat, and the culprit for his delicious scent.

I pick up the amber glass bottle and inhale. It's locally made. Cedarwood, bergamot, smoke, citrus, the label says. Whatever it is, it threatens to dampen my panties every time I breathe it in. I leave his room behind and move back to the kitchen, and sitting down on a stool at the counter I scarf down some oatmeal and peruse his other notes.

One on the drawer labeled "*Cutlery.*"

One on the pantry labeled "*Dry food, help yourself.*"

Another on the pantry that says "*Don't eat my Pop-Tarts.*"

I smile. *Big mistake writing that, buddy.*

I drink my coffee, then make my way to the living room, scooting up to the comfortable sofa. There are Post-it notes with the remotes on the side table that say what streaming services he has. I open my favorite one up and scroll through his "Watch Again" catalog, selecting one of my own favorites, and settle in. It's midway through *Point Break* that Wade finds me curled up on his sofa.

His eyes flit to mine as he takes his cowboy hat off and sets it down on the bench near the door.

"You behave this morning? No cooking?"

I nod, trying to ignore the odd way heat covered my body when he asked if I'd behaved.

"Yeah, I'm not taking any chances of making it worse."

"I don't know who the 'Brads' are but they called you twice between the time I got your phone and plugged it in," he says. "I wanted you to have it in case you needed anything. I don't have a landline," he offers as what seems like reasoning for going into my cabin.

Always practical, always in control and always thinking of everything.

I'm starting to realize these are the cornerstones of Wade's personality.

Wade doesn't seem to be looking for an explanation but I give him one anyway.

I chuckle and then spill the tea. "The 'Brads' are one person, my ex. The numbers are any line he tries to call me from. I worked with him during my time at Bellingham."

"As in Bradley? The Bellinghams' son?"

"Yes. You know him?"

"Met him briefly when I was a teenager, but probably couldn't pick him out of a lineup now. A little spoiled, if I remember right. He told us all more than once he was the boss's son and he'd take over the ranch one day."

"Sounds about right, and he's still waiting," I say.

"None of my business, but why don't you just tell him to stop calling if you don't want to talk to him?" Wade asks as he starts pulling things out of the fridge and fills himself a glass of water.

I laugh because yes, it should be that simple. "I've tried that, he doesn't listen. Doesn't take no for an answer very well. I've been meaning to get a new phone, but I'm trying to save every penny right now and blocking his numbers didn't work so well. He calls less than before but it's still frustrating."

Wade's jaw flexes in thought as he grabs a knife and cutting board. "No judgment, I have lots of experience in the shitty ex department, but bottom line, Trouble, a man should always respect a woman's wishes, even if he doesn't agree with them." He says nothing more on the subject and then looks up at me and asks, "Okay then, you like pineapple?"

I smile at both his assessment and his way of not scolding me for dating someone who is clearly an asshole.

Wade makes quick work in the kitchen as I continue the movie. I watch him in my periphery, as he washes his hands carefully then rolls his flannel up over his forearms, the little knot between his brows deepening as he works, slicing up cheeses and fruits, placing crackers and meats on a wood board.

"Never took you for the action movie type." He nods to the TV as he sets the rather pretty charcuterie board down beside me and seats himself on the other side of it.

"My favorite kind of movie," I say enthusiastically. "The classics especially, the more action, the better."

"Well, we have that in common," he says as he helps himself to some of his offerings.

"When did you do"—I look around and nod toward the Post-its—"all this? Did you even sleep at all last night?" I ask.

A look crosses Wade's face, one I don't quite understand.

"Slept great." He leans into me, his voice deep. "Running on ninety seconds, Johnny . . . pure adrenaline," he says, quoting a famous line that Patrick Swayze's character says in the movie.

I gasp dramatically, then laugh. "Wade Ashby, was that a *joke?*"

"Nah . . . you should know by now I don't joke," he says, his face instantly unreadable again as he pops a grape into his mouth.

"Right, I forgot. Jokes bad, grunts and scowls good." I giggle.

He grunts with exaggeration at me and leans back into the sofa, relaxing his legs, but I don't miss it for a second. The full and devastating lopsided smirk that plays on his lips. A smirk that makes my stomach drop.

"Something like that, Trouble, something like that," he says, that smirk just enticing me where I sit. I can't do anything but stare at him for a moment.

It's like I'm seeing a whole other side to Wade Ashby, and try as I might I just can't seem to look anywhere else.

CHAPTER FOURTEEN
Wade

When I return home at five, Ivy is on the couch, her ankle on a pillow just like I instructed, and the crutches are beside her. She is determined, I'll give her that, and strong as hell.

I drop my hat on the bench, say hello and watch her use her strength to pull herself around the room, keeping her ankle elevated. She seems to do it with ease, and she also seems to have a hard time sitting still, another thing we just might have in common. She moves quickly, disappearing into her bedroom. I hate that I don't like the idea of her needing space, but I get that it might be odd for her to be here with me like this, making small talk all the time.

I let her be and make my way into the kitchen to wash up and think about some kind of a dinner for her. As I do, I marvel at the odd feeling of just having someone here when I come home. Lights glowing, sound. *Any* sound other than nothing. Someone to greet. I don't hate it.

There are two candles lit in the center of my coffee table that my mother put there before I moved back. They've never been used until now but fuck, it smells good in here. Kind of like Ivy but amplified. Vanilla and some sort of cookie scent.

Ivy surprises me a few minutes later and comes back into the living room with a smile, her hair now up in a big messy bun, the heavy worn gray hoodie I left her this morning on her petite frame.

"It gets cold in here," she comments.

"Fuck, yeah it does, sorry. I'm used to it. I'll make a fire." I move to the big old stone fireplace and get one going for her as she asks me about the day while she cues up *Die Hard*.

I fill her in as I move back to the kitchen and pull makings out of the fridge to start dinner. I watch her settle in on my sofa and I can't help but wonder what other movies she's watched, or how many of her smutty book chapters she managed to fit in when I wasn't home all day, maybe in the bath while she—

Fuck, Wade. No. Just no.

I force myself to focus and our silence turns comfortable. Just the sound of the movie and the crackle of the fire fill the room as I roll my sleeves up and get to work on some quick chicken penne. I've always been capable in the kitchen—not only do I love to cook, I simply had to, because Janelle would burn water if she tried to boil it. If I wanted to eat anything other than grilled cheese sandwiches, I had to become resourceful. It was useful knowledge and my mother had made sure us boys knew our way around a recipe.

"I made my bed and tidied up a little," she says as I grimace at her.

"Y'er supposed to be sitting. Elevating."

"I don't sit well, Chief. I stopped when my ankle started aching, don't worry."

I nod and pop my AirPods in, and turn on David Allan Coe as I get in my cooking zone.

Thirty minutes later, I stand back and admire my handiwork.

Fuck, if I ever fail as a rancher I'm pretty sure I could absolutely kill it as a chef. I deliver her plate and take my seat on the other end of the sofa with my own.

"Oh God . . ." She moans that tempting sound again as she chews her first bite. "This is delicious," she mutters as she takes another.

I let myself eye her up when she isn't looking, wrapped up like a little burrito in the corner. The dark hair that's escaped her bun sits wispy around her face, and she looks way too good right now in my clothes. Speaking of which . . .

"CeCe is going to head to your cabin when she's done at Olympia today, she said she'll FaceTime you and you can instruct her on what to bring you for the next few days."

She nods. "She's already messaged me. I gave her a list. She should be here anytime."

Not even two bites later, the telltale sign of CeCe's headlights shine through the front window.

"Knock knock, delivery." CeCe's voice sings through the space as she opens my front door toting two good-sized duffle bags. Nash is trailing behind her like the puppy he is.

"Well, isn't this cozy . . ." Nash chuckles while I mentally berate him for being such a cocky son of a bitch.

Ivy smiles a megawatt smile at CeCe that almost takes my breath away as I watch it light up her whole face.

"A Not Angel home delivery service," Ivy remarks.

"Hell yes, and this delivery service comes with the help to put everything away too . . . Ooh, Mama's chicken penne? Don't mind if we do," CeCe says, already grabbing herself and Nash plates down from the cabinet.

"Guess this is a dinner party." Nash smirks as CeCe loads his plate up and he stuffs a piece of garlic bread into his mouth.

CeCe and Ivy ramble on while they eat, about random things going on in town, changes to Olivia's boutique. The fact that Gemma, Cole's shitty excuse for an ex, has a new boyfriend. Small-town gossip at its finest.

Nash and I make our way to the kitchen when we're done eating and I pour us both a bourbon. I grab my Pop-Tarts out of the pantry, open a package and pop two in the toaster. We lived on these things when we were young

"So, you have a house guest for a few days?"

"Appears that way, yep," is all I offer back.

"Fuck it, I'm just gonna ask. How the fuck is that gonna go?" He swirls his glass and takes a swallow.

I look at Ivy in the next room as I answer. Her face is animated, pretty, soft. A far cry from how it looked when I found her on my porch last night. She looks comfortable and she looks too damn good in my living room. I avert my eyes to the sink as I start to fill it with hot soapy water.

"It seems to be going alright so far. She's already looking better," I say, pulling the Pop-Tarts out of the toaster and passing one to Nash, he takes one from me and takes a bite.

"Must be all that tender loving care you're giving her," he says as he chews, smiling big enough to show me he's on to me, as if I'm that obvious.

"Fuck sakes, it isn't like that," I mutter under my breath, but I don't deny it. I am looking after her; it's the right thing to do. "I'm doing what I need to do for the ranch—she's got to be better to train. I would do it for anyone."

Nash grins again, and even though he isn't really my brother, sometimes I feel like he knows me even better than Cole does.

"Whatever gets you through the day, Sergeant," he says as he claps me on the back.

He thinks he's so smart. What the fuck does he know?

CHAPTER FIFTEEN

Ivy

"**A**re you feeling comfortable here?" CeCe asks as we put away my things.

"Oddly, yes," I answer honestly.

"Wade acts tough but somewhere in there he's just a great big softy," CeCe says to me as she hangs a few sweaters in the small closet.

She's brought me everything I asked for, tights and yoga pants because jeans will be too structured for the next few days, big sweaters, my toiletries and pajamas, and my beloved two books that I'm currently reading so I can take a break from the TV.

"That one is spicy." She points to the "why choose" I'm reading that just came out a few months ago.

"I'm only fifty pages in, don't spoil it," I say to her.

"It takes a bit, but when they get together, damn. I had to wake Nash up before I took care of myself." She laughs, and I laugh with her.

She's nothing if not honest, and it's something I love about her personality.

"Great, I guess I'd better read it when I'm alone so I don't do something stupid," I blurt out, then instantly regret it.

CeCe's eyes grow huge, she raises an eyebrow and then she starts laughing.

"You got a little crush on my brother?"

"No . . . I . . ." I stammer. "I mean, he is a good-looking man. I—fuck." I throw my hands up, not knowing what else to do.

CeCe laughs. "You're so busted."

I am, yes. It certainly doesn't help my go-to flick roster that he's being so damn nice and sweet, not to mention cooking me dinner with his strong arms and AirPods in like he's on *Top Chef*. Correction: World's Hottest Top Chef.

"The fact that you even tolerate him is a wonder, when he's so cold all the time." She giggles.

I know my face is still red from blushing so I may as well stop trying to hide it and own it.

"He's actually been really nice. I mean, as nice as Wade gets. He's warmed up to me a little bit I think. He even made a joke today," I say.

"Stop lying." CeCe laughs as she disappears into the bathroom to put my makeup bag and toiletries on the counter. "Didn't even know he knew any jokes."

"I mean it was lame but I'll take it," I say, laughing now too.

CeCe looks like she is thinking for a moment.

"You know, it might be good for him to have someone around for a few days. I worry about him. Janelle really screwed him over. Maybe having you to work with, possibly becoming his friend, will remind him what it's like to have human connections again and that they aren't all bad. I always hope that he can find someone worthy of him one day. Janelle never was." CeCe tucks a piece of hair behind her ear and the massive diamond on her left hand catches the light, momentarily blinding me.

"Goddamn, that thing is like a beacon," I tell her, grabbing her hand to admire it as we giggle.

"What the fuck, Trouble?" I hear Wade call out before he

even gets to my door. He's clearly annoyed as he knocks, pushing the already-open door.

CeCe and I both start to laugh at his stern demeanor. But I notice something more. His hands are on his hips and he's taken off his flannel. Wade's standing before us in his black t-shirt tight to his strong torso and upper arms, his hair is perfectly wavy and poking out slightly from under his backward hat, and a dishtowel is slung over his shoulder. Even pissed off, I admit openly to myself that Wade Ashby is . . . really *hot*.

"Uh-oh." CeCe giggles. "Dad's here to give us shit."

He grunts then turns his eyes to mine.

"The fuck are the rest of my Pop-Tarts?"

"Oh shoot, was I not supposed to move them?" I ask innocently as CeCe falls back on the bed in laughter. "I'm not sure what cabinet I put them in, you may have to check them all." I giggle.

"You wanna play, Trouble? Let's play," he says, his tone dark.

CeCe laughs even harder, but me? I just sit there and take note of all the ways it makes my body tingle when his voice does that threatening, commanding thing.

CHAPTER SIXTEEN
Ivy

I huff out a breath and look at the clock. The blaring blue glow reminds me I'm not getting enough sleep. It's three a.m. but I'm wide awake lying here. Restless and way too turned on after reading half my book before I fell asleep. CeCe was right. I could use a half-naked Wade right about now—even just to look at while I took care of myself would do. Behind the privacy of my closed lids, I picture the way the muscles in his back flexed under the ink there when he moved, how he looked hovering over me when we fell on my bed, his hard body almost pressed against me . . .

Shit. How inappropriate would it be to get myself off in Wade's spare bedroom with him sleeping down the hall?

Twenty minutes later, I realize it's inevitable and I'm not going back to sleep. I get up, throwing on my shorts, then, grabbing my crutches, I make my way out to the living room, trying to be as quiet as I can so I don't wake Wade, but I'm immediately startled the moment I enter the space. Wade's already here, lying back on one side of the sectional sofa, his long frame stretched out, taking up the entire thing. His eyes are closed and he's breathing softly. The end of *Baby Driver* is playing on the TV.

He's only wearing dark sweatpants that hang low on his hips, dangerously low. My mouth turns to sand as I let myself take in the sight of him. The blanket that must have been covering him at some point is now on the floor. The noticeable bulge in his pants is a feast for my eyes and his muscled body glimmers in the light of the TV, one powerful arm stretched behind his head.

And the way his lips look right now . . . I bite my bottom lip to stop myself from breathing out an involuntary moan. He just might be the sexiest thing I've ever seen. A tight coil of heat begins to form in my low belly as I let my thoughts take over. I imagine myself running my tongue over every crevice of his chest. I *should* turn around and go back to my room. *I really should.* I bargain with myself. Ten more seconds of taking in the sight of him and then I'll go back there and take care of myself, because fuck it, there's no turning back now. It has to happen or I may spontaneously combust.

Okay, so I stand there a little longer than I planned, because fifty-two agonizing seconds later he stirs and I can see the outline of his cock move in his sweatpants. Goddammit. He's packing a fucking weapon in there.

Stop looking, Ivy. Jesus. What the hell is wrong with me?

I start to turn to make my escape but one of my crutches scrapes across the trim and Wade shoots up, rubbing his eyes with the heels of his palms.

"Christ. What are you doing up?" he asks as he adjusts himself, looks at the clock, then covers his lower half with the blanket.

Too late, I already got the full view.

"I couldn't sleep, just felt like maybe watching a movie."

He blinks at me. Can he tell how flustered I am right now? All I can think of is scaling him like a tree.

Wade runs a hand through his hair and stares up at me, his sleepy green eyes mesmerizing me from across the room.

"There's one thing that helps when you can't sleep," he says, his voice so deep, so enticing.

Fuck, Chief, tell me what it is.

"W-what?" I stutter.

He stretches . . . Jesus, that body . . . those abs . . .

"Ice cream," he says.

Oh. My desperate pussy dies a little. I almost whimper but I manage to control myself.

"Sit," he commands as he gestures to the other side of the sofa. Even that turns me on.

He stands, his hardened cock still a bit obvious even as he tries to conceal it.

I feel like I might be actually drooling.

As he walks into the kitchen and flicks a light on, I make my way to the sofa and lean my crutches against it. I look up and really take in the sight of him. His sweats are hanging just low enough to let me see the two dimples in his lower back, over his perfect ass.

Yep. Definitely drooling.

"What's your go-to topping?" he asks as he scoops chocolate ice cream into two bowls. The simplest action that causes his upper arms to flex perfectly. "M&M's or sprinkles?" he adds. "Ivy?" My name on his lips forces me to blink.

Did I answer him?

No, I didn't because I'm still just standing here. Staring at him.

"M&M's," I say quickly, forcing my gaze up to his face.

Wade's eyes meet mine, tracking my gaze down his body. He looks up and smirks, before shaking his head. I instantly realize he knows I was staring at him.

I'm fired. He's going to fire me.

I spin around in utter humiliation; there's no taking back the way I was just eye-fucking him. I stand in silence for all of ten seconds. Wade doesn't speak but I hear him as he begins to move toward me. I squint my eyes closed in anticipation of my termination, then a strong arm reaches around my body as his spicy scent envelops me. Just as my pulse starts to accelerate to deafening levels, I open my eyes to see a sundae and spoon in his hand as Wade holds my treat in front of me.

I take them from him, and spin around as best I can only to find him towering over me. Heat fizzles up my skin like Pop Rocks melting on my tongue as Wade's eyes rake over my face then land on my mouth.

His throat bobs as he swallows, and for just a fraction of a second it makes me wonder if it's possible that he could want me the way I want him right now. He blinks, then moves silently back to the kitchen to grab his own sundae as I let my legs give out like they've been begging to for the last three minutes. I sit down on the sofa below.

"Looks like we share the same guilty pleasures," he says as he sits down beside me and manspreads, just to torture me further.

My face must show my worry because he actually smiles—the first real smile I've ever seen him wear. One that takes my goddamn breath away.

"Action movies and ice cream," he says, amused.

Oh, those guilty pleasures. The cold ice cream slides down my throat and I need it. It's way too fucking hot in here.

Wade says nothing else as he pulls up *Lethal Weapon* and we eat our ice cream in silence.

I look to the thermostat on the wall beside me. It's only seventy degrees in here. It looks like I'm the problem. I think I need to get out of this cabin, and fast.

CHAPTER SEVENTEEN
Wade

"What the fuck is this?" I ask as I pull the front door open to the three Not Angels on my porch.

"What does it look like? It's a party, Sergeant." Ginger Danforth pats me on the chest as she breezes by me with two bottles of wine in one hand.

"Fuck me," I grumble as CeCe and Olivia Sutton pile in behind her carrying brandy and more snacks than the grocery store has on its shelves.

"Ivy couldn't come to Sangria Sunday so we brought Sangria Sunday to her." Ginger smirks as she starts unloading all the mixings of sangria onto my counter. "Even brought our own bartender, and we're putting a Camilla Danforth twist on it tonight—coconut rum, the way my mama makes it." She gestures to the door and I see Nash coming through it with a look of *sorry, bud* on his face.

Ivy stands from the couch where we were just having dinner, smiling wide at the girls like she's really fucking happy to see them, and why wouldn't she be? The only person she's really seen in four days is me. I try not to appear annoyed that our quiet dinner and *Ocean's Eleven* is over as I gather my plate.

"Is this alright?" Ivy asks me. Her blue eyes taking in my shift in mood immediately.

I soften my gaze. It's not her fault they came barging in.

"Totally fine, Trouble. You could use a fun night." I pat her shoulder.

She's healing up just fine. Even walking around on her ankle a little, she says it rarely hurts unless she puts a lot of pressure on it. I've been doing a good job of keeping her fed, keeping her ankle iced and keeping her company as much as I can, especially every night around three or four a.m. when she appears in my living room in search of ice cream and action movies. After the third night I was just ready for her, ice cream in hand and *The Equalizer* ready to play.

Mercifully, she's been wearing actual clothes, unlike the first night when it took every inch of my willpower not to fuck her ten ways from Sunday on my sofa, but you can bet your ass I burned every inch of her into my mind. The way her silky soft skin begged me to lick every bit of it, the way her chest rose and fell with every breath, her pebbled nipples begging for my touch as her pouty lips fell open and the pink of her tongue darted out to wet her bottom lip when I stood over her. I've never been so overcome with an urge to take a woman in my life. I don't even know how I sobered myself up. Sheer fucking strength that should've earned me a goddamn medal.

"Y'all are so sweet!" Ivy squeals.

"Way to give me a warning," I say to Nash as I re-enter the kitchen.

"I didn't even know what we were doing until I got in the truck," he says, holding his hands up in surprise.

He gets out a knife to slice lemons while CeCe gives him a kiss on the cheek and Ginger and Olivia pour snacks into bowls to bring to the living room.

"Besides, you could use a guys' night anyway, a break from playing house nurse. We're gonna go to the big house to watch the Titans game with Pop when I'm done making the sangria. Got some of that craft beer from the brewery on 21."

"Sorry I'm late, y'all. Fucking Gemma can never be on time," Cole grunts as he bounds through the front door.

"Someone needs to remind her that her daughter should be her damn priority," Ginger pipes up instantly from the living room, a heated look on her face.

"Maybe you could, I've tried fifteen hundred times," Cole grumbles.

I pat him on the back—thank God Mabel has one reliable parent.

"I have half a mind to smack her around a little bit," Ginger says as she turns and grins at CeCe and Olivia. "Like CeCe tried to in the summer."

Cole shakes his head at Ginger. "Fuck, that is not the answer." His gaze moves to Ginger's and his brow furrows.

"Maybe not, but seems like the one that would be the most fun." Ginger giggles, the other girls chiming in with her.

Cole scowls at her. "Every damn time the pot needs stirring, there you are in the middle of it with a paddle trying to lure in your army." Cole doesn't miss a beat as he acts out stirring a giant paddle, while pointing at Ginger.

"I'm glad I can keep things exciting for you, Mr. Ashby," Ginger retorts, winking before turning her gaze to Nash. "Better make us a few pitchers if you're leaving, Nashby," she adds as she pops a raspberry into her mouth.

Cole turns to grab her arm. "If I have to drive your ass home tonight, I'm not stopping for pizza or whatever food you're craving when you're drinking, so you best be on good behavior tonight, woman," he says to her as her grin grows wide.

"Aw, honey." Ginger looks at him with a *who are you*

fucking kidding? face, then frees her arm and pats him on his jaw. "Of course you will, but don't worry, I'll only call you if the other men in town on my call list are unavailable." She shrugs with a sweet smile then heads into the living room.

"Fucking little vixen," Cole says as he shakes his head and pours himself a drink.

How these two can go from having each other's backs to bickering like an old married couple in one second flat, I'll never know.

Nash and I have been telling Cole for years they need to fight out their aggression between the sheets. It's obvious everything Ginger Danforth does is just to get a rise out of Cole, because she basks in his attention like a cat lying in the sun when he gives it to her.

I chuckle at them and run a hand through my hair as I turn back to the kitchen.

Suddenly everything in the room goes quiet and all eyes are on me.

"Did Sarge just fucking laugh?" Nash asks, his eyes wide. "I haven't heard that since 2009. Swear to Christ."

"Fuck off," I retort.

"Been since high school for me." Cole grins, raising a hand as he searches through the snacks, finally settling on some Twizzlers.

"I didn't even know he had dimples until last week," Ivy chides.

"He has dimples?" CeCe chuckles, everyone else following suit.

For some reason, just this once, I can't help but give up and laugh with them. Maybe I do need to loosen the fuck up a little.

Nah, fuck that.

CHAPTER EIGHTEEN
Ivy

I've never had friends, not really—none that I could ever really trust anyway. When I was a teenager, I never had the time to do all the normal things girls my age were doing. I was working and studying to get a scholarship because I knew at a young age that was the only way I was getting a college education.

I imagine if I had, this is what it would have felt like. Gossip and girl-talk, a fire in the fireplace and Wade's rustic lamps the only lights in the room, *How to Lose a Guy in 10 Days* mixed with delicious drinks, snacks and way too much info about each other's sex lives. Girls that come to cheer you up when they know you're down and out. Girls that have your back like a little squad. A little army of sunshine. That's what these three are and the way they've welcomed me into their circle, I'll be grateful for as long as I'm on this ranch.

"So, let's just call out the elephant in the room, Ivy. What is this little arrangement with you and Sarge?" Olivia asks.

I look at all three of them and feign total innocence, because I am innocent, aren't I?

"No arrangement, he's just being kind. I'm going back to my

own cabin in a day or two," I reply, popping a chip into my mouth.

"The way Wade Ashby is looking at you these days is . . . different, not kind. Different than I've seen him look at a woman in a long time," Ginger chirps.

"I was starting to think he had given up on women," Olivia adds.

"He's my boss," I say, looking straight at CeCe. The last thing I want is her or anyone in this family thinking I have ulterior motives where Wade is concerned. Secretly, it really frustrates me that I'm having a hard time not thinking about him lately.

"I said that once," CeCe snorts, and the other girls start laughing. I should've known she wouldn't think badly of me either way.

"Boss or not, he looks at you like he's ready for a one-way ticket to Ivy-town." Ginger chuckles as she gets up to grab more sangria. "Refill?" she asks.

I nod and hand her my almost empty glass.

I don't know what to say here—too much info and it might get back to Wade, and I'd die of embarrassment. Too little and they'll know I'm full of shit. Having girlfriends is sort of a tricky thing.

"We, uh . . . get along pretty well. There are moments I think he's annoyed with me and then there are moments where we just feel in sync if that makes sense."

"It does," CeCe says. "You two will be working awfully close for the next while. And as my mama says, time has a way of working these things out." She winks, and I sigh, relieved she's so easygoing.

"Whether he's your boss or not, the fact remains, he is a single cowboy," Ginger chirps from the kitchen.

"Say it." Olivia looks at Ginger. "We all know you're going to."

I look at Ginger, confused as hell, as she hands me back my glass, full to the brim of Nash's delicious sangria with Ginger's Mama's twist.

"Now you've just ruined it," Ginger says.

"Fine, I'll say it. Save—" Olivia starts.

"No, no, it's my saying," Ginger interrupts, looking me in the eye. "Look, Ivy, Wade is hot stuff, always has been. I'm just saying, if the opportunity presents itself, save a horse. Scientifically, it will probably help you train better, because you'll be less stressed out and even more in sync. It's practically a no-brainer."

Olivia laughs as CeCe groans.

"God, this town is too small. I need to be related to less of the single men around here." She laughs, and I smile in spite of myself.

"Ooh, speaking of single men, let's prank-call Cole and tell him we did something illegal." Ginger giggles as she pulls her phone out of her purse. Because we've all had one too many this seems like an excellent idea to all of us.

We wait with bated breath as the phone rings and she holds it out on speaker so we can all hear. The sounds of Nash and Wade yelling at the football game in the background come through.

"You don't have a very reliable list if no one else would come get you, Vixen," is what Cole answers with, and I wonder if Ginger knows exactly how tightly she grips this man's balls with every word she speaks.

"You were the first I called, baby. I need a man of the law, we tipped Mr. Saulito's cow."

The three of us snicker as silently as possible. We are clearly excellent at this.

"Don't quit your day jobs to run out and become actresses," Cole says, totally monotone over the line.

"Really, come save us, baby, they're gonna haul us off to jail." Ginger sounds like an actress in a 1950s southern drama as she speaks.

"Four tipsy-ass women, that have a combined weight of four hundred and fifty pounds, one of whom has a twisted ankle, tipped a seventeen-hundred-pound cow?"

"We're stronger than you think, Cole," Ginger says, now hot and bothered that he doesn't believe her as the rest of us silently die laughing.

"I know you're fucking strong, woman. But I can hear your damn cronies laughing in the background. They aren't as inconspicuous as they think. I am a cop, remember? I spot bullshit pretty easily."

"Goddamn, you guys need to work on your incognito!" Ginger yells at us. "We'll do a better job next time of convincing you. Also, I definitely am gonna need that ride home, so come soon. Ta-ta, Law Daddy."

"Fuck, I'll be there at eleven," Cole says before hanging up as we cackle.

"Speaking of saving a horse, when are the two of you ever just going to do it already? It's obviously destiny," I blurt out.

All three of them turn to look at me.

Shit. Was I not supposed to say that?

CeCe scoffs, "As if, they're way too close for that." She looks at Ginger to confirm. It takes her a second, but she glances from CeCe to me.

"Definitely. I'm not saying I haven't thought about it, I'm only human, but if I let him into my Garden of Eden, things will never be the same. Besides, he's a complicated soul, and furthermore, I don't get down with fuckboys," Ginger says.

I smile at her, but I'm not sure I believe her.

"Ew . . ." CeCe swats her.

"What! He is, what do you think he does in Lexington?"

"I don't know, goes shopping? Takes in the nightlife?" CeCe asks, not even believing it herself.

Ginger snorts. "He goes shopping, alright. Pussy shopping, the kind where he doesn't ask to stay over after."

"There's my cue to exit the room." CeCe stands to head to the kitchen, and Ginger eyes me with a smirk.

I can tell as plain as day that there's not a chance she wouldn't welcome Cole into her self-proclaimed Garden of Eden if she had her opportunity.

But like I said, I've never had friends, so I just wink at her. Her secret is safe with me.

CHAPTER NINETEEN
Wade

By the time I get home on Wednesday and start dinner for us, Ivy is animated and full of chatter. This has been our routine for the last week. Dinners, drinks, snacks, talking ... okay, mostly Ivy talking, while I listen intently through every action movie I can load up for us, about nothing and everything—our childhoods, her training plan, places we've been, college, music, food, you name it. It's nothing too personal, but feels very personal just the same.

After spending these nights with her, I feel like I know Ivy a little better, and everything I know about her I like, and fuck, she's becoming more difficult every day to put out of my head. You think it would be weird sharing a home with someone you barely know, but in this instance, I feel more at ease around her than I did with Janelle after six years of marriage. I've found myself almost excited to leave the office and come home the last few nights. And that isn't a good thing for me when it comes to not giving in to this little mini Ivy obsession or whatever this is.

"What am I going to do when I get home and have to go

back to boring dinners?" She smiles up at me as I hand her a steaming bowl of my family's favorite—okay, Mabel's favorite—deconstructed chicken pot pie topped with homemade biscuits.

"For a fee, I could leave a plate on your doorstep," I say, only half kidding because I like cooking for her.

Mostly, I like the face she makes when she takes her first bite and realizes she loves it. Her throat makes the cutest moaning sounds and her eyes roll back just a little. It makes me wonder about the other times she'd make that face and those sounds.

"Oh my God, I would pay for it," she says, giving me the sound I want as she takes her first bite. "You made these biscuits from scratch?"

I scoff as I take a bite. Fuck, that *is* really good.

"Don't insult me, Trouble. There's no other way," I say, disgusted she'd think I'd use a box mix.

She holds both hands up in truce, and I look up at her as she smiles. She's gotten a little more comfortable. Maybe too comfortable, since she's wearing those little gray fleece pajama shorts again, the ones I wanted to tear off of her the first time I saw them. And just to further torture me, tonight she's wearing *my* red bandana, the one I gave her to dry her tears her first night at my place. It's tied into her wavy hair like a little scarf, and I couldn't give a fuck to ever get it back. Something of mine that close to her is doing something to me I can't really put into words.

"Sorry, I would never want to insult the chef and risk never getting fed like this again." She takes another bite.

I won't tell her there's probably no risk of that. I'm pretty sure I'd cook for her anytime she wants.

"Oh, I also talked to a handful of potential jockeys today . . ." she starts.

The conversation I'm trying so hard not to get used to

continues as we talk about Nashville and the auction while we finish eating.

Reluctantly, I let her help me dry dishes afterwards because her ankle is a lot better. Also because she tells me if I don't let her help with something, she's going to eat all my Pop-Tarts while I'm sleeping tonight.

I listen to her hum to herself while she works. By the time we're done and I'm heading for the shower, she promises to finish cleaning up and get the movie ready for us.

There's a simplicity to this I can't really comprehend. Oddly like we've been doing it for a lot longer than a week. When I get to the shower, I'm grateful for a few minutes alone. I'm strong, but my willpower is wearing thin, and my balls are a different level of blue than they've ever been before, just from spending every night sitting five feet away from her.

By the time I'm dried off and tossing on my sweats, I have a plan. I'm going to go to bed early. It's her last night here, then we'll go back to normal. I'm taking her things to Blue Eyes for her after work tomorrow, and she's even going to spend some time in the barns before we head to Nashville on Friday.

But when I reach the living room, I see that Ivy has slid the coffee table out of the way and has a big nest of throw blankets and pillows from the couch in the center of the room, on the area rug in front of the fireplace. She's holding a bag of candy and popcorn in her hand.

Fuck me. What plan again?

"*Fast X*?" she asks with a smile.

We've watched the first nine over the last few days.

"I mean, I can't go home without watching the final movie. That would be a travesty."

I don't even hesitate. I grab us two waters from the fridge and make my way over to my own personal nest of cock torture as quickly as I can.

"You should take the wrap off, Trouble, let's have a look," I say to Ivy an hour later, when we're mid-movie, as I pop a handful of popcorn into my mouth.

I watch as she unwraps her ankle carefully.

She pokes and prods at it, sticking a long, silky leg out and flexing her foot. I have no idea how but even that makes my dick twitch.

"It's almost better," she says, observing. "A little tight maybe, but I'd say ninety percent better."

Don't do it, Wade. Don't you fucking do it. I look up at the ceiling for a split second.

Fuck it. I'm doing it.

"Give it here, I'll rub it out for you." I motion for her to bring her foot to me.

"I haven't shaved my legs today." She giggles. "They might be prickly."

"Fuck, if you think I care about that, you're dead wrong," I tell her.

She bites her bottom lip and contemplates for a minute. I wonder if she may not trust me enough to even want my hands on her. I berate myself for once again not knowing how to keep any sort of boundary with her, but before the thought can leave my head she's scooting across the floor and putting her foot into my lap.

I reach over, bringing her slender ankle into my hands. I start by pressing my thumbs into the arch of her foot, which feels tiny in my palms. Even her goddamn feet are pretty. A few seconds pass and she moans softly while I try to keep my breathing under control. Heat slinks up my forearms with the feel of her bare skin on mine and the sight of her pretty pink toes in my lap.

"Do you fink they'll ever make another one of veese?" Ivy asks through her own mouthful of cinnamon hearts. I chuckle at her mumbling.

"I don't know. It depends on whether or not Vin Diesel can get an acting job somewhere else," I answer, trying to think of literally anything other than my swelling cock against my sweatpants. "And FYI, your legs aren't prickly in the slightest," I say.

In fact, I'd like to run my tongue over them.

She giggles. "God, that feels way too good, I might have to hire you."

"It'll cost you," I say without thinking.

Ivy's response is barely more than a whisper and shocks me just a little. "Oh yeah, well, whatever it is, I'd be willing . . . just add it to my tab. Daily dinner and foot rubs. Gawd . . . that feels good," she says, almost in a sort of pant.

The tone of her voice is even more husky than normal and sexy as fuck.

That voice threatens to ruin me.

"I think they can always convince Vin to come back, but they'd have to leave The Rock out, apparently they don't get along," I say, keeping this lame-ass subject going. "And The Rock would kick Vin's ass, that's why they made *Hobbs and Shaw* and Vin wasn't in it," I mutter as my thumb traces her calf.

"I think Vin is stronger than you think," she says.

"Not a chance he could take The Rock."

What the fucking hell are we even talking about?

I don't have a clue, but I can play this game all night, the one where we talk ourselves through whatever this is, especially now that my hands are creeping past her knee, kneading her skin like I can't touch enough of her. I can't stop. I don't want to stop.

The slightest little grin plays on her lips as her slightly fuller lower one, the one that was put on her face by God Himself just to taunt me, meets her teeth as she thinks, and she narrows one eye in a squint.

I slide one finger up just slightly over her inner thigh, then circle the back, squeezing tight as she lets out a breathy moan. I may as well dig my rock-solid dick a grave with that sound.

"This is something you should do, get massages. I see how tight your shoulders are at the end of the day. I don't know how good I'd be at it but I could try to return the favor," Ivy offers quietly.

I sigh. "I think it would take a lot more than a little massage to work out the weight in my shoulders," I reply, realizing that sounded a lot more like an invite than I planned.

"Oh I know," she says mischievously. I look over at her, she's grinning ear to ear. "Or . . . you know what works to relieve tension?"

Fuck me. She looks way too enticing right now to ask me that.

"How about a little tussle? Blow some steam off, Captain Grumpus?" she queries, right before she tosses a pillow and it smacks me square in the shoulder.

I blink, shocked, then register what she's doing.

"Oh, you're done for, Trouble," I growl, leaping on top of her and gripping her tight around her waist as she squeals with delight. Before I know it, I'm pulling her down below me so her small frame is completely caged beneath mine.

Her laugh is contagious as I tickle her into a whimpering pool,

"Mercy . . . mercy . . . Wade!" She giggles.

"So you're a tough little thing but the fucking moment I find those ticklish spots you're begging for mercy? I gotta say, I'm a bit disappointed you caved so easily."

She's pushing her blanket against me to fight me, my own laughter filling the space around us bringing hers on, and fuck, it feels good to laugh, especially with her. Even with her still slightly injured ankle, Ivy is strong, catching me off guard. She sends me to my side, and I flop down onto my back as she falls between my legs.

"I'd never really say mercy, Wade. It was all just my war tactic, throwing you off guard so I can get the better of you, and it worked," she taunts, her breathing heavy and jagged as her hair brushes my chest through my t-shirt.

There's no denying for either of us how hard my cock is right now.

"Maybe so, but you're not gonna win, Trouble. I grew up wrangling my brothers."

"I grew up wrangling horses," she retorts as she struggles to pin me down.

I roll my eyes and pretend to yawn in mock boredom.

"Okay, you're going to force me to actually make an effort here?" I ask.

She scoffs at my taunting words but I wrap one arm around her waist and effortlessly flip her over, pinning her below me again, my one hand holding both her wrists easily above her head.

Our laughter putters out at the same time and the room is silent. The fire crackles. Ivy looks up at me, her cheeks flushed, pupils blown out, her pink lips parted and begging.

The only other sound in the room is our breath rising and falling together and my thunderous heartbeat in my ears as I become torturously aware of the warm space I'm settled against between her thighs. A low growl rumbles in my chest as I fight my conscience.

The angel on my shoulder is telling me to stop, sit up, move, go to bed, anything, before I make a mistake I can't take back.

But the devil on the other tells me that this moment? Her body pressed against mine, her sweet breath so close to the tip of my tongue, isn't something I have the strength to walk away from.

Ivy's glassy blue eyes drop to my lips at the same time she shifts her hips, her legs parting slightly, welcoming me in, and I know as sure as fuck that the devil's taking this round.

"The way you're looking at me right now, is this *your* war tactic?" Ivy asks, her voice shaky. I adjust my hips slightly and the tiniest moan escapes her lips.

"And just what way would that be?" I ask, as my pulse hammers in my throat. "Like I want to find out if you taste as good as I think you do? Like it's the *only* thing I'm fucking thinking about day in and day out?"

"Yeah . . ." she whispers. "That."

I dip my head even closer, my lips just over hers as my next words come tumbling out, hoarse and deep, before I can stop them. "Find out, Ivy . . . Say *mercy*."

I let my gaze trade between her eyes and her juicy fucking lips that are right there, so close. Ivy's breathing shallows, her lips pop open slightly, her pink tongue wetting them, and I see it, the second she gives in, her voice so quiet I barely hear it, but I do.

"Mercy . . ." she whispers at the same time I drop my face to meet hers.

My lips devour hers without one ounce of uncertainty, licking, tasting, claiming. Fuck, do I want to claim her. She tastes so sweet, her sugar scent melts on my tongue as her eager lips match mine effortlessly. My heartbeat pulses harder the more I search her mouth with mine. I pull back slightly to run my tongue along her plump bottom lip as she whimpers.

"I was right. You taste fucking delicious," I groan.

I want her permission to explore and she gives it to me, enticing me as she wraps her legs around my waist, coaxing me closer with the slow, languid sweep of her tongue into my mouth and another moan. My hands leave her wrists and find every inch of her body they can. I grip the side of her neck, sliding my thumb down from her jaw, pressing it lightly to the center, feeling her throat work as she swallows the deep groan that leaves my chest.

Her fists grip my t-shirt, tugging at it as she runs her hands under it, over my sides, leaving a blazing trail as she goes. I press my cock into her shamelessly and the sound she makes into my mouth in response almost does me in entirely.

Thunderous knocking startles us both. And we just lie there for three or four seconds frozen, looking into each other's eyes.

"Wade!" More pounding.

"Fuck," I growl into her lips, pressing my forehead to hers for a beat, both of us catching our breath.

"Why is it locked? It's fucking cold out here," Cole bellows from the other side.

I sit up and straighten myself up, looking back down at her, legs still spread wide, knees bent. I'm willing myself the strength to pull it together and answer the door even as Ivy's disheveled appearance and swollen lips tempt me to ignore Cole and get right back to kissing her. A finger darts up to touch her lips and a grin plays over them.

"Delay of game, Chief." She giggles.

I might fucking kill Cole.

CHAPTER TWENTY
Ivy

hit, shit, shit . . .

Did I kiss him or did he kiss me? Does it matter? It was the best, most panty-melting kiss I've ever had, and it answered my question. Wade Ashby is, in fact, capable of losing control.

I straighten myself up as best I can after that as Wade stands up, moving all the blankets back to the couch and sliding the coffee table into place. He adjusts the bulge in his sweatpants in an attempt to hide it, but he doesn't do it well. I side-eye him as I run a hand through my hair.

"You better hide that weapon better if you're planning on answering the door right now," I mutter with a smirk.

He grunts the most frustrated sound, and adjusts himself a little more, pulling his t-shirt down to cover himself as best he can.

As he moves toward the door I cover myself with the blanket and haul the bowl of popcorn from the table into my lap. I have never been so into a movie as when Cole storms into the living room.

"She's moving in with him? She didn't even tell Mabes

they're serious yet and she's moving in with him. I had to hear it from *him* of all people? If I fucking murder Gemma, will you promise to raise Mabel like your own?"

He is fuming, I've seen Cole grumpy but I've never seen him angry. A chill runs up my spine at the fury that protects his only daughter. He startles when he realizes I'm on the couch.

"Fuck, Ivy. Sorry, I didn't even realize you were still er— here," Cole says as he takes in the scene before him. It must seem innocent enough. He doesn't even flinch at it.

"I'm going home tomorrow," I say as a lame explanation.

"We're watching a movie," Wade adds, clearly no better at this than I am. "Calm down, I'll grab you a drink," he says, patting Cole on the shoulder.

"She's up to something, I know she is. I fucking knew it when she all of a sudden decided to actually show up on her scheduled weekend. So help me fucking God if she's using Mabel as pawn to lure some fucking boyfriend in I don't know what I'll do."

I stand and grab my crutches—although I'm hardly using them anymore. This is a conversation for family only. "I'll leave you to it, boys. I'm gonna take a shower and then head to sleep early. For what it's worth, Cole, you're a great dad. If I can see it after only a month, everyone else can see it, including Mabel. She knows who she can depend on, trust me," I say, hoping to calm him even a little.

My eyes meet Wade's across the room, longing and the same confusion I feel reflecting back at me. "Good night, boys," I say quietly.

"Thanks, Ivy, that means a lot," Cole says back, oblivious to what he almost just walked into, before continuing with his rant.

Wade nods before I turn around and leave the room, the feel of him between my legs still fresh in my mind, but I leave knowing that this was a one-off. A result of forced proximity and one fleeting moment. Wade is my boss. I need this job. I can't go back to Jellico.

The hot water tumbles down my skin like a soft rain as I close my eyes and just let it run over me. I smooth my slick hair as I remember the feel of Wade's warm stubbled jaw under my hands, his plush lips against mine.

God, he's a good kisser, exactly how he is in his everyday life—sure and firm, controlling with a side that feels like he'd give to me in a way I have never felt. His strong, powerful arms wrapped around me, his large hand cradling my throat. I've never felt more tended to.

The ache between my thighs is a sweet torture I can't resist or smother no matter how hard I try. I let my fingers ghost a hardened, aching nipple in the hot water and I shiver. I really wanted him, I wanted him like I've never wanted a man before—granted I've really only been in a real relationship with Brad. My few and far between one-night stands since college don't really count.

The intense way Wade's mouth claimed mine told me instantly that Wade Ashby would play my body like an instrument. Without thinking, I detach the shower head from its clasp and turn it to massage mode, trailing it over my breasts. I let out a moan that can't be contained as I imagine his callused hands raking down my bare, wet back, kneading my skin, as if he were in this shower with me. I roll a nipple between my fingers and the fire in my low belly ignites.

Sliding the shower head down over my waist to my clit

pushes my breathing to hasten as I press my free palm against the wall. Wade is behind me; his lips pepper kisses down my spine and two fingers slip into my aching pussy.

He works his fingers expertly to a curve that presses every sensitive spot I have.

"You've wanted me from day one, haven't you, Trouble? You wanted to pull that towel down the day you came into my house unannounced and take my thick cock between your lips," he asserts, his voice deep and challenging in my mind.

"Fuck, yes I did," I whisper, water sprinkling against my lips.

"And now, you want me to fill this tight little pussy with every inch of my cock?" he asks.

"Yes," I whimper, my face pressed against the shower wall as I work the water pulsating from the shower head against my aching swollen clit.

His cock stretches me perfectly as he drives into me from behind, his big hands gripping my hips in a bruising hold. I work the shower head against my dripping core faster, more, deepening my fingers as far as they'll go. In my mind, they're Wade, fucking me with every single ounce of desire I feel for him.

I move the jet up, just a fraction of an inch but it's enough to send me reeling as I let out a muffled cry, tumbling, falling, exploding from the inside out with Wade's name on my lips while I do.

The water starts to run cold as I come back to earth from the best orgasm I've had in, well, maybe ever. I place the shower head back in its holder and towel off, squeezing the water from my hair as I dry off and stare in the steamy mirror at the woman that just got off while the man she was thinking of sat in the next room.

So much for staying professional.

CHAPTER TWENTY-ONE
Wade

"Need a hand?" I ask Ivy as she comes toward my truck wheeling her small navy suitcase that's seen better days behind her.

"Sure, Chief." She smiles at me. And it's the good morning I missed at four when I woke up and she wasn't here, so I watched *The Terminator* and ate my ice cream alone. I've barely seen her since Wednesday, when the kiss felt round the fucking world we shared almost broke me.

Okay, the truth is I've been avoiding her, trying to get my head straight before spending the next three days with her. Trying to keep a grip on all this because it's starting to feel like I'm losing it. I have pep-talked myself to death, reminding myself Ivy is my employee and I have to keep control.

Except, I'm not sure I even have any anymore. The fucking minute Cole left, I made a beeline for my shower and fisted my cock with the vision of her plump lips wrapped around it, her husky sounds humming eagerly against me. The reality that it could never happen between us resurfaced faster than my cum could circle the drain. After everything she's been through with her obviously shitty ex and her family, I won't be another person in her life that just takes what they need from her. And let's face it, I'm not exactly prepared for anything complicated right now with everything sitting on my plate.

I hand her a Spicer's coffee in exchange for the bag that has more than a few weathered corners and some definite wear. As I load it into my truck, the tag falls forward. *"Property of William Spencer."* That name hits me square in the chest like a bullet. A familiar sort of grief washes over me at the tiny remnants Ivy holds onto desperately from her father, the same way I hold onto my own dad's fishing pole that I still use when I fish, just so I can welcome the memories of fishing Cave Run Lake as a boy that come back to me, or how I keep his cowboy hat and his old truck I still drive that he gave the best advice in. I set my jaw to keep the sting away from the bridge of my nose. I might be the only person she knows that understands just how valuable this old suitcase is, and it makes complete sense to me why she totes it instead of buying a new one.

I climb into the driver's seat and take my hat off, tossing it to the back.

"I think we should talk," I say at the same time Ivy says, "Is this gonna be weird now?"

We both smile, then Ivy giggles, taking her plump bottom lip between her teeth. All the filthy things I want to do to her and those soft, pouty lips run through my head no matter how hard I try to stop them.

"You have a mighty tricky way of winning a tussle, Chief," she accuses. "Kissing your opponent into submission is kind of like cheating, just sayin'."

I scoff. "In true Trouble fashion, you welcome the kiss then blame me for it. I see how it is."

She laughs, feigning shock.

"I'm innocent here, you were the one that kissed me," she jokes. She knows she's full of shit, and fuck, I can't control myself around this woman at all so I blurt out, "I was between your legs, I could feel how badly you wanted that kiss." I point back and forth at her. "These pretty innocent eyes aren't fooling anyone."

She gasps then swats me, and I chuckle, scrubbing my face with my hand.

"We've been spending a lot of time together," I say, trying to convince myself. "But, all I do is tell every ranch hand on this property that they need to keep their hands to themselves, and then at the first chance I get, I kiss you. So, I'm sorry."

I expect her to agree, or say it's okay, but as usual when it comes to Ivy, I expect wrong.

"I'm a big girl, I knew what I was doing. It was both of us—as you so eloquently pointed out, you were between my legs, and Wade, you aren't wrong, I did want it."

Fucking Christ, this woman's mouth.

We sit for the longest beat in history just waiting to see what the other will say.

She eventually shrugs and breaks the silence. "Let's not sweat it. Let's just say it's . . . human nature?"

I blow out a tortured breath.

"Human nature?" I query. "Huh, that's the excuse we're going with?"

"Yep. Seems plausible. Whatever gets us through the day without you wearing that guilty look on your face." Her cocky little smirk taunts me as she points a finger in my direction, as if she's fully in on the secret that I'm lying to myself about her. "So, we're gonna be friends then, yeah?" she asks, extending a hand for shaking.

I take it, closing around her soft fingers with my hand, and even that proximity still feels like too much.

"Friends," I reply, clearing my throat.

"Can't go back . . . so, let's just . . . move forward." Ivy does her seatbelt up and looks at me expectantly. That went a lot easier than I thought it would.

She pulls out her phone to check the time and I remember that I have a present for her. I reach under the seat of my truck.

"Also. Here," I say, handing her the small white box.

She takes the new iPhone from me hesitantly and stares at it in her palm. The silence lasts too long.

"It's the newest one. New phone number and you're on the ranch's plan. If and when your time is done here, you can transfer it to your own name. Mine and my family's numbers are in there for you. When you're ready, I can help you add who you want, if you need me to."

She blinks and her mouth falls open slightly and then she starts to ramble. "Wade. I didn't tell you that story about Brad to make you feel . . . I was going to buy one, they're just expensive and I'm trying to save. I'll pay you back. I can buy my own—"

"Listen, just . . . fuck . . . you are the only one that should decide who calls you. Your personal space is your fortress, okay? Just accept it. You need to have a reliable phone through this training anyway. Preferably one we can set your email up on," I say firmly, poking fun at her dinosaur of a phone.

Ivy says nothing but her eyes say it all. She nods, knowing it's not worthwhile to argue with me.

And I can't help but add, "And for what it's worth, assholes that clearly don't take no for an answer need to hit the road. This will make it easier."

She reaches over and puts her arms around me. "Thank you, Wade. Really. This might be the most thoughtful thing anyone has ever given me."

I breathe her in for one second before she pulls back from me, and how fucking pretty she looks this close to me almost stuns me. She averts her eyes and moves back to her side of the truck.

"Right . . . so, for the sake of keeping this friends thing going maybe don't look at me like that," she says.

"You either," I say, because the smile she's wearing feels like a reward. One I can't help but want to earn every way I can.

The almost-four-hour drive passes easily. We fall right back into the same type of conversation we were having in our nightly movie fests, and as the AT&T building comes into view, Ivy is a picture of relaxation, and so fucking beautiful. Bare feet up on my dash, a warm fall breeze flowing through the window swirling her hair around her face as she sings a Lainey Wilson song like she wrote the damn thing.

I can't help but think that deciding to make a derby run might just be the best impulsive decision I've ever made.

I hold that feeling all the way to the Omni Hotel. The lobby is a bustle of activity, country music plays through the open space and a fire roars in the large central fireplace even though its seventy-two degrees outside.

"Reservation for Ashby," I say as I get my ID and credit card ready, slapping both on the marble countertop. Beside me, Ivy hums along to the music playing in the lobby.

"Of course, Mr. Ashby, we have your room ready for you, you're on the seventeenth floor. You'll be staying in an executive king suite."

"And the second room is still adjoining?" I ask errantly, putting my cards back into my wallet, just to clarify that I will in fact have to suffer with Ivy so painfully close.

"Uhh . . ." The attendant fumbles with the mouse and clicks through a few screens. "Second room?" she asks. "I only see one reserved room here, Mr. Ashby."

CHAPTER TWENTY-TWO
Wade

I blink, and Ivy gulps beside me. I smile at the young girl.

"There must be some mistake," I say politely. "I booked two rooms—two adjoining kings."

More clicking through various screens on the clerk's side of the counter are deafening, as my heart hammers in my chest while I search for my reservation on my phone.

"I'm sorry . . . it's only my second day. I can get a manager . . . but, Mr. Ashby, I only see one room here and we're booked completely full through Monday. We'd be happy to comp you the night for the inconvenience."

The thought of sleeping in my truck in the parking garage passes through my mind. I've slept in worse places. A few more minutes of the same before she's looking up at me with nervous eyes and no way to rectify the loss of the second room.

"It's fine, she can take it," I say. My words calm the flustered girl, I pass her a twenty-dollar bill for her trouble, then turn to nod at Ivy to assure her I won't try to stay with her—or worse, that I planned this. But the moment I face Ivy her hand darts out and rests on my forearm. Her violet eyes full of confidence.

"*We'll* take it," she says in a tone that tells me her mind is set. I open my mouth to protest but she shakes her head and mouths quietly, "It's fine."

It's nowhere near fine. It's the furthest thing from fine, but for some reason I don't disagree. I nod back at her.

One room? One fucking bed? Yep, I'm fucked. Fucked like an alcoholic trying to withstand his own personally crafted bottle of one-hundred-year-old bourbon.

When he hasn't had water in days.

In a desert.

On a midsummer afternoon.

Fucked.

I look up at the ceiling as the elevator door closes and we're alone in the small space. My hands are balled into fists as I restrain myself. I speak to push my dirty thoughts from what the idea of sharing a room, of sharing a bed, with Ivy is doing to me.

"I think we both have a goal here and—" She turns to face me, her eyes stunning me as they focus on every inch of my face, saving my lips for last. "I want to do my best for you. I want to be focused on training," she mutters, as if she's trying to convince herself too. The only problem is I am not even listening to her because her gorgeous eyes render me stupid.

"Fuck, I didn't plan this room thing," I retort as the elevator doors open. "I hope you know I would never put you in this position," I continue as I hold the keycard over the sensor.

"Of course I know that, Wade."

I push into the room and maneuver around the massive king-size bed that seems to be screaming at us from the center of the room, like a neon sign is hanging overhead that says *"Incredible fucks happen here."*

"I'll sleep on the sofa. Christ, I'll sleep in the bathtub, Ivy, if it will make you feel comfortable."

The air is so thick between us you could cut it with a knife, but because this damn woman never ceases to surprise me, she starts laughing. Not a little chuckle or giggle, an all-out, no sound exiting her body as she drops to the bed and tears form in her eyes laugh. When she is finally able to breathe, her laugh fills the air like a clear sound and it's so contagious that I start to laugh too, but I have no idea why we're even laughing. I can't stop, I'm right there with her as her hand covers her beautiful smile while she catches her breath.

"All you try to do is keep total control and . . . they put us in . . . they put us in the same room, with one . . . with one . . . bed?" She laughs hysterically for a few more minutes, then wipes the tears from her eyes. My cheeks hurt from laughing along with her; the irony isn't lost on me either. I drop to the small sofa across from the bed.

Ivy stands and moves toward me. I breathe her in as she pats a hand to my face, her knee brushing against the inside of my thigh, and I wage an internal battle with myself not to slide my hands up the backs of her thighs.

"I know what we need."

Fuck.

"We have a full day of viewing tomorrow and the auction after that. We'll be working all weekend. We should have some fun too. We're going out on the town; it's not even dinnertime but fuck, I could really use a drink and I'm sure you could too. I'll have a quick shower, I'll be ready in a half hour," she says as she flips her suitcase open on the bed, and I catch my breath.

To no one's surprise, a few rogue scrunchies tumble out. Of course she would need twenty different colors and patterns for a three-day trip.

Ivy pulls some things out then disappears into the bathroom to freshen up, her long shimmery hair cast over her shoulder as she goes.

I *should* do a number of things. I *should* sleep in my truck tonight, I *should* get my shit together and realize that if we're both going to stay focused through this, I have to push past this little crush. But because I know I have to endure the whole weekend with her, I pick up one of her scrunchies off the bed and bring it to my nose, breathing in the scent of her. I'm like some kind of a fucking animal when it comes to this woman, and I wait for the shower to start running in the bathroom.

Without a thought in my head, other than *I need to fucking cum now*, I unbuckle my jeans and pull my already rock-hard cock out. I wrap the soft, blue satin scrunchie, the exact color of her eyes, around my dick and then I spit generously into my palm. The depraved side of me takes over as I close my eyes. The silky fabric encompasses me as I begin stroking my cock with it. An unmatched fervor takes hold, a part of her wrapped around me, it's too much to bear.

I fist myself in quick, intentional pulls while I imagine nothing but her incredible body in that shower only ten feet from me, hot water dripping over her perfect tits down to the taut skin of her waist, and further still to the sweet little berry I want to suck between my teeth at the apex of her thighs. I would fucking worship her, I would spread her plump ass apart in front of me while I watched my cock fuck into her sweet soaking cunt over and over.

My eyes screw shut as a sort of haze lines my vision. *"Fuck,"* I mutter, gripping the edge of the wall with my free hand as I give a final tug before spilling myself all over my hand and her scrunchie.

I take a minute to recover and listen to hear that the water is still running in the bathroom. I blow out a shaky breath.

It's official. I have fucking lost it. I need a fucking drink, and this scrunchie?

Well, that's definitely fucking mine now.

CHAPTER TWENTY-THREE
Wade

"Can I get you anything else, cowboy?" our server asks. She's young, blonde, and very flirty. She's wearing the standard Twelve Thirty Club attire, which is where we've landed for dinner. She's Cole's type to a T, not mine, and she's been doing her damnedest to get the best tip possible since we sat down.

The thing is, I wouldn't even look twice at her because Ivy is sitting across from me wearing a blue strapless dress the same color as her eyes, her hair pulled back high on her head in a ponytail, and all I can do is stare at the way her graceful neck curves to her shoulders and think about how badly I want to get my mouth on it.

I may have cleaned myself up physically after I ruined her scrunchie, but mentally, I still haven't recovered.

"Looking for dessert?" The server leans down to pick up my empty plate, and I avert my eyes from her tits that are practically in my face. I swear, I hear Ivy snort from across the table.

"We're good. Just the bill, thanks," I say as she stands back up straight and gathers Ivy's plate as well.

"Too bad." She grins at me, attempting to be as sexy as possible.

"I'm cramping your style." Ivy giggles when the server is out of earshot. The sun streams in the window behind her and lights her up like a goddamn halo.

I look down to my drink than back up to find a smug look on her face.

"You know she was flirting with you, don't you?"

"Meh," I say nonchalantly

"It's not your fault. Something happens to women in Nashville. They're all looking for a cowboy," Ivy comments.

"Good thing I'm not a cowboy."

"Rancher counts. In fact, I think it's just the hat, you could be a tax attorney for all they care, as long as you wear those jeans like that and carry that hat around, you're eye candy."

I don't miss her comment. I lean back in my chair and fold my arms over my chest.

"Are you checking out how I look in my jeans, Trouble?"

"I mean . . . I'm in Nashville too," she says, and my cock twitches.

Ivy's eyes flit to my phone on the table as it buzzes for the third time since we've left the hotel. For the third time straight, it's fucking Janelle.

"You got yourself a case of an ex that doesn't take no for an answer too, boss?" Ivy takes another drink, then errantly licks some of the salt off the side of the glass, which in itself threatens to brick me up under the fucking table like a teenager.

I look away and flip my phone over, ignoring Janelle again.

"A word of advice, you can be the good man you are without sacrificing your own sanity. That's the positive thing I learned from Brad. You can learn something from Janelle too. Stop looking at your time with her as a waste, and look at it as a stepping stone to what you want and what you don't. All you have to do is set that boundary with her for good."

I run a hand through my hair and blow out a raspberry.

"Fucking hell, didn't know this dinner came with free therapy."

"Gotta earn my keep somehow, Chief." She smiles then adds, "So, Mr. Rancher . . . back to the hotel, or you got other ideas?"

Oh, I have other ideas alright. Ones that tell me I need to keep myself out of that hotel room as long as humanly possible. I look across the street then back to those violet eyes I can't get enough of.

"You like Johnny Cash?" I ask Ivy.

She smiles wide. "Who doesn't?"

"Let's be tourists then," I say.

I've been here before and seen it all, but somehow with Ivy everything feels brand new.

When we've gone to every single touristy place we can, staying for the longest time at Studio B while Ivy tells me how much her father loved Elvis and a handful of stories about him, stories I actually find I want to hear because somehow when she tells them I'm interested, we finally get back to the Omni. Only Ivy doesn't seem quite ready to go upstairs either, and it's only nine-thirty. We decide to sit in front of the massive fireplace in the lobby, and she tells me I need to buy her a drink, which turns into three more for her to my one. We listen to live piano music and talk, and I laugh at her dancing in her seat to an ultra-slow piano rendition of "Thank God I'm a Country Boy." The way she exaggerates her moves is ridiculous and incredible all at once.

I can't shake the feeling throughout the night that every time we look at each other, it's like we're asking which one of us will cave first. It's never going to be safe to go upstairs together, but we have to at some point or we'll be waking up in the lobby.

By midnight, Ivy is fairly drunk. Funny as all hell, but drunk nonetheless. I'm learning drunk Ivy has no filter between her brain and her mouth, one more side to her I never thought I'd see, but like now that I do.

"Seventy-eight dollars! For just a few drinks?" she says as she eyes the bill when the server drops it on the table.

"You're not in Laurel Creek anymore," I tell her as I lift my glass and finish the rest of mine finally.

Ivy narrows her eyes. "You know what I think?" she asks.

"What?" I play along.

"I think I like this Wade Ashby, outside of Laurel Creek."

"Oh yeah?" I ask.

"Yeah, you're carefree, no one's placing their burdens on you . . . I mean, I've seen you smile at least three times." She says it so exaggeratedly that I realize I really have a fucking reputation.

I lean toward her across the table.

"I'll tell you a secret. I don't think my smiling today has any-thing to do with what city I'm in, Trouble."

Ivy averts her eyes and drains her glass, then looks down to the receipt on the table. If I didn't know any better, I'd say she was almost nervous, and fuck, I *like* that I make her that way.

That little bit of fear I see in her eyes ignites me. She should be afraid—if I ever got my hands on her I'd never let her go.

"Well, that's rather expensive, even for Nashville." Her eyes light up. "Oh I know!" she says like she's just thought of the best idea. "Maybe you could just make those convincing *fuck me* eyes you gave me at this server, and she'll give you a break. She likes you." Ivy slings the strap of her purse over her shoulder and leans in. "They all like you, you should use that hotness to your advantage."

"*Fuck me* eyes?" I ask, enjoying her theatrics.

"That's right, don't act like you don't know." She guffaws and waves a hand at me. I see just how free she is right now, how open. The thought of her like this is downright fucking dangerous for me.

"Those dark, smoldering eyes you gave me right before you kissed me? You could've made me do anything you wanted in that moment," she says with the softest rasp to her voice.

My jaw falls slack for a brief moment before I get it together as she giggles at my reaction.

"Okay, time for bed," I tell her as I drop a hundred-dollar bill on the table and help her stand.

"Yes, time for bed." Ivy grins. "One bed."

"I'm sleeping on the sofa, the bed's all yours, Trouble," I tell her as we wander the hall to the elevator.

She laughs, and reminds me the sofa is half my size, which it is. I watch her curvy form in front of me as she walks, then move in beside her and hit the button for our floor. She flips from nervous to brazen in one second flat. *Alcohol.*

Standing right in front of me, she uses her thumb and forefinger to tweak my chin.

"You think I couldn't resist you in my bed with me? Just because your face is perfect?

She thinks it's her I'm worried about?

I just chuckle because seeing her blunt and honest like this is even fucking adorable.

"Even this stubble here," she says as she skims her finger down my jaw. A simple touch I almost have to close my eyes just to withstand. "Everything is just so . . . symmetrical, like you aren't real. It's extremely satisfying and kind of infuriating," she says as her hand stays resting on my face just long enough for my body to register her touch.

I place her hand back down at her side.

My cock is going to disown me soon with all the fucking torture I'm putting it through.

"You probably don't even try. You probably just wake up like that," she rambles.

"Don't give much thought to a beauty routine," I tell her.

"Exactly, and you still look like that. *Infuriating*." She throws her hands in the air in drunken animation.

Upstairs, I reach into my wallet and pull out our room key, swiping it over the lock and pushing into our room.

"Well, I'm not a heathen. I do use moisturizer, and a good shampoo and conditioner," I tell her as I take my hat off and run my hand through my hair, before dropping it on a nearby chair.

She giggles and doesn't miss a beat. "Well, duh . . . gotta keep yourself smelling all delicious and whatnot," she says as she waves a hand over me and kicks off her sandals, pops her suitcase on the bed and reaches back to unzip her dress right in front of me.

As she does she mutters something that sounds like, "*It's fine . . . we're all adults here.*"

Jesus Christ. I look up to the ceiling and will myself to wait for her to enter the bathroom before I look back down. That was my plan, but when it comes to her, I have no willpower, so when she turns to look back over her shoulder and says, "I think it's stuck. Can you help me, Wade?" I get to her in less than one second flat.

"You're gonna get all this hair caught," I tell her as I pick the long ponytail up off her back and bring it to my nose, breathing her in, reminding me of her scrunchie that was wrapped around my dick only hours earlier, then I place it over her shoulder.

I stare down at her from my full height. She's so unspeakably close to me. It would take so little to bend her over the bed, flip her dress up and give in to whatever the fuck this is. I take a breath to steady myself but that doesn't work. She smells too fucking good and her skin has a sort of dewy shimmer I can't explain. As I fiddle with the zipper and pull the caught fabric out of it, I almost stop myself from freeing it just to get one more second of breathing her in, but the temptation of undressing her wins.

I pull the zipper down to her waist and her entire back is exposed. Inked vines dance down her skin from her shoulder blades along the column of her spine, etched with words so tiny I'd need to be a lot closer to read them. They're Ivy vines. They spread out over her tailbone and disappear into her black lace panties that I currently can't stop staring at.

Blink, Wade. Blink.

"All done?" she asks so sweetly, I instantly sober myself up.

"Yep," I reply, clearing my throat.

Ivy spins around, holding the structured top of her dress up over her full breasts, and smiles up at me. Somehow, my hands are on her shoulders, she's warm and so fucking soft under them. I let my eyes trail over her, her collarbone, the curve to her ear, the pulse that beats there, her full lips, and when I land on her eyes, they're glassy.

She smiles at me. "Wade, we agreed you wouldn't look at me like that," she says, a little slurry, reminding me how much she's had to drink. Way too much for me to touch her like this. It makes the decision slightly easier for me to slide my hands down her arms and let go.

"Thanks for your help," is all she says, way too innocently, before she spins around and heads for the bathroom, her entire silky back on display, screaming at me that she never had a bra on under that dress all night before she disappears behind the bathroom door.

When she comes out, she's dressed in another Eric Church tour t-shirt, this one cut at the neck into an off-the-shoulder version, and those little shorts she wears just to torment me. I've got her suitcase away, her bed turned down, and water on the bedside table for her, but I am already changed into my sweats and tucked in—crammed in, really—on the sofa beside the window. The only light is the one beside her bed.

"Drink some of that water before you go to sleep," I tell her as she pulls her ponytail out, her long hair tumbling down over her bare shoulders, and she yawns.

She lifts the bottle up, looks at it and then looks back at me, and suddenly I feel very much on display, with no shirt on the sofa. The way her eyes hungrily roam my body is like a shot straight to my groin.

"Have to be in control of everything at all times?"

I lie back on the sofa to break her gaze, extending an arm behind my head.

"Just drink the water."

"Yes, sir," she says, not realizing how those words from her lips affect me.

As she shuts out the light, I can almost hear her smile as she says, "Night, Chief."

I feel my jaw tense as I try so hard to keep myself on this couch, I'm afraid I may pop a tendon. I close my eyes and will myself to sleep. Because we both need it. She is probably going to be hungover tomorrow, and I'm going to be exhausted from staying up all night thinking of the way she looked holding that dress up with one hand as the outline of her perfect tits were on full view.

I focus on her breathing as she drifts off to sleep, thinking that will be less of a distraction than the images in my head, but I'm wrong. The throaty little sounds she makes while she dreams have me bricking up ten feet from her. Everything about Ivy Spencer distracts me, and I've been doing my best to fight it for way too long.

I just don't know how much fight I have left.

CHAPTER TWENTY-FOUR

Ivy

"What's his hip number?" Wade asks me the next morning as we slide into the first line of ten outdoor stables at the Tennessee Bred Yearling Sale.

I quickly pull the list of thoroughbreds up and scan it. "543, Book One stalls."

Wade nods. It's a sea of people, owners leading their horses out into the corrals for potential buyers to view. Wade clutches our guidebooks for the Book Ones and Book Twos.

I'm fighting a tired haze after how much I drank last night, but I don't know if I would've made it through without the alcohol.

"Essentially, it's like the NFL draft," he says to me. "Hip 543 or Rustling Winds is a Book One. We would be paying upwards of one million for him. But you're right, with his bloodlines we got a damn good derby shot."

I nod.

These are things I've only heard about and researched; his knowledge is firsthand. I will be letting my gut guide me, going by feel of the horse and his personality.

"There are a few others I want to check out in Book Two, the second-highest class of breed. Even the Book Threes. No one really knows the perfect formula for a winning racehorse."

Wade takes in the horses we pass as we walk, always watching for something no one else sees. In that respect we are very similar; I do the exact same thing.

I watch as his green eyes observe, deep in thought before he speaks, teaching me, and even that is hot. "You hear the saying 'it's best to find a diamond in the rough'? These are all diamonds, even the Book Threes, it's just finding the right one," he tells me.

I nod as I keep up with his long legs. If he sees a horse he likes we stop for a moment and take notes.

I stop in front of one that catches my eye at the end of the row. He's beautiful, maybe the most beautiful horse I've ever seen in real life. Bellingham had good riding and breeding horses but nothing like the one we're here to see today.

"Crescent's Landing," I say, watching the horse.

Wade stands back watching me relate to the horse. I observe him and try to make eye contact with him for a few minutes, reaching my hand out to touch him, and he pushes his face toward me, asserting his dominance.

"He's pretty, but he's too jumpy," I say, after a few minutes, writing him off.

"That's it? One glance and he's out?" Wade asks, not judging. He seems genuinely curious as to why I would snub a Book One so quickly. "His sire came in third in the Breeders' Cup in '19 . . ." He begins reading his stats from the book.

I'm only semi-listening to him, we've drifted into the next row now, and the most beautiful chocolate filly and I are having a moment. She's timid but regal, a Book Three. Her stature just says she's a queen, and I instantly love her.

"I don't really go by stats, Chief. I go by their hearts. I can

142

usually tell just by watching them if they're serene but also a fighter, and that has to come naturally. You can't train the heart."

We've reached the filly now and I note her name and hip number.

I smile, my eyes filling with warmth for her as my dad flashes through my mind. *Hi, Dad,* I throw up into the universe.

It's love at first sight. She comes to me instantly and I trace the lines between her eyes with my hand. Her stature is grand, like she knows a secret I don't. I like to think she's telepathically telling me *I'm your girl.*

"No training the heart, words to live by," Wade says, looking amused.

"That's right," I tell him. "Just like people. Your heart is what it is the moment you're born. Don't you agree?" I ask Wade without looking at him, I'm still having a moment with hip 211.

"S'pose so, Trouble, never thought of it that way."

I smile at the beautiful horse in front of me and I then let her go. We stand in silence for a beat before Wade clears his throat.

"She hasn't got anything really too noteworthy to speak of with her breeding. Her grandsire raced and won at Keeneland and Crenshaw Downs; he was in the derby but never placed in the top five."

"And she's a filly," I add. Everyone knows fillies rarely win the derby.

"I'm not too worried about that—their hearts may not be able to be trained but their bodies can be," Wade says.

"Again, just like people." I grin. "Think of all the things we do just because it's what we're trained to do, but it's not what's in our hearts."

"True story," Wade replies. "But yes, you're right. Last I checked, only a couple fillies have ever won the derby."

"Three," I correct, without looking at him.

I give her one last little pat. She's a beautiful creature and we'd probably only pay around a half million for her. I force myself to move forward, because as much as I think she could be the one, I would never ask Wade to take such a risk.

"If it was my money, and I had all the time in the world, my money would be on her, but it's not." I shrug. "So, let's go look for your surefire winner," I say, casting one more glance over my shoulder at my girl.

We continue cruising the aisles until we come to the horse we've been looking forward to.

"Well hello, Rustling Winds," I say to him.

He is strong and beautiful, I'll say that. I start at his feet and take in the sight of him. Moving over every inch to search for flaws and strengths. Is it wrong to judge a horse's personality the way I would judge a man's at first glance?

Probably, but do I do it anyway? Absolutely.

And I can already tell that this horse is the small-town superstar quarterback that everyone and their mother has told is a winner since the moment he was born. He's perfectly bred, but he knows it, and that may be his downfall or his triumph. Only time will tell.

"Probably run you more like 1.2 or 1.3," I say as I move to greet him.

He's wonderful. He isn't my girl, but I could definitely help make him a winner.

"I've received five texts from Nash this morning telling me to pay any price. He says his main contribution to help is with the upfront costs of the horse, so 'go big or go home,'" Wade says with air quotes.

I smile. For being the non-emotional ex-hockey player that pretends he only really likes CeCe, that man has a heart of gold and his love for this family is unmatched.

"Well alright, let's spend his money than, shall we?" I ask, a mischievous grin playing on my lips.

Wade grins back. He is a sight this morning. It's a wonder I made it out of that hotel room alive today when he wandered out of the bathroom in perfectly fitting jeans, a flannel and a thick Carhartt jacket, running his hands through his damp hair from the shower and smelling like the clean spice of his aftershave. Everything about Wade is big, manly and rugged. It takes everything in me not to stare at him and just simmer in the faces he makes, or the way his jaw works as he speaks, even the deep sound of his voice—

"We shall. You have a look down the next row. I'll go make sure we're registered for tomorrow's auction and double-check our seats," he speaks, interrupting my little daydream of him.

I nod and point to the row where I'll be when he's done. Taking in the horses as I pass them, any one of these could do it for us, any one of them could be our winner. I just have to believe I'm good enough to get them there.

"Ivy."

I freeze.

That voice. Instantly, the little hairs on the back of my neck stand up. I'd know it anywhere. I especially remember the last time I heard it, an inch from my face as its owner stood over me, seething, an evil look in his eye that I'll never forget. I pray I'm just imagining things.

"Ivy Grace." Again.

Fuck.

I close my eyes and take one deep breath before I turn around to face him, silently willing myself not to murder him before I even have the chance to help Wade choose a beautiful new horse.

"Brad," I say, bracing myself for a fight, hoping I can get rid of him before Wade comes back.

"What are you doing here?"

Why am I asking? I don't care.

"I'm here looking at another stud to breed with Mona Lisa," he answers, looking at me almost like he's seen a ghost as he mentions one of his ranch's prized mares. His hat comes off and he runs a hand through his dark blond hair.

He starts coming closer, and my fists ball up at my sides.

"I can't believe you're here." He's all soft and sweet, the way he always was for a time after we fought. It was how he gaslit me into thinking I overreacted to his behaviors.

"You haven't answered me or my family. All I've wanted to do is talk. After you . . . lost it that night, I realized why you'd think I'd try to hurt you and I forgave you. It took me a while but you don't have to be ashamed anymore. I really miss you. I'm not the enemy here, Ivy, all I've ever done is love you."

I throw a silent prayer up.

Dear Universe, if I stab him with my pen, you know why.

CHAPTER TWENTY-FIVE
Wade

I've never seen Ivy wear a look on her face that says she's actually angry. She's always a giant ball of happy, carefree sunshine, so to see her face now, staring at whoever the fuck this shiny cowboy is across the aisle, has me poised and ready to attack if necessary. Her eyes are dark and stormy. I start moving quicker, pushing my legs to move faster to get to her before he can.

Just as I close in, Cowboy Ken moves closer and tries to put his arms around her. The look on her face is sheer panic so I stand in front of her and smoothly extend my hand for shaking.

"Wade Ashby," I say as I physically feel Ivy relax behind me.

Cowboy looks up at me, startled like he has no idea where the fuck I've come from.

"Brad, Brad Bellingham," he says, taking my hand. I can instantly tell he's a wet noodle, just like his handshake, and I knew he looked familiar.

"So, can we talk?" he says, looking between Ivy and me, as if he's trying to figure out why I am standing between them. Ivy steps forward, and I wonder just exactly what went on between her and her former employer's son.

"I haven't answered you for almost three months—that should tell you that I don't want to talk to you, Brad. And I'm not going anywhere alone with *you*."

Wait, why the fuck not? My eyes zero in on him. *If he hurt her—*

"Ivy, it's all been a misunderstanding, I just want to—"

"I believe she said no, Brad," I bite out. "So that'll be all, but it's been mighty nice to see you."

Brad opens his mouth to protest, he seems to have a problem with understanding the word *no*, and I'm using every ounce of my self-control to not let my mind roam to why Ivy looked as angry and uncomfortable with him as she did two minutes earlier. Brad looks between us, back and forth for a second, and then he snickers.

"Got yourself a bodyguard?" he asks Ivy.

The fuck did he just say? He just made the stupid mistake of taking my politeness to mean I wouldn't take him out at the knees. I'm about to show him I can be a gentleman and still fuck him right up.

"Actually, I'm her friend. It doesn't seem like you are though, so I'm only going to ask you nicely one more time. It's time to give Ivy some space now." I give him the universal flick of the wrist for *get the fuck out of here*.

He looks at me, sizing me up. He's polished, his cowboy boots don't even have a single scuff. He's no match for me and I'm pretty sure by the look on his face, he knows it. If he even tries to breathe too close to her, I won't really give a fuck about how it'll look when I knock his ass out. But he sure will, because I can already tell appearances mean more to this guy than they do me.

Brad smirks, and something sinister I want nowhere near Ivy hovers in his eyes as he opens his mouth to speak to her.

"Yep. That's what I thought. Someone to threaten me with is just how you'd operate." His eyes snap to mine. "Ashby, yeah? Silver Pines," he says. "It all makes sense now."

My fists clench at my side as I try to remain calm. He isn't the sharpest tool in the shed, which is why he looks at Ivy and keeps talking.

"Fucking your way through another ranch? I guess that's your thing?" he says to her with a grin.

Well, that does it.

Before my brain allows me to even think, my fist connects with his jaw and sends him right back into the mud and horse-shit below him.

I crouch down, making sure the dirt stays on the bottom side of my boots. Speaking low so he's the only one to hear me. "I gave you the opportunity to leave here peacefully, Brad. It's been a long day already, and I really don't want to have to make a total fucking spectacle of you, so I suggest you stay down here in the shit where you belong until Ivy and I clear the barn doors, understand?" I pat him on the shoulder and then pick his hat up out of the mud and toss it at him, and it hits the fucking wet noodle squarely in his chest before I stand.

Our little show has now attracted a small crowd. He starts chuckling like the smug little prick I can already tell he is, even though his lip is profusely bleeding. The thought of this trash any- where near Ivy has my blood boiling, as I clench my fists and will myself not to hit him again and land him in the hospital.

"You're up, my friend. She's really good at sucking you in." He looks at Ivy behind me. "You're a good little tease, aren't you, honey?" Then back to me, grinning as he pulls a hanky from his pocket and holds it to his lip. Looking right at Ivy, he adds, "Thing is, she can't offer you much though in the long run, pal."

Fuck sakes. Why can't people just fucking listen?

One hand grips his shirt, the other connects with his jaw again. He's instantly dozy as some of our spectators gasp.

I stand and turn to Ivy to get her the hell out of here, but when I face her, she's shaking like something he said actually got to her and then she's hightailing it out of the barn as fast as her still-weakened ankle will carry her.

Ivy's legs are no match for mine and I catch up to her in two seconds flat.

"Did you get all the paperwork finished up?" she asks as her voice shakes, like she's trying to hold it together.

"Ivy—"

"I should've known he might be here. I'm sorry to bring this embarrassment to the ranch."

"Ivy—"

"I'm not trying to sleep my way to the top of anything—" she rambles.

I grab her arm and spin her around. We're in the parking area now and there is no one around. I grip her face and lower my voice enough to get her attention, I'm hoping it stops her from spiraling,

"I don't give a fuck about anything that excuse for a man just said. I know you don't have some scheme to advance yourself on my fucking ranch, but I need to know, did he hurt you?"

One look into her eyes brimming with tears has me pulling her to my chest. I silently will myself not to go back and kick that motherfucker in the face. Ivy allows me to pull her in, molding her small frame into me. She fists the back of my shirt as if I'm her safety net. The tears threatening to spill since we left the viewing area come tumbling out with a force I can barely keep up with.

I settle her in, sigh and stroke her long silky hair, holding her tight to me, steady.

"I've got you. You're safe. Let it out."

An unmeasured amount of time passes as Ivy sobs into my chest. The sound of gravel crunching and people approaching brings her out of it. She pulls her face back from my chest and sniffs.

"I'm sorry." She tugs at my flannel. "I ruined your shirt," she adds, smiling through her tears.

I scoff. "Don't give a fuck about the shirt."

Ivy looks up at me. "Can we just get out of here now?"

"If that's what you want," I tell her as we turn and walk the short distance to the truck. I want to ask again, but I don't want to pry. Partly because if he did anything remotely like what's rolling through my head right now, not only will I kill him, I won't regret it for a second.

"Brad wasn't just my boss's son or some fleeting ex," Ivy offers as we get into the truck and I turn the ignition over. "We dated for five years. It's a part of my life I never want to go back to again. I was weak. It was emotional abuse; I know that now."

I speed up, needing to get the fuck out of here. *Now.*

"At the time, I talked myself into believing he was just trying to watch out for me, to help me be the best person I could be. I know how silly that sounds, but he was very good at manipulating me. It started small, offering critique on my clothes, questioning how faithful I was, questioning my whereabouts when I wasn't home. His family—especially his dad—never really accepted me; I always got the feeling they thought Brad was too good for me. The only one that was kind to me was Brad's sister, but even she did whatever Brad wanted. I always felt like less around them."

"Jesus Christ," I say, scrubbing my face with my hand, flexing it. *Fuck, it hurts.* I look down to see the blood on my knuckles and try not to think about how good it felt to hit that fucker.

"Then it progressed, moving to my work, how I trained, what I could never do right. After a couple of years, I was thinking of ending things. It was apparent we weren't even on the same page. I wanted to get married and have a family one day and Brad just didn't. I began a plan to leave him. I wasn't really happy, but then everything was . . . derailed. It was around that time that I found out . . . well, kind of devastating news." I look at her, not knowing what to expect. "Basically, it may be hard for me to have children. Without getting into it too much, my body will probably not allow for a full-term delivery even if I conceive. It will be *very difficult* is what I was told. Brad seemed almost happy at first, but in the days following . . . well, he said some harsh things to me about not being able to carry on his family name"—she fiddles with her purse strap as she talks—"and that he was staying with me when another man may not. A few times after that, whenever he was really angry at me, he . . . he said I 'wasn't worth anything in the long run.'" She uses air quotes around her words, and I want to kill him. "Which is why it hurt me so much to hear that today. It just brought it all back. And he knew it would. I let it get to me even though I know now I shouldn't. I know better." She shrugs.

I reach out instinctively and drop my hand into the middle, allowing myself this one thing. Just this one moment, to touch her any way I can. I stretch my pinky finger out and wrap it around hers as she speaks. She doesn't flinch, or move, she takes a deep breath, like it settles her, and continues. *This motherfucking waste of existence.*

"Ivy, he should've been fucking consoling you, been there for you, not making you feel like you weren't enough." I look out the window and debate; I'm not that far.

"Can I go back? I want to go back . . . I'm going back," I say surely, moving to pull over and turn the truck around. Ready to hightail it back to the parking lot and put *Brad* through the fucking ground.

"No. Please, it won't change anything and will just run your family's name through the mud."

"Maybe so, but it will make me feel a whole lot better."

"Wade." She tightens her fingers over mine. "Please keep driving."

I grit my molars to keep from saying every fucking cuss word in the English language, but I do as she asks and continue driving, because right now it's not about me, it's about her. But I can't help but add, "I better never see him again."

Ivy nods. "Fair enough, but he isn't worth it." She squeezes my hand. "I know that now. When we met he seemed so together, so stable. He was older than me, almost thirty to my twenty-four. Looking back now, I know that even affection and intimacy were a game for him," she says.

I wince but force myself to listen and appear calm.

"He would reward me with it, or take it away to punish me, and it wasn't even really good." She blushes but grins with her admission. "He used everything as a weapon. It was all a mental game."

I grit my teeth again to physically force myself from spewing a barrage of cuss words Ivy doesn't need to hear right now. I will myself to just listen to her, just be there for her, but at the same time, I only have so much self-control when it comes to this woman that I'm starting to feel the need to care for and protect.

"I'm going to drive a little faster now," I tell her. "I have to. I need to get as far away from here as possible."

She nods and looks out at the passing countryside on the way back to Nashville as she continues.

"I'm not telling you this to be my savior. I know my worth now, even if my fate is to never carry a baby to term, and he should've never treated me like I was less. I started going to therapy, I was really fighting with my own self-worth after a few years of being under Brad's thumb. My father, he raised me to be strong, and I felt like I was letting him down, if that makes sense. After six months of going to therapy in secret, I admitted to myself that

Brad was, in fact, emotionally abusing me. I was still in contact with my former mentor Peter from the American Quarter and Thoroughbred Association—again, in secret. Having male friends was a fight, even ones who were my father's best friend and old enough to be my own father."

Fucking hell.

"Peter said he saw the changes in me and was worried about me. He's the one that sent me the ad for your trainer position. Seeing that ad gave me hope for a fresh start, a chance for me to live a life away from Brad and start over—to follow my dreams and to never let anyone fuck with me ever again. I made my mind up and promised myself and my dad, *never again.*" She looks at me for a fleeting second as if to see if she should continue. I slide my hand up to rub her shoulder, and nod.

"The night I tried to leave Brad, the night I drove to Laurel Creek in the summer, I packed my car. I was planning on going before he got home but I had told him I was going to visit my mom in Jellico . . ."

Ivy's eyes are a million miles away, and all I want to do is crush myself to her and tell her it's going to be okay.

"It was a Thursday. On Thursdays, he always went out with the boys, but for some reason he came home early. He was more than a little drunk, which is when he was the nastiest. My trunk was open in the driveway, and all my belongings were inside it. I was just inside for one more minute to verify I had everything with me. If I hadn't gone back in, he would've been too late and I would've been gone. When I came out, he was standing beside my car; he knew instantly what I was doing."

Ivy closes her eyes as if she's trying to scratch the memory from her mind.

"He grabbed my purse from my hand and took off into the house, told me I wasn't leaving, and once inside he dropped it and came for me. H-he pressed me up against the wall, spewed terrible things I'm not willing to repeat. Something in me just snapped. The look in his eyes, the way he was holding me. His hand came up and I remember thinking *he's going to hit me*."

Holy fuck, I will fucking kill him.

"I kneed him hard between the legs to defend myself. He went down like a sack of potatoes." She smiles through her tears, and for that split second I know she's proud of herself. I squeeze her shoulder even tighter.

"I could've run then, but I didn't. I didn't stop hitting him. I kept going, kept hitting him to let him know never to touch me again."

Fucking right she did, my little spitfire.

"I couldn't stop myself—every bit of anger I had boiled to the surface. I might have killed him, I was looking around, look-ing for something to hit him with if he got up and came after me, but my dad's voice stopped me. I swear I heard him say '*you're better than this, angel, leave now.*'" Another fat tear slides down her face as she bares her story to me, and she swipes it away instantly. "So, I ran as fast as I could to my car, I got in, took off and I never looked back. Showed up on your doorstep two days later and the rest is history."

I let out a breath I didn't even realize I had been holding, and pull over to the side of the country road we're driving on just as the sun starts setting. It's been a long day and I just need a second to look at her. Thinking of the way she came to my ranch, with nothing but some belongings and hope. Fuck, am I glad she put up with my shit and stayed.

"I'm sorry you went through that. But fuck, if you've never told anyone else this, if no one else knows this story, I want you to know I'm so goddamn proud of you, proud of you for getting the help you needed, proud of you for being brave enough to take a stand against him before he could hurt or violate you." I use my hand to cup her jaw, my thumb tracing her cheekbone.

"You never need to be afraid of him again. I would never let him hurt you."

Ivy's hand comes up to grasp mine at her cheek and she smiles, her eyes still glassy from the tears.

"That's the thing, Wade. I don't need anyone to come to my rescue; the only thing that even remotely scares me is that when I finally snapped, because I held all that in for so long, I could've killed him for the way he treated me, and not regretted it for one goddamn second."

Definitely not the response I expected, and fuck, I don't know how it's possible, I think I might be even more crazy for her than I was five seconds ago.

"But you did look awful hot and bothered out there, protecting my honor," she adds, smiling. As usual she's shifting gears in two seconds flat. Just the tone in her voice changing slightly has all the blood in my body rushing through my veins faster. Ivy's such a beautiful whirlwind and she's always one step ahead of me.

The thought of anyone making her feel like she isn't enough sets off a rage in me like I've never felt. But the most prevalent thing I feel? Pride.

She's got this, she doesn't need me to handle it for her. I've never known a woman quite like her before. It's goddamn refreshing.

She's so fucking strong.

CHAPTER TWENTY-SIX

Ivy

"You still seem tense. Have another, Chief," I say hours later as I motion for the bartender to come to our end of the bar.

The Saturday night crowd at Luke's 32 Bridge doesn't disappoint. It's a wide open space with a center bar, and right now it's full of people ready to party country-style.

We're only two drinks deep and I'm reminded for the second night in a row why I love Nashville so much. The crowds, the sounds wafting out of every single pub down Broadway, the genuine country music roots that bloom here for a while, only to be plucked and given to the masses, then replanted with the next crop of talent and nurtured until they, too, are ready.

"Nashville's your town," Wade says as he sips his shot of bourbon.

The butterflies I felt before around him are now drunk and out of control in my stomach, as he stares into my eyes in the dark bar. It felt so good to share my story with someone today, and the way Wade just listened and consoled me will sit with me in my heart for a long time. I'm glad the first person I told was

Wade. I never knew I needed to get it out until I did. Now, I just feel . . . free.

I smile up at him, trying to ignore how gorgeous he is tonight. Faded jeans and his perfectly fitted flannel shirt, hugging tight to his upper arms, and he's wearing that damn Titans hat again, backwards. He's the picture of rugged, masculine perfection.

"I love it so much," I say to him. "Think of the talent that played in this very bar, in the bar next to us, the one across the street. Hell, this man on stage right now could be the next big country superstar. Only time will tell," I say as the bartender approaches.

I hop up on the rail to get closer so he can hear me. "Two more." I smile at him and he nods, passing me another two Nashville-sized "shots."

We turn our backs to the bar and watch through the crowd as the rugged-looking singer on stage moves through his own rendition of "Fire Away" by Chris Stapleton. He's good enough that the bar gets louder, dancing and singing along.

I sip my drink, and let the warm fuzzy feel of the Jack Daniel's in my glass vibrate with the music through my body for the next few songs, as Wade keeps watch from just behind me at a standing table, sipping his own drink a lot slower than I sip mine. I need this release. I've been so pent-up for him, while he has been the picture of cool, aside from the five minutes he let go and kissed me on his living room floor. I can't stop the visions of Wade looking so goddamn sexy in every setting from flooding my mind while the singer starts his version of "Like a Wrecking Ball" by Eric Church.

I sway my hips to the music, my flowy black sundress hiking even higher as I raise my hands over head, and I let the sultry music vibrate through me at its own frequency, feeling that perfect blend of tingly and warm. The crowd is so thick in the dark bar I can barely see the stage, and the drunken chatter is so loud that I don't realize I've drifted a little further onto the dance floor.

The crowd sings the chorus and I sing right along with them as I feel large hands run down my sides. I instantly hope that they're Wade's, but I realize quickly the hands around me aren't his as they move nervously around my waist and the scents of vodka and expensive cologne fill my senses. This man's cologne smells nice but it isn't Wade's earthy, spicy scent.

"Watching you move out here makes me feel like you need a partner," a deep voice rasps into my ear. I pull back and meet the eyes of a tall, young cowboy.

I open my mouth to speak.

"There you are," Wade says, posting up beside me like a guard dog. "Need another drink, *sweetheart*?" he asks, loud enough for the man in front of me to hear, then looks to him as if he never even noticed him standing there.

"Can we help you with something, bud?"

"Nah, sorry, man. I thought she was alone." He nods and disappears into the crowd as I start laughing and swat at Wade.

"*Sweetheart*?" I ask, one eyebrow raised. "I wouldn't take you for the *sweetheart* type."

Wade passes me a shot and nods, offering me the salute, to which I hold it in the air.

"To us, getting the yearling tomorrow that'll win you a derby."

Wade holds his glass up and then knocks it back in one fell swoop. *Impressive*. I follow suit, swallowing the burn of the whiskey down my throat.

"I could be the *sweetheart* type," he says, looking genuinely offended as he places our glasses on a passing waitress's tray.

I laugh. "Nah, I picture you more like the *come here, woman* type," I say, mocking his voice.

Wade wraps his arms around my waist and starts moving with me to the music.

"After the heartfelt nickname I've given you already? How could you ever think that about me, Trouble?" he asks, thinking he's pretty funny, looking down at me with that smirk on his face I can't get enough of.

I try not to notice the way my insides pool into fiery ash with our bodies pressed together like this. We're on a dance floor, of course we're going to have to dance.

I laugh with him for a moment as I let my fingers trail the hair at the nape of his neck. Wade's eyes shine in the dimly lit room as his thumb traces my lower back while we dance to the singer crooning his version of "Sand in My Boots" by Morgan Wallen.

"All good, Chief. I'm starting to realize that grumpy is your love language, so I'll choose to let it flatter me—but how do you know you didn't just stop me from meeting my soulmate in that cowboy?"

Wade makes a scoffing noise.

"He was not your soulmate," he says, his jaw flexing.

I raise an eyebrow. "How do you know?" I challenge.

"You think *that* guy was your soulmate?" His brow furrows, and his jaw tenses even further. "The guy that came up to you and touched you before he even said hello to you? He's your soulmate?"

I giggle.

"I suppose not," I say with a smile, as one large hand of Wade's pulls me even closer, his hips press into me possessively and the other hand slides up my back, through my hair. His head comes down over my ear, and my breath hitches in my throat as my thighs clench together.

"A man like that is nowhere near good enough for you, Ivy," Wade whispers, his voice gravelly and deep, but crystal clear in the noisy bar, sending goosebumps down my neck. My breathing increases and my skin is suddenly hyper sensitive against my clothing. If he keeps whispering to me and holding me like this, I'm pretty sure he's going to ruin my panties.

"You need a man who takes the time to know *you*, not just the way you look." His lips hover painfully close to the bottom of my earlobe.

"You need a man who can handle your sassy little attitude, not be threatened by it, *and* give it back to you tenfold," he says, his breath warm on my neck.

I whimper into his chest as he slides his hands back down my sides, firm and sure, resting them at my tailbone in such a way that has me clenching my thighs together and wishing he'd slide them down even further. His thumb traces lazily again, sending shivers up my spine.

"And you're the man who knows what I need?" I ask him in a shaky whisper. The loud bar is no match for the sound that vibrates through Wade's chest. It sounds like a low growl.

"I know you well enough to know he wasn't it," Wade says, his lips ghosting my skin as he speaks. "At the very least, Ivy, you need a man whose hands don't shake when he touches you." His lips hover in their place, bringing every nerve ending under my skin to life.

I whimper and turn my lips up to his ear. "You got steady hands, Chief?"

"Rock fucking steady."

I feel his hands circle my waist slow and sure, his thumbs running down the front of my abdomen as he holds me close. We both stand still on the dance floor, just breathing into each other's skin. I'm frozen with the pull between us and how close his lips are hovering over mine. It's at this exact moment that the stage lights brighten and blind us, and the opening strings to "Sweet Home Alabama" fill the air, breaking our spell as the crowd explodes around us. I pull my face back to look at Wade, his emerald eyes dark and anchoring me where I stand.

Fuck, I've never seen anything like him.

He grins at me, melting me from my head to my toes.

I grin back, a challenge in my eyes.

"Seeing as you don't want any other man out here on the floor with me, can you dance?"

His eyes shine back at me, accepting my challenge.

"Fucking right I can dance, *sweetheart*." In one swift movement, he takes hold of my hand and lifts my arm up over head, spinning me around in a perfectly executed twirl.

Of course, he isn't lying. Wade keeps me dancing for the next two hours, stopping only to champion me replacement shots before I even notice I'm thirsty, both of us sweaty and tipsy, as I sing along to every country song they rock the stage with. As he watches me move before him with a look I can't place, Wade's coveted dimples are on full display.

In this place, with no worries, no burdens, with me, the only thing I can think is . . . happy looks damn good on Wade Ashby.

CHAPTER TWENTY-SEVEN
Wade

"Fuck," I grunt under my breath.

Ivy snorts beside me. "Runs multimillion-dollar ranch, can't operate a key card?"

The green light signals the click of the door finally, and I look down at her. You'd think with her size and stature the drinks she had would hit her harder, but she seems as in control as I am, just feeling good enough not to care that my hand is still firmly planted around her waist, where it's been all night.

"Get your bratty little ass inside," I say as she laughs.

"Goddamn, I don't remember the last time I had that much fun." Ivy kicks her boots off and lifts her sweaty hair off the back of her neck as she putters to the window, tossing her purse on the bed and grabbing a water from the mini fridge. For someone so accident-prone, there are times Ivy moves with the grace of a dancer. Something about the way her toned legs make way for her ass that would fit so fucking well into my hands drives me wild. I blink when I notice her noticing me staring at her ass. *Fuck.*

Ivy's fuckable ass–1.

Wade–0.

"See something you like, Chief?" she asks, her eyebrow raised, hand on her hip, reminding me that Ivy and alcohol makes me want to fuck the sass right out of her mouth, and goddamn it would be a beautiful sight.

"Go take a shower," I say gruffly, needing her out of my sight line. "I'll take my turn when you're done."

She nods, and after another big gulp of water she grabs some necessities and heads into the bathroom while I pace the room and ask myself how in the actual fuck I'm making it through this night.

Thirty minutes later, the hot water pours over me. I need it. I'm pushing my limits of self-control to the extreme. When I saw that no-more-than-twenty-five-year-old cowboy's hands on her, I had to stop him. There was no thought, I just reacted. I can't have her but I don't want anyone else to have her either. I shut the water off and wrap a towel around my waist, wiping the steam from the mirror as I step out, and I have a silent conversation with the man I see there.

Yes, she's fucking perfect, I mentally tell him. *In every way, but you can't have her. Don't be one more person to expect from her. You need her for the ranch. You can't fuck this up.*

I look around the bathroom and berate myself when I realize I didn't bring any clean clothes in here with me. I sigh and make my way out of the room. *Nothing she hasn't seen before.*

When I come out of the steamy bathroom, Ivy is in the bed; her hair is dry now and she's tucked right in, a little bag of cinnamon hearts in her hand and *John Wick* on the hotel TV.

"They have a whole action movie section," she says, her eyes lingering on me just long enough to taunt me. Makes me want to drop my towel and give her something to really look at.

"Need clothes," I tell her.

She nods. Covering her eyes with her hands.

"I won't look. Scout's honor," she says, a little grin playing on her lips as she flashes me the peace sign. My jaw falls momentarily slack. She has no makeup on but her plump lips still have the prettiest pink hue to them. They're the most enticing lips I've ever laid eyes on. My cock instantly starts to swell, because at this point, I'm willing to admit that it's a given that when Ivy is around, I'm hard.

"Be right back," I tell her as I grab my boxers and my sweats. I force myself to go into the bathroom, and I close the door almost all the way, knowing I'm only going to be a minute and run a brush through my hair. As soon as I'm done I run a hand through it to loosen it up.

I drop my towel and have a conversation with my cock to simmer down. I'm hard as fuck as I'm imagining running my hands through Ivy's hair, sticking my cock down her throat, gripping her tight and fucking her face until my cum is leaking down her chin. Everything about her drives me wild.

And now I'm fucking rock solid. And my hand is on my cock. The internal battle within me wages on as I tell myself to pull my boxers on over my naked body, but the way her hands were up over her face left her perfect tits on display, and those pebbled little points under her silky tank were just fucking begging to be pulled into my mouth. *And now I'm stroking my cock.*

"Fuck." I make the decision to take care of myself before I try to go back out there and watch a movie with Ivy; it's the only way I'll get through. The creak of the door makes me pause the tug on my cock. I don't turn around, I just look up at her over my shoulder in the mirror. Ivy stares back at me; her stance is calm but her breathing and the look on her face says she's here for a reason.

CHAPTER TWENTY-EIGHT
Wade

I watch Ivy's throat work into a gulp. It doesn't take much to see that I'm nowhere near fucking done in this bathroom.

I expect her to back away, cover her eyes, back up, but none of that happens as we stand suspended like this for a length of time I could never measure. Me stroking my rock-hard cock, naked with my back to her while she watches in the mirror. The only sound is her breath as it increases when she takes in my size, probably registering that I would fill her like she's never been filled.

Ivy's breathing continues to shallow as she moves closer to me, until she's standing right behind me. I brace myself for something, anything, but I never stop my fist on my cock.

After all, she came in here.

Her delicate hands start at my shoulders and run down my arms. The moment her fingers connect with my skin I know there is no fucking going back. My eyes nearly roll back in my head just with her touch alone. I continue to work my cock with one hand and white-knuckle the counter with the other.

"What happened to not looking?" I smirk at her in the mirror over my shoulder. Only one of her blue eyes is visible from behind me.

She swallows, and her next words come out shaky but still confident. "Truth is . . . well, I've never really been a scout, never even known one so, um . . . upholding their honor doesn't mean shit to me."

Fucking Christ.

I spin around and stand over her, looking down at her from my full height, and I nod to her to look down.

"Then own it. Fucking look," I order.

Ivy does exactly what I tell her to do and looks down. Her tongue darts out to wet her bottom lip as she pants in front of me, her eyes flitting back to mine.

"Wade . . ." she almost whines. A question lingers there, one I'm so fucking ready to answer.

I run my knuckles over her jaw with my free hand, never stopping the stroke on my cock as I tower over her and bring my mouth down as I cradle the side of her face to pull her closer still. I take a deep breath and inhale her. Sugar and cinnamon sweetness.

"I've fucking tried, Ivy. But I'm just exhausted trying to pretend I don't think of touching you every fucking second. See, I knew you were trouble, yet all I've wanted to do since the moment I met you is show you how to behave," I tell her, and a moan escapes her lips. "Every man has his breaking point," I say as I run my knuckles over her cheekbone, my other hand still working my cock that is so desperate to fuck.

"Now, you came in here, so tell me you want it. Tell me to stop being a gentleman. Tell me to be the man you're in here looking for, Ivy."

I slide my thumb across her bottom lip and slide it into her mouth. The heat and warmth of her consumes it as she doesn't hesitate to take it in.

"Just say the word," I tell her.

Ivy blinks up at me, wraps her arms up around my neck

intentionally, and whispers the one word that takes away every ounce of control I possess. The one word that threatens to ruin me.

"Mercy . . ."

I growl in response, releasing my cock and wrapping my hands around her waist, and I let my mouth fucking consume hers. This kiss isn't careful, it's a torrid clash of lips, tongue and teeth as my hands slide fervently over her warm body, up under her shorts, as I squeeze her pert ass the way I've wanted to for so long, and it's a handful, just the way I like it. The moment I squeeze, she pushes herself further into me and I groan against her lips as she whimpers into mine.

Sweet heat and pressure licks up my hips and spine like lava as I lift her and carry her to the bed, depositing her onto her knees. Ivy reaches one hand up and places it on my tense jaw; the other moves between my legs and connects with my cock. She presses her palm against me and lets out a tiny gasp as I dip my head back down to hers. My tongue searches every corner of her mouth eagerly, just letting the sugar of her spread over my tastebuds for all of a minute as I grip her hips and pull her as close as I can. Moments pass like this as I savor every part of her mouth. I grab her hand from my cock and place her open palm under her lips.

"Spit," I growl, which makes her eyes grow as big as saucers. *Fuck, I'm so fucking hungry for her.*

She doesn't question me, she listens like the good girl I already know she is and spits into her palm.

"Again," I say, knowing she has a lot to cover. She listens and spits again before returning her hand to my cock, desperately trying to meet her fingers around it, failing miserably because I'm too big for her and that makes me beyond desperate to fill every tight hole she has. The rhythm of her hand over my cock, for even a few fleeting moments, sends a deep groan through my chest into her mouth, which she swallows down eagerly.

"Can I?" she asks as I lick and suck her juicy bottom lip into my mouth.

She's about to meet the side of me she may not be ready for but I'm too far gone to hold back.

"Can you what?" I ask.

Ivy moans as my thumb and forefinger find each of her nipples through her flowy, silk tank.

"You want to suck my cock, Trouble?" I ask her.

"*Fuck* yes, I do," she whines. "I just don't . . . I haven't exactly done it before, not really."

I freeze, dead. *Wait, what?*

"It's just . . . any men before Brad were just one-offs, and he . . . he never wanted me to."

The fuck? A man that doesn't want his dick sucked should never be trusted, is my first thought. My second is that if I'm the lucky bastard that gets to be the first to stick my cock down her throat, well, I'll take that badge with fucking honor.

I kiss her lips. Fuck, I'll never get enough of them.

"I've got you. I'll teach you what to do," I say as I slide my thumb over her lip. I'm so fucking hard it hurts as she slinks down the bed to a sitting position and looks up at me expectantly. Her legs spread wide on either side of my standing ones. I push them open even wider just because I like the way it looks.

She's just the perfect height to press her lips to the head of my cock. I take a moment before I let her, to tilt her chin up to face me and take in the vision below me. Savoring it. Ivy looks so fucking beautiful and innocent. Her violet eyes stare back up at me, her cheeks are flushed, her pupils blown out, her lips already swollen from kissing me.

She's the prettiest fucking thing I've ever seen, just waiting for me to paint her lips with my cum. I slide my hand to the side of her face, letting my fingers rest in her hair as my thumb traces her cheekbone down to her jaw, then finally I pull down her bottom lip and hold her mouth open.

Fucking stunning.

"Stick your tongue out, Ivy. Show me where you want my cock," I tell her as she moans and does just as I say. Popping her mouth open wider, she darts her pink tongue out to wet her juicy fucking lips. Pre-cum leaks from my tip for her in anticipation of her mouth anywhere near me.

"More," I tell her, showing her how to give me the space I need. I drop my cock on her tongue.

"Suck," I command.

Her tongue comes up and swipes against the head of my rigid cock. I suck a breath in through my teeth with the contact. Her eyes never leave mine. The sight of her like this almost makes me lose it, but I somehow, someway, control myself, finding the will, because I want to fucking enjoy every second of her first real blow job.

"That's it, now wrap those pretty lips around me while I slide my cock into your mouth, and I want your eyes right here," I say as I point to my own.

Ivy nods, and wraps her hand around my base, using her tongue over the head of my cock. She moves slowly, like this is all new to her, and it's almost too much to take. Her bubblegum lips surround me as her tongue swirls the underside of my shaft. The heat and warmth of her mouth flood my senses as she moves her tongue the way she does when she kisses me. I groan. She's already better at this than she realizes.

I feast on the sight before me.

"You look fucking incredible with my cock in your mouth," I tell her.

I pull out just to give her a moment to breathe.

"I'm going to give you more now. Just relax, I'll tell you what to do," I say as I grip her hair with my fist and let myself slip into her mouth deeper. My head falls back; I feel like I may have just died and gone to my own personal heaven as I hit the back of her throat.

Ivy gags and sputters around me but that doesn't stop me.

"Take me deeper, and lick here when you do, slowly," I say, stroking the underside of my cock. She does exactly what I tell her to and she gags some more, fighting to catch her breath. I fucking love it.

"Fighting me like that only makes my dick harder, makes me want to fuck your throat deeper."

She *moans* with desire around me, and the vibration of her hum ripples through me in waves.

Fuck me. I want to do bad things to this woman.

"Atta girl, you like choking on my cock, don't you?" I growl as I fuck between her lips.

Ivy moans again and nods, her eyes huge and watery as I slide in and out of her mouth, hitting the back of her throat and staying there for a beat with every deep thrust as I grip the back of her head through her hair, letting her strands tangle through my fingers.

She whimpers around me as a tear spills out and over her cheek. I dart my thumb out to catch it before it falls, licking it off. Even her tears taste good.

I no longer feel like a man, I'm a beast that wants to bring every single part of her to my mouth.

My eyes roll back as she gets herself into a rhythm like she was born to suck my cock, trading between long languid flicks of her tongue and sweet pulls that have her cheeks hollowing out around me. Minutes pass like this as I revel in her hot mouth. Every dirty thought I've ever had of her brims to the surface with my impending release until I almost can't take it any longer.

She moans again in a quiet hum as she increases her pace around me, stroking me as her spit trails down my shaft with the depth I'm taking her, claiming her, fucking her beautiful face.

"That's it, such a good girl," I tell her as my thumb strokes her cheek while she works to take all of my cock.

"I'm going to come, Ivy, and you're going to swallow, understand?"

I'm so fucking close . . .

She nods and whimpers around me as my vision turns static. I use her hair to pull her face back slightly. Her jaw falls slack, her lips barely touching my cock, and she looks up at me with hooded eyes and sticks her motherfucking tongue out with a smirk and I lose it.

Hot ropes of cum jut out and land in her mouth, on her lips, and her chin. Some form of *fuck* and *such a good fucking girl* leaves my mouth mixed with murmurs of her name as I come back down to earth. I look down at her, dragging my thumb across her chin and swiping my cum that escaped her lips back into her mouth.

"Every last drop," I say as she takes my thumb and sucks it off like a dutiful little pupil while I groan. My cock already begs for more.

I pull her body up to me by her arms and crush myself to her. Tasting myself in her mouth as I do, and it drives me to the brink of insanity.

She moans into me.

"Wade, I'm on . . . fire. I need . . . I need—"

I chuckle into her lips.

"Trust me, Ivy, I already know what you need. What you should be worrying about is me never letting you get off your back once I get you there." I kiss her lips, almost gently, as I grin into them.

I realize she has no idea what she's in for.

I'm only just getting started.

CHAPTER TWENTY-NINE
Ivy

Fucking Christ Almighty, if I'm going to die young, let it be with Wade Ashby hovering his incredible body overtop of me, pressing his huge, and I mean *huge*, cock against me.

I no longer have a choice; if I lose my job after this or if it's awkward, I give zero fucks. It will be worth it. Something I decided the moment I pushed open that door and saw him stroking his cock. I've never seen a man do that before so confidently, I've never seen a cock as big as his, and I just couldn't look away, even though I knew I shouldn't be in there.

"You taste so fucking good," Wade says into my lips as he kisses me so deeply, so intently, I'd swear he's won awards for kissing. Gold medal winner right here on top of me. A fucking Olympian.

His tongue sweeps against mine in slow, delicious strokes, searching my mouth in a way I've never been kissed as his hand grips my jaw then trails down to my throat like it did the first night his lips met mine. His thumb strokes the center lightly as I realize it's very possible his large hand would actually fully wrap around my throat with ease if he chose. Maybe that should scare me but it doesn't at all, I think it turns me on even more. Wade moves back to look at me. His eyes trace the lines of my face, saving my lips for last.

"I'm going to fucking worship you tonight," he says, kissing me, his voice deep and full of gravel.

I moan into his lips.

"Please . . . yes, please," I beg. It's all I can say. I have no train of thought. I'm only existing in this moment to pray for his hands on me the next.

"I love hearing you beg, Ivy, you have no idea what it does to me," Wade says as he trails his tongue over my bottom lip, sucking it roughly into his mouth, holding it there for a few seconds before releasing it with a tiny popping sound.

"Since I can't seem to keep myself under control at all when I'm with you, if anything is ever too rough I need you to promise to tell me. It's the only way this will work. If it's too much, just tap my thigh."

Little jolts of fear ripple down my spine, but the need I feel for him outweighs it tenfold. I look into his eyes—they're serious and pleading. It's in this second that I realize Wade Ashby has a darker side. Call me a masochist but I feel no fear, only need. No matter what Wade says, I know he would never, ever hurt me. The only thing that surprises me is that until tonight I had no idea that the thought of him being a little rough with me *wouldn't* scare me—in fact, I may even *want* it.

I nod to him, still moaning under my breath because Wade's hand has moved down the column of my throat, under my tank to my breast, where he pinches my nipple then swipes his thumb over it and rolls it between his thumb and finger, like he has nothing but the time and energy to torture me for hours.

"I'm going to need to hear the words, Ivy. I don't fuck around with consent." *Of course he doesn't.* "Tell me this is what you want," he commands.

"I want you, Wade, so fucking badly I can hardly see straight. That work for you?" I quip, as a deep delicious heat coils in my low belly.

His fingers swipe, pinch, roll.

Can you come from someone touching your breasts? Because holy shit, that feels good. A dark growl erupts from Wade's chest as he sits me up and yanks my tank top off, tearing it in the process, and his hot mouth moves down my body. His lips find one nipple while his free hand finds the other, like he needs to take care of both of them equally, expertly, before his lips move to my shoulders, my arms, my neck. He devours me with open-mouthed ravaging kisses, nipping across my body, biting down then kissing over the pain like he has a thirst that can only be quenched by my skin. He's everywhere and simply not enough places all at once, as I pant for more.

Wade moves back up to kiss my lips as his hand reaches into the waist of my shorts, gripping my hip, kneading it in a deep hold as he centers himself between my thighs and presses his cock against my aching clit. How wet I am is obvious, I'm sure he can feel it through the layers of my panties and shorts still between us.

I shamelessly grind into him as my neck arches back. Visions of his cock filling me overtake me. I might die if he does this for too long; the slow delicious roll of his hips is like tossing gunpowder into a flame. He's so unhurried, so intentional.

Just as I'm about to beg him again, his fingers slide to my center, pushing my thin cotton panties aside. He sucks in a breath and mutters, *"Jesus, fuck,"* when he feels that I'm positively dripping.

"This all for me? You're fucking soaked," Wade states as he practically rips my shorts and panties from my body. I lie beneath him, naked and panting.

"What did you expect with the way you've been touching me? It's all your fault," I whisper as Wade smirks into my lips.

"Drip down my hand, I welcome it. I fucking love it"—a kiss—"I can't wait for you to drip down my cock."

Oh God . . .

Wade's eyes rake over my body; he seems to take in every single stretch of my naked flesh with a hunger in his eyes I can't explain. I move to cover my hips and stomach instinctively. I was never self-conscious until Brad, but he preyed on that, and I'm just now learning to be comfortable in my curves and in my own skin again.

"Don't you do that, don't cover yourself with me, ever. You're fucking perfect, Ivy, goddamn perfection, got it?"

I nod, warmth flooding my chest, his praise lighting something in me I never knew I needed.

Wade pushes one big finger into my soaked pussy and my back instantly bows off the bed. The sound I make earns me a groan from him, igniting me all on its own. He smirks down at me when he realizes how much he affects me, like he knows a secret I don't.

"I'm going to ruin this tight little cunt tonight. You will love every second of it, but one thing I won't do is rush this." His fingers make quick work of bringing me to a precipice.

"I'm going to get you there slowly. I'll give in when you're ready to trade me your fucking soul for my cock," he says as he adds another finger, sweeping his thumb over my aching clit.

I'm going to come all over him, and he's barely touched me.

He looks down at me as he takes in my writhing form. I'm panting wildly and I don't even care how it looks or sounds.

"Look how fucking pretty you are, your body just begging for me to fill you."

This man's mouth. I can't handle these words—they're going to send me right off the cliff I'm desperately clinging to. Wade expertly fucks his fingers into my pussy as I whine around him.

"That's it, come for me. Show me what a beautiful mess you can make of my hand," he says as I scream out, "*Oh God*, Wade, *fuck*." While fireworks ignite behind my eyelids, my entire body quakes as I break and shatter, doing just what he says, dripping down his hand and corded forearm. Wade lets my breathing return to normal levels as he plants one single kiss under my earlobe then whispers, "Just one thing . . . the only name you call out when you come is *mine*, Ivy. I don't even want to hear God's name on your lips. He has no place in my bed with you, understand?"

I nod.

"Good girl. Now, you can give me another one. Spread these thighs."

Holy fuck, who is this man hiding behind Wade's unassuming exterior and how the hell do I keep him?

CHAPTER THIRTY
Wade

Ivy whimpers and pants like she can't take one more second of anticipation as I settle myself right between her thighs. I'm about to make a permanent home here. I use my hands to start on either side of the prettiest pussy I've ever seen, pressing her legs wide open before me.

"Don't be shy, not with me," I tell her as she whines my name quietly, begging me to lose myself in her.

I kiss her swollen clit as she shudders. Just once, to get acquainted with my new home.

"My name on your lips is like music to my ears. I can't wait to make you scream it all fucking night long." I suction my mouth around her clit, sucking it into my mouth just to allow myself my first real taste of her. She's the fucking sweetest sugar there is. I groan as her back arches and she makes the most tempting sounds I've ever heard while her hands move to my hair, pulling tight as I grind my hard-as-fuck and aching cock into the mattress below me.

"Fucking exquisite," I mutter, and then I get to work, like eating her dripping cunt is the only job I've been put on this earth to do. I slide the flat of my tongue against her, firm tortuous flicks over her, doing just what I said, taking my time while I push two fingers into her. My mind runs wild. I fantasize about the moment it will be my cock forcing her to stretch around me.

"*So* fucking tight," I say to her, almost ready to blow all over the bed. I move a hand up to one of her breasts and pinch her nipple between my fingers as she bucks her fleshy hips into my face, smothering me with her arousal and thighs, but I'm stronger. I push back, deeper, harder. Fucking my tongue into her as she screams and moans that she can't take it anymore and that she's going to come.

"Let go, Ivy, soak my face. Fucking *suffocate* me, and say my name when you do," I tell her and she does. Crying out some form of my name mixed with unintelligible words just as I wanted, her fingers tugging at my hair and clawing at my shoulders until I'm sure they're bleeding. Giving me just enough pain to beg her for more, because that little bit of pain is just what I want, what I crave from her, and somehow, already, she seems to understand that.

I let my tongue gingerly trail over her soaking slit, gathering her cum on my tongue, then I rise to meet her face and kiss her. Ivy's tongue laps against mine, eagerly, already my needy, dirty girl.

"You're so fucking sweet, Ivy. It's going to be impossible for me to ever stop burying my face between these thighs," I tell her as I kiss her.

She's moaning into my mouth and already angling her hips up to meet me like she just can't get enough as I circle her clit with slow, shallow sweeps.

"It's yours," she manages.

"What is mine, Trouble?" I ask her, loving that she's this desperate for my hands on her. Her eyes open and focus on mine for a split second.

"My soul . . . Take it, Wade," she whimpers. "Just give me what I need."

Fucking Christ.

"Such a greedy fucking girl, I'm going to give you my cock, but it's going to be a tight fit so I need you to breathe and do exactly as I tell you, okay?"

She nods hesitantly. "I trust you, Wade, just don't split me in two," she says as my tip graces her entrance.

Fucking hell, even that feels like fucking heaven.

"There's never been anyone since Brad. I'm clean and . . ." she offers with a tiny little shrug. "I'm on birth control."

Fuck, I was so lost in her I hadn't even thought about a condom.

"I'm clean too," I say, then I kiss Ivy both to assure her and to give her one more second to say no, one more second to back out before we change everything. But she doesn't, she kisses me back and angles her hips up enough that the first full inch of my cock sinks into her, causing us both to moan. *Fucking Jesus Christ.*

"Deep breath," I tell her, and then I sink into her deeper as she gasps and pants below me. "Again." I coax her to breathe, kissing her softly. "You're doing so good, I'm so proud of you, Ivy. You're taking my cock so well," I tell her.

Holding myself up on my forearms, I grip the sides of her face, pulling it to mine to kiss her softly, trying to calm her. I sink further. "That's it," I tell her as she takes a deep breath and pulls me in a little more while I breathe out a shaky groan.

"Fuck. Ivy. *Fuck,*" I grunt as I push even further, pressing my forehead to hers, still gripping her face.

"Is that . . . all the way?" she asks, her eyes begging me for honesty.

I kiss her, before teaching her to embrace it.

"You can take more. I'll fill you so full you'll never want me to leave you empty."

She nods, and that fiery sass I'm obsessed with shines in her eyes.

"More then," she says with confidence.

I grin back at her. "Such a little brat," I say as I give her no more warning, and I kiss her as I bury myself in her to the hilt before she can change her mind.

"Holy, motherfucking *fuck,* Wade," she says. "You're too big, you feel . . ."

"Don't ask me for all of me unless you're ready to take it all, Trouble." I kiss a line down her throat and pull her nipple into my mouth, then trail my middle finger to her clit between us, circling her for a beat to bait her, to beg her body to adjust to me. She's so fucking wet. *So fucking tight.*

"You feel . . . you feel . . ." she mutters again, losing the words.

"*So fucking good,*" I breathe out for her because holy fuck, *this pussy.* This pussy might just be the death of me.

"Yeah . . ." she pants. "That."

I pull myself out halfway and drive into her again fully as she cries out. She's so full and I've never been so crazed.

Every single ounce of me is molded with her sweet, tight pussy like tongue and groove, and I decide I want to die right here, buried deep inside Ivy. I start slow, savoring, dragging myself out and pushing myself back in, staying rooted in her for a few extra seconds every time, circling my hips there to give her swollen clit the friction it needs to drive her fucking mad.

Her moans become louder as her legs wrap up around my waist. Nails dig deeper into my skin as I slowly, deeply, deliciously fuck my cock in and out of her with the restraint of a goddamn saint, and just as I'm sure her body is ready and she's begging for more, I start to really move. Ivy cries out, my name mostly, every time I withdraw then bottom out inside her.

I move slowly at first, controlled. Taking my time to just *feel* her. To bask in her.

I do this until I can't be gentle with her any longer; her pussy is the fucking brass ring. Beads of sweat form between us as I grip her thigh tight and hold her still, taking all the control as I lose the place where we connect.

We're no longer two. Just one. I stay in these moments with no idea how I hold it together. My cock deep in Ivy's pussy with nothing between us, just her skin on mine, is nothing short of supernatural. I slide my hand up to her throat and grip under her jaw, pressing my mouth to hers as I fuck into her harder.

She whimpers and moans beneath me. I squeeze a little tighter, testing her, and I feel her walls clamp down around me like a vice. I wait for her to tap my thigh as I tighten my grip on her throat, but she doesn't. Her legs begin to shake as she chases her high and I'm right there with her, I'm higher than I've ever been, with no hope of ever coming down.

"Soak my cock now, Ivy, come," I order.

"I'm going to, and Wade?"

"Yeah?" I grunt, while I do everything in my power to hold it together as my balls tighten to an incomparable level at the vision of her beautiful body below me.

"I want you to come too, and squeeze my throat tighter when you do." She says it so innocently that, instantly, I'm a fucking goner.

My vision blackens as my release fires up my shaft and spills into her, at the precise moment she clamps down around me and comes all over my cock, each of our movements turning sloppy and shaky as her name leaves my lips and mine leaves hers. A dull buzzing fills my head as I come down and still jerk inside her.

All I hear is silence and our breathing. I'm pretty sure I might be dead. If I'm not, I want to be because there's no greater heaven than this. Buried in Ivy Spencer, with my shoulders bloodied and her arms around me.

CHAPTER THIRTY-ONE
Ivy

"John Wick Keanu would take Neo Keanu any fucking day," Wade says as he grabs the can of whipped cream and drops a good dollop on top of his ice cream an hour later, when we're nested in the messy king-size bed, with *John Wick* 2 and ice cream.

I take a bite of my own sundae; it's pretty good for being a room service sundae, but only because Wade went and hunted down a can of whipped cream and M&M's for us while we waited for the delivery, finally coming up victorious from the gift shop, muttering something like, "What kind of sundae is it without M&M's?"

I look up at him as I eat and try to talk some logic into him.

"I don't think so, John Wick is brute force, Neo outsmarted people. Think of the complexity of the entire *Matrix* series," I say as I lick whipped cream off my finger.

Wade drops his spoon into his bowl and looks me dead in the eye.

"I'm seriously rethinking everything that just happened here, I don't think it can happen again," he says, shaking his head as he points between us. "You've lost your damn mind, woman."

I stick my tongue out at him. "You just like John Wick Keanu because he's grumpy, he's your soulmate. If you think about it, you'll know I'm right," I say, shoving a bite of ice cream into my mouth.

Wade leans back in bed, his naked torso on glorious display as he sits in just his boxers and shovels his ice cream into his mouth. I smirk as I watch him; his brow is furrowed like he's actually pissed I could ever say John Wick isn't the best version of Keanu Reeves. Even annoyed, he's fucking incredible-looking.

Just as I suspect, he's not done arguing his point. He leans forward.

"Another thing . . . He's only smart in *The Matrix*. In the real world, Neo is just a typical computer nerd." I laugh as he continues. "You're fucking with me, you can't possibly think he'd stand a chance against Wick, take it back."

I start to giggle.

"Not a fuckin' chance, Chief." I shrug, looking intently at my ice cream, acting totally oblivious to his annoyance. To be honest, I don't give a shit about any of it. I just like getting him all hot and bothered.

Wade sets his bowl down, his eyes darken and he looks at me like he's going to pounce on me. I shrink a little, cause damn, he kind of looks scary when he looks at me like that.

I set my bowl down and start to slowly crab-creep across the bed away from him.

He cocks his head and narrows his eyes at me.

"You fixin' to run away from me right now?"

"Maybe," I say, ready to bolt off the bed just to fuck with him. We were heading to the shower anyway when we finished our ice cream.

A split second passes where we just stare at each other, each of us trying to guess what the other is about to do.

"If I catch you before you get to that shower, I fuck you."

My breathing instantly accelerates with his words.

"I thought you were rethinking this?" I say, pointing between us. "I've shamed you with my action hero choices, remember?" I taunt him as I creep another foot backwards, never taking my eyes off of his.

Wade swipes the whipped cream off the side table with force and I flinch.

"I lied."

I'm gone before the words finish leaving his lips. Moving as fast as my ankle allows, through the sitting area to the little bathroom beyond in five seconds flat. I just get my hand on the shower knob and turn the water on when one strong arm wraps around my waist and lifts me right off the ground.

I yelp.

"Too slow. I mean, I fucking walked here, Trouble," Wade says.

Cocky motherfucker.

He drops his lips to my ear from behind me.

"And I wasn't finished eating, but I still feel like something sweet." His lips trail down my neck. "So now, it's you."

"So what you're saying is, even though you caught me, I still win?" I laugh as Wade pins me up against the vanity and spreads my legs with his knee.

"What I'm saying is, you're a little brat and you leave me no choice but to fuck that sass right out of you."

A trail of cold skims my spine as whipped cream hits my skin, before the can is set down on the counter beside me. My pussy instantly throbs.

"I fucking love your tattoos." Wade's eyes blaze a trail over the ivy vines that weave over the center of my spine and extend outwards at my tailbone, over my hips. I love them too. As much today as I did the day I got them back in August, once I got the power to leave Brad. *"If you can't run, then walk, if you can't walk, then crawl, but whatever you do, you have to keep moving forward"* by Martin Luther King is etched throughout the vines. They remind me of my strength; they remind me to move forward no matter what.

"So fucking sexy, they're a target for my lips, my teeth . . ." He bites under my shoulder blade where they begin, then slides one finger all the way down, almost to where they end. "And for my cum."

His tongue comes down to swipe the whipped cream off my back. I whimper with his words—God, they do something to me. He has barely touched me and I'm desperate for something, some sort of friction as he presses his hard cock against my ass, but I can't move. Wade's legs are still holding mine apart, he knows I'm entirely at his will.

His thumbs come down my back, pressing into my skin on either side of my spine hard, as I pant, but I want him to press even harder. He reaches my tailbone and digs his thumbs into it, gripping me tight. I push my ass against him. My body begging.

His big hands move and knead the globes of my ass as he spreads me further apart. A finger trails over my soaking slit and I whimper. It's not enough.

"I've imagined this view since the first day I met you," he admits.

I look at him over my shoulder in the mirror. Steam is filling the bathroom now as the shower runs behind us. Wade's upper arms flex as he grips my hips and pulls me taut against him.

His eyes are hungry, dark; he looks so damn beautiful, it hurts.

He opens his mouth to speak and I expect something dirty, but instead, he simply says, "Ivy, I've just never seen anything as pretty as you. You're like a goddamn work of art, a masterpiece." He says it almost sweetly, before two fingers are thrust into my pussy so deeply, I cry out. I rock against them as best I can as Wade holds me. I'm well beyond shame; I just want to come and this man holds all the power.

My eyes roll back as the shaking of the whipped cream can sounds again, and then it's sprayed just over the cleft of my ass and down, stopping right before my pussy. I still can't move. The ache of the vanity biting into my thighs isn't even noticeable compared to the ache between my legs. Wade spreads me wide and then drops to his knees behind me. I feel his teeth on my skin, biting a path up the inside of my thigh. The pain makes my pussy ache more. He settles in and then I feel his tongue against my clit. I try to clench my thighs and push my pussy into his face, but his strength keeps me right where I am. He moves to the whipped cream and licks some off of me and I cry out.

"Mmm . . . fucking dessert," he groans as he trades between my pussy and the whipped cream. He doesn't lick the mess he made off of me in one fell swoop. He takes his time, tiny little flicks of his tongue clean every drop of the sugary topping, and by the time he's done and the whipped cream is gone, I'm a boneless, panting mess, gripping the countertop so hard my hands have gone numb.

Wade reaches around me and lifts my head by gripping my throat. His cock is so hard against my back I beg him to fuck me in little whimpers.

The smirk he offers me in return is of a man in complete control.

A man in his element.

"Look at us, look at this woman," he orders, watching me in the mirror.

I look at the woman I see there—she doesn't look like regular me. Her breasts are heaving, nipples hard and aching for touch. Her eyes are partly closed and glazy, her cheeks are flushed, her lips parted as she breathes in tiny little breaths, her hair is wild.

She looks . . . sexy, so confident and strong, desirable. She holds all the power, and that thought is fucking electrifying. I want to be her more often, with *him*.

"So desperate . . . so needy for me . . . such a fucking beautiful sight," Wade says as he kisses a trail down my shoulder, then his hands come down around my waist again, spinning me to face him, kissing me as he lifts me up easily then begins walking. He deposits me in the hot shower, never breaking his kiss on the way.

I gasp when the warm steamy water hits my skin. Wade presses my back up against the tiled shower wall before he slams his cock into me with no warning. My eyes fly open and I try to cry out, but no sound leaves me as water hits my cheeks. I wrap my legs around him.

"Fuck, Ivy." Wade sets his pace and begins to fuck me hard and fast. "So fucking perfect."

My head falls forward against Wade's shoulder as his hand slides up the back of my neck. Gripping my wet hair, winding his hand around it, he uses it as leverage to pull my body to him, fucking me so deep, so hard, I feel I might fall apart all over him already.

"Such a good fucking girl, giving in to me, giving me all that sass," he whispers into my shoulder, and something about those words sets me off. I pull my face back and kiss his lips.

"Fuck me as hard as you want. But, Wade, you'll never fuck the sass out of me," I say breathlessly, pressing my palms behind me against the ledge on the shower wall. I take back control of my body, fighting the way he pulls me down to him, moving how I want, only giving him what I allow, and he stills, gripping me at my hips and running his hands over me, and he does something I don't expect.

He lets me.

He moves into me under my lead, he tells me how pretty

I look riding his cock, how well I take him. He tells me my pussy was made just for him, and every word of praise pushes me higher, closer to the orgasm creeping in from every corner, every cell, every nerve ending. My entire body is on fire for Wade.

Just as my high takes hold, he whispers, "Come, Ivy, come for me." It's a command and I feel it, the struggle of power between us, both of us knowing there's nothing about this either of us can control.

The feeling is otherworldly, godlike. I look into his deep green eyes that are so dark now, so stormy. I fight my release with everything in me.

"Make me," I say in a moan as he growls at me, growing inside me even more.

Wade wraps his hand around my throat, pulling my face forward to kiss him as he groans my name into my lips, forcing the air from my lungs with his hand.

"I swear to fucking Christ you were sent here to test me, Ivy. You have no idea the restraint it takes me not to lose control while you fall apart all over my cock," he says in his low tenor.

My body quivers as my breath is taken, yet his hand gets tighter. Dots line my vision just at the precise moment he spills into me. I let go.

I come with him, and it's the most earth-shattering orgasm I've ever felt. The moment my eyes roll back and close, he releases my throat, allowing me to suck in a deep breath. I breathe out the moan I couldn't under his hold.

The water hits my lashes as Wade pulls me to him tightly, wrapping his arms around me, holding me up completely.

"Fuck, I change my mind. I'd never want to fuck the sass out of you anyway, Trouble. I think it's my favorite thing about you."

CHAPTER THIRTY-TWO
Ivy

The rustling of newspaper wakes me from the deepest sleep I think I've ever had. I don't even remember falling asleep. The last thing I remember is Wade cleaning me with a warm cloth after he took me again once we got out of the shower. Then, he scooped me up in his arms and kissed my forehead before sleep took us, with me molded under the crook of his arm like it was carved out just to fit me.

One eye flutters open, threatening to close again until I see *him*. Wade is sitting at the little table in our suite in the sun, wearing only a pair of light gray sweatpants and thin rimmed black glasses, his brow furrowed, hair disheveled and wavy, the scruff of his jaw a little more noticeable than yesterday. He's deep in a read of an article in *The Tennessean*.

My pussy aches at the sight. I'd never found glasses on a man attractive until I saw Wade Ashby wear glasses, but add in shirtless and the hazy morning sun? This sight is almost too much to bear. A smile plays on my lips as I stare at him when he doesn't yet know I'm awake.

The way his throat bobs as he swallows, the wide powerful spread of his shoulders, and arms. How he seems entirely too large for the table but fits somehow regardless. There is a dark and silent beauty to Wade Ashby I'm not sure anyone else in this world has ever really appreciated. Always the leader, always the one everyone relies on. But underneath it all? Under that gruff, rugged exterior lies the sexiest man I could ever dream up. The way his lips claimed me, how his body moved seamlessly and expertly with mine, sends heat to my core when I haven't even had my morning stretch yet. He lifts a steaming mug of coffee to his mouth, and wraps his full lips around the rim. I have no control over the tiny moan I let slip out.

The sound instantly brings his attention to me and his eyes flit to mine. A smile breaks out across his face and my breath hitches at the sight. He's fucking spectacular, and at this moment, cocky as hell, leaning back in his chair. He knew I was staring at him.

"Morning, Trouble. Coffee?"

"Please," I manage to croak out as I turn my head halfway into the pillow and grin, my cheeks heating.

"Too late, you're already busted." He smirks. "Don't worry, I did the same, but you slept through it when I was ogling you," he says, chuckling, and I start to giggle imagining Wade watching me sleep.

He takes his glasses off and sets them on the table, then places a porcelain mug that matches his own under the Keurig on the counter and fills it with coffee, while I silently scold myself for clawing up his back and shoulders the way I did. I would apologize but I think he liked it.

"You snore *really* loud, but you're cute so I'll forgive you," he says, handing me my coffee in bed. Working together has its perks. No need to tell my boss how I take my coffee after a one-night stand when he's brought me one on many occasions in the morning.

"I do not snore."

"You do, woke me right up." I can't tell if he's kidding or not.

I laugh, and run my free hand through my very messy, very knotted-up hair.

"Well, I'm going to blame you and that city bus full of passengers you're packing that you assaulted me with last night," I say as I set my coffee on the bedside table.

Wade laughs harder than I've ever heard him laugh as he jumps onto the bed over me like a tiger on the prowl and pulls me right down under him, before kissing me on the tip of my nose.

"I didn't hear you complaining last night. In fact," he says as his lips meet my neck, "I'm pretty sure your words were more like, deeper"—*oh God*, another kiss to my collarbone—"more"—another kiss—"harder, Wade, please."

. . . and now I'm wet again.

"Don't remember any complaining though," he says as I look up at him, stunned by the dark beauty of him.

"I didn't want to make you feel bad is all," I say.

"Uh-huh, so if I reached into these sheets right now, I wouldn't find you wet for me at all then?" he asks as my breathing increases.

I moan involuntarily as his hand slides under and cups my breast.

"N-no," I stutter. "Dry as the Sahara Desert."

He grins into my lips at the challenge.

"Mmhmm," he says as his fingers slide through my already-dripping slit.

"You're a terrible liar, and I'm hungry as fuck," he says as his lips move down my waist, to my hips, and my breathing increases.

Turning my head to the side, I notice the clock on the wall

"Wade!" I cry. "We have to be at the auction in an hour."

Wade's unfazed as his lips meet the inside of my knee, and he lifts his chin to eye the clock. "How much time do we have before you *absolutely* need to start to get ready?" he asks, a deliciously devilish grin playing on his lips.

"We need twenty minutes to get there," I say as I try to think. I *really* try, but his tongue is moving dangerously close to my core and it's killing my brain cells the closer he gets. His tongue flicks over my clit and my eyes roll back. "Fuck," I moan.

"Come on, Ivy, focus. How much time?" His voice is doing that thing again, deep, bossy, commanding.

"I can't . . . think when you're doing . . . that."

"I seem to remember when I met you that you said you were really good at multitasking . . ." *Fucking hell.*

His teeth graze my clit and I nearly fold in half.

"Well . . . I need a shower, so . . . I maybe have ten minutes," I finally manage to breathe out.

Wade settles between my legs and looks up at me.

I almost cry at the beautiful sight.

"So much time . . ." And then he disappears, burying his face in my pussy as I cry out in response. Strong arms hook around my thighs and pull me down the bed, pressing me further into his face as he laps me up like I'm his favorite flavor of ice cream. His expert tongue goes between fucking in and out of my pussy and sucking my clit into his mouth as two fingers push into me, curving to hit the spot I'm now in love with. Wade doesn't move slowly this morning, he gives me no reprieve, begging me to lose control, begging me to come, which I do within what feels like seconds because Wade Ashby was put on this earth to eat pussy and I never even stood a chance.

"Holy fuck . . . *Wade*," I scream as I grip his hair between my fingers, my legs spasming around him as he burrows his face in further so he doesn't miss one drop of what I offer him.

He kisses my clit gently as I try to remember how to breathe properly. A dizzy haze overtakes me.

He smirks between my legs.

"Breakfast of champions, and still got time to spare," he says as he rises and taps me twice on my ass.

Is this real life?

The yearling auction is sensory overload. A sea of people, agents, ranchers, corporations. The chatter is off the charts by the end of our second break. We're small potatoes in this world, especially having been out of it so long. My new phone buzzes in my back pocket. I pull it out right away.

MRS. POTTER

> She's ok, was still sleeping, her phone was dead. I left her a note with your new number so she knows it's been you texting her. Going to go back later and see if she wants to get cleaned up and go to the market with me.

> You're a godsend, thank you.

MRS. POTTER

> I don't mind helping out. One of these days she's going to come around dear, you'll see.

> I sure hope you're right.

MRS POTTER

> Don't give up on her. I'll let you know how the day goes.

"Everything okay? Wade asks with concern, taking in the face I'm wearing.

I worry about her so much I'm sure it's obvious.

194

"I've been trying to get in touch with my mother all morning with no success. Every time that happens, I fear the worst. I think maybe she drank too much and hit her head, or she left the stove going and burned the place down, or any number of other terrible things. So I did what I always do, I reached out to her neighbor Mrs. Potter, to pass on my new number and to make sure my mama is okay," I say with a small smile.

Wade nods, reaches over and tucks a piece of hair behind my ear. I turn my face toward his palm, already craving his touch again.

I have to wonder if somewhere in there he hates the thought of her in some way, knowing that his best friend's parents died at the hand of a drunk driver. If he does, he doesn't show it.

My phone buzzes again, interrupting the moment. I open the email and then turn the face of my phone to show Wade, lighting up the subject. I grin.

"We may just have our jockey. Not just any jockey. Rowan McCoy, the nephew of the jockey that raced for your dad in 2006. He wants to come to the ranch and meet with us after we secure our yearling," I say to Wade.

Wade nods, dividing his attention between me and the numbers that are now flying out of the auctioneer's mouth. I just know he's calculating the day's worth. The tally which they've been keeping today so we can guess just how much Rustling Winds will go for.

But Wade doesn't ignore me; he lets me know he hears me by resting a hand on my mid-thigh and squeezing gently. His fingers are so large they fall in between my thighs, and my core aches with just that simple contact alone before he returns his hand to his lap.

Part of me is glad he isn't freaked out about what happened last night; the other part is, well, freaking out.

CHAPTER THIRTY-THREE
Wade

I don't know how the fuck I'm supposed to concentrate on anything with this woman beside me all damn day in a gauzy pink linen dress and black fucking snakeskin boots. All I can think about is making up an excuse to sneak Ivy into the nearest lockable room and then fucking her into another dimension.

She's like a drug I'm hooked on and can't get enough of after just one night.

I'm not an inexperienced man. I've had a good amount of sex in my life, but nothing has ever felt like her, like us, together. Not even close, and waking up beside her, that sugary-scented hair spread out all over the bed, her ivory skin peeking out of the sheets. Fuck, I can't wait to take her home and wrap her up in mine.

"Hip 211, Robicheaux Ranch incorporated, Louisiana, 'Angel's Wings,'" the auctioneer says. I take in the shape of the filly as her stats and family bloodlines are read. I already know them, by memory now.

I knew this was our horse the moment I saw the way Ivy looked at her yesterday. If she's going to train a winner she has to believe in the horse we choose, and she believes in this horse. I could instantly tell they had a bond. Even right now, she looks like she's about the jump the rails to go and give this horse a hug. The auctioneer starts the bidding at one hundred thousand and I raise my number. Judging by the last ten horses of her stature, the price will go up in increments of twenty-five to fifty thousand because she isn't really a front runner.

I raise my number again.

"Wade, what are you doing?" Ivy asks rhetorically, knowing I won't be able to answer until the bidding is over.

A few more calls and we're already at three hundred and twenty-five thousand. I'm willing to go up to seven hundred thousand. I've already discussed it with my mother, Nash and Cole over text, and they're all in. Of all people, it was Nash who said he'd trust Ivy to pick our horse blindfolded, and even though her words didn't choose Angel's Wings as her own, her eyes did. Ivy isn't the only one with intuition, and I saw it immediately, a yearning and connection between her and this horse that she simply didn't have for Rustling Winds or any other horse we saw.

"Six-seventy-five going once, do I have seven? Seven?" the auctioneer calls.

The older man I was bidding against keeps his paddle down. I look back at him, and because it can't hurt, and I'm comfortable enough in my own skin to pimp myself out just a little, I look right at the auctioneer and toss him a winning smirk just like Ivy suggested, willing him to call it for me.

He meets my eyes and speaks. "Six-seventy-five, going twice. Sold to Silver Pines Ranch, Morgan Brant agent," he says, mentioning the agent we're using to broker the deal with.

When I put my number down and look at Ivy fully for the first time, she's holding her hands over her mouth, and I instantly think I fucked up.

"Are you not happy? Was this not the one? I—fuck I thought, I was sure—" Her hand comes down and settles on my forearm.

"My dad used to call me *angel*." She smiles simply at me, tears line her eyes and it's like a punch to the gut.

I smile and squeeze her thigh.

I didn't fuck up. I did good.

Real good.

"I felt a connection but I just . . . I wouldn't want to make you take this chance—" she says.

I internally breathe a sigh of relief and kiss her forehead.

"It was meant to be," I promise her. "She's the one."

But she's not convinced, and I can tell it's not for fear of the horse, it's that Ivy isn't used to people doing anything solely because they believe in her.

"But fuck, are you sure? She's not a surefire bet, Wade, not like Rustling Winds," she says, her eyes flitting between me and our new horse almost nervously.

I tilt her chin up to me, bringing her eyes to mine. I can see the worry she's wearing and I'm not fucking having it. Brad, and anyone else that ever made her feel like she wasn't enough for one fucking second, needs to have their head knocked.

I use the voice that tells her this is no longer a discussion. "Ivy, it's done, and she's the horse I want too."

She huffs out a breath, looks to the horse being led out of the sale ring then back up to me. "You must be crazy, Wade Ashby."

She's right, I am crazy, but not in the way she thinks.

"Call me whatever you want, Trouble. But I'm not worried one bit. I'm not betting on the horse. I'm betting on *you*."

CHAPTER THIRTY-FOUR
Ivy

"I sent Rowan the stats on my Angel baby already, he seems excited."

Wade looks at me and opens his mouth to speak but I cut him off. "Yes, my girl already has a nickname. I'm so excited to start working with her I could die." I smile wide, and it must be contagious because those dimples I cannot get enough of are in full force on Wade's face.

"There are a few others we could work with if he passes," he says as we walk. "I've already sent out emails to a few to introduce us, just in case."

I nod, although I don't think we'll need to—Rowan seemed very interested in working with Silver Pines.

"There she is, go see her." Wade rubs my back, giving my shoulder a little squeeze, and points with the documents and the book in his other hand to Angel.

As I start to walk, he motions with his head for the registration table in the next building.

"I'll go call Morgan and get us settled with the auction house and the forms for the AQTA. You visit with her, get acquainted, I'll be right back," he says, leaving to call our agent.

I greet Silver Pines' new baby—my new baby—and spend the next few minutes reiterating to myself over and over that I can do this, that she's the one, that my gut instinct is right, that we didn't just spend over half a million dollars on the wrong horse. The moment my hand connects with her my confidence returns. I instantly know I can work my magic with her

"You are the one, ain't you, baby?" I ask her.

My phone buzzes in my pocket, pulling me from the moment.

GINGER

What do you call a woman horse?

I smile. I'm starting to love having friends.

A filly, until she's four. Then she's a mare.

GINGER

Fuck yes, well, like I always say, if you want something done right, get a woman on the job. 👊 Especially an angel filly.

OLIVIA

Yes, angel energy. You've got this Ivy!

CECE

I had to tell them. Congratulations!

News travels fast in this family

CECE

I held it in as long as I could, Nash told me this was the horse a few hours ago, I'm so excited for you.

A few hours ago? We just bought this horse forty minutes ago. My cheeks heat as my brain registers that Wade made this decision with them before we even sat down at the start of the auction. And for some reason, that feeling warms my whole body from the tips of my toes to the top of my head, and scares the shit out of me all at the same time. He's so sure in his belief in me, I'm going to have to live up to that now.

GINGER

We're gonna be the hottest bitches the Kentucky Derby's ever seen.

First we have to train her and win a shit load of preliminary races. I'm freaking out a little.

OLIVIA

You and Angel's Wings are gonna knock 'em dead. She's already a badass and so are you

GINGER

You've definitely had a productive day today babe. Maybe your boss will give you some kind of bonus for finding the right horse?

CECE

Please, I beg you, message this shit in private

OLIVIA

They've already been there all weekend, who's to say he hasn't already?

GINGER

CeCe, earmuffs please

CECE

FFS Muting this chat

GINGER

At this point, I feel like you just plain owe it to us to find out if he's the type of man we've always thought he is. Definitely BDE, and maybe a bit of a freak under that serious scowl.

OLIVIA

Agreed.

GINGER

Remember when we used to peek out the crack in CeCe's bedroom door when we knew he was in the shower?

OLIVIA

Those two seconds he walked by with a towel on the way to his room were worth putting up with CeCe going on and on about leaving Jason Westman the whole summer before college.

GINGER

Ivy you are the one, young grasshopper. Save a horse, purely so we can put the topic of Wade's BDE to rest.

CECE

You two are such assholes. I knew you were using me all those years.

GINGER

We've put our time in. We deserve to know now, just sayin'

I have no plans to be your Not Angels science experiment. And for the record, Wade has been a perfect gentleman today.

GINGER

What about yesterday? ••

I suppress a giggle and put my phone back. Just as I do, my eyes find Wade two stalls away, all finished with his phone call. As I stand frozen, watching him walk toward me with his sure, steady pace, a flannel jacket and his tattered cowboy hat low over his eyes, my heart rate begins to speed up. Nothing about him seems unintentional, or nonchalant, not even his stride.

His jaw sets as his eyes meet mine and he smirks at me. BDE? Check.

CHAPTER THIRTY-FIVE
Wade

"This is the training schedule," I say as I place my spreadsheet on the coffee table in the den at the big house. "We'll need to train all through the spring and summer," I tell my family at our usual Monday night dinner.

Ivy and I have just come back from Nashville, and of course they all want the dish on Angel's Wings.

"There's a place in Sarasota we can take her to record her workouts and obtain her gate card, so she's qualified for racing, I want to take her there in early February if you all agree. The sooner we can make her comfortable with the noise, the other horses, the sooner she'll be ready for her juvenile racing year. I hope to have her springing from the gate by next Christmas," Ivy says to my family across the table from me.

It's a big goal, but if anyone can do it, it's her.

I let my eyes drink her in when no one is watching. She's wearing a pair of light blue jeans that hug every curve she offers and an off-the-shoulder white sweater. Her hair is hanging loose and the wisps that trail her graceful neck have me wishing I could lift them up, wrap those strands around my hand and suck her skin right into my mouth. I've buried myself in her seven times in the last forty-eight hours, but even that isn't stopping me from wishing I could lure her into the dark hallway and bend her over the closest side table.

"... and she's regal and confident and so goddamn beautiful. Isn't she, Wade?" Ivy asks me as she shows photos of Angel to the family.

I nod and sip my bourbon. "The most beautiful," I say back, watching how she swipes her hair behind her pretty little ear, not even thinking about the damn horse.

Mama moves to the kitchen so she and CeCe can mix together a spinach salad.

"I hope y'all had time to have a little fun too," she says to us.

Ivy looks straight at me and raises one eyebrow. It's a look that tells me she's about to be a brat and it makes my cock twitch every fucking time.

"Y'all wanna hear something mind-blowing?" she asks, biting her bottom lip.

I give her a look of warning.

Cole instantly looks up from the other side of the sofa.

"Fuck, yeah," he says

"Wade *danced* at Luke's 32 with me," Ivy says, looking at me with that grin on her face that says she knows how much my family is going to bust my chops over it, but still, she adds with a little smirk, "All night long."

Mama grins without even looking up from the dressing she's making.

"You're good for him then, darlin'. He used to love to dance."

Fuck my life.

My mother's smile grows as she looks up and points her spoon at Ivy while she talks. "Remind me to show you a home video real soon of him and Cole singing karaoke and dancing their little hearts out one fine Christmas morning."

"Goddammit, Mama." I run a hand through my hair.

Cole laughs as if he wasn't just as ridiculous as I was at that age, while he takes a big swig of his drink. Fucker used to act out Justin Timberlake's dance moves like he was entering goddamn *American Idol*.

"I think I sort of remember that Christmas. Wade was in his Lonestar phase," CeCe pipes up, holding a carrot to her mouth like a microphone. She sings the chorus of Lonestar's biggest hit in the wrong fucking key.

Amateur.

"I'm a confident man," I say, raising my glass. Fuck them all, I'll own it. "I sang the shit out of that song for a twelve-year-old. A lot better than that piss-poor performance," I chirp at CeCe, and knock back a shot.

"Her voice is straight from heaven itself," Nash coos into her ear as he kisses her.

Cole makes a vomit sound and pretends to crack a whip.

"My fucking sentiments exactly. I seem to remember you talking all sorts of shit about CeCe Rae back in her Shania days," I say.

Nash is a cocky motherfucker and doesn't take one second to say, "I was a stupid kid then; I didn't mean it. I always thought she was a great singer."

"Thank you, baby." CeCe kisses him on the nose as Ivy giggles from across the table.

I shoot her a text as CeCe impersonates Cole next, singing Justin Timberlake, and I'm grateful I'm not their target for five minutes.

> You have no idea what kind of punishment I'm gonna rain down on you for that later.

I watch her as she feels the buzz of her phone in her pocket. I'm transfixed on her face as she pulls it out. Watching the corners of those beautiful lips turn up into a half smile as she types, as pretty as sin.

TROUBLE

I'm sure that smart TV of yours has built in karaoke if you want to punish me with soft, croony country music?

You can bring any music you like. You have no idea how much I can make you suffer.

TROUBLE

But we're not in Nashville anymore. Don't you think it's about time to behave like adults and co-workers? We got that out of our systems didn't we?

Fuck no. Not even fucking close.

Should've thought of that before you wrapped those lips around my cock.

TROUBLE

Actually, if I'm being honest, all I can think about is wrapping my lips around your cock.

Christ.

I nearly choke on my bourbon as I read her answer. Ivy leans back in her chair and crosses one leg over the other, looking straight at me like she's untouchable. The joke's on her if she thinks I wouldn't haul her ass into the main floor bathroom and prop her up on the sink while I fucked that tight little pussy into next month.

> You're looking awfully confident with all these people around, and as much as I like that, you know what I like more?

TROUBLE

> What?

> The look you're going to wear later when my fingers are tangled in that long, thick hair and I'm fucking the back of your throat.

I look up at her to find Ivy shifting in her seat and I instantly know that she's wet and desperate for my cock to fill her.

Pop clears his throat beside me, jump-scaring the shit out of me. Where the fuck did he come from?

"Set the table . . . *Chief*," he says quiet enough for only me to hear, as he hands me the cutlery, looks between Ivy and me and winks.

Fucking Christ. Observant old man.

I swipe the cutlery out of his hand and adjust myself as discreetly as possible while Pop shakes his head and heads back to the kitchen.

Across the den, Ivy leans back in her chair and sips her bourbon while she giggles.

As I set the forks and knives down in their place on the table I feel my phone buzz.

TROUBLE

> Can't fucking wait.

And now I'm hard.

CHAPTER THIRTY-SIX

Ivy

"So what are your first steps with her?" Cole asks me as we clean up from dinner. I've stayed back to help clean up while Wade and Haden work on the stall that my new baby is going to call home very soon.

"Getting her comfortable with all her tack, a rider, and gate schooling—and then, if all goes well, workouts begin. Rowan will get used to working with her and then we'll take her to Florida and see if she's got what it takes."

"Three months, is that enough time to get her ready for testing?" Cole asks with genuine interest.

"I think so, they've been working with her a bit at Robicheaux Ranch—they've been warming her to the saddle, working with her a little. Time will tell." I grin, Cole nods.

"So, y'all will drive?"

"Probably, Florida isn't that far. We'll have gear to bring and Dusty can tow her with the diesel," I say, mentioning the monster Ford truck the Ashbys keep for hauling.

"Spending almost ten hours in the truck with Wade. Whatta treat." Cole chuckles as he wipes the counter down.

They look very similar to each other, as brothers should. Cole's just an inch or two shorter than Wade, and has Jo's friendly eyes. Wade is all sharp angles and smoldering.

"Something tells me Ivy doesn't mind Wade's company too much. I mean, I haven't seen you swing at him yet and you've even been his roommate," Nash says while he places dishes in the dishwasher.

I shrug. "I'm getting used to him."

"Takes a special kind of soul to work for Wade, he's very . . . particular. There were days Sam wanted to sock him one," CeCe says from her place at the island, reminding me my time here is limited. Last I'd heard, Sam was planning on returning to work in April.

"Ever since Janelle, he's just always had a big old chip on his shoulder. Wade was always the serious type, but still . . . before her, he was kinda fun," she adds.

"I'm glad he's got a new endeavor to focus on, keeps him busy," Nash says as they clean. "He was with Janelle a long time, and I know she's not done with him yet."

"I'm hoping he'll tell her to hit the bricks for good if she comes back again." Cole shrugs and pops the rest of his cookie into his mouth.

"Not if, *when*. The moment she's done with what the town has to offer, she'll be back begging for Wade. He was way too good for her, and the moment she realizes what she gave up, she'll be back," Nash corrects.

I listen to them all talk about Janelle like she's the female version of Brad, and my heart goes out to Wade, he does deserve so much better than that.

"Maybe he's already let her go," I offer without thinking, ignoring the knot in my gut at this conversation.

Nash looks at me in a way that feels too knowing and then speaks.

"The funny thing is I don't even think he loved her by the end. Janelle is just really good at manipulating."

"Here's to hoping his Janelle days are over," Mama Jo quips as she sweeps. "I'm still holding out hope for him to meet a nice girl. He deserves to be happy," she adds as she smiles at me.

I clear my throat.

"Thank y'all for dinner. It was delicious. If it's all the same, I'm going to go see if Wade needs a hand readying anything for Angel," I say to them all.

Jo makes her way over to me and pinches my cheek gently. How an almost sixty-year-old woman can look this good will never cease to amaze me. I hope I'm still as hot as Mama Jo when I'm older.

"You're welcome anytime, honey, we sure are grateful you're here."

I smile back at her. "I am too."

"Big day tomorrow." She grins as I pop my cowboy hat on. "Sleep tight, say goodnight to Wade for me," she singsongs as I head out.

I can't help but notice the little gleam in her eye as she says it. A gleam that says Wade's mother may have some idea that something is going on between us.

The air is unseasonably warm for early November as I make the short walk from the big house to the main barn just after dusk. I struggle over the events of this weekend and the predicament I've got myself in. Involved with a man I work with, *again*. Wade isn't Brad, and this whole situation is different. Wade treats me like I'm his equal, and as gruff as his personality seems I know there isn't a mean bone in Wade Ashby's body. Still, I'm leaving at some point soon, I'm a stand-in. Where does that leave me and my boss when I have to go across the country for another job?

I blow out a breath and try to shake free of my overthinking. Something I always do. We're just having fun, we're attracted to each other and it's just sex. Really incredible, mind-blowing sex. Wade is a man like any other, right?

And as long as we're smart about personal-work boundaries, there is no reason we can't keep a good working relationship and still have some fun together. I can stop at any time if said mind-blowing sex gets in the way of work.

I've almost got myself convinced as I remind myself of all the ways I'll be able to keep the perfect work-sex balance with Wade when he comes into view on horseback.

His cowboy hat shields the last of the day's sun from his face, his flannel sleeves are rolled up to his elbows as they usually are, showcasing those strong forearms while he grips his reins tight with one hand and with the other holds the reins of another steed who's trotting happily beside him. His body moves effortlessly with his horse Apollo, as if he was born on horseback. His perfectly worn in Levi's are hugging his powerful legs all the way down to his boots. The biggest Tennessee-made cowboy boots I've ever seen.

He spots me and smirks at me as he gets close enough for me to see those beautiful green eyes.

"Ride with me," his deep tenor commands over the empty field.

Who am I kidding? I am so screwed.

CHAPTER THIRTY-SEVEN
Wade

"See if you can keep up, Chief," Ivy says as she hops up onto the steed I've brought her, Sheffield. And then in one split second, she's gone, holding her cowboy hat to her head, her hair flying out behind her like the wings of a raven.

I knew Ivy could ride fast, but what I didn't know was how fucking beautiful and effortless she would look doing it. I squeeze my boots around Apollo, signaling him to speed up to catch the little spitfire.

For someone who just healed up an ankle she doesn't seem to have any worries of getting hurt. That tells me either she's damn good on a fast horse and she knows it or she simply has no fear. Either answer is just as fucking sexy as the other to me. We ride like this for some time through the property until I finally breeze by her. She might be fast and impulsive but I'm good with the long haul and know how to work my horse better than anyone.

"Gotta pace him," I call as I pass her, winking as I tip my hat.

Ivy grunts the cutest little sound as she catches up to me at the same time I slow, so we can ride side by side at an easy jog.

"Your family's land is so beautiful," she says as the sky begins to litter with stars.

We are almost at my favorite spot on our 650 acres. The large pond we learned to fish in as boys with my dad. There is a tiny cabin at the base of it where we'd camp in the winter to ice-fish. It feels like a late summer night out here tonight, as Ivy comes to a halt when the water comes into her sightline.

"Stunning. This is all still yours?" she asks

Hard to believe when she puts it that way. Mine. My job to carry on his legacy.

"Yep," I say.

"That's a lot on your shoulders, isn't it?" she asks. "How do you feel about that? Is it a weight you welcome or weather?"

I blink because fuck, in my entire life no one has ever asked me that before.

"It's my birthright," I answer.

Ivy rides over to me, circling the space where Apollo and I have stilled.

"That's not what I asked you. What I asked was, do you *want* it?"

I huff out a breath and try to be as honest with her as I can.

"Sometimes." I pull ahead and move closer to the water, watching the moon shine off of it for a second. "I have to do this, there's never been another choice. My dad got sick and passed so quickly. Cole was already the Deputy Sheriff, now he's fixing to become Sheriff. I could never sell it, it's the way I feel the closest to him, it keeps him alive, if that makes sense."

"Perfect sense, actually," she answers immediately. "But what I mean is, what about *you*, Wade? If you could keep this dream and still have something for you, what would it be?"

I have to deep-dive into any dreams I had for this place, because it's been a long fucking time since I've thought about it. I shrug and decide to be honest with her.

PAISLEY HOPE

"I always wanted to build, maybe add some more cabins, and offer weekend escapes. Maybe a rustic barn to house weddings. Bring in more income by running this place as a destination as well as a ranch. We have the land to add a hospitality side."

Ivy flashes me a moonlit megawatt smile.

"That's fucking genius, you know that, don't you? Why aren't you doing that? With this view of Sugarland? It's picture perfect."

I shrug, pulling my hat up to rub my forehead. "It's been a long time since I've considered what I wanted, Trouble."

She laughs and starts off in the direction of the barn.

"Sometimes you need to forget about what everyone else wants, Wade. Follow your own dreams. From what you and your family have said about Janelle"—I wince at her name—"she didn't allow much time for you to think about yourself. Sounds like you've been only giving to her and to your family, and somewhere in there you stopped giving to yourself. Gotta fill your own cup sometimes too." She looks out to the water for a beat, then back to me, breaking the comfortable silence between us.

"If you want to make this beautiful place into something other people can enjoy, do it. Where there's a will, there's a way, my dad always used to say."

"Sounds like a smart man," I comment as I ride beside her.

"He was . . . the best man I ever knew." She's got that distant look in her eye again for a second before her smile returns.

"Race ya back." And then she's off.

But this time, I'm using my knowledge of this land to my advantage. I take off more west, close enough that I can still see her but knowing there's a break through the trees that cuts across the field. I ride hard and fast back to the barn, with Ivy finally catching on and chasing her way behind me.

By the time I make it back, I'm a hundred feet ahead of her and dreaming up all the ways she's gonna reward me for my win.

CHAPTER THIRTY-EIGHT
Ivy

"You cheated, Wade Ashby," I yell as I finally make it into the barn.

He's already untacked Apollo, acting like he's been back for hours.

"You're fucking slow, Trouble. I was thinking about a nap while I waited."

I narrow my eyes at him, which seems to amuse him even further.

"I want a rematch! I could've beat you if you would've played fair!" The competitive side of me is actually slightly annoyed as Wade closes the gate to the corral and makes his way over to me while I dismount.

He chuckles when I breeze by him like he isn't even there, and I add Sheffield to the large pen to cool off.

"I never took you for a sore loser," Wade observes, folding his arms across his chest.

"I didn't lose! You cheated," I say as I shut the gate and take my riding gloves off.

Wade grabs me the moment we enter the long hallway of the small barn, pressing me up against the wall. It's quiet here;

there are no animals in this part, only equipment. The sound of insects outside and our breath fills the air.

"I'm definitely not . . . kissing a cheater," I mumble as Wade's tongue traces the column of my throat. I turn my face to the side, and I feel the cocky fucker grin, like my challenge only turns him on more.

"Look, Trouble, you can stay mad at me all you want, for *your* loss." He pulls my chin up to meet his gaze and tips my cowboy hat back enough to press his lips to the corner of my mouth. "I'll even rematch you anytime, anyplace, but don't think for one second you're getting in the way of me sinking into you right now, cause I've been thinking about nothing else all fucking night."

And then his lips are on mine. My fight dies the second his tongue sweeps into my mouth and dances with mine. Leather and spice mixed with the minty-ness of his breath overtakes my whole being. His kiss is demanding, claiming and deliciously slow, as his fingers lace with mine at my side, pinning me deeper to the wall with his hips. I can feel him hard already through his jeans against my abdomen. Wade parts my legs with a knee and trails his finger down my cheek to my jaw, under the curve of my ear.

"I thought about it on the drive home." He pulls my sweater down to expose my shoulder, a low groan escaping his lips before he takes a bite, sucking my skin into his mouth, then releasing it as he moves over my collarbone, dotting it with kisses. My sweater hits the concrete floor as he pulls it off and his fingers find my pearled nipples effortlessly through the lace of my strapless bra.

"Thought about it all through dinner too. Do you know how hard it was for me to stop myself from taking you into the next room and fucking you right then and there?" His voice is gravel in my ear as heat pools in my panties with the expert way he's working his fingers against my nipples.

I whine again and inch myself closer in his cock.

"And you were such a little brat tonight. Do you know what happens to little brats, Ivy?" He pinches my nipple. Hard.

Oh fuck. Why is this so hot? How can a man be this good at this?

He reaches down and cups my pussy through my jeans, pressing the heel of his palm into my clit, and all I can do is whimper.

"They get fucked, hard," he rasps, as just his finger and thumb pop the button on my jeans, and I'm in sensory overdrive because his other hand is still working slow torture with one of my nipples. Wade yanks my jeans down, dropping to his knees and sliding the denim down to the floor, pulling the flared bottoms off over my boots. He looks up and lets his eyes rake over every inch of me, standing before him in just my bra, panties, my cowboy boots and hat.

"Well, that might be the hottest thing I've ever fucking seen," he growls as he stands and yanks a rope down from the wall and spins me around.

I moan as he does, and his cock presses into my ass and I rock against it desperately. It's like he's training me to crave him, to beg for him. If that is his plan, it's working. I've never wanted anything more.

Holding my hands over my head, he wraps the rope around my wrists, securing them to the open barnboard above me, in a taut line that gets tighter when I pull my wrists toward me. His lips meet my shoulder blade as I pant. I need him to touch me, somewhere, anywhere.

"You want to taunt me? Tease me? Make me hard before we even sit down to the fucking *dinner table*?" he asks as his fingers trail under the back of my thong, sliding downward to the cleft of my ass as he grips my hip tight with his left hand. A tight slap lands on the fleshiest part of my cheek, stinging me.

A growl rumbles low in Wade's chest at the same time I moan. My pussy throbs. Another stinging slap catches me off guard, before he stands back and admires his work,

"Fuck, my handprint looks good on you," Wade says as he grips me tightly, then trails a finger down through my soaking slit from behind.

"Mmm." He growls an animalistic sound as he feels the mess I'm making between my thighs. "You like it rough, don't you, Ivy? You're so fucking wet."

"*Fuck*, yes," I breathe out.

"Spread these thighs for me as wide as you can now. I'm fucking desperate for this sweet cunt," he says as he pushes my legs apart with his boot. "But first . . ."

I feel him pull my hat from my head and replace it with his own.

"The only hat allowed on your head while I bury my tongue inside you is *mine*."

"Holy *shit*." I bite my lip to keep from yelling as Wade drops and does just that, burying his face deep in my pussy, spreading me even wider to give himself more access as his tongue darts in and out of me, lapping against me as his face rocks into me. He grips my ass and spreads me wide as his tongue continues its assault. Two fingers curve into my most coveted spot and I'm begging to come within what seems like seconds.

"Fuck, Ivy, I could survive everyday only eating this pussy," Wade growls as he flicks his tongue relentlessly over my clit. "Fucking morning, noon and night, and I'd never tire of you."

"Wade!" I scream as I start to fall apart. My pussy tightens around his hypnotic fingers and I'm practically hanging from my tethered place to the wall. I know the only thing that is stopping the rope from cutting the circulation completely off in my wrists is his strong hands at my hips, and his face.

"Don't hold back, Ivy. Come on my tongue with my name on yours."

Stars explode behind my eyelids as I screw them shut. Every cell in my body is alive and buzzing with Wade as an intense orgasm centers inside me.

I'm whimpering obscenities, curse words, his name, *yes, please*, among other things I couldn't even tell you, all the while he never stops, never slows, working his tongue into me, proving quickly that there's truly nothing he loves more than feasting on me.

I open my eyes as my breathing begins returning to normal, but Wade gives me no time, he pulls the hat from my head and uses the pad of his finger to circle my clit. I'm so sensitive that every time he touches me, I shudder and my legs almost give out. My wrists are so tight against the rope that it burns, but I don't care about the pain. I don't even really feel it. All I feel is Wade's finger tracing a line up my slit, and then I hear the sound of his buckle and his jeans hitting the concrete floor. One large hand reaches around and grips my hip tight, squeezing my flesh there, pulling me taut to him; the other moves to my hair as he twists it around his fingers, as he drives into me with one violent thrust and a beast-like growl.

"Fucking *Christ*, Ivy."

I can only moan in response; I may as well not even have legs because they have ceased to remember how to work.

Wade holds me up, lifting my body and giving my wrists a little relief against the tight rope holding them. He somehow pushes himself even further into me, that last final inch. Stretching me, begging my body to accept him.

"So fucking wet. So fucking tight. So fucking *perfect*," he mutters as he drags his cock out slowly, almost all the way, then slams back into me again with a long drawn-out growl and a "Fuck . . ."

I moan and bite my bottom lip. His hands reach to my front and pull the lace of my bra down, letting my aching breasts bounce free, finding my nipples as he fucks into me roughly, all the while peppering my shoulders and arms with the softest, sweetest kisses I've ever felt. It's too contradictory, but in this moment, I can't imagine anything on earth that could possibly feel better.

Wade uses my body like a toy to fuck himself. His slow unhurried movements are never-ending, and every time I get close to orgasming all over him he somehow knows, and stays in me for a beat longer than he should.

"Wade . . . please," I beg.

"Please what, Ivy? Let you come?"

"Yes, please, Wade . . . please," I whine, almost in tears.

I feel his lips turn up into a smile against my back. "Not yet, baby." His lips graze my ear and my breath stops as he whispers, "This is what heaven feels like, let me take my time."

Oh God. Sir. Yes. Sir.

He groans as he continues to circle his hips within me.

For how long? Who knows? Every time Wade bottoms out in me he stays longer, at a slow steady pace to drive me fucking insane as his finger finds my clit. A sort of floaty haze takes hold of me. One small stroke against my aching bud of nerves, and the jolt of pleasure and need has me tightening around his cock, begging him to spill into me and let me come in return.

I moan and whimper as he uses his free hand to finally untether me from the wall. I fall, my back into his chest in a boneless, sweaty heap as he holds us both up and circles my clit, sliding his other hand up to my throat, turning my face to cover my lips with his own, absorbing my cries in a sloppy, aggressive kiss while I spiral out of control.

I never thought sex could be this natural, this unhinged. I want him to dominate me, to hold me down and have his way with me, whatever that way may be. With each thrust, Wade goes deeper, harder. The sound of my own arousal and the in-and-out of him fucking me is pulling me further and further into the abyss of Wade. My mouth falls open in a soundless cry.

"Fuck, Trouble, when you whimper like that, I can hardly take it, you take my cock so fucking well."

I can't contain the sounds that leave my lips as he stops moving, buried to the hilt in me. I try to move but his strong hands hold me in place, one at my hip, the other around my throat.

"Remember when I said I would make you suffer?" he asks, moving again.

God, I want to die like this.

"Yes," I whine.

"Do you think you've suffered enough?" he asks.

"Yes. Fuck yes, Wade . . . please," I say.

"You want to come?" he asks in a whisper as he completely stops moving. My pussy pulses around him as he does. "Then beg me. Beg me to paint your insides with my cum, Ivy."

"Please . . ." is all I manage, trying to move in any way I can, but he's too strong, holding me too tight.

"Please, what? You always have so many fucking words, use them. Make me believe your plea," he says as he draws slowly out of me.

Oh God.

"Please . . . fuck . . . please, let me come . . . Wade . . ." I whine. I take as deep a breath as he allows. As his hand grips my throat tighter and dots spread across my vision I realize what he wants so I give it to him. I'd give him anything right now. I whisper, "Mercy . . ."

The groan that comes from his chest is approval.

"Such a good fucking girl, Ivy," Wade growls as he somehow

grows even more inside me and pinches my clit—once, then twice—as I'm combusting from the inside out.

I come with a cry that Wade absorbs with his own lips, allowing me small bursts of air to keep me from passing out as he falls apart with me, biting me on the shoulders, my neck, my lips, anywhere his mouth can connect.

"Fuck," he grunts. "There isn't anything more beautiful than watching you come all over my cock."

A single tear escapes my eye while he comes, then mercifully, he releases his hand. I inhale fully as a whole-body shudder consumes me. Wade wraps his strong arms around me tight and tenderly uses one finger to shift my face back up to his, kissing me gently on the lips, massaging my marked wrists with his other hand as if he's making sure they're okay.

"Heaven." He mutters the single word as a statement, a label.

Yes, if this is heaven, I never want to come down to earth.

Thirty minutes later, we have ourselves put back together and the horses in their stalls for the night, when Mama Jo rounds the corner of the main barn, in full riding gear and a cowboy hat.

"Evening, Mama," Wade says.

It's not lost on me that if she had come thirty minutes ago and entered the barn, she would've seen me tied to the barnboard while Wade fucked me into oblivion.

"Hey y'all, I was coming to visit River Rising, thought I'd be alone," she says, probably surprised to see others in the barn after dark.

I know enough from Wade that River Rising was his father's old horse that placed in the Derby in '06. Grief settles in my stomach for this woman, her loss, the relationship everyone says she had with Wyatt, all gone forever. Her visiting Wyatt's horse when she's alone pulls on my heart strings.

"Kinda late, ain't it?" Wade asks as he pulls her into a side hug.

Jo shrugs. "I like to ride him on warm nights and chat with Daddy. And it's only eight thirty." She grins. "What are you two doing here still?" Her eyes move between us with questions that make me want to drop her gaze, and quick.

"Making sure everything is set for Angel's Wings," Wade says at the same time I blurt out, "Wade took me for a ride."

Mama Jo's eyes meet mine. Wade grins.

"I mean, we rode separately, together."

Wade speaks instantly, covering for my awkwardness. "Kicked her ass in a race back from the pond too, although she won't admit it."

I narrow my eyes at him. "He cheated."

"Knowing the land better than you isn't cheating, Trouble." He wraps a rope around his corded arms as his veins ripple while he works. I wish I was the rope.

"I was resourceful," he says, winking.

I scoff.

Jo laughs. "You love that pond, don't ya? Did Wade tell you his daddy took him fishing there when he was a boy?"

"He did." I grin, glad she seems to be letting me off the hook for now.

She reaches up and pats his face. "Wade always said he couldn't wait to take his boys there when he has them one day, and do the same."

Wade looks down to his mom, and grief of my own hits my heart, but the idea of Wade with kids warms me. He would be the best dad to the world's cutest, most controlling little babies.

"Well, that never happened," he says.

"Oh hell, baby, you're only thirty-four, plenty of time for all that. You'll have your babies there one day, you'll see. I know it," she says, sure as the sun rises as she passes by me, squeezing my hand.

"Night, darlins," she quips as she saunters down the row.

Wade looks at me with an apologetic look for his mother saying something she could never know would torment my heart. Before she's even around the corner he's pulling me close.

"Come on, dirty girl, let's get you cleaned up. We have a date with *Ocean's Thirteen* and some ice cream."

I smile up at him, right before he kisses my lips.

Yeah, I could get used to this.

CHAPTER THIRTY-NINE
Ivy

"Rowan's in? For sure?" Wade asks as he opens the shower door in his bathroom.

This bathroom is similar to the one I used when I stayed here but larger, and the shower is the entire length of the wall. Built for two, really.

"So he says, just wants to meet as a formality. He's coming tomorrow."

I lose my bra and turn to step in with him, as he runs a hand through his hair while the water soaks it, and my mouth waters at the sight of Wade, wet and glistening in the shower. I stand watching tiny droplets of water trickle down his muscled chest like a Plinko board.

I don't know how long I stand there for, taking him in from head to toe, but it's long enough for Wade to notice and look at me questioningly.

"Coming in this century, Trouble?" Wade asks, grinning at me like the cat that ate the canary, obviously loving that I can't take my eyes off of him.

I make a face at him while I step into the steaming space as he spins me around and lets the water wet my hair, running his hands down it.

"I can wash my own hair you know . . ." I say instinctively.

"I know you can, but I want to do it. I love this hair—just the sight of this hair trailing down your back does something to me. Makes me hard all on its own. I would fuck this hair if I could."

I turn to look up at him, and plant a kiss on his jaw, giggling at his ridiculous words.

"If I didn't know any better, I'd think you do this on purpose," I observe while the hot water slides down his chest, entrancing me once again.

"Oh yeah, what's that?" He chuckles as he turns me around, grabbing his shampoo and squeezing some into his palm before rubbing it into my hair.

"It's your life war tactic. You seem all unapproachable and nonchalant about everything and everyone, but underneath it all—figuratively and literally—you're hot, insanely hot, actually, and when you let it out, you have kind of an incredible, addictive personality. People might actually like you, if you let them."

He grunts behind me, a sound that says he's half annoyed with me, half impressed.

"I don't need people to like me, I like my horses and less than ten people, as long as they like me back, and that's enough."

I sigh as Wade's large hands massage my scalp with his sandalwood and rosehip shampoo. It smells just like him: incredible.

"Feels good, hmm?" he rasps into my ear.

"Yes, so good," I say honestly.

Wade pulls the shower wand down, the exact replica of the one I used to make myself come in his other bathroom, and rinses the shampoo from my hair.

"I don't do it on purpose, I'm just not very good with people," Wade confesses. "There's always so much on my plate. I don't really have much left for niceties."

I giggle. "I don't buy it; I get the feeling you just don't *want* to let people in. If you do they might let you down, like Janelle did."

A moment of deafening silence passes as he rinses out the conditioner. I find something so sexy about the fact that this rugged cowboy has the matching sandalwood and rosehip conditioner in his shower.

Just as I start to worry I got too personal, he answers.

"And I get the feeling you're not used to people helping you with anything, and it makes you nervous when they try. You might get too used to it. Sometimes it's okay to let people take care of you."

I grin at his astute observation. "Well, aren't we the pair then? Each of us behind our metaphoric walls."

"Seems so," he says as he reattaches the wand to the shower head and I giggle at my own dirty memories.

"What's funny?" Wade asks as he hands me the soap and rubs shampoo into his own hair. He looks like a photoshoot as he scrubs it out.

"Just reliving my romance with your shower head," I say innocently, just to torture him as I wash my body.

Wade stops dead in his tracks, water rinsing his body wash from his shoulders, down his back. The need to trace the lines with my tongue overwhelms me.

"My shower head?"

"Well, not yours, mine, technically . . . when I stayed here."

Wade smirks, that haunting gleam in his eye returning that I can't get enough of.

"Elaborate," he says as he finishes rinsing himself, his cock already starting to thicken with the idea of my story.

The water rushing down the drain is the only sound as I contemplate my admission.

"You have a great massage setting. I used it to make myself come one night while I stayed here . . . two nights . . . three—"

227

"You only stayed here seven."

I huff out a breath. "Okay, four nights."

Wade's jaw goes slack as he looks at the shower head, like a battle is being waged in his mind, then he detaches it swiftly, turns it to massage mode and offers it to me, his expression dead serious.

"Show me."

My mouth falls open. I blush, and his knuckles trail over my nipple.

"Just where was I when you made yourself come, Ivy?" he asks, his voice doing that lower-octave thing that instantly makes my lady bits come alive.

"In the next room."

Wade moves closer to me and physically places the shower head in my hand as he dips down, his lips meeting my ear. I moan as his stubbled jaw grazes me.

"Don't be embarrassed, Trouble, I ruined one of your scrunchies with my cum once. I wanted you just as badly as you wanted me, right from the start."

I blink at his admission. Only confidence radiates from him, as if coming into my scrunchie is the most normal thing on earth.

"Now, show me," he says, with no room for argument.

I do as he says, using the water to trail over my body while Wade instinctively grips his hard cock with one hand and fists my hair with the other, tipping my face up to him so he can whisper in my ear.

"And tell me exactly what you were thinking about while you got yourself off in my house like the dirty little slut you are for me?"

I moan as the water hits my aching clit, closing my eyes, partly so I don't have to look at him and partly because it feels so fucking good already.

"You," I admit.

"Say more," he commands as I begin to circle the shower head, little jolts of lust scorching up my center.

"I . . . imagined you pressing me against the wall," I say as I feel large hands grip my shoulders and spin me around.

"Like this?"

"Yes."

Wade's hand runs down the center of my spine. This is so dirty, so deliciously fucked-up, that I'm telling my boss how I got off to him in his own shower and he's moving to act it out with me, but then again there is not a chance in hell that I'm stopping.

CHAPTER FORTY
Wade

"Then what?" I ask Ivy as I take in every muscle in her back before me, the inked vines that dance down her spine and descend down her hips, the two tiny dimples in her lower back that her wet hair is grazing. I slide my cock between her ass cheeks as she keeps the sprayer on her pussy.

She whimpers.

The thought of her in the next room making herself come with me in her mind is fucking electrifying.

"Then you asked me if I wanted you to fill my tight little pussy with every inch of your cock, and I held the water . . . here," she says as she holds the jets over her clit. It startles her and she lets out the fucking cutest little whimper.

My dirty fucking girl.

"Mmhmm . . ." I mutter as I use my thumb on the little rosebud in the center of her ass as she works the shower head over her pussy. The need I have to fill every hole this woman has every minute of every day is downright shocking to me.

"Do you?" I ask.

"Huh?" she says, dazed, and her whole body shudders when my thumb presses against her wet puckered asshole.

"Do you? Want me to fill your tight little pussy with every inch of my cock?"

"Every goddamn minute," she answers without hesitation while I lose the tip of my thumb to her and groan. One day, my cock will take its place.

She cries out with the feeling, but it's not lost on me that she rocks backward, *into me*.

"Fuck, Wade . . . I've never . . . no one has touched me there before."

I grin behind her. "Just one more thing for me to teach you," I say.

She whimpers into the shower wall with need.

"Just the thought of you hiding in my shower, making yourself come with my name on your lips, drives me fucking wild."

Ivy moves the shower head in circles as her legs begin to shake.

Nope, not yet, she isn't.

I take the shower head from her, and turn her around so her back is pressed against the tile, holding the wand in my own hand, still keeping it over her clit but teasing her with it, only giving her a few seconds of it before pulling it away. My lips find hers, slow and hungry, as her palm connects with my shaft and I bite down on her lip.

"I was almost there," she moans.

"Only I finish the job, only I make you come, got it?"

She looks up at me with fire in her eyes. "I thought I just told you I can take care of myself?" Her mouth turns up in a smirk and I want to wipe it from her face with my cock down her throat.

"See, that's the thing, Trouble," I say as I use both my finger and the shower head to move shallow circles over her clit.

She moans.

"You're lying to yourself. You can't take care of yourself, not entirely," I say as I shove two fingers into her soaking cunt.

She whimpers and leans her head against my chest in defeat.

"Because whether it's by my cock, or your own fingers, or this shower head, I'm still the name you cry out when you come."

I drag my teeth across her jaw, and pull her sweet skin into my mouth as I move the wand and press against her soaking slit with my rock-hard dick.

"That's a bit . . . overly confident, don't you think?" she breathes out. Her words are strong but I'm physically holding her melty body up as she pants below me.

"Not overly anything, baby, just taking ownership over what's *mine*." My fingers move in and out of her tight heat, slow enough that she begins writhing for more when the water finds her clit.

"Are you . . . saying you own me?" she manages to ask as her eyes roll back in her head and her nails dig into my back.

"Right now? Sure fucking looks like it."

I use my free hand to tilt her chin to me, those violet eyes open, glazy with lust, little droplets of water sitting on her long lashes, her hair wet and matted, water dripping over every part of her.

She's absolutely fucking incredible.

"How I make you come tonight, how I make you scream my name. That's what I fucking own, Ivy." I kiss her lips. "And you want me to own it whether you admit it or not."

I place the shower head back in its home and anchor Ivy's body against the wall with my own as water tumbles over us. I grip her slippery hips tight and then, lifting her, I lose myself to her tight soaking cunt against the wall without any warning.

Her mouth opens in a cry as she quivers around me; she's offering me no friction but gripping me so tight with the very feeling that threatens to be my undoing.

"Ready to admit it yet?" I ask, as I drag my hands over her and look down to feast my eyes on where we connect.

"I . . . deeper . . . more," she chants incoherently as she claws my shoulders.

I grin and grip her hips so hard it will surely bruise her as she whimpers, pushing myself into her further, sliding my hands up to knead her shoulders as she wraps her legs around my waist fully while I pull her body down to meet mine. Hard, fast, unforgiving.

"Yes!" Ivy cries as my cock throbs inside her,

"Fuck, look at you. So desperate . . . aching for more of my cock. I'm going to make you come so hard you see stars behind those pretty eyes."

"Please . . ." She is losing her grip on my arms as I fuck her. I have no worry of hurting her, she wants it as hard as I can give it to her, her dripping cunt is my proof. My eyes threaten to roll back into my head with every movement. She feels . . .

"You feel . . ." I trail off, just losing myself in her for a second.

"So fucking good," she cries out.

"Yeah." I kiss her. "That . . ."

"Wade . . ." She moans my name as I piston into her over and over.

I see the fight in her while I fuck her, trying to make this last longer. As I tether my hands in her hair, I watch her fight begin to die. It's the most beautiful sight to see Ivy give in, because I know she never gives in easily to anything. To watch her submit to the pleasure I offer her every time I bottom out inside her is the reward I seek.

"Such a needy little brat. So eager. Your body begs for my cock."

"Yes . . ." she cries as I grip her hair hard, and tip her head back so my lips meet hers.

"Tell me, then, Ivy. Right now, in this moment"—I kiss her—"who owns this pussy?"

"*Fuck*," she calls out in a whine, eyes rolling back again.

"*Who*, Ivy?" I double down, driving her up the wall as my thumb pinches her hardened clit, sending her over the edge.

Her head comes forward, her beautiful eyes fall open and focus on mine for one split second. One split second where time and space cease to exist as she whispers, "You, Wade. You."

An unexpected warmth in my chest fires through me with her words. Overtaking me, consuming me completely as I drop my hand from her hair, unable to control myself.

My cock jerks and spills into her, while she falls apart around me, her pussy begging for every drop I have, pulling me deeper into her with every spasm of her tight walls.

"Ivy . . ." I draw out her name in a groan as I close my eyes and hit the wall with my palm to keep myself from blacking out. I have no idea how long I come for, only that it feels like it will never end. A tiny finger pulls my chin up to allow my gaze to meet hers, bringing me back to her, a coy grin on her beautiful lips.

"Looks like I might own you too."

CHAPTER FORTY-ONE

Wade

December

I stare down at my boots in the dirt while I wait for Ivy, leaning against the open silos door. For forty-seven days we've been doing the same thing, and this is the first day she hasn't been on time.

I know it's been forty-seven days because every morning Ivy reminds me how many days we've been training Angel's Wings for, and how many days to go until she has to be springing from the gate all on her own.

I shouldn't be surprised I'm standing here freezing my ass off though.

Ivy's been a nervous wreck all morning. She spilled her coffee all over her first flannel, messed up the time for a phone meeting with the AQTA, and now she's run back into the office just as we were ready to head to our practice track for Angel's big moment, muttering something about it "being windier out than I thought."

The sound of her boots clicking alerts me that she's moving toward me down the long hallway.

"Fuck, you're almost making *me* anxious," I say as she finally comes into view.

Ivy blows out a breath when she meets me, holding up a scrunchie, and she smiles.

"Couldn't find it. So fucking nervous," she says as we begin to walk.

Late due to missing scrunchie? This woman has lost it, but fuck, she looks beautiful doing it.

"She has to do this today. If she does, we're smooth sailing into January," she rambles, biting her lip. "Do you think she's had enough time?"

Her violet eyes look to me for the answers when she already has them all, but I don't mind. Being needed by her, I think it brings a kind of peace to me.

"Well, one thing is for certain, she'll do a fuck of a lot better now that you've got the scrunchie," I scoff, trying to calm her.

She swats at me as she pops it on her wrist before she says, "I'm allowed to be irrational today, there's a lot riding on her staying on schedule."

"She's going to do just fine, Trouble," I tell her, squeezing her shoulder as we walk.

The air is cold as it hits my face. I see Rowan McCoy the moment we approach the track, already waiting for us too. He signed on with us immediately after we brought Angel home and is our official jockey for Angel's run at the derby. He's been exactly what we were hoping he would be, and he and Ivy are working together perfectly.

Turns out they have a lot of the same, what I like to call *unconventional* approaches. So most of the time, it's the two of them teaming up and overriding my more old-fashioned ideas.

Ivy's beaming with pride for her baby as Angel gets closer, and she leaves my side to approach her. She nuzzles her, pats her, and speaks to her, just taking a moment to say whatever voodoo shit she thinks will help Angel finally enter, wait patiently, and then spring from the gate on the bell without any mistakes.

Ivy has moved slowly with her training, slower than I would've, only bringing her to the gate twice a week, always putting the horse first, never rushing her.

I don't teach Wade, I guide, she repeats constantly.

I pull my hat up and wipe my brow. With only four days until Christmas, this is her last chance to have Angel stay on schedule.

In my opinion, Ivy is a big fucking ball of nerves when she shouldn't be. She's stuck to her schedule with precision. It's been her goddamn life's purpose between her regular duties all day and keeping me satisfied at night. Well, as satisfied as I can be. I've realized in a very short period of time that no matter how much of Ivy I get, it's just never enough.

"Breathe," I tell her as she comes back to stand with me.

She nods, listening, and takes a deep breath.

If I ever had any doubts about choosing this horse—which I didn't—I surely wouldn't have them now.

Watching Ivy train her is like watching magic happen right before my eyes. They're like one spirit, the two of them.

"Should we go watch with the crew now?" I ask her, gesturing to the other side of the track for the best view as I squeeze her hand.

We go to the other side and meet most of my family there. Everyone is here at the ranch for our annual holiday cheer and appetizer night. I take in the bunch as they stand out in the chilly December air, chattering to each other about everything and nothing all at once.

"Let's get this show on the road, Mama forgot her winter coat," Ginger says with chattery teeth as Nash and Cole approach from the big house.

"Who the fuck is this guy? Cousin Eddie?" I ask, tugging on Nash's hat. He's rocking an army green trapper hat with ear flaps. Between that and his red and black flannel he looks like he's right out of *National Lampoon's Christmas Vacation*.

"Got some trees in the north field that need chopping after this?" I ask Nash. "Think you can take a break from cleaning the RV and walking Snots?"

"Fuck you, man, I'm in the holiday spirit," he grunts.

None of it makes sense until I see CeCe and Mabel come around the side of the barn, CeCe in the exact same coat, a smaller version, of course, and Mabel in a Christmas scrunchie that matches Ivy's, that Ivy gave her as an early gift.

Cole reaches out a hand and passes Ginger his big navy parka.

"Anyone ever told you to come more prepared, woman?" he bites out as she takes it eagerly from him, wrapping it around herself and pulling it tight.

"Why would I need a big uncomfortable coat? I walked from my house to the car, from the car to your door. I forgot we were coming out here to watch Angel dash from the gate."

"Spring," Cole corrects. "And that's a piss-poor answer. What if your car breaks down?"

Ginger thinks for a moment, as if that possibility has never occurred to her.

"I don't know. I live my life one moment at a time," she says as she buries her face into the fleece. "Besides, if I break down, some man of the law will have to come rescue me." Her eyes tilt up to his and I almost see him grin at her. I realize it's only because he's laughing at his own response before he says it.

"If it happens and you call me after your break down, you'll be standing by the side of the road shivering, and I'll be driving by, waving at you with my hot chocolate from my nice warm truck, holding up my winter fu—frickin' coat."

"I think that still counts, Daddy," Mabel pipes up

"You always have room for me in your passenger seat, Cole." Ginger smirks.

The sound of the gate closing interrupts their weird fucking banter as the ranch hands secure Rowan and Angel in the gate perfectly, and Ivy blows out a breath as she waits to see if Angel stays calm when the gate clicks shut.

"Holy fuckballs, I might need a drink before we ring that bell," she whispers nervously up at me. I drop my head to her ear so no one can hear.

"I can make that happen, but in my opinion, you don't need a drink, you just need to watch Angel show us she can do this, and then I'll reward you for doing such a good job later," I tell her.

"Hmm," she says as she takes her bottom lip between her teeth the way she does when she's contemplating something.

After being with her almost every minute of every day for over two months, I've gotten to know her on a level I don't think I've known anyone, ever. The best and worst parts? It's the most incredible feeling in the world when her lips meet mine, and also the most terrifying, because I know if I want to have anything more than what this is now, I not only have to find a way to keep her on my ranch when her contract is up, I'll also have to be ready to let her in and trust I could actually have something that won't end up like my marriage. As much as I should've thought all this through before I got to this point, I didn't, so here I am, one hundred percent in denial about the fact that this has gone way beyond some kind of physical attraction with Ivy. But, like the true man in denial I am, I just keep telling myself it will be fine and that I can worry about the way she makes me feel tomorrow. Forty something days and counting . . .

"Care to make it interesting?" she asks, her violet eyes full of mischief. Full of trouble.

"You want me to bet against my own horse?" I scoff incredulously.

"Please? I need a distraction and something to look forward to if she doesn't do well today—"

"If she doesn't spring, she still has weeks to train and get it right before she goes to the track in Florida," I remind her.

"Right, bet me anyway," she says matter-of-factly.

"Okay, Trouble, shoot, what's the bet?"

"If Angel springs out perfectly all on her own . . . you have to do anything in the world I want. If she doesn't, then I will do anything you want."

So what I'm hearing is, either way I win?

I look at her, and I see she needs this so I instantly agree. After all, anything Ivy wants to do to me or with me will be good for me, I'm sure.

"Deal," I say as we move to the rail posts to get the best view.

Ivy looks like she's about to blow her top at any given moment.

I slide my hand under the collar of her coat and place it on her shoulder, rubbing gently under the neckline of her Henley, letting the silkiness of her skin and her hair warm me. She's fucking adorable as ever in her trademark jeans, flannel jacket and cowboy hat. On her feet she wears tattered ivory Lucchese boots.

Haden records the length of time they stay settled in the gate. I'm pretty sure Ivy stops breathing as Haden moves to the bell.

"Hey." I squeeze her shoulder; she looks at me. "Sweetheart, she's got this."

Two more minutes pass and Angel still stays, just as she's supposed to. Ivy closes her eyes as Haden moves to ring the bell and the gates spring open. Rowan squeezes tight to Angel's sides with his boots and Angel springs from the gates into a gallop, burning down our track at an already impressive speed. Angel shows her confidence, and Ivy knows instantly that taking all these weeks not to rush her worked exactly as she planned.

My whole family starts hooting and hollering for Angel.

"Yes! Go, baby!" Ivy yelps, cupping her little mouth with her hands as if the damn horse can hear her from where we stand.

By the time they make it to the end of the track, Rowan is pumping his fist in the air with their victory and Ivy is practically jumping up and down and whistling, tears threatening to spill down her face.

I chuckle as I pull her into me in a side hug and squeeze her tight.

"That's my baby!! That's my girl!" she yells to me as I pull her even closer and kiss her on the top of her sugar-scented head, not giving a fuck who sees.

My fucking sentiments exactly.

CHAPTER FORTY-TWO

Ivy

"Well, deck the fucking halls, who's ready to light this place up?" Ginger says as she drops her purse on our table at the Horse and Barrel the day before Christmas Eve. She's the last to arrive and is outfitted in a scandalous red dress. Her dewy skin and long dark curls dance under a Santa hat.

Wade and I are already seated with Olivia, Cole and CeCe, with Nash keeping a close eye on us from behind the bar. But the moment Ginger arrives, she commands everyone's attention, including Wade's suddenly vocal younger brother.

"Apparently you, as always," Cole mumbles under his breath as he pushes a strawberry margarita to her across the table.

"Don't be such a scrooge, Officer. Thought I saw a mistletoe over there if you want to take a stroll?"

Cole scoffs but I see it, that one second where his eyes drink her in like she's his favorite brand of liquor and he's thirsty as fuck.

"I'm sure you got lots of options in that department, Vixen."

"Tons, of course, but I'll tell you what, Cole. Just because I'm feeling festive, you can be first up." She smiles as she tweaks his chin. She's one of those girls who is so goddamn pretty, it almost hurts to look at her, and no matter what Cole Ashby says, I'm sure he notices it just like every other man in this room.

"I need another drink," Cole half grunts. "Want another?" he asks Wade.

Wade knocks back the rest of his bourbon and nods.

"Me too, baby, we're celebrating tonight," Ginger says to Cole as he saunters off. "I told you wearing my boots would bring you luck! To Angel's Wings' first milestone, may her juvenile wins come just as easily. Also, babe, you look fucking gorgeous, you're glowing. Doing what you love looks good on you." Ginger smiles.

I look down at my navy strapless dress that had Wade sliding his hands under it after he came to get me when he was done working tonight.

Ginger raises her margarita, and we all follow suit while I blush at her blunt compliment. In truth, I'm probably glowing because I've never been so sexually satisfied in my life, although that might all change when Wade finds out what his loss of our little bet will entail tonight.

Wade's hand finds my thigh under the table and he gives it a light squeeze. Those damn butterflies I've been feeling for weeks surface instantly in my stomach.

"So, what's next?" Olivia asks as she smooths her tight copper bun. These three women look like a crew of Christmas cheer: Olivia's dress is hunter green velvet and hugs every curve she has on her tall leggy frame, and CeCe is the angel in a white sweater dress with a non-existent back that keeps Nash popping over to our table anytime a man in the bar that doesn't know she's his even remotely glances her way.

"Now we start more intense training before her juvenile season starts. Her first qualifying race—a practice, essentially—is in early February. She'll be tested before it," I say.

"And if she gets her gate card, we can move to nominate her for the derby, and her first juvenile race would be in September," Wade pipes up beside me.

"You just need forty points, right?" Ginger asks

"Yep, but it's not that easy to get them, and the more we have, the better," Wade starts.

"And the more races Angel has under her belt, the better off she'll be if she makes it to derby day," I add.

Ginger grins a kind of all-knowing grin.

"Look at you two, finishing each other's sentences—seems like working together so much is working out." She winks at me, wagging her crimson-painted finger between us, and takes a sip of her margarita, and by sip I mean half the glass.

"That's good to be in sync with each other," CeCe adds, turning to me with a genuinely sweet smile that I can't help but smile back at.

"You couldn't ask for a better trainer," Ginger says formally.

Wade's brow furrows, as if he's annoyed at Ginger. Not that he tries to hide the fact that we spend all our time together, I've just realized after the last several weeks that Wade Ashby doesn't like answering to anyone and he likes his privacy. We haven't talked about any of what is happening between us; we just keep moving through the same delicious routine. Train all day, eat whatever incredible meal Wade cooks us at night, then fuck like we can't get enough of each other until we pass out.

I haven't even seen my cabin for more than laundry and a change of clothes in weeks, and although I'm fighting through some serious feelings for my boss, I'm nowhere near ready to admit them, partly because I know I'm leaving at some point, and partly because I know I could probably never really give him the future he truly deserves. Those sons Mama Jo mentioned that he dreamed about have stuck in my mind on replay. Constantly reminding me of what we wouldn't have.

As if Wade senses my worry about the state of *us* with Ginger's words, he reaches over and grabs my thigh under the table again. I blink as I look down at it, noticing a word etched into his skin that wasn't there before. The ink is new, glossy, like he just got it done today. It sits perfectly between his thumb and forefinger in a slanted scrawl.

Mine.

My heart accelerates as I look up at him in question . . . did he actually? His eyes meet mine, then glance down to his hand, then back to me. The look in his eyes is all the answer I need. They're dark, claiming. The way he looks before he ravages me.

He definitely fucking did.

My breathing speeds up as Wade's lips come down, dangerously close to mine. My eyes flit around the table, but no one is even paying attention to us in the dark, noisy bar. He leans into my ear, his deep voice crystal clear, and he whispers, "Everything we do is only for us. What happens between me and you doesn't belong to any of them, but if you ever had any doubt what I see when I look at you . . ." He smirks, then adds, "You're going to look so fucking pretty wearing my collar, Ivy." And he squeezes my thigh tight, sliding his fingers under my dress.

My pussy throbs in anticipation as I try to stay calm.

"That thought scare you?" he whispers. "Or make you want to beg me for it?"

"A little of both," I whisper back truthfully.

"If you want to beg, you know there's only one word I need to hear," he says.

His eyes lock with mine, *mercy* on the tip of my tongue and I've only been here five minutes. The bar fades away around us until Ginger's voice breaks our trance.

"I need another. Where is that man?" She smirks, draining her glass.

"Asher's bringing refills for all of you," Cole tells her as he slides in on cue and crunches on a pretzel.

"You know me so well." Ginger nudges him with her shoulder as he rolls his eyes.

"I just know how fast you drink. It's been ten whole minutes, you're off your game tonight."

"What are you insinuating? Bite your tongue, please. In the last four days I've had three Christmas luncheons, sick kids in every corner of the classroom, break-ups, teen drama, and twenty-four 'If William Shakespeare was alive today' papers to grade. Don't shame me because I'm a woman who knows how to let loose after a long week, Cole Ashby. You're better than that."

Cole grins at her and holds out his upturned palm with a handful of pretzels.

"Aww, darlin', I'm so sorry," Cole says to her, his voice low and slow, yet somehow still taunting to her.

Ginger eyes him up and takes a pretzel from his outstretched hand.

"I'll take that apology, thank you very much, and keep them coming," she mutters as he slides the bowl over to her.

"When does Mabes come home from Gemma's for Christmas?" Wade asks Cole, turning Cole's mood instantly sour at the mention of his ex-wife.

"Tomorrow. I'm not giving up the Christmas Eve traditions Mabel is used to just because all of a sudden Gemma wants to pretend to be an adult and parent her. If she's still a parent next Christmas, we'll talk about splitting the time proper."

"I fink she's up to sumfing," Ginger says as she crunches on her pretzels. "Out of nowhere, after almost five years of being absent, she has a boyfriend and is a serious mama type? Uh-uh, mark my words, something is up," she continues.

"I agree," Wade says. "Who is this guy, anyway?"

"Brent fucking Wilson. Cop. Arrogant prick. Hit on CeCe

last summer," Nash says as he slides into the booth with the bartender, Asher Reed, close behind, carrying our margaritas.

I haven't had a lot of interactions with Asher, but I watch as he approaches. He might be the only man in this town as tall and as big as Wade. I remember Ginger saying once that he was the town fire chief. Dark Irish looks with wide deep gray eyes, and I don't think an inch of his visible skin is left un-inked in charcoals and black aside from his face. He's covered from his jaw to his wrists. His scruff on his face is thick. He looks like a larger and much more dangerous version of Chris Hemsworth in *Extraction*. Of course my mind goes to action movies as the basis of comparison.

His voice is deep and intimidating as he sets our drinks down, the slight Irish accent noticeable.

"Four strawberry margs," he says as he slides each of us one.

I can't be sure, but for a brief moment I think he slips something under Olivia's as he passes it to her, but it's so subtle I wonder if my mind is playing tricks on me. Olivia looks up at him and meets his gaze for a fleeting moment, then looks back at the table. I didn't even realize they knew each other.

"Goddamn, it's colder than a witch's titty in a brass bra out there!" Papa Dean calls as he and Mama Jo bound up to our table, snowflakes dusting his cowboy hat.

"Jesus, Pop. Way to make an entrance," Cole says as Nash gets up to slide two more chairs over to our already overstuffed table then disappears toward the front of the bar.

"Gotta make my presence known somehow. Can't let Blake Shelton here steal the show all night long."

He pats Wade on the shoulder, and I smother a grin.

"You been drinking? What the fuck are you talking about, old man?" Wade says as the table snickers collectively.

"Can I have everyone's attention please?" Nash calls through the mic on the stage. "We're going to be doing something a little different tonight, since tomorrow is Christmas Eve and we have a resident superstar in our midst," Nash says, pointing at Wade as two Horse and Barrel employees wheel out a massive flatscreen TV behind him.

"Motherfucker," Wade growls as he watches a server cart out a state-of-the-art karaoke machine next.

His eyes instantly take hold of mine in the dark bar as he shakes his head and clenches his fists. "I'm gonna fucking pummel him," he grunts, blaming Nash immediately for this.

I place my hand over Wade's forearm. "Actually, Chief . . . remember that bet we made the other day?" I smile up at him innocently, and I've never been more satisfied when his jaw falls slack, genuine shock lining his face as he realizes it was me behind this, right before he whispers so only I can hear.

"You're so gonna suffer for this, Trouble . . ."

I grin. "Death by swoony country music? I'll take my chances." I giggle as CeCe cracks up laughing beside me.

CHAPTER FORTY-THREE
Wade

Three more bourbons and a shot or two of tequila later, me and the boys are on stage singing our rendition of "Friends in Low Places" by Garth Brooks, and if it weren't for me we'd be fucking tanking it. By the end of the song, Cole's breaking off into an air guitar that would make Jimmy Page jealous, and Nash is making sexy-time faces at CeCe while he dances—correction, gyrates—on the stage.

Me? I'm zeroed in on the black-haired beauty at the table who's looking at me like she's a little turned on and a little afraid of what I'm going to do to her for making me sing karaoke to a room full of townies. It may be my worst nightmare, but I'm a man of my word if nothing else, and I'll get up here and make a fool of myself any day if it means I have her undivided attention like I do now.

Ivy rises from the table and takes to the dance floor with all the girls as we finish up, and a few of Cole's cop buddies take the stage and do their best with Luke Bryan's "Kick the Dust Up."

I take a breather at our table with a half-lit Papa Dean and watch Ivy move. That fucking navy dress might just be the death of me. Her hair is in a smooth high ponytail, showcasing her dewy shoulders, and the strapless dress is structured to her waist and then billowy to her knees, and all I can think about is hiking it up and driving my cock into her until she screams.

"Alright y'all, we're going to take a break, more karaoke to come after some house music," Nash says into the mic a few minutes later, as "Highway Boys" by Zach Bryan keys up on the sound system and Ivy moves hypnotically to the music as she sings every single word.

I take a sip of my bourbon as Pop nudges me in the elbow with his own.

"We're just going to pretend the two of you aren't knocking boots forever?" he asks.

I nearly spit my bourbon out.

"Fuck, old man," I reply.

He laughs, a big hearty Papa Dean laugh, the kind where his eyes almost completely squint shut.

"Boy, I'm old, I ain't dead. And that girl is looking at you like she's a lot more than your employee."

I scoff but have nothing to offer, because when I look at her on the dance floor, she is, in fact, looking at me like she wants nothing more than for me to crush myself to her, and fuck, it's a beautiful sight. Maybe the most beautiful sight I've ever seen.

"It's just none of anyone's goddamn business," I say, taking a swig.

"A girl like that doesn't come around often. If you don't snatch her up for real, someone else will. Just because you admit it doesn't mean it's destined for disaster. And, Wade, just cutting the shit for a minute because your pa would, all day long. Happy looks good on you," he says, way too seriously.

"Fuck, you're killing my buzz with all this mushy shit, Pop."

He smirks. "Case in point," he says, raising his glass toward the dance floor, where some fucking chump just dropped his cowboy hat onto Ivy's head.

I'm there in two seconds flat, while Pop cackles behind me from the table, and the second I make it to her I'm pulling the hat off of Ivy's head and putting it back onto his, hard.

"Wade, this is Nick, he works with Cole," she says with a friendly smile. "His hat matches my dress," she adds, obviously a little too tipsy to realize what he's insinuating by putting his hat on her head.

"Wade Ashby," I say, shaking his hand, gripping tight enough for his eyes to meet mine in question.

"Sorry, I didn't know you had a boyfriend," he yells to Ivy over the music as Ginger laughs.

"Wade is her boss, aren't you, Wade?" The cuss words that are running through my head at my little sister's half-lit friend right now are creative and plenty.

"I-I need a refill, and then I'm going back out to dance," Ivy says as she looks at me then heads for the bar, with Nick watching her go and not even hiding it one bit.

I lean over to him, not taking my eyes off her.

"You wanna keep those eyes in your head, I suggest you find elsewhere to look, yeah?"

Nick looks at me and grins. "I'm not the only one who wants her, I'm just the one that called dibs." He laughs and points to a table full of men in the corner.

Rage courses through me with the way he's disregarded her like she's a fucking raffle prize he just won. I look past him at the group he says was just bartering for Ivy. "Go tell your table of cronies, staring at a woman like that, it's just not fucking polite and I won't tolerate it. If I catch any of your eyes on her like that again, you'll have a hard time seeing your way out of here."

"Hey man, I don't want any problems, not when there's plenty of tail here, lots to go around."

Filthy fucking—

"You take care of your employees so well, Sarge," Ginger

251

croons in my ear, leaning over from where she and CeCe are dancing, laughing smugly.

I start scanning the bar as Nick scampers off.

"Christ, Ginger . . . find a hobby, yeah?" I mutter.

"Just trying to get you to admit it, Wade. For what it's worth, you two are great together," she says sweetly as I keep scanning the bar for Ivy, hating that she's calling me right out.

"She went toward the bathrooms." Ginger smirks, and the little shit is way too goddamn personal, but I don't have time to worry about her.

And right now I don't give a fuck who knows it, I'm a man on a mission as I beeline for the back of the bar.

CHAPTER FORTY-FOUR
Wade

I make my way through the sea of people, and all I can think of is getting to her. I tried not to act like a total Neanderthal, but the fucking moment I saw his hat on her head, red lined my vision and now I don't even give a fuck. I just need to get to her. To feel her lips on mine and I don't care who knows it. She's mine, and fuck it feels good to admit it to myself. Now I'm going to show her.

I nearly plow into her as I round the corner for the bathrooms. I stop dead in my tracks and look down at her.

She stands in the hallway just looking up at me for a few seconds, fire in her eyes. Ivy puts her hand on her hip and says, "You put him in his place? Tell him your *employees* are off limits? I don't know, that was a real nice hat, it really did match my dress." She giggles.

She's taunting me, trying to get me to admit I'm jealous, and fuck, I have no way to stop the words that come out of my mouth next in a deep growl.

"Don't fuck with me, Ivy."

She grins. "Touchy. Are you a little jealous, Chief? Got something you want to make clear?"

I grab her by her shoulders and press her up against the wall in the dark hallway, and my lips come crashing down on hers with a deep hungry need. Sliding my hand to the back of her neck, I grab her ponytail and tip her face up to allow me better access, my tongue swiping into her mouth, tasting the sugar I love mixed with strawberry, and I groan. She's fucking delicious.

"The only hands that touch this beautiful fucking body are mine—it's me you use when you need someone, got it? If I ever see another man's hat on you again, I'll be putting him through the floor with it."

She whimpers as her hands slide up my sides. She tips her head back and breathes out a moan as I touch her.

"You going to take me right here in the hallway then, Wade? Wrap that collar around my throat so everyone can see that I'm yours? Cause I'm so fucking wet for you right now I don't think I can wait another minute."

I bite back a deep groan from my chest as my hands slide over her dress and grip her plush ass through it. I push her into the stock room and lock the door behind us.

The glow of a pink neon sign in the room that says "*HAPPY HOUR*" is our only light, but it's all the light I need. I hoist her body up onto a file cabinet with one arm and pull her lacy white thong down until it hangs from her ankle. Flipping her dress up and dropping to my knees, I bury my face in her sweet glistening cunt, licking a firm trail up her center, sucking the sweet taste into my mouth. I hum a groan against her with desire and her whole body shudders.

Ivy's hands move to my hair and she weaves them in and pulls as she bites down on a moan.

"You're gonna have to be quiet, baby. Think you can do it?"

Her breathing is out of control as I stand and push two fingers into her pussy, feeling her warm tight heat squeeze around me as my mouth devours hers, taking her and the control, reminding her who she belongs to.

"I-I don't know."

I press my lips to hers, and sliding her thong fully off her ankle, I ball it up in my fist.

"If it's hard to be quiet with my fingers in you, you don't stand a chance when it's my cock." I grin at her in the dark. "I've got you, *sweetheart*," I whisper against her ear as I shove her panties into her mouth.

She accepts them greedily as I bring my thumb down to work in tight little circles over her aching little bundle of nerves.

I move my fingers in and out of her, in a quick rhythm, massaging that spot she begs for me to hit day in and day out. Her eyes flutter closed and I know this won't take long.

I loosen my buckle and lose my jeans in a matter of seconds.

"Oh no you don't, not yet, greedy girl. I want to feel this tight little pussy strangle my cock when you come."

I continue fucking her with my fingers and then I lean down to whisper in her ear. "I'm going to fill you so full you'll never forget I was here. So full you'll feel me everywhere."

Ivy moans into her panties and wraps her legs around me, pulling me to her. I slide my hands up to her waist and sheath myself in her in one deep thrust. We both let out muffled groans, her into her thong and me into her shoulder as I draw myself back out and push into her again.

"*Goddamn*, there's nothing on this earth like you," I mumble as her breath hitches around her panties. I push myself deeper, more, and I let the heel of my palm slide up to her throat and grip it tight, moving my thumb to cover her makeshift gag and hold it there.

I drive into her over and over as the cabinet hits the wall, alerting anyone in the hall to what is happening, but I don't give one flying fuck. I'm a crazed man, all I see and taste and breathe is Ivy as her pussy pulls me deeper and her nails bite my neck and shoulders under my t-shirt.

I look down in the dim room to where we connect and take in the sight.

"Such a good girl, my Ivy, taking all of me, now watch me fuck your sweet cunt, like the dirty girl we both know you are."

Ivy does what I tell her and looks down then moans, her legs quivering as she does her best to keep them tightly fixed around me, her heels biting into my skin.

"Fuck yeah, you like to watch. I know you do. You like to see how I take what's mine," I observe.

She nods, her eyes shining in the dark before she closes them, chasing her high.

Ivy whimpers and pants as I slide my hand fully around her throat and squeeze, using the leverage to pull her body down to meet mine as I fuck into her. I look up and see the word *mine* around her throat on my hand like a fucking banner, tears spill over her cheeks as she cries out into her thong, and fuck it's even prettier than I imagined.

I lean my head down to hers as I fuck into her hard, and pulling her thong from her mouth with my teeth, I spit it out then kiss her lips.

"Fuck it, scream my name, tell them all exactly who's making you come, Ivy," I tell her.

"*Wade*," she yells, giving the loud-as-fuck music a run for its money outside the door.

"*Mine*," I growl as my release barrels down my spine into my lower back like wildfire when I feel her clamp down around me. Her hands grip my hair so tight it hurls me toward the cliff and we fall off together. With me grunting her name and "*such a good dirty fucking girl,*" and her digging her heels into me and moaning my name as she rides out her high and her legs fall slack. I stay rooted in her for a beat, kissing a line up her tempting shoulders, I kiss her lips gently once, then twice.

She leans her sugar-scented head on my chest.

"So, I'm yours, then?" she asks with a hint of sass and sarcasm.

"Fucking right, you are."

"I didn't get you a gift as special as tattooing something on my body for you." She giggles into me, running a finger over my new tattoo.

"Fuck, you're the only gift I want," I say without thinking.

"Did you ever think, Wade? Maybe us together, maybe we're each other's gifts?" she hums, cracking my heart wide open.

All the depraved dirty thoughts still running through my mind for her while I'm buried in her mix with something else, something sweet, something I would never want to lose, a deeper connection than I've ever felt. It overwhelms the fuck out of me.

I want to say so much more, but instead I just say, "I think you may be right, sweetheart."

CHAPTER FORTY-FIVE
Ivy

Strong, warm arms wrap around my waist, pulling me close, my back to his front. I open one eye; it's dark out still. I peer at the clock that tells me what I already know. It's after 4:30 and Wade is pulling me close to say his usual good morning. The scruff of his jaw kisses through my hair onto my shoulder, and goosebumps follow in the wake of his lips.

"Fuck, I wish I hadn't set the time so early to be there," he groans into my skin, and I smile. Wade's voice is always devastatingly deep and sexy, but in the morning? God, it's on a whole other level.

"You sleep another hour. I'm meeting Dusty and Brent to unload," he tells me.

Thank God. He's wearing me out these days, I've never been one to sleep in but lately I'm stealing any extra sleep I can.

I know he's having a huge fence delivery today to start replacing a large section on the property, and I can easily sneak another hour of sleep in.

I settle my naked skin against him and sigh, my eyes still closed.

"I thought you had no time for that this morning, Mr. Ashby?" I mutter, feeling him hard and pressing against me.

"Fuck . . . I don't. And today, it's going to be a long-ass day without you," he grumbles into my skin. It's out of the ordinary; we aren't usually apart for more than thirty minutes on any given day.

"Mmhmm," I hum into my pillow. Wade's bed might be the biggest most comfortable bed on earth, always smelling as delicious as he does.

"I am going to get through everything this morning to meet the boys at noon for ax throwing," he tells me.

I nod, still sleepy.

Christmas may be over but it seems there is always something to celebrate on this ranch. Today is CeCe's bridal shower, and I'm surprised they haven't shut the whole town down for it. Wade is meeting Nash and Cole later, and I have my own tasks with Rowan and Angel before heading to the big house for the party.

I rock my ass against him, suddenly feeling a little more awake.

Wade groans into my shoulder as he peppers it with kisses. These are my favorite moments, before the sun is up, cradled in his strong arms, and my heart aches with the feelings that overwhelm me daily. The constant question of *how long will I have this for?*

A light tap comes down on my ass cheek as he grunts.

"Have to be there by five, Trouble, and you know it. Stop being a little brat or you'll be paying for it later." I feel him slide out of bed with a final kiss on my shoulder.

"Can't fucking wait, Chief," I mutter.

I listen to the comforting sounds of Wade moving around the cabin, and when the front door closes, I hear the sound of my coffee brewing as I let sleep take me for another thirty minutes.

"What time is too early for mimosas? I mean, it is a bridal shower and I'm still single, so I figure now?" Olivia asks, and shrugs as she considers cracking open a bottle of Moët and Chandon mid-morning.

Ginger swipes the bottle from Olivia's hand and giggles as she passes it behind her to Cole, then straightens out her maid-of-honor floral pin above her left breast.

Cole blurts out, "Now's a bit early," at the same time Ginger says, "Never too early."

I grin and watch the two of them lock eyes for all of one second before Cole grimaces at her, but he begins untwisting the wire around the bottle anyway. Ginger's either really good at pretending she doesn't notice the way he looks at her, or she's truly oblivious.

"Just need you to use a little muscle before you go, baby." Ginger smiles sweetly.

Cole's grimace dies as he continues to work on the cap for her. She's just really good at pretending, I decide.

The faint slow pop from the champagne echoes in the big house living room, which has been turned into a sort of whimsical, rustic lounge for CeCe's winter-themed bridal shower. White flowers are everywhere, and comfortable pastel lilac and muted mint chairs are placed throughout; twine lanterns grace every flat surface with flickering flameless candles even though it's only 11:30 a.m.

CeCe is checking on every single detail with Jo, both of them moving in sync together, laughing and chatting as they straighten out every glass and ensure the dessert bar is laid out perfectly. Spicer's Sweets has outdone themselves. Cupcakes and cake pops line the table, chocolate-covered fruit and cookies are abundant. Everything is a picture of simple, rustic perfection.

"She's the easiest bride on earth to stand up for because she insists on planning everything herself." Olivia leans into me and giggles as Nash gulps beside her.

"This is just the beginning, my friend." Cole smirks at Nash as he passes Ginger back the open bottle. "You're just along for the ride, bud. Watch this."

Nash's eyes widen like he's truly a little afraid of what Cole will do.

"Nash doesn't like where you've placed the gift table, he thinks it should be closer to the window, so we'll just go ahead and move it?" Cole asks CeCe as he chuckles.

CeCe spins around, looking for Nash in our small group, her eyes narrowed like she's on a mission to set him straight. Nash raises his hands to her before she can speak.

"He's just kidding, baby, the gift table looks perfect where it is. I'd never dream of moving it," Nash says quickly, cuffing Cole around the back of his head as Cole laughs. "You trying to put me in the shit house? Fuck."

"Should've eloped," Cole retorts.

The doorbell rings, and CeCe smiles wide as she makes her way over to us to shoo the boys out. She's the picture of grace in a white, linen dress that reaches the floor. It's strapless, elegant and flowy. I don't think I've ever seen her look so beautiful. The rest of us are wearing soft pastel colors as requested.

"That's our cue to go meet Wade," Nash says as he pulls CeCe close and kisses the top of her head, muttering something the rest of us can't hear. The look in his eyes is intentional and full of so much love.

"It's time! Let's go, girls!" Jo says like she's Shania herself, as she cocks a hip and raises her arms up before she lets in the first guests.

"Don't forget to make sure you're back at three-ish," CeCe instructs Nash and Cole in a voice that says *don't mess with the bride*.

"Around when? Seven? I got it," Cole says without missing a beat, as Ginger grabs his hat off the sofa and stuffs it into his chest.

"Stop trying to wake the matrimonial beast and do as you're told," she scolds.

"You need to let out some aggression, Vixen? Where are your manners?" Cole chuckles.

Ginger gives him a look of *you're done for* as he pulls one of her long curls then puts on his baseball hat. He acts cocky, but something tells me he knows he could never take her on.

My phone lights up in my hand with Wade's name.

CHIEF

Five hours to go until I get you alone, the day isn't the same without you Trouble.

Ginger scoffs from beside me when she sees it and my smile, her chocolate-colored eyes dancing with our secret.

"My only question is, why? We all know. We're all adults here." She nudges me and looks at me expectantly. There's no arguing with her that Wade and I definitely have something serious happening.

"It's not a secret, I just think it's almost like if we have the talk, it's real, and then he takes the risk of putting his heart out there, if that makes sense? And Wade's just private. I think we were just both planning on . . . having fun, and now . . . I don't know what we are. I don't know what to tell you."

Ginger's giggle is contagious, and I have no choice but to smile back.

"Listen, Janelle did a number on him, hurt him and left him when he needed her most," Ginger admits.

I nod. "I know the feeling, maybe that's why I haven't forced the talk either," I say honestly.

"He is private, always has been, but the way he looks at you . . . the way you look at him . . . Gawd . . . it has to be hot. Tell me it is?" she asks as she grins.

I smile back, loving the way that I can actually speak freely about him to someone.

"The hottest fucking thing ever. Wade is . . . fuck . . . I have no words," I gush.

Ginger squeals and then leans in, whispering, "I knew it. Goddamn, I knew Wade was a freak under that serious mask he wears. Don't you know? There's an old wives' tale that says once a girl has a bossy rancher, no other kind of man will do?"

I laugh. "I am starting to believe that."

"Look, maybe a couple of months ago you were having fun, and now that you've had that fun, I think you have to talk about it. Wade Ashby isn't the 'let people in' type of guy, so if you're in his inner circle, I would plan to stick around for a while. In other words, that man is not letting you leave this ranch."

I sigh—it feels so fucking good to be honest.

"I would love to stay. In fact, I'm dreading leaving. Once we get Angel's nomination squared away, maybe then we'll talk. I want to, I just, fuck, how do you even start that conversation?"

Ginger blows out a deep breath "You need a girls' day. When do you leave for Florida to get Angel's gate card?

"A week from now, next Wednesday," I breathe out in a sigh.

"I think you need a day out, manis and pedis on Saturday maybe? Just the two of us? You can settle the mystery then."

I look at her, narrowing my eyes to understand what she means.

"BDE?" she says, using her hands, pulling them apart to gauge Wade's size. "Tell me when."

I laugh at her; she never seems to worry about a thing, and just being around her is calming.

"You don't really need to tell me . . . towels don't hide much." She winks then giggles, and I laugh back as she hands me a mimosa. It must be too early because the smell turns my stomach. "For what it's worth, I've never seen Wade this"—she searches for the word, tapping her bottom lip with her first finger—"settled, happy." Ginger winks at me as she lifts her glass.

"So, to being happy." She takes a sip, and I follow suit as she shrugs the conversation off as if she has no doubt everything will just work itself out.

I swallow another sip but it almost makes me gag. I decide that's enough morning champagne as I watch the guests start to pile in, setting gifts down and hugging each other.

Ginger turns and squeezes a tiny woman she calls "Nana" as the lump in my throat grows. A pang of want washes over me. I never envy much, my fate is my fate, but what I wouldn't give to have a family like this to stand beside me, to be there for me when I need them.

"Come on, newbie, time to meet the town," Olivia says, appearing from behind me. She locks arms with me, grinning and pulling me right into the crowd.

Two hours later, the living room at the big house is filled with laughter and squeals as CeCe puts her head in her hands and her cheeks turn a deep shade of pink. She's front and center amidst a sea of boxes and wrapping paper, on her second-to-last gift.

Ginger is writing down the items received in every single card dutifully beside her so CeCe—and Nash, CeCe is convinced—will have an easy time writing thank-you cards out later. Jo is on the other side, playing a gift Santa of sorts. I crane my neck to try to see what is so funny about the gift CeCe is holding. She holds open her palm at Ginger's coaxing. It looks like a tiny silicone rose. Ginger's endearing and very innocent little grandmother smiles and speaks up over the crowd.

"It's the newest model, dear."

"Granny Dan! You . . . shouldn't have." CeCe laughs, still blushing and trying to hide the gift from her mother's prying eyes.

"I'm your mama and I'm old but I'm not stupid," Jo giggles.

Granny Dan holds up a finger as if she's trying to sell the device CeCe is cradling in her hand for a living. I grin instantly, knowing what it is finally, and can't believe this little old woman that looks like the Queen of England purchased a vibrator from God knows where? Would a woman that age use the internet?

"The best part about it is that it's very tiny and inconspicuous, a lot easier to keep in small spaces, and if you ever lose it the average person won't even know what it is." She winks as a doubled-over Ginger starts into a story about CeCe losing her not-so-inconspicuous vibrator in the town's car depot.

I laugh along with them. Ginger's story and CeCe's guests' laughter fade to the background as I see my phone light up in my lap with Wade's name again. Just his name on my screen ignites something in me. I'm not used to spending the day apart from him.

After almost three months of working side by side, day in and day out, it feels odd.

A tsunami of emotion I know I've been fighting washes over me, crushing me. It settles deep into my bones. I can't figure out why I'm so damn sappy all of a sudden. Is it the setting of being at a bridal shower? Whatever it is, I can't shake Ginger's words as I open my phone. She not only said that Wade is happy, he's settled, because of me.

A thousand moments flash through my mind as I search for that truth. The way he brushes my hair off my face in the morning, to kiss me on the forehead; how he is now the proud owner of every streaming service known to man, so our well of movies doesn't run dry. How he drives all the way to Lexington to buy M&M's in bulk from Costco for our ice cream nights. My fresh towels in the bathroom for my shower and my coffee brewed for me before he goes to the barn on the mornings when he's got to be out there earlier than I do. Even just those moments when I hear his voice in any given space, it makes me feel warm and whole just knowing he's around, and it hits me sure and swift. That *is* real happiness.

A kind I've never felt. I open his text up and smile. It's taken me way too long to admit it to myself but I think I'm in love with Wade Ashby, desperately in love. And if I do, in fact, have to leave him and Silver Pines behind anytime soon, it might just threaten to destroy me.

CHAPTER FORTY-SIX
Wade

> These boys are actually telling me *Mr & Mrs Smith* isn't a romance movie and I need some backup

TROUBLE

The audacity. It's clearly an iconic love story.

> Right? And it's one we haven't watched together yet, how can that be? I thought we'd watched them all.

TROUBLE

No clue but that's a damn shame. Tonight's movie then?

> Sounds like a date.

TROUBLE

I'll be the one in my pajamas on the left side of the sofa.

> I'll bring sundaes, and Trouble?

TROUBLE

Yes?

> It isn't formal, no pajamas required.

My chest heats and I smile wide just thinking about what's to come. The simple perfection of the night ahead. Aside from the meal I have planned to make and the meal I'm planning on making out of Ivy, just sitting parked in my place on the sofa beside her, low lights, a shitload of blankets and snacks is the place I crave the most. It's the place I look forward to when I leave the barn at the end of the day more than any other.

"It's your turn, lover boy," Nash calls to me, holding out my ax for throwing at Woody's—Laurel Creek's local bowling alley and newly added games room that features ax throwing, escape rooms and a small arcade for kids. None of the locals know that Nash financed the revamp for the owner just to keep the downtown vibrant and alive. So far, it's going extremely well and has boosted the local businesses surrounding it, including the Horse and Barrel.

Nash, Cole and I have ventured here for the afternoon to bide our time during the shower of the century. Haden has tagged along and looks up from our table, and grins at me with Nash's words, a knowing grin he's given me before.

"You're one to lecture me on employee-employer relations," I retort back, pointing at him with my beer bottle in hand.

Nash chuckles.

"So, it was a certain horse trainer you were grinning at over there? Exactly what I thought. Sex is one thing, having something serious with someone is quite another. Is this serious? We all know it's been going on for a while," Nash says to me.

"And we're all jealous," Haden adds.

"Speak for yourself. I already have the perfect woman," Nash pipes up, and Cole shakes his head.

I snatch the ax from Nash as Haden chuckles as he sips his beer. I approach the line to take aim at the wooden board marked with rings and targets.

"I don't care what anyone says, men and women can never

truly be just friends for long without either going their separate ways or fucking. End of story. Especially when the woman looks like Ivy Spencer," Haden guffaws, like the idea would be impossible. I guess since I can't keep my dick out of her for more than a few hours at a time, he's technically right.

I grit my teeth regardless. The image of Ivy in Haden's mind is something I'd like to wipe clean with my boot.

"Careful, Hade, don't piss Sarge off, he's still heavy in his state of denial," Cole mutters, chiming in.

"Hey, he's the boss, he has the right to do whatever he sees fit for the ranch," Haden chirps from the table.

I let the ax fly and it hits just on the outside of the board, nowhere near the center or the killshots. The three of them holler at my shot. Nash because we're playing in teams and he's my teammate, and the other two because my shitty aim just helped their game immensely.

"I like this. Keep talking about his *employee*—for some strange reason it seems to piss him off. We might have a shot at winning," Cole tells Haden.

Naturally, Haden doesn't miss a beat.

"I'm just saying, if what takes *doin'* to make the ranch have its best year in ten is Ivy Spencer, Sarge, I say go ahead and take one for the team. None of us will blame you." His laughter is deep as he pushes me further than he should.

Fuck this.

"Killshot," I warn them, before I toss my next ax and hit the killshot dead on. "Eight points, fuckers," I mutter, then turn to face Haden, my jaw tensing as I strive to keep myself calm.

"And if you mention Ivy like that again, you'll be finding out how quickly my size thirteen lands right up your bony ass," I bark out.

Cole and Nash cackle away beside Haden; they love nothing more than to see me fired up.

Haden stands and pats me on the back.

"Don't go getting your size fucking double xl boxers in a twist, I know it's natural for you to defend her. I'm sure you'd stick up for me like that too, Sarge. Wouldn't you?" He grins.

Nash takes his shot next and hits one of the targets, lets out a little "fuck yeah" then turns to me.

"In all seriousness, we know you and we just want you to admit it to yourself, that you care about her, we can all see it. The way you look at her, it's like a lit-up neon sign is stuck to your forehead that says, *'I'm fucking obsessed with Ivy Spencer.'* You deserve to be happy, so don't let her or a potential future like that slip through your fingers," he says, like the sappy fucking romantic my sister has turned him into.

He and Cole grin like the shit disturbers they are.

"We're just getting your goat, you prick. You gotta choose sometime to settle down, you're getting up there." Cole smirks as he pops a nacho into his mouth.

"You're five years younger than me," I deadpan.

"Yeah, maybe, but at least I don't need to inscribe the word *mine* across my hand so I don't forget who's cock I'm fisting." Cole motions the universal gesture for jerking off and I look down at my newest ink and shake my head.

"I, for one, am appalled," Nash jokes. "I doubt your cock wants to be objectified like that."

"That's what I'm saying!" Cole adds. "Have some respect. Your cock's feelings matter."

Nash leans back then continues. "He stuck with you through the dry years . . ."

"Jesus fucking Christ," I mutter.

"Look, the honest truth is, we really just love to see you get that mushy little grin on your face whenever Ivy's anywhere within a fifty-foot radius of you." Cole chuckles.

My phone lights up with a new message from Ivy on the table, and at the precise moment they see it, they double over with laughter. I shake my head at them but I can't help but grin back.

"I rest my case." Cole points at my face.

Just as I feel like the afternoon can't get any more awkward than discussing the state of my love life with my brothers and my employee, the high-pitched tell-tale laugh of Janelle fills the air.

Motherfucker.

"We're not letting Janelle chase us out of here, we've got one more game, we're playing it. Just ignore her and her crew," Cole pep-talks me as Janelle saunters over to us.

I just got this woman out of my life for good in December when her financing came through, but she just had to walk into the bar I'm in on a goddamn Wednesday afternoon. She's with two women I've seen around town. They wait at the bar area.

"Well, well, well, if it isn't my favorite husband."

"Ex-husband," I correct.

"Actually, you're just the person I want to see, Wade. I was gonna call you tomorrow . . ." She looks at me, waiting for me to ask why, and when I take a sip of my beer instead of biting, she continues. "So, they finished the roofing job and I'm a little short for the remainder of the cash. I was hoping you could help me out."

I pull my hat up and rub my forehead. Of course she is. "Goddammit, Janelle, you had a refinance, you were supposed to set that money aside."

"How was the cruise? You know, the one you went on with Gemma last month?" Cole asks with a knowing and cocky look in his eye. He told me she went with Gemma to the Bahamas; Gemma bailed on Mabel's school play to go.

The funny thing is that Gemma and Janelle never even liked each other until they became our exes and started working together. Seems they bonded over the break-ups and formed a little anti-Ashby-men club. I shoot Cole a look that says *why the fuck did you have to poke the bear?* He sees it and shrugs.

"The cruise was just lovely, Cole, and none of your god-damn business, but thanks for asking," Janelle retorts, her blue eyes narrowing, not disguising her disdain for the way my brother has always called her out on her bullshit.

I study her face as I watch her. It's mid-afternoon and she already seems tipsy. She almost has a weathered look about her now, as if her years of drinking and partying have started to finally catch up with her. That would torment her to her core.

Her biggest fear is getting older. She's only in her mid-thirties but she looks quite a bit older. Comparing her to the delicious, vibrant woman I crave every moment of every day just seems so different now. Watching how incredibly confident Ivy is and the glowing beauty she emits daily reminds me I'm dealing with vastly different women. One is self-loving and the other self-loathing.

For a moment I feel really fucking sorry for Janelle. This will probably always be her life—alone, searching for the next man to make her feel good about herself, never getting that from within. I smile to myself.

Fuck, I'm starting to sound like Ivy. "Love the earth and your body" *and all that shit.*

Cole makes a face at Janelle and she back at him. I let out a sigh, and not wanting to make my business public, I grab her by the elbow and pull her into the hallway to the restrooms.

Without even looking at him I already know Nash is shaking his head; he can't stand Janelle.

"Janelle, you're thirty-five years old, you have to start looking after your finances better. The house is yours, not mine. I'm not your husband anymore. I'm sorry, but you're on your own this time."

Janelle blinks in shock. She tosses her long bleach-blond hair over her shoulder.

"Wade, I'm almost two thousand short."

I can see the panic on her face. She reaches a hand out and tries to touch my chest. I instantly shrink away from it and grab it just as it brushes against me, placing it back down at her side. Only one set of hands touches my body, and they sure as fuck aren't Janelle's.

I set my jaw and settle in my stance.

"I guess you'll have to take some more shifts at Snippets," I say firmly, mentioning the hair salon she works at. "Or sell some of your expensive shit—your shoes, your purses. But you have to be the one to figure it out this time. I'm not putting one more penny into that house, it isn't mine anymore."

"Wade, you can't mean that," she scrambles, and I see the anger welling up in her eyes. "I can always count on you. It's your home too. In fact, I've been thinking about you, a-about us, all the things I did when we were together. I was wrong treating you like that." She shrugs pathetically, and one giant tear threatens to spill over her cheek.

How did I never see how manipulative this woman was before? Janelle moves closer to me, trying to entice me. It does the exact opposite. It does nothing but fucking turn me completely off.

"I was hoping we could maybe give things another shot? I-I think I'm ready to settle down, maybe have a family, and there's no other man for me, Wade. I'm still an Ashby. I haven't changed

273

my name back because, truthfully, I was hoping there would still be another chance for us. I guess I just couldn't let you go. I still think about—"

I can't help myself, I start to laugh—out loud and hard.

Janelle blinks, and for a moment I feel like she might actually take my hint and stop talking.

I'm wrong.

"This isn't funny. I'm pouring my heart out here, Wade. You gonna tell me you don't think about giving things another try?"

I blink for a moment, actually asking myself if she's serious.

Holy fuck, she is.

"Janelle. That's never going to fucking happen. We're divorced for a reason." I look her in the eye so she knows I'm serious. "I don't love you anymore, and Christ, you were a fucking terrible wife to me in the end."

"You don't mean that, Wade—" She pauses as the light bulb goes off in her head "Wait, is there someone else?"

I grin at her, because there most certainly fucking is, but mine and Ivy's business isn't hers.

This feeling is so goddamn freeing.

I really and truly don't give one single fuck about her problems anymore.

"To put this as simply as I can, your problems aren't mine anymore. Can't pay the roofer? Maybe take out a loan." I pat her on the shoulder like I would a buddy, then turn to leave, but glance back at her before I do.

"And by the way, you most definitely are not a fucking Ashby. Get on changing that, yeah?" I leave her standing in the hall alone, and for thirty full seconds she doesn't move or say anything, then she storms by me, grabbing her girl crew, and barks out something about me not deserving her as she blasts through the front door.

Nash watches Janelle go, then looks back at me as I return to the boys and take a swig of my beer.

He chuckles and says, "Closed that door—fucking slammed it, actually." And then he offers me the biggest grin I've ever seen him wear.

I grin back.

Yeah, I did, and fuck does it ever feel good.

CHAPTER FORTY-SEVEN
Ivy

The Ashby big house has turned into an after-party of sorts. All the boys have moved the fifty rental chairs out and returned them to the party supply store, and loaded the mountain of gifts into their pickup trucks, getting ready to deliver them to Nash and CeCe's house. Us girls are cleaning, eating candy leftovers, and singing along to Jo's country playlist as we finish our chores together.

You'd never know there were seventy people here this afternoon. Papa Dean wanders in from sweeping off the front porch for Jo and takes a deep breath, tossing his hat on the row of hooks on the wall at the front door.

"Well, Jo? Pizza for dinner from Muldoon's?" he asks, mentioning the town pizza joint, as we all begin to drop down on the sofas, taking a moment before we head out.

"Hells yes, this mama isn't lifting one more finger for the rest of the day, who's coming for dinner?" she asks as she sinks down onto the couch beside me and smiles at me while tightening her high ponytail.

"I'm in," Cole pipes up. "Just gotta grab Mabes from her friends' and we'll be back."

"We are too," CeCe adds.

Jo nods and turns to me, in question.

"Thank you, but I'm actually really tired. I think I'll head back to my cabin." It's not a lie, but really, I just can't wait to be alone with Wade after this day apart. I glance at him as he vacuums the front foyer and wonders if he missed me just as much.

"Of course, thank you for all your help today, darlin'."

I nod and smile back. Nash and CeCe come back into the room, just as Wade finishes up.

"We're all set, we're just going to drive this to our place and then come back for dinner. Wade, you following?" Nash asks.

Wade's eyes flit to mine across the room, I expect him to say nothing, but he makes his way directly over to me.

"I'll be back in a half hour," Wade says to me, reaching down to kiss my lips right in front of everyone, once, then again, lingering a little longer on the second kiss. I assume he did it without thinking, but when he looks at me I know it was on purpose.

"Just . . . fuck." He sighs. "I didn't want to wait one more second to do that," he says, melting me from my head to my toes.

I look at him, then around the room that has completely ceased activity to gauge my reaction. I open my mouth but don't get a word out.

"Thank Christ, are we all allowed to know something's going on here now?" Dean blurts out, pointing back and forth between Wade and I.

Everyone in the room stifles a laugh, except Ginger who outright snickers as Wade grunts.

"What do you mean, Pop? Wade's just really dedicated to his work," Nash says as CeCe smacks him.

Cole doesn't say a word, but I notice his grin as he picks up the last of the gift bags to head out to Nash's truck. Olivia and Ginger snicker a little louder with no shame.

"Laugh it up, fuckers," Wade says, then turns to me and

drops his cabin key into my palm intentionally. "You go to my place and I'll meet you there. Ignore them." He looks up at all of them. "This is why I don't tell any of you anything."

CeCe's smile fills her face as she winks at me.

"Immature little pricks," Wade adds as he heads out the front door and laughter fills the house.

Try as I may, I can't stop myself from laughing with them. I guess secrets can only last so long on this ranch.

CHAPTER FORTY-EIGHT
Wade

The house is dark when I pull up to it ninety-eight minutes later. Just to fuck with me, Nash needed me there for an hour to help with every little thing he could think of before they went back to the big house, rearranging the guest room in his house to turn it into a wedding gift room of sorts. *"Let's just move this sofa to the garage, oh and bring the table in to set the gifts on."* All with the world's cockiest smirk on his face. I knew what he was doing, now that he'd seen me give in and kiss her—he was trying to get me to admit how badly I wanted to get back to Ivy, that this is serious between us.

Well, fuck him, I'm almost thirty-five years old, I can kiss whoever the fuck I want and I'm not giving into him. As much as I want to yell it from the rooftops, what happens between me and my girl is our business and our business alone. Until we have this talk, I'm sure as shit not having it with anyone else.

I push open the door and make my way into my dark foyer, carrying groceries I had to grab on the way back to make Ivy dinner. A soft glow emits from the kitchen. Just as I toe my boots off and enter, I see her.

Ivy standing stark fucking naked wearing nothing but my tattered old cowboy hat and high heels.

"Oops, looks like I forgot to get dressed, cowboy . . ." she says innocently, and it's sexy as fuck.

She starts to walk to me, but the heel of her shoe gets stuck in the floorboard and she almost topples over, naked. I catch her with the arm I'm not holding groceries with and steady her. She looks up at me from under her hat, startled.

"So much for being all mysterious and graceful." She giggles as I help her stand. "I tried," she says as she shrugs.

I chuckle and kiss her lips. They're soft and welcoming.

In fact, they don't just feel like a welcome.

They feel like *home*.

"You are fucking adorable," I tell her

"Hold on, I can save it." She laughs as she backs up and cocks her hip out, posing before me with every stunning curve.

Yep. That'll do it. My dick instantly hardens with the need I feel for her. Beautiful, brilliant, funny as hell, smart-mouthed, always a little clumsy her.

All of her. Every last bit.

My hungry gaze roams over her ample curves for all of ten seconds before the groceries in my arms hit the floor and are forgotten in a heartbeat. Then I'm across the room, scooping her up and dropping her onto the counter.

Ivy yelps when the cold butcher block meets her warm naked flesh as I press my hard cock into her hot pussy. I look down and see just how wet she is pressed against the denim of my jeans. I groan into her mouth as I devour it. Tasting her tongue while I grip either side of her jaw, kissing her in the rhythm that drives me wild as her lips match mine effortlessly.

My fingers are lost to her thick hair as Ivy's legs tighten around my waist. She tugs at the snap buttons on my flannel and slides her hands down my arms as she pushes my shirt off. Her fingers graze over my chest, her touch like fire over my skin. Every single cell in me is buzzing with the feel of her. My need to settle between her thighs almost hurts as she moans into my lips when I pinch a pebbled nipple between my thumb and finger, rolling the little bud between them, then bending down to suck it into my mouth.

"I missed you today, baby," she whimpers into me, and my chest tightens with her words.

"Fuck . . . I missed you too."

So fucking much, I don't even know if I can imagine a time when you're not here.

"Show me . . . just how much you missed me, Wade."

A low growl rumbles in my chest; she has no idea what she does to me, but who am I to not give my girl what she wants?

I trail my lips over her shoulders, and my hot breath covers her skin, across her neck, over her nipples, and for a moment I let my teeth graze each one as she cries out and pushes her hips against me, shamelessly begging for friction. I rub her thighs and slide my hands further up the inside of them to her tight wet heat at the apex, using my thumbs to spread her pussy wide, then I drop to my knees and lick a trail up her center with the flat of my tongue.

Ivy moans my name into the quiet of my cabin and it echoes through me. I hum a groan against her as she laces her fingers into my hair and pulls tight. It ignites me. I lap up every single drop of her sweet, soaking cunt into my mouth, reveling in the feel of her soft thighs hugging my face.

"Mmm, I missed your taste . . ." I tell her, and I mean it as I bring my mouth down over her.

"Tastes like mine," I say, pulling her clit into my mouth, getting high on just the sweetness of her alone. I curve my arm under her ass and pull her down closer to my face, holding her in place as I begin to feast on her pussy.

"Ivy, I'm going to make you come, but you have to trust me and you have to let go when the time comes," I tell her.

Ivy's back arches as I add two fingers into her, curving them against the spot that will get her just where I want to take her. Her hips rock over me as she rides my face, as she gets into the rhythm she wants. I flick my tongue over her while I fuck into her with my fingers slowly, just to torture her a little until she's panting so hard I know she's about to come apart, and I want it.

Fuck, do I want it.

I push my tongue deeper, and she cries out as she begins to quiver around me.

"Wade, it feels, I don't know what this is . . . I can't," she says.

"Yes you can, Ivy. Just let go, trust me. Come . . . and make a mess of my face when you do." I continue to fuck my fingers into her, giving her no reprieve, just a steady pace to ruin her. The moment she clamps around them to come, I pull them out quickly, moving to her clit as she comes with a cry and my name, soaking me in the process, just like I knew she could. I smile into her and kiss her pussy as she shudders, scrubbing my face with my hand.

"Such a good girl," I mutter as she shivers.

"Wade . . . what was that? Did I . . ."

"Yes you did, and it was the hottest fucking thing I've ever seen."

I would give her a moment, let her come down from what her incredible body just did, but I'm a greedy motherfucker so instead I just pick her up and carry her to my room and deposit her on my massive bed. I lose my clothes and kick them aside, then stalk toward her and kiss her like I can't get enough of her. And I can't.

"You ever actually fucked a woman wearing your cowboy hat before?" she asks with a little grin, climbing on top of me, once again a step ahead of me that turns me instantly savage for her.

I crush my lips to hers in a scorching, hungry kiss, then pull her bottom lip between my teeth.

"Never," I say back. "But seeing as you're fixing to ride my cock right now, I'd say that's about to change."

Ivy moans as my fingers find her nipples, and I toy with her while she grinds against my cock, covering me in her slippery arousal. I let my finger slide to her center, circling her clit long enough to cause her head to fall back. When it does, she holds my hat on her head as her juicy lips part in a moan and it looks like every fucking fantasy I ever had.

"Fucking Christ, Ivy, you're so goddamn wet," I mutter as I sit up and kiss her from her collarbone to her earlobe, stopping to pull it right into my mouth, biting down. I groan.

Ivy's fingers thread through my hair and pull as she hisses at the feel of my teeth biting into her flesh.

"You like pain, Wade?" she whispers, knowing that I do.

A low growl vibrates through my chest as I take her other earlobe between my teeth and bite down. She cries out as I lick over the bite and then she pulls my hair harder in response.

"Two can play that game . . . I know a secret," she whispers. "You like it even more . . . it makes you even harder when I hurt *you*." She tugs my head back tight, running her teeth across my jaw before biting down, hard.

Fuck, this woman was fucking made for me. She moves back to my lips. I groan into her mouth as she kisses me, pulling my hair even tighter as her tongue moves with mine in perfect harmony. She bites down on my lip as I knead her thighs and her ass in my hands. From this angle, the fleshiness of her hips is so exaggerated, I just want to bite every fucking delicious part of her.

"Did that hurt too much, baby . . . ? Mercy?" she moans.

"Never," I growl as I slide a hand up her jaw, settling my thumb beside her lips. A small, almost evil laugh comes from Ivy as she turns her face to take my thumb between her lips and bites down. I suck in a breath, desperate to fuck.

I pull her body down to take what I want, what's mine, and slam my cock into her, but she stops me, then moves her lips to my neck, planting soft, sweet kisses down it before biting into my flesh again, keeping my skin between her teeth as she rocks her hips over me. I growl in response and lay a little slap to her pussy.

"Fuuuck . . ." she moans with the sting. My girl loves a little pain just as much as I do.

"I'm about to wreck this tight little pussy right now, Ivy. It's not going to be gentle. It's going to be fast and hard," I warn her as she moves over me. "Because you drive me so fucking crazy that I just can't stop myself." I move my face down to pull a pink pebbled nipple into my mouth, letting my teeth trail over it, biting just enough to make her whimper as I desperately try to maintain control.

"Yes you can, but not quite yet . . ." Ivy whispers with that little bit of sass in her sweet husky voice that sends me to the brink of insanity.

"First, I need to know how bad you want it," she whispers. "How badly you want *me*, Wade . . ." Her hips roll over me, slippery arousal slides up and down my cock, but she never quite positions herself to allow me to slip into her like I want to . . . like I'm goddamn desperate to.

"Tell me how badly you want to fuck me . . . *beg me*," she whines as I'm threatening to come just by the feel of her pussy sliding over me and her words.

Fuck . . .

"I don't beg for anything . . ." I fight her, holding onto that control as long as I can.

Nails bite into my chest as she continues to move, closer, then stops, repeating her motions until I'm so close to finding my way inside her, it's fucking nothing short of maddening. Ivy kisses me deeply, the sweetest little sounds coming from her throat that tell me she's desperate for me too. She takes my lip into her mouth again and bites, this time hard enough for me to taste blood on my tongue. I hiss in response.

"All you have to do is say it, Wade . . . then I'm all yours. Say it . . ." she moans, and the sound vibrates through me. Ivy rises up just enough to allow the head of my cock to sink into her and then she stills. I grip her hips to pull her down but fuck, the little brat angles herself back just enough to stop me again.

"Ivy, *fuuuuck* . . ."

She brings her face down to mine, kissing me, smirking into my lips as she slides her hands up through my hair, dragging her nails down the back of my neck, all while she continues the delicious roll of her hips. I watch, entranced, as she sits up and leans back, which pushes her tits out as her nails land on my thighs and rake over them as she rocks against me. Her hot wet pussy is my fucking kryptonite and threatens to make me blow all over my stomach just from her sliding herself back and forth against me.

I suck in a breath through my teeth.

"It's only a word, baby . . . no big deal. Say it . . . *beg*." She rolls her hips, riding me without letting me in.

I groan. The bite of her nails rakes up my arms, and she leans forward so her mouth is just over mine. I try to nip at her lips but I miss as she pulls her head back just enough. I growl at her and she whispers.

"Say it, and I'll let you fuck me as hard as you want."

Just like that, I'm a fucking goner as the word she wants to hear rolls off my tongue.

"Fucking . . . mercy . . ." I whisper as she whimpers in approval, and then I'm thrusting my cock into her so deeply and surely I feel like I might pass out.

"That's what I wanted. Such a good boy, Chief," she hums in a moan, and fuck, the way those words resonate with me is something I neither understand nor want to forget. As if she's degrading me and turning the power back over to me all at once.

Hearing them, mixed with the feel of her tight pussy around me, sends me reeling, my eyes screw shut and I threaten to come on the spot as I push myself into her further, inch by inch.

"*Fuck, Ivy* . . . Fucking Christ, woman," I grunt. "You feel so goddamn good."

Ivy breathes out a moan as I stretch her. She feels better than good. She feels like she's made just for me.

"That was a dirty little trick. You're going to be begging for relief from the way I stretch your sweet cunt now," I say as her tits find their way to my mouth. I pull each of them in, begging her tight channel to allow me into a space we both know I'm always too big for as I slam into her from below. Her pussy tightens and she feels so docile and small in my arms.

"Please, Wade . . . so full . . ." she moans.

Fuck yeah, she is. She's full to the hilt and I love when she is, more than I've ever loved anything else. I give myself just a moment, just to feel her, to take one second before I let myself really ravage her.

I'd sell my soul to the devil himself to live inside her forever.

I slip her off of me, flipping her over so she waits on her knees for me. Pushing my hat off her head, I grip a fistful of her hair and hike her hips up, taught to meet my cock as I slide my hands down over the globes of her beautiful ass.

"Grab the headboard, Ivy, and you better hold it, really fucking tight," I warn her.

She moans and does what she's told, gripping tightly to it. The moment she does, I start to fuck.

I don't hold back—after her little show, I can't, I don't have the strength. I drive myself into her tight little pussy from behind her as she white-knuckles the wood. My headboard rocks into the wall as I fuck into Ivy, holding her body tight to me as she moans and whimpers while I take what I want, what I need, what's *mine*.

The only sounds in this room are the growls that escape my chest out of desperation for her, our skin slapping together and her sweet gasps of pleasure. My hand curls up around Ivy's throat from behind, her custom collar locked in place as I continue fucking her, hard. I pull her back up to my front, turning her face. I press my mouth to hers as I feel her pussy close in around me and she begins to quake after only a few passing minutes.

"Wade . . . I'm going to . . ." she whines. *Already, I love it.*

"Nah, baby, you're going to come slowly," I tell her. I want to draw her pleasure out, to savor her and every single second inside her.

I rotate my hips slowly, letting her feel every single stroke as I move in and out of her. Every cell, every single atom of our joined bodies. Ivy's moans become deep and throaty as her nails bite into the sides of my thighs, a wickedness in her movements that says *you can hurt me as long as I can hurt you.* But it only makes my dick harder, bringing me closer to my high with every gnash of her nails against my skin. My balls tighten, as I slam inside her again and again.

"Come now, Wade, and baby, tell me that you're mine when you do." She moans her last words, and holy fuck, I'm coming, hard. My grip around her slender, biteable neck deepens as I kiss her. I'm in a never-ending spiral, my release reaches out from every corner of my body, centering through me in slow motion as I hover on the edge of kissing her and choking her, her nails digging deeper into me with every wave that consumes us.

"Holy fucking Christ, Ivy. *I'm entirely fucking yours,*" I groan into her just as her eyes roll back and shut. I loosen my hand on her throat, letting her inhale.

Our breathing is synchronized as we come down from our high like we just ran a marathon together.

Ivy leans fully back against me, her head settling under my

jaw. A buzzing euphoria washes over me. I have no idea how long I stay inside her, still. Moments? Minutes?

The softness of her. This feeling. This warmth.

"Wade?" Ivy asks, breaking the trance I'm floating in.

I open my eyes and look down at her perfect, flushed face as she tilts it up to me.

"Yes?"

"Was my dinner in those grocery bags you dropped?"

I drop my head to her cheek and kiss it. "Yes, Trouble, I just have to make it."

"Okay, I'm kind of hungry now, can we eat?"

I chuckle into her shoulder.

Anything you want, baby.

By the time I've almost finished creating a meal that would challenge Bobby Flay, still half surviving on the euphoria of her, Ivy's showered and is curled up on the couch blankets up to her cute little chin, her hair the only real visible part of her I see as I grate fresh parmesan onto our manicotti. When I'm done, I take the final swill of bourbon from my glass and put my earbuds back in their case.

I talk away to her as I make my way into the living room juggling our plates, napkins and cutlery. "Are you planning on sitting up, sweetheart?" I ask her.

It's when I round the corner of the sofa that I fully see her. Blankets up under her chin, the most relaxed and beautiful look on her face. Ivy is completely out cold before we've even had dinner. Her lips are parted and she's breathing softly, like a little sleeping angel. I set the plates down on the coffee table and drop to the chair across from her, just to stare at her for a few seconds before I wake her to eat. The reality settles with me that's been staring me in the face this whole time.

Whether Sam comes back or not, I'm making a place for Ivy here—any job, any task she wants. Hell, if she asked me to quit running the ranch so she could do it I would. Anything to keep her nestled into my sofa just like this every night when I come home.

Before Ivy, I was only existing day to day, going through the motions. I wasn't living; she's my missing piece. There's nothing more I could ever possibly want or need than these simple moments with her. A life with her. Ivy's weaved her way into the threads of my heart; she's been training it this whole time without me even realizing it. To love again, to take a chance. To believe in a future, a future with her, however that looks. One where I let myself be happy and I'm not afraid to let her love me back.

My heartbeat accelerates and squeezes in my chest as I realize there are two things I've never been more certain of than I am at this very moment.

One: I'm wildly in love with Ivy. I not only love her, I *need* her, the way the moon needs the sun to set every night just so it can rise.

Two: There's no me without her anymore—she just doesn't know it yet.

CHAPTER FORTY-NINE
Ivy

"Ivy . . ."

"Ivy . . ." a voice says again. A firm, warm hand rubs my arm and my eyes fly open. I look at the clock. Seven a.m. Thursday. The only day we don't get up at the crack of dawn because Cole handles the morning chores and I don't have to be at the barn until eight. After Wade made me the dinner of my dreams, before we made our way to bed where he reminded me one more time how hard it is going to be to ever leave here, I fell into a fast, deep sleep, so much so that I didn't even wake up through the night, much less to my phone buzzing on the nightstand just now. I pick it up just as the call ends and heads to voicemail. I focus and jolt up in bed. Wade, sensing something is wrong, jolts up beside me.

"What is it?"

"Fourteen calls from my mama. What the hell?" I don't even have time to rub my eyes before it rings again. Dread fills my soul as I answer.

"Mama," I say frantically. "What's wrong?"

"Ivy . . ."

I blink at the voice that doesn't fit on the other end of the line.

"Brad?" I ask, not knowing how to make sense of anything right now.

Wade growls beside me.

"Where's my mama?"

"She's been in a car accident."

"What?" All the blood drains from my face and I feel like I'm floating. "Where is she? Why did they . . . ?" Wade grips my thigh to settle me. I breathe.

"Where are you?"

"She's in x-ray. We're at the hospital in Pendalton," he says, mentioning the hospital a few counties over from Jellico. What was she doing so early in the morning near Pendalton?

"She's asking for you, she's in and out. She's got a pretty good bump on her head and her wrist is all fucked up. I think the glass cut her up a bit too. I've been trying to call for almost an hour," Brad adds.

"Fucking shit, shit, shit." I'm somehow already standing as I mutter under my breath, and so is Wade, tossing on his own clothes as I do and he has no idea what's even going on yet.

"I'm on my way," I say and then I hang up.

An hour and fifteen minutes later, Wade and I are pushing through the doors at Pendalton Community Hospital. It's a miracle I even have shoes on; I don't even remember the drive here, I just know I have to get her into a program. What if someone else was hurt because she was drinking and then got behind the

291

wheel? What Wade must think of her. He hasn't really spoken other than to ask me if I'm alright or tell me she's going to be okay. After a thirty-minute phone call with Cassie to fill her in, where she proceeded to tell me this isn't the first time my mother has driven drunk, I was grateful for the silence because if I tried to talk after that I would've burst into tears.

As I'm speeding through the waiting area, I'm muttering under my breath, "I should've been here. I should've made sure she got the help she needed."

"You can only help people as much as they want to help themselves," Wade whispers in my ear, squeezing my shoulder as we make our way to the reception desk. I don't know if he heard me mutter that or he was just assuming he knew the thoughts running through my head, but just those words threaten to make me lose it. I've already lost my dad; I can't lose my mom too.

I make my way across the small emergency waiting room to a glass enclosure. The nurse behind the reception desk has dark curly blond hair and types quickly into his computer, ignoring my existence. I wait a few minutes and then begin to tap my nails on the counter without thinking, Finally, he finishes and looks up at me, pushing his glasses up his nose as he speaks.

"Are you looking for someone?"

"My mother, Glenda Spencer, was brought in a few hours ago from a car accident."

He nods and goes back to typing. "She's being stitched up right now, and your fiancé is here. You can go back to see her, Room C-22."

I don't miss Wade's grunt at the word *fiancé*. Nonetheless, he slips his hand over mine to remind me we're in this together, and we start to move. I realize somewhere in the back of my mind that this will be the first time Wade meets my mother. The last time I saw her was in November and she was a little worse for wear when I went home for a visit. I've meant to get back more, we've just been so deep in training. A wave of embarrassment for my mother's addiction and guilt for her choices washes over me—that is until I turn the corner to my mother's room and see Brad at her bedside looking like he's actually worried, waiting for her to return from being stitched. Now the only feeling I have is rage.

Wade posts up beside me like we're a unit waiting to attack when Brad stands. I can feel the anger radiating off of him as he squeezes my hand.

Brad wastes no time and comes over to me quickly but Wade is quicker.

"That's close enough, tell us what happened and then leave."

Brad scoffs, but Wade doesn't waste one millisecond entertaining him; he towers over Brad and grips his shirt collar tight. I can see the restraint in his eyes. Brad's hat tumbles off his head to the floor but I don't move. Part of me wants Brad to know he isn't going to fuck with me anymore, and Wade is doing a mighty good job of showing him just that right now, so I let him for just a moment.

"We're not going to fuck around here, no more games. I know every single filthy fucking thing you did to her, and I'll tell you that it's by the sheer grace of God and the fact that we're in a public place that I'm not pummeling you into next week right now. The only words out of your mouth will be what happened to Glenda, and then you will fucking leave before I put you in the room next door. Is that fucking clear?"

"Look, I don't know what she told you, but I never treated her poorly. I loved her when no one else—"

"Wade, let him breathe so he can tell me what happened," I say as calmly as possible. I've heard enough. A true narcissist never admits they're wrong. "He isn't worth it," I add.

Wade lets go but he's emitting steam as he backs up one foot and sets his jaw expectantly.

Brad picks up his hat and dusts it off nervously as he talks. "EMS called me this morning. They tried your phone number that was listed in your mom's phone as her emergency but it was disconnected." He eyes Wade as he says this, then looks back to me.

"I've talked to my mom with my new number—this makes no sense," I say.

"She still had your old one in there listed as Ivy, I had to search through her text messages to find you—your new number is still just a number. My ranch number was the second point of contact, so they called me. I came right away, and when I got here and figured out your number, I started calling you."

You'd almost think he was genuinely concerned, but I know him better than that, this is just a means to an end to get to me. He never cared about my mama when we were together and he sure as hell doesn't now.

"Miss Spencer?" A man's voice calls to me from the doorway, I spin around to face him.

"Yes?"

"I'm Dr. Terry Evans, I have been treating your mother this morning."

"How is she? Is she—" How do you ask if someone is drunk without making them sound terrible.

"She's okay, she almost hit a deer, around five this morning, swerved to miss it and got a nasty bump on the head when she hit the ditch. Her airbag has given her a fair bit of fabric burn, and I had to set her wrist as it was broken in two places." I wince, having my ankle just sprained was painful, I can't imagine breaking a bone in two places. "We also had to give her quite a bit of blood, she lost a lot to a cut on her leg and she's a rare type—AB negative. EMS thinks it was about sixty minutes before anyone noticed her and called it in."

"Like a blood transfusion?"

He nods in response. "Yes."

"Was anyone else hurt?"

The doctor looks at me with a question in his eyes.

"No, she was alone, and she's doing well, all things considered. A little shaken up, of course. They'll be bringing her down momentarily. I'd like her to stay a night or two to keep watch on her."

I look from Wade to Brad and then back to the doctor, not wanting to ask this in front of either of them but not really having a choice.

I close my eyes and go for it.

"Is she . . . was she . . . under the influence?"

The doctor flips open his paperwork and skims through it. "She's been very coherent, I wouldn't think so, no. Ah yes, here we are, your mother's blood alcohol level was zero."

She wasn't drinking? Zero? I don't remember the last time I saw my mother where I could say her blood alcohol level was zero. Is she trying to quit drinking again?

"That's what I was going to tell you," Brad says from behind me. "She said she's seventeen days sober. She was going to an early morning AA meeting in Pendalton."

Tears well up in my eyes as I wish that this could be the time she makes it through. The doctor smiles and nods.

He isn't out the door for more than a few seconds when I turn to speak, fire rising in my gut. I've been tiptoeing around this for months, but if my mama can be so strong all on her own, so can I.

"Brad, thank you for answering that call and for reaching me. I'll be sure to remove your number from her phone, but I don't ever want to see you again. You were terrible to me, you abused me and I won't forgive you. Don't contact me anymore. Don't use my new number. If you do, or you get your family to, I'll be seeking a restraining order." I cross my arms over my chest and stand as strong as I can for eight in the morning, on no coffee and a shit ton of adrenaline.

Wade stands firm beside me, and I know it takes everything in him not to hit Brad, but he doesn't, he just rubs my back, maintaining his control as he speaks, backing me up.

"And Brad, if you ever have a time where you forget what Ivy just said, I'll break every bone in your fucking body just to remind you, and you know what? My smile will grow with every single snap."

Brad motions to get the hell out of this room; his jig of the caring ex is up and he knows it.

"She's all yours," he mutters, squeezing by Wade and out the door.

"That's fucking right, she is," Wade says in a tone I wouldn't ever want to fuck with.

I breathe out a sigh, knowing that this may actually be the last time I see Brad. He would never want to run his father's name through the mud, and a restraining order would do just that. I am wiping a tear off my cheek, reminding myself Brad Bellingham isn't worth one single tear, just as my mama comes around the corner in a bed on wheels being pushed by a nurse.

I go to her immediately and hug her as best I can. Her face does have fabric burn on the entire left side and her wrist is in a cast. Her one eye is black and blue and she has what I assume is that nasty cut the doctor mentioned wrapped on her thigh, but she actually looks healthier than I've seen her look in a long time. Her eyes are bright and free from under-eye bags, and her smile is clear and full.

"Baby, I'm so glad you're here. That was the scariest thing that's ever happened to me. I'm sorry I didn't add your number in properly and Brad had to come," she whispers in my ear.

I let her go when the nurse clears her throat.

"I'm supposed to get Mrs. Spencer set up so she can rest. Pain meds will make her sleepy."

As if on cue, my mom yawns, and the nurse must sense my

hesitation because she turns to me and says quietly, "Give me twenty minutes to settle her, go get a coffee, then you can sit by her side." She pats my arm and smiles. "She's going to be just fine. Looks worse than it is."

It's those words that sucker punch me right in the chest, so much so that the moment we're outside the door, I break and Wade pulls me in close to his chest as I cry, stroking my hair and murmuring how strong I was and how proud of me he is.

I pull back from his now-wet shirt, and he wipes my tears off my cheeks.

"She was sober, she is sober. She was just trying to do the right thing and she stayed there all alone for an hour? She must have been terrified," I sniff.

"She's okay, she got here and she hasn't had a drink in over two weeks, Ivy, that is something special."

I nod; she's never made it that long before. As far as I know, the longest she's made it without a drink since my dad passed was eight days. I look into the room while the nurse and personal support worker help her get comfortable.

"I just feel so helpless, I wish there was something I could've done, something I could do."

Wade tucks a piece of hair behind my ear and kisses my forehead.

"Come on, Trouble, I've got something we can do."

CHAPTER FIFTY
Wade

"You never cease to surprise me, Chief," Ivy says as she munches on a giant chocolate chip cookie in the hospital cafeteria.

She runs a finger over the little cotton bud taped to the inside of her elbow.

"I've never donated blood before. We have the same blood type, my mom and I." She smiles. "I should do it more often—knowing how rare our blood type is, it's needed."

I look up at Ivy from my text conversation. I grin at her; she looks happy now, calm. I would do anything to see her like this all the time and know I was the one responsible. I'm planning to make it my fucking life's purpose.

"Nash makes us go every year, ever since his parents died. I think he feels like he might be able to help someone else in their same situation," I tell her as I continue my conversation with my mother over text.

She nods and stuffs the last bite of cookie into her pretty mouth.

"I get vat," she mumbles around her cookie, and then takes a big sip of her juice. "I have to talk to the hospital about getting her into a rehab program. I have some savings and she needs it. She's done so well . . . if she had help, she might really have a shot at getting and staying sober. I'd hate for her to be on her own while we're away over the next couple weeks and do a backslide."

I'm already three steps ahead of her but I don't want her to worry about all this right now. I just want her to be with her mom.

"Wade, does it bother you to know her past? Do you think of Nash's parents, that someone like her was responsible?"

The way she says it tells me it's been on her mind for quite some time and it has bothered her, and I hate that with every fiber of my being. I reach across the table and grip her hand tight.

"What happened to Nash was terrible. A freak accident. Alcoholism is an illness, Ivy. At least that's the way I've always looked at it. It was Nash's parents' time to go. You have to stop carrying her burden on your shoulders. Promise me you will."

"I'm sorry, I'm so damn emotional about this. Maybe because I'm struggling with the pressure of Angel's training too. I don't know. I will do my best. I promise. I just . . . the idea of one day having my mama back, being close to her, the one I looked up to and loved when I was a kid. The pain of that is a lot to bear. I want it so badly. I just feel like I can't be in all the places I need to be at once, and I don't know how I can change that and still have a career."

"You never know what the future holds, Ivy. You should put some faith into it all, and trust you're where you're supposed to be. Fate might just come through, and maybe it will work out the way you hope," I say. "Jolene Ashby words to live by," I add.

This makes Ivy grin.

It's something I never believed before Ivy came into my life. I used to believe a man made his own fate, but now I'm not so sure, because Ivy is so much more than I could ever dream up on my own.

299

CHAPTER FIFTY-ONE

Ivy

I look up from my phone when my mother stirs beside me. I've been sitting with her for two hours just watching her sleep. She looks so peaceful. We look much the same, same black hair, same eyes, she just has been through so much. My daddy used to say she was the most beautiful woman in the world, but the world's just worn on her now.

Wade has gone to handle some ranch business and make some phone calls with the promise he'll return with some food before lunchtime. I think secretly he just wanted to give me some space to be with my mama. She reaches over and pats my hand when she wakes, and when I look in her eyes they're clear and loving.

"You thought I was driving drunk, didn't you?" she blurts out. My mama has never been one to beat around the bush.

I smile.

"I was worried, yes, I had no idea you were sober, Mama, I'm so goddamn proud of you." My voice breaks and she reaches for me.

"I wanted to show you, not tell you. After so many tries I wanted to make sure you knew this time I was serious. I was really struggling last night. I was lonely, thinking of you and Daddy and Cassie. All the years I let pass me by. All the years I drank away."

I squeeze her hand. I can't even imagine her plight.

"I wanted to drink so goddamn bad. I keep my one bottle. My backup bottle. It sits on my counter and reminds me that I can drink it if I want to. So far, for the last seventeen days, I haven't. But I still want to every day."

"What do you need, Mama? The hospital has an outpatient rehab program, it's a month long, you're already off to such a good start—"

"Who can afford that, honey? It's probably thousands of dollars."

"Some of it can be covered by the state; the rest, well, I have some savings—"

"Ivy Grace Spencer, you will not spend your hard-earned money so I can go to some hoity-toity rehab. I'm doing okay on my own. I was trying to get to a meeting when that deer came out of nowhere. I don't know why I didn't remember your daddy's words."

I smile because I know the ones she means.

"Never swerve for an animal because they'll end up walking away and you'll be in the ditch—" my mom starts.

"—just slam on the brakes and hold that wheel for dear life," I finish.

We smile at each other, and I realize there is so much of my father that still connects my mother and I, and maybe we should start using that to bond us instead of pushing each other away.

"I wish I could be closer to you. We're just so deep in training this horse right now."

"You'll do no such thing. I'm fine where I am. Look, if I had the money I'd go to the rehab program, but I don't, so I have to want it badly enough and work through it in my own time."

I nod.

"Can we talk about something more fun?" She grins, a spark of my old mama in her eyes. "Who is this absolute *hunk* of a man that is escorting you three counties over at seven in the morning?"

I blush.

"My boss, but he's also so much more. We're close." I'm struggling to label whatever Wade and I are.

"I never had a boss that looked at me like I hung the moon." She looks at me like her next statement is obvious. "That man is in love with you, Ivy Grace. He watches you like he's ready to take on the world for you at a moment's notice." My mom laughs then grimaces, holding the sore side of her face.

"It's how your father used to look at me." She smiles and snuggles her head back into her pillow.

I lower my eyes from her gaze, and another round of unpredictable tears fills them.

"I'm in love with him too, so much, but . . . I know he's going to want a family one day, and I'm just so afraid I won't be able to offer him that."

"Does he know it may be tricky for you to carry a baby to term? Has he told you it bothers him or that he's worried about it? You could find a surrogate, adopt; there are ways, honey."

"Yes, he knows, and I know that." I sniff. "He hasn't said anything about it, but I think that's because this thing between us went from a fling to something more when neither of us were looking. I don't know what the future holds, I'm leaving his ranch soon—"

"Baby." My mama looks at me and smiles a soft smile. "Take it from me, if you won't take it from anyone else. If a man is going to love you with his whole heart—and that man does, there isn't a doubt in my mind—never, ever let that go. Do everything you can to hold on to that for as long as you can, because you never know how much time you have with people."

I blink, and more tears spill over my cheeks.

A soft knock on the door interrupts us. I stand to wipe my tears away as the doctor enters the room.

I move to stand, but static begins to line my vision and an intense wave of nausea washes over me, creeping up my throat so fast I gag and grip the wall. I compose myself and look up at him.

"Sorry, doctor, I think I need to sit for a second. We gave blood, I'm . . . dizzy," I say, putting my head down into my hands.

"It is normal to be a little woozy after. How long ago?" he asks.

"About two and a half hours ago . . ." I mutter

"Hmm. That seems like it's a little long to still feel woozy, but maybe with the adrenaline of the morning. Just stay put, don't stand on my account."

I start to feel better as the blood returns to my cheeks.

"That's just been happening on and off . . . I'm in an intense time with my job . . . and I haven't been eating the best," I tell him.

"Stay seated, please. I just wanted to check in on your mother. Glenda, are you comfortable speaking about your sobriety with your daughter here?"

"Of course," my mom says to him.

He nods. "You were mentioning you have been sober and were worried about your family thinking drinking may have had something to do with this accident?"

My mom nods and smiles at him, then turns to me.

"I filled him in that I'm sober, because for once, I'm proud of myself."

"You should be," the doctor tells her and me, looking back and forth between us.

"There is a program you could enter right from here. We even offer transport—"

"Thank you, but Ivy and I were just talking about that, I just simply can't afford that right now—"

"That's the thing I was coming to tell you about, the state will cover some and I just found out that the hospital donor program has some availability. I didn't think we did but when I checked, we've added some new donors recently. The program is to help people in your situation. You qualify in every aspect, and we'd be happy to help you apply, I think you'd be approved right away."

My mom's eyes fill with tears, so mine do as well naturally, and I hug her.

"Yes, we'd like that," I say.

"When will we know?"

"We may know by tomorrow if we process the application today. I'd like you to stay a day or two anyway, Glenda, so we can keep an eye on that concussion, and we could arrange for you to leave here and head straight there if you like? Probably Saturday. I can give you some info on the center in the meantime."

I turn to my mom. "I could get anything you want to take with you, and I can fill Mrs. Potter in, I'm sure she'll keep an eye on things for you."

My mama nods and the doctor writes a few notes down.

"I'll have the nurse come back to help you fill out the forms shortly. Until then just rest and I'll leave you two to visit." He looks through his paperwork again.

"And, Miss Spencer, if I may say, I am the main doctor here, but I also run a family practice right across the street. Since you're going to be around over the next couple of days, pop in to see me, I can draw a little more blood from you, make sure you aren't lacking in something that's making you dizzy . . . could be something as simple as low iron." He shrugs.

Although having any more of my blood taken sounds like the last thing on earth I want to do right now, I agree.

"Yes, thank you, I'll come tomorrow morning on my way in here, give myself a day to rest after this." I smile at him, pointing to the cotton bud on the inside of my elbow, and he nods and smiles before saying goodbye to us and heading off to his next patient.

He no sooner exits than Wade appears in the doorway looking so perfect, so settling, and his gorgeous masculine features flex as he stands there in a pair of perfectly fitting jeans, a white hoodie and his backwards Titans hat. Even having rushed to get ready this morning he looks like casual perfection. I feel my heart melt even more when I see he has food with him and a tea for my mama.

His eyes meet mine and I see it, the way everyone keeps telling me he looks at me. I bask in it for a brief moment before my mother speaks.

"Come in," my mother says to him, breaking the silence. "I'm Glenda Spencer, and I hear you're Wade. I'm sorry we didn't really get a formal introduction earlier; I was still pretty out of it. I understand you've been getting to know my Ivy."

Wade looks at me as he answers her. "I have, she is pretty great . . ." He gives me the smirk I literally can't get enough of, then turns his eyes back to my mom.

"Ivy said you like tea? Two milks?"

"I do." She is already a goner for him—I can tell by the smitten little grin she's wearing. Who wouldn't be? Wade Ashby is the definition of dreamy.

"Thank you for coming with her this morning," she says as she accepts her tea from him.

I stand, but I have to steady myself a little before I make my way over to him.

"What's wrong?" he asks instantly, panic lining his face.

"I'm just a little dizzy. The doctor said it's probably from donating."

Wade meets me in the middle of the room and grips my elbow.

"I brought you lunch, that should help," he says, holding up the most delicious-looking club sandwich I've ever seen.

My stomach grumbles at the sight. I look up at him. "That sandwich looks like everything I could ever want right now," I tell him.

He shrugs and then smirks at me.

"Just out here making your dreams come true, Trouble."

Goddamn, isn't that the truth?

I don't think I could ever love this man more than I do right now, standing in front of me, offering me something as simple as that lopsided grin and a club sandwich.

All I have to do now is tell him.

CHAPTER FIFTY-TWO
Wade

"This place is state of the art. There are yoga classes for my mom to take, therapy sessions, grief counseling, and an excellent meal plan."

I pass Ivy her ice cream sundae in the center of my bed as she scrolls through the website for the treatment center her mother is heading to. She isn't giving me any information I don't already know, but I listen to her animated chatter intently anyway.

"And then, if she makes it through to the other side of this, I need to spend more time with her. She used to work with my dad, helping with the animals, maybe she could update her knowledge and work again. You know she used to craft too, she was really good at making blankets, hats . . ."

I smile down at her, and the hope she has in her eyes makes me hope her mother can do it.

I lose my shirt and get into bed beside her. Before Ivy started sleeping here, my room always felt lifeless. The deep walnut cabin walls against the rustic log headboard Cole and I made last summer. The navy blue bedding covering my California king-size bed. Everything was neat and cool. Now that she sits in the center of it, there is life here, it's warmer, and crawling in beside her naked little body every night, wrapping my arms around her, is the only place on this earth I truly care to be.

"Support is the most important thing. I just have to figure out how to do it all with Angel's juvenile year ahead." Her pretty features knot as she thinks about the responsibility on her shoulders. It's a look I know well because it's one I wear most days, wishing there were more hours than twenty-four to get things done.

"We'll figure it out. Where there's a will, there's a way, right?" I ask as I use my thumb to swipe rogue whipped cream from the corner of her mouth and lick it off my own thumb.

Her eyes turn to mine and she smiles.

"You remember my dad's words?" It's the simplest statement but I blink at her. I hadn't even thought. It just seems to me, we're in this and everything else going forward together.

"Ivy, I remember everything you've ever said to me. In case it isn't obvious, I'm fucking crazy about you."

She kisses my lips. "Meh, you're alright." She giggles.

I'm grabbing her ice cream from her and setting it down on the table, ready to show her just how crazy she actually is for me too, when my phone buzzes on the bedside table.

"Fuck, I'm waiting on something," I say, as Ivy sits back up and happily starts munching on her ice cream again, continuing her read through Walnut Grove Rehabilitation Center's website. And it's the text I'm waiting for.

BOSS LADY

I talked to the contractors, they're coming in the morning. You're doing the right thing.

I know, I just don't want to put any pressure on this yet, so it stays between you and me until it's done.

BOSS LADY

One thing I know for certain is you can't ever be too loyal. I know you're not the heart on your sleeve kind, but Wade at some point you have to try to trust the universe has your back.

Thanks for the Ted Talk.

BOSS LADY

Stop being a smart ass. She's going to love it. You'll see.

You know this because you're always right?

BOSS LADY

Because you've got something special here. Because that girl loves you.

BOSS LADY

Also because I'm always right. *Wink face*

I set my phone down and look over at Ivy; she's leaning against my headboard, knees bent, iPad in her lap. Her hair is pulled up high on her head in one of her scrunchies and the strap of her tank top hangs off her shoulder just slightly. Her mouth opens into one of her cute little yawns and something about how she looks is so easy, so natural.

All my worries about taking such a big step for her disappear as I settle in with Ivy in my bed, in *our* bed. Her arms come up around me and I instantly know I am doing the right thing.

And fuck, my mother *is* always right.

CHAPTER FIFTY-THREE

Ivy

By Saturday morning, I'm up early, ready to head to Jellico and then to the hospital to see my mother off to her new rehab facility.

The ranch is quiet when I head over to the barn to see Wade before I leave. The only sound is hammering coming from Spirit, the cabin two over from mine. Wade has contractors working on some of the worn-down cabins on the property over the next few weeks. The sun isn't even up yet and the air has a spring-like quality to it. This is my favorite time to be at the barn, I know Rowan is already out working with Angel and Dusty on our practice track, and he'll be leaving before us for Florida. My brain is buzzing as I enter the silos office; there is so much riding on this gate card, so much riding on my mama.

It all floats upward when I open Wade's door and see him deep in thought, wearing his glasses with a pencil between his teeth. He's looking at blueprints for the first cabin that is being worked on. His cowboy hat is off and his hair is rustled. His warm leather and spicy scent fills my senses, and I feel the need to just hug him. His eyes rake over me when he sees me, setting something off in me without him even touching me. He smirks at me—we're matching, both of us in black and gray flannels and blue jeans.

"Are we just boring and predictable now?" I ask as I approach him.

Wade pulls his glasses off and sets them and his pencil down on his desk. He takes his plush bottom lip between his teeth and looks at me for a split second before he comes around the front of his desk with that lopsided smirk, wrapping his strong arms around me as he plants a kiss way too aggressively for six-thirty in the morning and his public office on my lips. Still, I can't stop the feeling that envelops me from my head to my toes, desire stretching to every nook and cranny of my being.

Wade chuckles and then moves past me and closes the office door, turning the lock and tipping the blinds shut. I stand frozen as his hands skim down the arms of my shirt from behind me. He pulls the scrunchie from my hair and tosses it on the floor to God knows where.

"The last fucking thing we are is boring and predictable, Trouble," he whispers in my ear, swiping my hair to the side and kissing my neck, instantly heating my insides as his breath and lips caress me.

"Did you actually think you were going to come into my office to say goodbye this morning in that tight little shirt with those perfect fucking tits on display and I wouldn't feel the need to fuck them?"

"I guess I just assumed you would be able to be professional," I whisper, as his hot lips meet the side of my neck, then move to my earlobe, pulling it into his mouth and biting down, hard. My pussy throbs and I clench my thighs together.

"The way you make me feel is anything but professional . . ." Wade's hands come around my front and palm my breasts, and my hardened nipples beg for his touch against the fabric of my bra.

I turn my face to the side, his lips landing on my cheek in a light kiss.

"Tell me how I make you feel, Wade?" I taunt with a small smile.

I love to be his undoing.

One swift yank on my shirt and every snap comes undone, and my breasts bounce free as he pulls my bra off and tosses it.

His finger swipes and pinches a nipple; the feeling is a shot straight to my already heated core.

"You make me feel . . . fuck . . . completely fucking out of control, Trouble."

I moan as my head falls back onto his chest. Wade doesn't let up, teasing my nipples as he reaches down and presses a palm against my pussy through my jeans. I whimper with the contact and press my ass into his hard cock. I reach behind me and cup him through his jeans between us, panting with want, wishing he could do away with all our clothes as quickly as he got rid of my shirt.

Wade spins me around and lifts me with one arm, swiping papers off the lowest part of his desk with the other then dropping me down onto it. He frees me of my boots and jeans with one hand as the other tangles in my hair while he kisses me deeply, searching desperately every corner of my mouth. I'm putty in his hands, begging for him without saying a word. *Use me, take everything I have, just make me come. Please.* Wade pulls back and takes in the view of me on his desk before him. He loses his boots quickly and unbuckles his jeans and kicks them aside, pulling off his shirt and standing naked over me from his full height. He's godlike and so beautiful, wearing a teasing smirk on his face.

His thumb comes out and drags across my bottom lip, then he presses it into the corner of my mouth before pushing it between my lips. I suck his thumb all the way in, looking up at him through my lashes. He groans in response. The sound rumbles from his chest.

"Be my good girl and push those perfect tits together," he orders.

I bite down on his thumb as he hisses, then I smile sweetly.

"Anyone ever tell you that you're bossy, Wade Ashby?" I ask.

"Yes, and don't pretend you don't love it." His lips meet mine. "Now, shut those pretty lips, do what you're fucking told and take my cock like a good little slut," he whispers into them, sending a fresh wave of goosebumps over my flesh.

I moan as his knuckles graze my nipple, because he's right, I fucking love it, so I do as I'm told.

Wade

Fuck, I could come just at the sight of Ivy right now, her eyes hooded, lips swollen from kissing me and her ass pressed against my desk. Her glistening cunt is on full display, and like the good girl she loves to be she's pushed her tits together, waiting patiently for my cock to slide between them. I reach between her legs and run three fingers over her dripping slit. She sucks in a breath as I coat myself in her arousal, using it as lube.

"Fuck that tight little pussy with your fingers while I fuck your tits."

I take over for her hands, pushing her tits together, then I slide my dick between them. She moans like it's the one thing she wants most in the world.

"I love it when you're this fucking needy before breakfast," I tell her as I start to fuck between her tits. My head tips back with the initial contact. Every part of her feels incredible. I look down to where she inserts one finger into her tight pussy, then two, as she grips my desk with the other hand. Her eyes fall closed, and she lets out a breathy moan as her body shudders. I lean down and spit between her breasts, then rub my cock all over them. She quivers everywhere when she feels it.

"*Fuck,* Ivy . . . even your tits fit my cock like they were made to take me."

"Wade . . . this is so hot. I'm going to come already," she whines as she shifts between fingering herself and circling her clit.

"No, Ivy, you're going to be a good girl and wait until I give you permission to come."

She moans my name as my head tips back and I close my eyes. The combination of watching her fuck herself and the soft warmth of her around my cock pulls me to the precipice. I'll never fucking get enough of this woman. I push myself for one more minute of this euphoria but she feels so fucking good like this I can't stop. Her free hand reaches out and grips my ass, sharp nails bite into my skin as my name leaves her lips, and heat ripples up my spine like tossing whiskey on a flame.

"Please, Wade . . . I'm going to."

I want to tell her to wait, but seeing her naked in the middle of my fucking desk drives me over the edge as she digs her nails into my skin.

"Eyes up here, Ivy, open your mouth and stick out your tongue. You can come when I come."

She opens her eyes and gives me the sass I fucking love.

"Thank you, *sir*," she says as she comes apart and it does me in. My cum juts out over her chest, her chin and her lips. It's fucking glorious. My cock jerks and pulses between her breasts and I slow my pace as her eyes stay fixed on me. We sit like this for a moment as our breath returns to normal.

I look down at her, the beautiful mess she is, still not quite ready to look away.

"You look . . ." I say, taking in the sight of her, at a loss for the right words.

Ivy laughs as she looks down to her cum-soaked chest.

"A bit messy right now?"

I groan as I swipe my first and second fingers over her chin and bring my cum to her lips, swiping them back and forth, painting them with me. I just stare at her for a few more seconds.

"No, baby . . . I was going to say you look . . . fuck, I'm so fucking in love with you, Ivy."

Ivy's mouth falls open.

Okay, maybe I shouldn't have told her I love her for the first time with my cum all over her and my dick between her tits, because the look she's wearing right now is one of shock. But fuck, I can't help it. I love her. I love every single goddamn thing about her and she just looks so beautiful, so *mine*.

"Did you just say you love me?" she repeats as we separate and she still sits frozen.

I bend down and kiss her lips, tasting myself there; it's mixed with her and the taste of us together is incredible.

"Yes, I said *love*. I love you, Ivy, and I don't throw that word around lightly. I fucking love my world when you're in it. I love working with you every damn day, I love talking to you, I love seeing what faces you'll give me when I say something that shocks you, I love making your coffee in the morning and your dinner at night. I love when these lips curve up into the prettiest fucking smile that lights up my whole universe." I kiss her lips again, hovering there.

"Most of all, I love who we are together. I love *us*." I say it as simply as I can.

"I . . . Wade . . ." she stammers.

"Shhh. I didn't tell you to hear you say it back. I just wanted you to know."

And I mean it. I know she's afraid—the last man she gave her heart to hurt her deeply—but I'll wait as long as she needs me to. I grab a warm cloth from my private bathroom and clean her up. She dresses and searches the floor frantically for the scrunchie that tumbled out of her hair earlier, but it's nowhere to be found.

She was supposed to leave for Jellico thirty minutes ago before I came at her like a lion hunting his prey. I put her out of her misery, reach into my drawer and pull out a red scrunchie from my small pile and pass it to her.

"Here, I have a few spares." I grin.

Ivy's eyes shift to mine. "You keep my scrunchies?"

"Never know when you might need an extra ten," I say sarcastically. "So, I keep them on hand when you leave them behind."

Ivy makes her way over to me, taking the scrunchie from me, reaches up on her tiptoes, planting a kiss to my lips, and she looks down at the scrunchie then back up to me.

"I love you so fucking much, Wade Ashby," she says softly, as a kind of peace I've never felt settles in my chest.

I have no words, so I just kiss her again.

The funny thing is, I didn't even *need* to hear it back.

As long as she keeps on looking at me the way she is right now for the rest of my life, I could die a happy man.

CHAPTER FIFTY-FOUR
Ivy

"This is an outpatient program. It's totally voluntary. You have the choice whether you stay or you go. You'll be able to call your sponsor, although you'll be appointed one in-house, and you'll be able to have your cell phone and visitors."

My mom nods, and even with her swollen, bruised eye and the fabric burn on her forehead and cheek, she looks fresh after an early morning shower and ready to start her treatment as we pack up the things I've brought her from her trailer.

I was shocked to see it clean when I arrived. Plants watered, dishes done. Mrs. Potter assured me she would go in every few days and run the water, check the heat, make sure everything is in order. I haven't been around with our intense training schedule, I've just been too busy, but Mrs. Potter informed me things have been quiet around my mom's since Christmas.

More often than not, she's seen her lights out early every night. She said they've been drinking tea together almost nightly on the porch. I wonder just how long she's been working towards getting sober, and then I remind myself it doesn't matter. She's here now and she looks eager to get on with it.

"Being in Williamsburg you'll only be forty-five minutes away, so I'll come see you after we get back from Sarasota."

My mom pats my hand and calms my worried eyes.

"Ivy, baby, you've been looking after me for a long time. You come whenever you can—training a horse for this race is a dream of yours, focus on it. Be in the moment. I'll be okay this time." She hugs me with a strong hold that tells me to trust her and have faith. I see a glimpse of the mother I remember, the one that held me when I was sick, the one that laughed with my father, a lot. The one that cooked us dinners and helped us with our homework. Between this turn of events and Wade's confession to me this morning, I feel like I'm finally in the right place in my life for the first time maybe ever. Moving forward.

"Your transport is here, Glenda." Dr. Evans smiles from the doorway. "We can help with your bags."

I smile back. "Thank you for helping set all of this up for her," I say as I extend my hand for shaking. He obliges and shakes back with a "My pleasure."

Tears prick my eyes as my mama looks at me, ready to leave. I hold them back; I'll save them for later. Right now, all I want is for her to go and heal. I grab my mom's last bag and make my way to the door behind her, hugging her and telling her one more time how proud of her I am before she disappears into the backseat of the transport van. As the van starts out of the loading zone, I let out a breath of relief. *Please let this be the time.*

"Miss Spencer." I jump when I hear Dr. Evans's voice behind me. I didn't even realize he was still there. "There's just one more thing I want to talk to you about, before you go." I turn back around as he motions to two chairs just beyond the waiting room.

"Let's sit," he says.

I assume he wants to tell me about my bloodwork, and I quickly go over in my mind how much money I have available in my checking account as I figure he may want me to settle some of my mom's bill before I leave. But he doesn't.

Instead, he asks me a question that brings my entire world down around me.

"Are you aware that you're pregnant?"

I blink and grip the bottom of the chair for stability, the room suddenly reeling around me.

Pregnant? I can't be.

My breath accelerates as I realize I *can* be. Calculating the days since my last period. *When the fuck was it?* Am I that woman? The one that doesn't even realize she's pregnant because she's living in a sex fog with a hot bossy rancher? Am I a fucking Lifetime show? I just might be. Was it in December? Yes, I had my period in December. At the beginning of it. And now it's February 2nd. My heart skips a beat and then sinks to my feet. The thought of carrying Wade's baby is a dream I can't even let myself fathom.

"I . . . no, I don't think . . . I am? Are you sure?" I ask, panic brimming in my chest.

"I'm sure that you are." He smiles at me.

My heart sinks, already breaking for this potential loss before it comes.

"I've been so busy I didn't even realize I was late. I'm on birth control," I say.

Dr. Evans seems unfazed.

"Have you taken any medications over the last couple of months? Anything out of the ordinary?"

I think back. *Besides an incredible amount of sex?*

"Only vitamins, and I've been taking some natural remedies to help keep my immune system strong through flu season." He looks at me, so I elaborate. "Extra Vitamin C, Mullein, St. John's Wort, Echinacea . . . A few others, because after Christmas I had the stomach flu, it was quick forty-eight hours."

He nods. "That could do it, and sometimes even natural meds can interfere with the pill, and sometimes the pill just doesn't work one hundred percent effectively.

"After you said you had been dizzy and nauseous, I had a hunch to check for it when we ran your panel, and sure enough I was right. I think you're right around seven to eight weeks along, judging by your hCG levels. You're also a bit low on iron. So we can get you on some with a good prenatal vitamin."

Before I understand what is even happening, tears are filling my eyes for a child I already love so much and I'm afraid I may not meet.

"I take it this is unexpected. Do you need . . . to talk to someone?" Dr. Evans asks.

"No, I . . . it's just, I'm not supposed to . . . I can't carry a baby to term."

Dr. Evans's brow furrows as he glances down to his folder.

"Why not?"

I fill him in as he writes in his notes while he listens to my story.

"I'd like to schedule you for an ultrasound. Check for the heartbeat and see how the baby is, check everything out really. Your levels are great right now. Did you ever get a second opinion on your fertility?"

I shake my head, not even allowing the hope to register, not to mention this might be the last thing Wade wants in life right now. He says he loves me, but does he love me enough to make it through this loss with me?

"Would your previous doctor be able to be contacted for his notes?" Dr. Evans extends a box of tissue for me to take one. I do, gratefully.

"Yes, I believe so." I nod, wiping my eyes with the tissue and taking a deep breath.

"Let's schedule that ultrasound. We'll know more then. I'll grab some vitamin samples and schedule you a time. I'll be right back," he says.

The moment he leaves, the floodgates open for a child I haven't even lost yet.

CHAPTER FIFTY-FIVE

Ivy

I go through the motions as I make my way back to town to meet Ginger at Annalise's Nail Bar for our girl date. A girl date I don't know if I can handle right now. I'm too emotional, until the moment I walk in the door and Ginger squeals and pulls me into the most comforting hug ever. Now I'm thinking maybe these next couple hours are exactly what I need before I face Wade. Before I change everything between us.

"I was wondering if you were going to stand me up, babe. I've already had almost one glass of champagne without you." Ginger smiles at me with her perfect smile

"I'm guessing people don't stand Ginger Danforth up often," I tell her, taking my place next to her.

"How is your mama?" she asks. "Champagne?"

I shake my head. "No thanks, just orange juice, I have a lot of work to do this afternoon when I get back." *And I'm pregnant* . . . It repeats in my mind every other second as if I could ever forget. "And my mama is . . . okay. Off to her new facility. I'm hoping it helps her," I finish.

Ginger squeezes my hand. "Timing is everything, babe. You can think you know what you want, you can think you have control, but you don't, maybe it wasn't your mama's time before. Maybe this is it."

"I hope so. I just have to get through Florida and then I can spend some time with her, let the training hands take a little more on with Angel for the next month or so. This is important."

"Speaking of which, you're wearing my boots on Thursday—they're the good luck boots."

"Deal." I smile as we both get a sudsy foot bath.

I spend the next twenty minutes listening to Ginger tell me all about the drama Cole is going through with Gemma, how he's worried she might try to get more time with Mabel now that she's showing signs of actually trying to be a mother. Hearing her talk about him tells me she's a lot more involved with CeCe's brother than even CeCe may know. If I wasn't such a wreck right now, I would be more curious as to what the actual story is with them, but I'm realizing my heart is elsewhere during this visit.

"Oh fuck," Ginger says as she takes a big gulp of her champagne. "You might want to reconsider one of these." She holds up her glass.

I'm about to ask why when I follow her gaze to hear the bell for the door chime and find two pretty—and loud—blondes walking into the nail salon. The loudest one is talking, like she's letting everyone know she's arrived. She's tall and leggy; she almost looks like a more weathered version of Margot Robbie.

Ginger leans in. "That's Janelle, Wade's ex-wife, and she's a goddamn treat," she whispers as the taller blonde's eyes lock with mine across the room. They narrow as if she's asking herself how she's never seen me before. As if she knows everyone in town and I'm clearly the outsider.

"Well, well, well, look what the cat dragged in, literally," Ginger says as Janelle and her friend cop a seat right beside us.

"Long time no see, Ginger. Time to find new friends now that CeCe is hooking up with her brother from another mother?"

"Time to make yourself look prettier on the outside because there's so much to make up for on the inside?" Ginger smiles so sweetly at her I almost giggle.

"Janelle Ashby," the woman says, extending a hand to me. "You must be new in town; I haven't seen you before."

"Ivy Spencer," I say, wishing I could just teleport back to the ranch away from the last encounter I could ever need today.

"Spencer. Are you the new horse trainer on my husband's ranch?"

"Ex-husband," Ginger corrects.

Janelle ignores Ginger's comment and eyes me up and down, really looks at me, and something in me makes me want to smack her. Maybe it's the mama in me rising up.

"I am the new horse trainer," I say. "It's nice to meet you, can't say I've heard much about you from Wade."

Ginger snorts beside me and raises her hand for another glass of champagne.

"Ivy is helping Wade train a derby horse. She has a real gift, something fresh and totally new for Wade, which is just what he needs in my opinion . . . in the training department, that is. Wouldn't be surprised if he decides to keep her on the ranch for a long time," Ginger says, a *fuck you* glimmer in her eyes.

Janelle looks me up and down. I see it on her face as it registers with her, the moment she realizes Wade might just be more than my boss.

"Well, those Ashby men sure have a lot of women hanging off them, don't they? Speaking of, how's Cole, Ginger? Has he finally managed to get through every woman in Kentucky so he can give you that pity fuck you've been begging him for, for years?"

Ginger smiles at her.

"Oh honey, wouldn't you like to know. But I'll never kiss and tell—I'm a lady, unlike some of the trash just hanging around town these days."

Janelle just laughs an evil little laugh at Ginger and leans her head back, closing her eyes before she speaks. "You know, I noticed how good Wade's looking these days, told him as much the other day," she says as she lifts her feet into her own sudsy bath.

Before I can stop it, my blood instantly boils as I ask myself when she saw Wade. He never mentioned it. Then I scold myself for being jealous.

"Well, that ship has sailed—so sad for you. Too bad you didn't notice that when you were still his wife," Ginger quips, not missing a beat.

Janelle opens her eyes and looks at both of us. "Wade's understanding, that man is loyal to a fault. Been really thinking a lot about him lately, you know. We were talking about giving things another go when we were at Woody's the other day for ax throwing."

Wade's day out with Nash and Cole comes to mind, and I wonder just what was said between them. I know Wade was there; I did not know Janelle was.

Ginger laughs this time, a clear laugh.

"Janelle, that would never happen. Wade may be loyal but he isn't stupid. He would never give you another chance."

Janelle leans back in her chair and closes her eyes again, as I ask myself if anything she's saying is true. She sure seems confident when she smiles and singsongs, "Never say never, Gingy."

After Ginger and I leave the nail bar and the world's most awkward pedicure with Wade's dreadful ex-wife, Ginger proceeds to tell me a million times as we eat our lunch at the local hot spot that Janelle is a compulsive liar and a drama queen, and I shouldn't give one word she says a second thought.

The funny thing is, I know that. I know how Wade feels,

and if I know one other thing about him it's that he's honest. I know he would never be interested in his ex-wife, but part of me, the part that is the self-preserving side and feels I can only rely on myself, tells me that maybe she can offer him something I can't. Then again, maybe that's just my insecurity talking considering the way I'm going to have to make this fun little relationship we've got going very real, very quickly. Too many thoughts run through my head to comprehend.

So now, I've just been sitting here for the past hour staring at www.baby.com on my phone, in the Sage and Salt parking lot, reading that mine and Wade's baby is about the size of a kidney bean and trying to figure out how to face him. I know I have to go back to the ranch. We're getting Rowan and Angel ready for Florida today, but for some reason every time I go to start the truck, I freeze.

I try to talk myself up, thinking of the advice my dad would give me in this scenario. As I dry my tears and try to straighten myself out, I remember. This man is different from any man I've ever known. This man isn't Brad. If this baby isn't meant to be, I'll make it through this. The question is, do I do it on my own and weather things as they come? Or do I make Wade suffer with me? Or do I just wait a few weeks and see what happens, what my ultrasound says?

One thing I know is certain—I've always only been able to count on one person, myself. To rely on someone else seems terrifying and my head is such a mess right now.

I reach down and run a hand over my still-flat stomach. To the naked eye, nothing is different, but in my heart, I know I'll never be the same.

Let's go, little bean. It's you and me. Let's go home.

CHAPTER FIFTY-SIX
Wade

"They're only little once and I want to spend as much time with them as I can. At least until they start school."

"I totally understand, and I appreciate how much notice you're giving me here. Can't say I'm surprised; I wouldn't want to leave those little faces every day either," I say to Sam as she pushes her double stroller back and forth while her five-month-old twins sleep. Her dark hair is pulled up on top of her head, sort of the way Ivy wears hers, and she's comfortable in tights and a big Nike hoodie.

She looks happy. Tired, but happy. I can't say I'm surprised at the reason she wanted this meeting today—to tell me she isn't coming back to work full-time—and I can't say I'm really sad about this news either. A small part of the dread I've been feeling every day as I glance at the calendar above my desk has dissipated immensely in the last thirty minutes. This makes things easier. Maybe now it won't be so hard to convince Ivy to stay on my ranch as the official head trainer.

"So, Ivy is working out fantastic?" Sam asks as she pulls a blanket up over twin number one.

I nod. "She's doing a great job here."

"Do you think there's a chance she'll stay on?" Sam asks.

"I'm not sure," I say truthfully, hanging up the rope I was wrapping around my arm on a hook outside the barn.

"Can I say, Wade? On a personal note, you seem . . . relaxed and less grunty than usual. Whatever you're up to these days, keep it up. It looks good on you." She smiles at me, and I just sort of do a weird laughing scoffing thing in response.

As if speaking about her manifests her out of thin air, Ivy's truck comes into view down the long driveway of the ranch. Sam looks at me. "Speak of the cute little devil."

Ivy eyes us cautiously as she parks in front of the barn and moves her sunglasses from her face to her head. Seeing her outfit reminds me of this morning, her body glistening with my cum as I told her I loved her. Maybe I'm just depraved, but just the thought alone makes my dick twitch in my jeans. Now that I've told her how I feel about her, I might never stop.

"Long time no see," Ivy says to Sam with a big smile and a hug. The last time she saw her was during the two-week overlap when Sam showed Ivy the ropes here before she went on maternity leave.

"Motherhood." Sam shrugs.

"So, got your return date set?" Ivy asks, her glance bouncing between Sam and me.

"Actually, Sam's just given me her notice as our head trainer. She's going to step back from her role here to stay home with the twins, and she'll come back in six months maybe and do some part-time training for us on weekends, maybe with the younger classes," I say, my eyes locking with Ivy's. Her mouth falls open slightly as Sam laughs and says, "Hope you don't have another job lined up. This big guy might need you around here for a while."

"I—that's great for you, to stay home with them a little longer." Ivy's eyes flit to the restless little ones in their stroller.

"I was just saying to Wade, I can't get back this time, I want to soak up every second," Sam says, brushing a little tuft of dark curls off one of the twins' forehead.

"I bet," Ivy says, taking her bottom lip between her teeth.

I decide this is a good thing for Ivy; she says she'll have trouble having kids, but maybe seeing the way Sam is with her adopted babies is a good thing. I watch as Ivy's face turns up in the sweetest smile for one of the twins, and hope she realizes she can still have this experience even if it looks a little different for her. The way it looked different for Sam.

"Nap time is over I suppose," Sam says, bending down to check to see if the babies are wet. "Shoot, I have almost an hour's drive back; do you mind if I feed them and change them first?"

"Of course," I say, gesturing to the big house. "Our house is yours. Mama Jo will be thrilled to see the babies."

Sam looks up from the stroller to meet Ivy's gaze. "Do you want to give me a hand?" she asks.

"I'd love to—if you need me, I'm all yours." Ivy smiles, then looks at me.

"Go ahead," I tell her. "I'm pretty well wrapped up down here today, just waiting on Angel's daily report." I eye her carefully, but nothing about her says she isn't okay. In fact, she looks genuinely excited to help Sam with the babies.

"Devin works from home. I normally have his help, so doing this alone is new to me," Sam gushes.

Ivy nods, and Sam unclips a car seat from the stroller and hands it to Ivy. "You can have Amelia, she's the calmest. I'll handle Hurricane Annie."

Ivy laughs and looks down at the little cooing bundle.

"Are you gonna go easy on me, Amelia, if I help your mama feed you?" she asks, running a finger down Amelia's soft, chubby little cheek. A feeling of need washes over me as I watch her, a need to give her this one day, to do anything to make her happy.

Ivy turns to head up the steps to the big house. Amelia coos at her happily from her seat, and I don't miss the way Ivy's face lights up when Sam turns back to her and says, "You're a natural."

Two hours later, Sam is gone and Ivy and I have Dusty and Rowan ready to head to Florida with Angel. Ivy's been quiet all afternoon since her visit with Sam. I try to give her a little space and chalk it up to her worrying about her mother. She's talked to her twice so she knows she's there and settled in, but of course she'll worry about how she's doing. I also can't help wondering if being with Sam affected her today too; it's been an overwhelming day for her, to say the least.

When we get back to my cabin, I'm talking to her about random things—Florida, what movie we're going to watch tonight, what kind of dressing she wants for her salad—but she's distracted, and something else I've never witnessed.

Quiet.

"Ivy . . ." I say after I ask her a direct question about the paperwork for Angel's derby nomination.

"Hmm?" she says, looking up at me from where she's standing at the living room window watching the sun sink behind the hills. She's nervous, and I can tell something more is going on.

"You didn't even hear me, did you?"

"Sorry, Wade." She sniffs, but says nothing else, which is again, highly unlike her. It's at this moment I realize whatever is going on with her isn't about her mother or Sam, and I'm going to find out what it is right now.

I put my kitchen tools down and walk to her, placing my

hands on her shoulders, bringing her to my chest. I just hug her for a moment.

"I was right, you do give the best hugs," she says, causing me to chuckle.

"What?"

"Nothing, Wade. Just a hunch I had about you once." I kiss her head.

"Are you going to tell me what's going on in your mind?" I ask

"I'm just dealing with some things today. I don't get surprised very often . . ." Ivy says randomly, before she looks up at me and smiles through fresh tears.

I have not a goddamn clue what she's mumbling about, but I can see the fight on her pretty face. Like she wants to tell me something or ask me something.

"What's going on, Trouble? I don't mean to sound like a prick here, but there's never a time where you aren't talking. If you're waging a war in that pretty head of yours over something, let me fight it with you."

A feeling of worry floods me as it occurs to me. It may be what I said to her this morning. Was it too much, too fast for her?

"I'm just . . . overwhelmed right now." She sniffs. I get it, because the need I have to protect her overwhelms *me*. I kiss her lips and she lets me in, reaching her hands up around the nape of my neck, letting them settle there in their place as they always do.

"Was it being around Sam today? Was it too much? Did she say something that upset you?"

"No, Wade, she was great, it's just . . . I want that for you so badly. A future like that, a family . . ."

None of this makes sense.

"We could have that if you want, however that looks for us."

"Wade, why do you have to be so perfect?" she asks as she wipes away a tear. "I mean, don't you just think it would be easier with someone else for you? Simpler? Even when you were with Janelle, it would've been easier. She could've given you a future, a family."

I scoff, *like fuck.* I look down at her and realize she's actually serious.

"Where is all this coming from, Ivy?" I ask.

Ivy breathes out a gentle sigh and turns to face me.

"I saw her today at the nail salon—Janelle. She said she talked to you, told you she might want to try again and I couldn't help but wonder . . . I mean, I know how you feel about me, but if you want a family . . . maybe someone, not necessarily Janelle but . . . maybe that would be better."

Wait . . . the fuck?

I set my jaw and take a breath, placing my hands on my hips. I try to stay calm. The fact that Ivy could even be threatened by Janelle and her lies, making her second-guess our future together, even momentarily, is too much for me.

Fucking Janelle.

"Ivy, I did see her, at Woody's the other day, but not in the way you think. She showed up while we were there. She came in and asked me for money."

Ivy thinks for a moment and chews on her lip.

"Did she tell you she wanted to try again? To start a family with you?"

I run a hand through my hair.

"Yes. She did, but that's what she does. She uses people. I was just someone she needed something from. And to state the glaringly obvious, I don't love her, I love you. I'm certainly not about to let a bullshit encounter with Janelle let you push me away. You have nothing to worry about with her, or anyone else ever, trust me."

Ivy moves further away from me and stands staring out the

window. For a long moment it's just silent, and I am still standing here with no fucking idea what is going on.

"I just . . . Wade, I'm not myself right now. I think maybe I'm going to sleep at my own cabin tonight. I need . . . a night . . . to clear my head, to just think, everything is happening so fast and I don't know what the future holds . . . my job, how that's going to look now . . ."

I look up and breathe for just a moment, panic rising in my gut.

"Ivy. You have a job here, for as long as you want, I told you that today." I sound like I'm pleading because I am. Pleading for the future that's right at my fingertips.

"Don't leave," I beg.

She turns to face me and I can see it in her, her fight with whatever she's struggling with, her own internal battle, whatever's living in her mind.

"I'm not upset with you, Wade. I just . . . don't know what's to come. I just need to sleep. Maybe things will look more clear to me in the morning."

She moves to grab her purse and her jacket. I feel like I'm watching in slow motion. I want to stop her, I want to grab her and tell her she isn't going anywhere, but another part of me says to let her go, to give her the space she needs to calm down, to realize she's talking batshit fucking crazy right now, thinking I'd ever go back to Janelle or anyone else for that matter.

Before she opens the door, she looks up at me. "This isn't your fault, Wade. It's mine. I let things get too messy, we work together, this whole thing is just so . . . complicated now, maybe too complicated."

My mouth falls slack. *What the fuck is she saying?*

"You can't possibly think that, Ivy," I say as I grab her arm to get one more second with her.

She looks down where my hand holds her then back up to my eyes.

"Don't tell me what I think, Wade. I had five years of a man telling me what I think."

It's those words that make me let go and watch her walk out my cabin door, because if there's one thing I *can* show her, it's that I'm fucking nothing like the man she was with before.

I'm pacing.

Fuck. Pacing and drinking . . . and pacing some more. By midnight, I've gone over all of this a million times and I can't fucking figure out for the life of me what happened today between Ivy and Janelle that got Ivy so spooked. She knows how I feel, she knows the last thing on earth I'd ever do is leave her to go back to Janelle. I'd rather fucking sleep on the barn floor naked for the rest of my life than sleep in Janelle's bed.

I run a hand through my hair as I walk outside to my front porch, holding a half-empty bottle of bourbon because everything in my goddamn house reminds me of her. It's cold outside but the fresh air feels good as I stand and stare two hundred feet down the path at Ivy's dark cabin. I let every encounter I've had with her register with me. Everything she's ever told me runs through my mind as the burn of my bourbon slides down my throat.

How she's never been able to rely on anyone, how it's only ever been her against the world. How everyone she's ever loved has let her down or left her in some way.

And then it hits me like a fucking bolt of lightning—she's pushing me away before I can let her down, this is all too real to her. The fact that we're happy. Really fucking happy. My words this morning and now that Sam isn't coming back, it's even more real for her. She could have it all, but she's trained *herself*. To think she doesn't deserve it.

I knock back the rest of my bourbon as I realize just what *my* job is.

To show her how fucking worthy she is of all of it. To show her that when she needs me most I'm going to be there, right there with her, every goddamn second, telling her it will be okay. Even when she's too vulnerable and afraid to tell me she needs me.

A light flickers on in her cabin, letting me know she's still awake, and before I even realize what I'm doing I'm moving down my porch steps in my t-shirt, not even bothering with a coat, as fast as my legs will carry me to her.

I make it to her cabin in less than thirty seconds. I'm just raising my hand to knock, but before I can the door swings open. Ivy's standing before me, her eyes are puffy, there's a tissue in her hand, shoes on her feet. I planned what I would say but when I look at her now, ready to come to me, so fucking beautiful it hurts, all I can manage is, "Baby . . . fuck."

I move into her cabin and pull her small frame into my arms. She doesn't fight me, she clings to me, fisting the back of my shirt.

Her voice is quiet against my chest. "I'm so sorry, Wade. I know you would never want . . . I know you love me. I'm just really scared."

I kiss her head, her face, her arms wrapped up around my neck, any part of her I can get my lips on, and I just breathe her in. I take a moment to brush her hair off her tear-stained face and cradle her cheeks in my hands. I kiss her lips.

"Ivy, I can't even spend four hours away from you. I don't know what you're scared of, I know something is going on in that mind, but all of that can happen while I'm sleeping beside you. Because fuck, I never want to go one night without you."

I pull her in again and whisper in her hair, her sweet sugar-scented hair, the hair I love so much.

"This. Us. This isn't like anything either of us have ever had before. You can take as long as you need, sweetheart, and when you're ready to talk about whatever this is, I'll be here, waiting, every fucking time."

She pulls her face back and looks up into my eyes for a split second.

One tear spills over her cheek before she whispers, "Wade . . . I'm pregnant."

My grip on her tightens involuntarily. Two little words.

Two little words that pull all the available air from my lungs and will forever separate my life into equal parts, the parts before this moment and the rest that is to come.

My breath hitches and I feel like time stands still.

I look into her eyes, and I know as sure as my heart beats that it's no longer gravity holding me firmly to the earth beneath my feet.

It's this woman and the child she carries.

My child.

CHAPTER FIFTY-SEVEN
Ivy

I compare the quiet in this moment to the seconds before a race begins. One moment there are thousands of people waiting with baited breath, you could hear a pin drop it's *that* quiet, the next the bell rings and all hell breaks loose when those gates fly open and the horses are off.

Only the gates never open. Wade stands before me, eyes wide, full of a thousand questions. He pulls me to his chest but he doesn't speak, and after a few seconds he paces into my living room and he drops to the sofa, his legs spread wide as he leans back, one arm resting on his thigh as the other scrubs his face. It's like I just put my cowboy into shock.

In true Ivy fashion, I start to ramble.

"I know I'm asking a lot by telling you this," I start to say, trying not to cry *again*. I can't help it because apparently pregnancy makes me an emotional trainwreck.

"Not because you wouldn't love this baby, Wade, because I know you would. In fact, imagining you with him or her makes my heart physically ache . . ."

He still doesn't speak, he just looks up at me, so I take a seat directly across from him on the coffee table and take his hand.

"The reason I'm asking a lot is because by telling you this, I'm possibly asking you to suffer heartbreak with me, and I'm sorry . . . I'm so sorry . . ." I trail off.

"I know we're new . . . I know this might be the last thing you expected. I even thought about not telling you, keeping it to myself so if it's not meant to be, you wouldn't have to go through this with me, but then I knew. I knew you'd *want* to go through it with me."

Something about those words seems to pull him from his trance. Wade drops to his knees and pulls me into his chest in one quick movement, holding me tight.

"How long have you known this, Ivy? How long have you been dealing with this on your own, sweetheart?" He pulls back and cradles my face as he asks, looking down at me, kissing my lips once before I can answer.

"Just since this morning."

He breathes out a sigh of relief with that.

I tell him the entire story as he listens intently, never once stopping the stroke of my cheek with his thumb. Before I can fully finish speaking, soft kisses meet my forehead, my cheeks, my lips, my shoulders through my hair. Everywhere he can dot kisses, he does, and he doesn't stop, as if the love he gives me has a direct correlation to how my body will accept this pregnancy, and maybe it will?

Wade smiles at me, a real fucking smile, and it's like sunshine breaking through the clouds.

"Don't you dare apologize to me for this . . . because this? This is fucking incredible, a miracle. We don't know what the future holds, but we're in it together, sweetheart . . . no matter what comes," Wade says, and I don't miss how his voice almost breaks when he does.

I breathe out a heavy sigh of relief as he pulls me back in.

"My dad always used to say there are two ways to look at

something, the way you're afraid it will turn out and the way you *hope* it will turn out. We have to stay positive," he whispers in my ear. He pulls back and looks at me again like he just doesn't quite know what to do with me.

It makes me giggle as I watch him, behaving almost like a squirrel, a really *big* squirrel, not able to decide which direction to go in.

"Do you have your own doctor?" he asks, raking a hand through his hair.

"No, my doctor when I left Jellico was Brad's family doctor. And I will go for an ultrasound next Monday. Dr. Evans offered."

"Monday," he repeats, nodding. "A week from now?"

I nod in response.

"I'll be maybe nine or ten weeks then, by the doctor's calculations, and we will be able to hear the heartbeat." I shrug sheepishly, and Wade's eyes snap to mine.

"Heartbeat?"

"Yes . . ." I answer.

Wade kisses me again, takes his large hand and places it over my abdomen, then he moves his face down to talk to my belly and I die a slow death from how fucking adorable it is.

"How can you have a heartbeat, little one? You can't be bigger than a penny in there."

"A bean, actually," I say as Wade's eyes come back to mine. he's still on his knees before me.

He looks back down, and takes in the sight of his inked hand resting against me, and he smirks and whispers the word that covers his child. "*Mine*," he says, then kisses my belly.

I feel my heart shatter, there is no going back. I'm a total goner for this man.

"You get cozy in there, bean. Your mama is your home, and she'll be the best home, you'll see," he whispers before he kisses my stomach again, then rises to kiss my lips.

"I know this is a lot. Are you—"

Wade's mouth comes down on mine, smothering my last words. The kiss is full of all the love he says he has for me. He kisses me like he may never have the chance again, before pulling back and looking into my eyes.

"I don't know whatever made you think for one fucking second that it's you against this world, but it isn't, it's you *and* me. If I haven't made it clear enough for you, Ivy, there's everyone else and then there's us. And this little bean"—he runs his fingers over my abdomen—"is part of us now. Not only am I not going anywhere, if anyone ever tried to keep me from you two, I'd set them on fucking fire to stop them. I will always protect *us*."

Wade looks at me with so much hope in his eyes, it almost does me in. It almost makes me believe this is possible.

"You just give me all your burdens, all your worries, I'll be the steady, for both of you." He kisses my cheek. "I'll do anything you need." A kiss brushes my other cheek. "I'll even share my Pop-Tarts with you."

I smile through my tears and kiss him.

"Besides, I have a feeling maybe we have a shot here," he says.

"Oh yeah?" I ask. "Pretty confident, are you?"

"Fuck yes, this baby is an Ashby," he says as he kisses my neck, his voice commanding.

"And let me guess, you're going to tell me *Ashbys never quit* or something like that?"

He chuckles as his lips find my neck.

"No, baby, we never follow the rules."

I laugh, a real laugh for the first time in what feels like days, as Wade's lips trail my neck to my lips and then he kisses me deeply.

"I never want to miss you like that again—no matter what

happens from here on out, we are in it together," he whispers in my ear, and his deep commanding voice has me clenching my thighs together just from the sound. "Tell me you understand."

I nod just before his lips meet mine.

He pulls his face back.

"That's my good girl," he says, with a kiss that sets me on fire.

I let my hands move through his hair and pull, hard enough to make him suck in a breath between his teeth. The way I missed him for just those few hours settles into my chest; there's not a chance in hell I can ever live without Wade Ashby.

He pulls me up by my wrists and we start to move toward my room, but any hope we have of even making it to my bed fails as Wade's hands roam down my sides, slow and intentional as he presses me into the wall.

CHAPTER FIFTY-EIGHT
Wade

I kiss her with so much need that I lose myself to her completely. To this woman I love more than my own life.

The mother of my child.

Ivy moans as my tongue trails the column of her throat. I nip gently along her sugar-scented skin and I feel her swallow; the need I feel to connect with her right now is so fucking intense it pulses through my blood like a drug.

My hand slides into her shorts, to her already wet pussy, as I spread her thighs apart with my knee, anchoring her against the wall.

"Jesus Christ, Trouble, are you trying to kill me?" I ask as I find out she has no panties on under her little fleece shorts. I slide my middle finger into her, and her pretty mouth pops open in a moan.

"Not a bad way to go," she murmurs into my neck as she whimpers with my touch.

"You have no fucking idea what you do to me . . . is this going to be okay . . . ?" I trail off, asking her permission because fuck, I have no idea what's allowed and what's not with early pregnancy. *But fucking hell, it better be allowed.*

She nods and smiles at me.

"We're good." She giggles as I pull her shorts from her body before her words even leave her mouth. She kicks them off her ankles as she leans up to kiss me and presses her perfect tits into my chest. Everything about her is warm and soft against me. Something about my need now feels more profound, like she's really mine—part of me lives within her now, and I can't explain why but that thought alone makes me feral for her.

I add another finger into her and unbuckle my belt with my other hand, losing my t-shirt as Ivy pulls it over my head. I should take her to her bed, but fuck, I'm too desperate for her to even move. I can take my time later, but right now, I need to just be inside her. I lift her small frame up the wall.

"Wade . . ." she moans, her tongue darting out over her juicy bottom lip as she props one arm up onto my shoulder, pressing her pussy against me. I feel how wet she is and I take my bottom lip between my teeth, sucking in a sharp breath. Her free hand comes down between us and wraps around my hard cock. She runs the tip of me through her soaking pussy, as desperate for me as I am for her, and we both moan into each other's lips; it's the only sound in the quiet space.

Ivy's eyes shoot to mine right as I'm sliding into her, they grow heavy as I stretch her and she's sinking down onto me, and a whimper leaves her lips as the familiar warmth of *us* floods my chest.

"You feel . . . we feel . . ." she tells me, gutting me, because fuck, *I know*.

"So fucking good . . ." I trail off, at a loss for words.

"Yeah, that . . ." She breathes out with the tiniest smile as her fingers move to tangle in my hair.

I move slowly, effortlessly, letting her surround me, letting her take me, like she already has, taken me and made me completely hers. My hands roam her silky skin and I just *feel* with everything in me. I feel like I've never felt before. I look down to where we connect and groan at the sight, watching us move together.

Up . . .

Down . . .

"So beautiful . . ." I say, working her hips with my hands. "I'm fucking home inside you, Ivy," I whisper as I fill her as deeply as I can.

"That's good, Wade," she says in a breathy moan. "Because I never *knew* home until I found you."

My eyes screw shut with the sheer force of her words as my mouth comes crashing down on hers. I groan into her, drinking her in as I feel our bodies work together, mine to withdraw and hers to pull me back in.

She shudders around me, her eyes flutter closed.

"So fucking *mine*. Always." I claim her.

"Yes, baby . . . I'm yours. And you're mine," she chants in a moan as she works herself up and down my cock like she was fucking made for me.

I grip the sides of her body, holding her still as I take over. I fuck into *my* perfect pussy. Ivy threads her fingers tighter through my hair and leans into me, running her lips across my jaw, nipping my skin with her teeth when she reaches my earlobe, my cock pulses inside her with the sting. My hands roam her body as I inch her up the wall with every thrust, her tits bouncing against me. When her hands leave my hair and slide down my arms, biting into my skin, I kiss her deeper. It's messy, chaotic, and perfectly us, as our bodies move in sync against the wall.

She whimpers and starts to clamp down around my cock.

"Wade . . ." she whimpers. "Don't stop."

"Never . . ." I tell her, as I grunt with the pleasure of her begging to come.

"I'm going to . . ." she mumbles as her eyes flutter closed and her head falls forward.

"Come, Ivy. You're fucking stunning when you come, it's the most exquisite sight I've ever seen," I tell her, watching her mouth form into a perfect little O as a deep breathy moan leaves her.

"Fuck yes, Wade . . . more," she whines, and it sets me off as our bodies tangle together and her ankles twist tighter around my waist.

Heat licks across my skin, my head lolls back as I grip her hair, winding my fingers in it. I kiss her with so much fervor her breath catches as I spill myself into her with one more deep thrust, just as she comes all over my cock. My fingers dig into her hips and my free hand is wound in her hair, holding her here. Tight to me. Right where I'd like to keep her forever.

We breathe in unison when it's over and I press my forehead to hers. The connection between us feels unbreakable. It's harmony. It's the fireworks and goddamn harp strings I've seen in the movies as I realize this is it, this is my life forever. She is my purpose. I'm hopelessly hers as long as she'll have me.

"I love you so goddamn much. My everything," I tell her, feeling the need.

A special kind of high that I'm realizing I only get from four words in the entire English language settles in my chest as she whispers, "I love you, Wade."

CHAPTER FIFTY-NINE
Wade

A week from now isn't going to do, and I told Ivy as much last night. There is not a chance I'm making her wait another week to see that everything is okay with our baby. I'll be getting her an appointment before that. I've never really been a praying man, but I will succumb to begging the universe for this baby. I'm willing this to be—the way my mother does. Manifesting everything she wants in life and always telling us to, telling us it works. I never gave it a thought before, kind of thought it was all just bullshit, but right now I'm manifesting the hell out of this because I never knew it until those words left Ivy's lips, but I *want* this. I want it more than anything I've ever wanted in my entire life. I won't even let myself think of a different outcome.

After we went back to my house, *our* house, we talked long into the night about the hows and what-ifs, as we ate our ice cream sundaes and watched *Under Siege*. I could see it in her eyes, the fear of letting this hope register with her. The fear of wanting it. But I'll do it for both of us, because somehow I have a feeling this is the future we're meant for. Her and me and this life. It's the simplest purest form of happiness there is.

By nine a.m., I'm ready to go. I have an appointment set for us with Dr. Miller's practice. She's been our family doctor for thirty years and I trust her with everything I have, including Ivy and our little bean. She agreed to take Ivy's appointment for me today as a favor, but promised to hand Ivy over to the other doctor in her practice so that Ivy can have a doctor of her own. After hearing she was with Brad's doctor for a long time, I felt like that was important. Ivy deserves her own doctor, her own way.

I find Ivy when I'm ready to leave at the barn talking to Haden and Dusty while they clean.

She's got her hair in a big high ponytail and is wearing tights and a UK hoodie. I wonder if she'll always take my breath away the way she does now, and I find myself hoping with everything in me that a round little bump will be filling out that hoodie very soon. I can't fucking wait to see how much more beautiful her body becomes as my child grows in her.

"The boys are going to finish up for you," I say when I approach her. I pull her to me and kiss her. Haden and Dusty don't even really look up but I see a smirk on Haden's face under his hat. He knows to respect me enough not to make any comments. I fill them in on some other things I need completed before Haden leaves to take care of his other responsibilities.

Nash and CeCe round the corner of the barn just as we're saying our goodbyes to the boys.

"Mark July 22nd on your calendar, we just filled in Mama, and we're going to have the best bachelor/bachelorette party in Vegas before that!" CeCe says as she smiles wide at Ivy, giving her a hug when she enters the barn.

"July 22nd? That the big day?" I ask, giving Nash the weird kind of hug/handshake men do when they're happy for each other.

"Yep, gotta plan our wedding around your horse's race schedule, because we want you both there for every part of it and when that racing starts, we don't want to miss any of it."

"Good luck to you, try to keep the bride beast tamed, and whatever you do don't pick anything without asking her." I grin.

"Shut up, I'm not a control freak, Wade," CeCe says.

Nash looks at her and chuckles like she must be joking but when she looks back he stops laughing immediately.

"You are a little bit, but it's an endearing kind of controlling, little firefly," Nash says as he pulls her to him.

CeCe winks at Ivy and shrugs.

She goddamn well knows she's as controlling as I am, but will never admit it.

"I heard Sam isn't coming back, does that mean you're here to stay?" CeCe asks Ivy, but she also looks back up at me for an answer.

"I'm hoping so," Ivy says, and when her eyes meet mine they're full of a secret only the two of us share. "I wouldn't want to go anywhere else," she adds with a shrug and a smile.

As Nash and CeCe scamper off to get their horses ready for a ride, Nash yells around the corner, "Have a nice day, love-birds," before the sound of their snickering fills the air.

"This is going to feel a bit chilly," Dr. Miller says to Ivy as she squirts a gel on Ivy's abdomen. Ivy is a ball of nerves and so the fuck am I.

"Just try to relax and we'll see what we can. I've had a look at your files from your previous doctor. I see his notes on your physicals, but I can't see anything in there at all about your cervix being weak, and he's since passed away so I can't even ask him."

"He was old when I saw him last, it was a couple years ago," Ivy confesses. "I didn't even know he had passed on."

I squeeze her hand as she relives the time in her life I'm sure she'd rather forget.

"God, I have to pee so badly." Ivy giggles as the doctor starts moving the wand with pressure against her abdomen.

Dr. Miller grins. "If you're not far enough along, we'll have to try a transvaginal ultrasound, but we'll try this first. And sorry, it makes it easier for us to see, pushes everything to the forefront if your bladder is full. This won't take long."

We watch as the doctor clicks away on her computer while she maneuvers the wand around.

The room is dead silent save for the constant clicking.

"Just taking some measurements," the doctor tells us, sensing our nerves is my guess.

After what feels like an eternity, she turns the screen around to face us and smiles.

"Seems you're right around eight to nine weeks along. You've got a little mover in there." She laughs as she points to the tiny little figure wiggling all over the screen that actually looks like . . . like a little bean.

"There is the baby's heartbeat, it's good and strong . . . and your lining is plenty thick, everything looks . . . good. I must say, I don't see anything here that would ever make me speculate you couldn't carry this baby to term, Ivy," she says. "But we'll run more tests to be sure."

A sob escapes Ivy's throat as she blows out a breath I think she was holding that whole time, and I smile down at her beside me, then kiss the top of her sweet head.

"What? Wade . . . did I just dream that?"

I chuckle and kiss her lips.

"No, sweetheart, you heard right. Looks like little bean is

already pretty set up in there," I say as I let the most love I've ever felt in my life wash over me.

We stare back at the screen and let ourselves become mesmerized by *our* baby, a perfect little mix of each of us. He or she wiggles around some more before the doctor interrupts us and tells us we'll need to come back for another ultrasound around twelve weeks. She gives Ivy instructions to rest, eat well, avoid stress, and tells us it's all very standard. She says there's no reason Ivy can't keep assisting with training as long as it's from the ground.

Ten minutes later, as Ivy heads off to get dressed, Dr. Miller prints me off three pictures of little bean and hands them to me. I stare down at the most incredible photo I've ever seen, in total awe, before placing that little masterpiece in my inside jacket pocket, right over my heart. *My little bean, I can't wait to be your dad.*

CHAPTER SIXTY
Wade

The drive back to the ranch is quiet. Ivy sits, staring down at the ultrasound photos in her lap, and I see it in her eyes as she moves them back to the window and the sunny countryside.

It's halfway home when she finally speaks. "I think maybe Brad had his doctor lie to me," she says quietly.

I breathe out a sigh and reach across the seat to hold her hand.

I fucking think so too. The caregiver in me wants to shelter her from this. In fact, the caregiver in me wants to drive to fucking Bellingham Ranch and demand answers even if that means beating them out of him, but that's not what Ivy needs right now. Right now, she needs me to be in control while I support her.

"It could be a possibility," I admit. "And even though Dr. Miller didn't say so, I can't shake the feeling she's confused by the whole thing too. The word she used about your ultrasound was *textbook*," I say honestly.

She looks up, nods, then stares out her window into the fields beyond.

"He knew I was thinking of leaving. It all makes sense to me now. He didn't want kids and he knew I did. He only would've done it for control. It's how he abused me. *Control*," she says again quietly, and I could kill this motherfucker for doing this to her.

"If I'm on the pill, and all goes the way it should, he gets what he wants and I don't get pregnant. Looking back, he was even cautious when we were . . . together. I wonder now if that was his way of being extra careful. It would just be a bonus for him if I thought I couldn't get pregnant, if I thought there was something wrong with me—it takes away my hope, then I'm that much more grateful to him for sticking by me when he can make me feel . . . less."

"I never want to hear that from you, even in a hypothetical setting, okay? Ivy, even if you weren't able to carry a baby to term, you would never be *less*. You know that, right?"

She smiles and pats her hand over mine.

"I do know that now. I didn't then."

My jaw flexes as I contemplate my next words.

"You know, if you say the word, I will drive there and get the answers you're looking for, happily." *So fucking happily*.

"I know," she answers simply, keeping her gaze out the window.

"But you don't need me to do that," I tell her firmly.

She looks at me for a split second.

"I don't? I just don't know how to handle this realization," she says, looking wounded. The pain I see in her eyes as she lets three years, the possibility of being lied to and feeling like she could never carry a child register with her—that look on her face, it almost destroys me.

I pull the truck over to the side of the highway and unbuckle my seatbelt, getting as close as I can to her. I grip the sides of her face, and kiss her softly on her perfect lips.

"No, sweetheart, you don't need me to handle this for you

352

because *you* are strong enough to tell me what you need in order to find peace with this, and I'll do whatever that is. If you never want to talk about it again, we'll never talk about it again. If you decide you want to somehow prove this is something Brad did, I will spend every last goddamn cent I have and every resource I can muster helping you do it."

"I know." She nods as a tear slides down her cheek.

"You said to me once, you don't need me to come to your rescue, and you were right. You don't, I don't need to be your hero, you're already your own fucking hero," I tell her as I kiss her again and place my hand over my child, letting the life radiate against my palm. "You left, you took control of your life, it led you here, to me, right where you're supposed to be," I remind her.

"I love you, Wade." She sniffs, looks down at my hand on her stomach and then back out the window. "We can't go back, only forward. Take me home."

I kiss her lips again and marvel at her fucking strength. I'm amazed by it. I'm in fucking awe.

"Whatever you want, sweetheart. I'm at your mercy."

As I bring her into my arms, into her place, and whisper to her how much I love her, I know that nothing matters but this. Her and I and our little bean.

Ivy is right—we can't go back, only forward, and you know what? There isn't a person on earth I'd rather leave the world behind with.

CHAPTER SIXTY-ONE

Ivy

"Stay still, if you're going to continue to grope me the entire time, your hair isn't going to be straight."

"Worth it," Wade says, not missing a beat, as he slides his hands up the back of my jeans.

Not a good idea when I'm standing over him with a pair of shears in my hand.

I bend down and kiss him on the lips and smile.

"You're the one that asked for this trim, remember? In your *dad era* now?" I say, recounting his words from this morning, when he came back to our Florida hotel room with new scissors and a comb and told me I simply *had to* cut his hair for him.

"I am, but fuck, that was before you were standing in front of me with your ass so close to my hands and your perfect tits in my face," he grunts, like it's painful torture I'm putting him through, which makes me smile in return.

"So greedy, Chief," I tell him, shaking my head.

"For you, always," he murmurs, as his lips come painfully close to my breasts through my shirt.

"We have to leave for the track in a half hour, if you want me to do this you have to stop trying to get my clothes off," I scold.

Wade clears his throat and straightens out, as still as a statue. My own perfect Roman godlike statue, as I run my fingers through the wavy, unkempt strands of his hair, following close behind with a comb, then my scissors. I'm not going to say he isn't tempting me with his freshly shaven, perfectly scented skin so close to my lips. It's not without effort that I don't climb into his lap, he's mouthwatering. But if I do that right now, he'll have really lopsided hair for the biggest moment in Angel's racing career so far.

The *start* of her career, actually.

"Okay, I'll be good. But if I do, that means I get to be as bad as fuck when Angel gets her gate card. The moment we walk through that door later. Deal?"

I giggle as he slides his hand up the inside of my thigh and tempts me even more.

"Deal . . ."

"You have to breathe." Wade rubs my shoulder ninety minutes later and the current I feel every time he touches me races through my blood.

I look up at him and smile.

"I know, it's just, I'm so fucking nervous," I blurt. I tap my feet, clad in Ginger's boots, and they kick the dust up under them in the Sarasota sun.

This track is unlike anything I've ever seen in the professional horse racing world. It is a practice course run as an exact replica of how a race will be for a horse. No detail spared, as owners and trainers want no surprises on their horse's first race day. The McKechnie Brothers Training Center has the market cornered for this, and if I didn't know any better I'd feel like I was at a real race. Angel's Wings has had two recorded workouts in the last three days, breezing or running close to her fastest, her best time being half a mile in fifty-four seconds.

The last two days have been a blur. I've been distracted, to say the least, trying to let everything sink in—this pregnancy, our future, my past, all of it. Thankfully the team Wade has provided me over the last three months to help train has really held the reins for me and done their best work with Angel leading up to this race.

I'm still not used to the idea I'm going to be a mother. But that news comes with a lot of self-reflection. I instantly felt like I had been lied to the moment I saw my little bean thriving inside me. Call it mother's intuition. For three years, I thought I couldn't have this, I just took what Brad's doctor told me at face value, accepting that he was honest. To hear our baby has just as good a shot as any of making it into this world was the greatest news I could ever hear, but I still felt I needed to mourn for the years in which I'd lost that hope—and for the future I never knew I could have. The future that is now a real possibility thanks to this incredible man beside me. Grinning down at me now like he has all the confidence in the world.

"There's no need to be nervous. Trouble, you've trained her well. She's got this, let's go watch for her." His brow furrows. "And walk beside me, I need to stop staring at your ass in that dress or I'm going to have to pull you into a hallway somewhere before this gate test and race even starts," he whispers in my ear, sending heat instantly to my core. It's already hot in Florida, so the return of my sundresses even for a couple of days is welcome compared to the early February cold in Kentucky. Wade isn't helping me cool down now looking at me the way he does when he wants me. A sight I'll never get over seeing.

We just manage to make it to the saddling paddock when

Rowan and Angel come into view as the announcer talks about Angel's bloodline, her chances and myself as her trainer.

I take a moment to greet her and nuzzle her, to connect with her in all the chaos to say, *"You've got this, baby girl."*

Rowan nods at us, his dark eyes always smiling. "We're as ready as we're ever going to be. One gate card coming up." He winks, and although I smile back, I think I might throw up.

Wade chuckles beside me.

"Come on, little mama, let's go sit. Can't do anything for her down here in the dirt."

I nod and follow him up to the owner's boxes, counting my breaths as I go.

We've just taken our places as the announcer's voice booms through the speakers. He talks about the horses in contention, their aspirations and the winners in their bloodlines as the evaluators, assistants and vet check Angel, her tack and Rowan. All taking notes that decide her fate.

A few minutes seem like an eternity until I see the evaluator give the thumbs up to the recorder, and I scream a little internal scream of joy as Wade rests a big hand on my thigh. So far so good, all she's got to do now is sprint right out of the gate and the rest is gravy.

That moment of silence takes over the small crowd as all the horses ready. I close my eyes and wait to hear the bell. The moment I do, I let them spring open to find the gates flying back. Just as she's been trained to do, Angel takes off like a bat out of hell.

"And they're off in the McKechnie Brothers Quarter Annual Simulation," the announcer begins as I grip Wade's hand on my thigh so tight my knuckles whiten instantly.

"Front runner *Cosmic Pines* trails up the center.

"Maine's Footprint has stumbled, and here comes newcomer *Angel's Wings* out toward *Cosmic Pines*, who's right there along with Tulsa Oklahoma's *Next Level* at the rail."

"Definitely gonna throw up," I say to no one in particular as Wade chuckles again and removes his hand to rub my back.

"You're so fucking cute when you're nervous."

"It's *Angel's Wings* quickly challenging up the inside. *Cosmic Pines* to take the lead as they round the first turn."

The announcer tells us Angel is neck and neck coming into the first turn.

"Yes! Baby! Go!" I yell.

"It's *Maine's Footprint* in third and the favored *Cosmic Pines* between *Angel's Wings* and *Next Level* as they make this run toward the half mile pole."

The horses stay in sync as they round the corner.

"Now, Ro, now," I say under my breath, as I watch Rowan shift his weight, signaling Angel just like we've trained at the exact moment, and I watch her pull through the corner and switch leads.

"Hells yes, baby," I say quietly as I pump a fist when Angel and Rowan start gaining on the others. Then I scream because there's not a shot in hell I can hold it in.

"*Angel's Wings* has taken the lead as *Cosmic Pines* now moves toward the quarter pole and drifts to the outside. *Footprint* has dropped back from his early efforts as they straighten away down the track. *Angel's Wings* is in front after three-quarters in just one minute."

I watch the track with baited breath. "You're turning blue. Breathe, sweetheart," Wade whispers to me.

Right, breathing is good. I blow out a breath but don't say a word, I just nod.

"*Angel's Wings* leads *Cosmic Pines* by two lengths now charging hard on the outside . . ."

Everything goes hazy.

"It's *Angel's Wings* still finding her way as they come down toward the final sixteenth with *Footprint* back and forth." The announcer becomes more animated in the last seconds of the race.

"*Angel's Wings* is leading home, *Cosmic Pines* has dropped to third and that is it! *Angel's Wings* has won it by a length!"

I am out of my seat jumping up and down and yelling, tears streaming down my face. It may only be a practice but it feels like the biggest win of my professional life as I jump into Wade's arms. He pulls me close, whispering he loves me, and I know just like he says, I'm right where I'm supposed to be.

CHAPTER SIXTY-TWO
Wade

> Everyone needs to come to the big house tonight for dinner, I have an announcement.

NASH

> It really never occurs to you that we might be busy?

> It's important and you're only ever four places, the ranch, the bar, Olympia or trailing behind my sister like a lost puppy.

COLE

> I'll be there, but I won't have Mabes with me, Gemma actually showed up today, second week in a row. It's a fucking miracle.

NASH

> I trail your sister maybe but I'm more like a German Shepherd, a big one, strong, there's nothing puppy-like about me.

> Whatever gets you through the day, bud

COLE

Are we supposed to act surprised when you tell us this sneaking around with your horse trainer is serious?

> That's not why I want to see you all. Just wait for fuck sakes

I grin. They think they're so smart, I will be surprising them.

NASH

Did he just openly admit it's serious?

COLE

Finally, fuck

NASH

About damn time

> We're allowed to have privacy in this family, you both should try it some time. Who I get into bed with at the end of the day doesn't need to be scribed on the fucking ranch wall.

CECE

Ooh I love announcements. We'll be there. I'm leaving the office soon.

CECE

@Nash I love you baby, but you definitely do follow me around like a puppy. Sorry not sorry.

> As I said.

NASH

A German Shepherd puppy. A mean one

CECE

Yes, of course baby

NASH

And wild, can't be trained.

CECE

The wildest.

This conversation has gone off the rails as usual.

NASH

Wade?

I'm going to regret this but what?

NASH

Remember the time you told me if a woman ties you up in knots to shoot you where you stand?

Fuck off.

NASH

No need to be hostile. Just wanted to say welcome to the club ☺

I put my phone in my pocket and make my way to my bedroom, where Ivy is finishing up on the phone with her mom, who two and a half weeks into rehab is doing excellent. Thriving with the treatment, in the coordinator's words. I gather by the way she's crying that Ivy has just told her the news about little bean. We just attended our twelve-week ultrasound and everything looks perfect, in the words of Ivy's new doctor.

We've been making space in my cabin for all of her things, which aren't many, just what she brought with her to Silver Pines

She hangs up the phone and sniffs,

"I'm never not crying these days ... especially when, Wade ... I *know*."

I look down at her, and swipe a tear from her cheek, genuinely not knowing what she is talking about, but that happens a lot when she's in a rambling kind of mood.

"Know?" I ask as I grab my keys off the dresser and put them in my pocket.

"I know. I asked my mom to get the name of the donor program that helped with her treatment, so I could send them a thank you," she says as I move in front of her and kiss the top of her head.

Shit. I never really intended for her to find that out.

I push her hair off her shoulder and use my thumb to rub her cheek as she looks up into my eyes.

"You're totally busted, Mr. Ashby," she says with a knowing look. "Angel's Wings Foundation?" she adds.

I nod. "Yes, it was technically created by the ranch and we didn't do it alone. Nash helped too. When I told him I was going to do it, he wanted to go in together. As far as the name . . . not only did it seem fitting, we had to think of it on very short notice."

"Why didn't you tell me?" she asks, not that she seems upset.

"Would you have accepted it? Or would you have told me you could take care of yourself?"

Her eyes narrow just a little and then a smile breaks out over her pretty lips.

"You just think you know me so well."

I chuckle and use one finger to tip her chin up to me and kiss her lips, feeling the tiny swell of her pressing into me as I hug her. I've never seen anything more beautiful than Ivy, her cheeks rosy, her belly beginning to grow with my child. I look at her with the other secret I'm harboring, and graze my knuckles down her cheekbone.

"News for you, Trouble, I do. And now it is a legitimate

foundation that will help more people for years to come in your mother's situation."

"Thank you so much," she says as she hugs me. "Thank you for caring for my family, Wade."

"Your mother is my family now too." I kiss her lips again just because I can't get enough of her as my phone buzzes in my pocket. I pull it out and check it, blowing out a breath.

"Ready for this? They're all on their way," I say to her.

She kisses me back, and takes a deep breath.

"Well then, let's go. Game face, Chief."

"You owe me twenty bucks." Nash grins at Cole as the room explodes with our news.

Ginger jumps out of her seat and hugs Ivy as she squeals.

"A little grumpy version of Wade, I can't wait. Do you think he'll come out scowling?" she asks.

I look down at her, my brows knotted in annoyance.

"Just like that, look at this picture, Ivy." Ginger frames my face as best she can from her height. "This is what you'll be birthing in exactly six months." She giggles as she nudges me with her elbow.

"Congrats, Daddy Wade." Olivia smiles.

"I can't wait to be an aunt again," CeCe gushes, hugging me.

I hug her back, marveling at the difference a year makes, both of us happy after starting over.

"Love looks good on you, Sarge," she says as Nash comes to her side.

"Ditto," I say back, pulling on her ponytail. "Now, if we could just get captain fuckboy to settle down."

We both look at Cole hugging Ivy as he says congratulations.

"Not a chance," CeCe giggles, shaking her head.

"You'll have a built-in babysitter in Mabel, that's for sure," Cole says as he makes his way over to me, shakes my hand then pulls me in for a little brotherly squeeze.

My mother follows suit.

"One more little voice to call me Nana? It doesn't get any better than that," she says as she takes her hug from me. She puts a hand on my face and looks up at me. "Your pa would be so happy you've found your person." Then she leans in. "Told ya you'd have boys down by the river someday."

"Or girls, but yes you did." I grin.

"I'm always right." She winks, heading into the kitchen to grab champagne and cake for us.

"And you remind us every chance you get, Mama," Cole calls out as she goes.

"You're next." CeCe wags her finger at Cole, and he scoffs.

"I've already got the only girl I need. I've got Mabes."

"And you always have Lexington," Ginger adds and giggles.

Everyone in earshot turns to her.

"What? A whole town is hard to give up, is all I'm saying," Ginger says innocently.

"Jealous?" Cole grins, turning his hat backward, then sits and leans back in his chair, folding his arms across his chest.

Ginger stalls for a minute and then retorts with a little more fire than warranted.

"Bite your tongue, Cole Ashby. I'm a lady." She crosses her arms and looks directly at him.

"Probably for the best anyway, he's a little afraid of you, he's told me." Nash grins.

Cole gives him a heated look so I chime in, "True story, he's definitely afraid of you."

"Fuck you both," Cole says at the same time as Ginger says, "He should be."

"I just have one question," Pop speaks up over all of us from the other side of the room.

We all turn to face him.

"Did anyone break the news to Wade that he's no longer the boss? Cause if not, I want to do it."

"I'm still the boss," I say immediately and with confidence, which for some reason makes everyone in my family laugh.

I look down at Ivy, who is giggling with them.

"I mean, are you really?" she asks, biting her bottom lip.

"You can be the boss some of the time," I say as I lean down to whisper to her as if I'm not totally under her spell. Which I am, every minute of every day.

"Whatever gets you through the day, bud," she says, laughing, giving me two thumbs up.

Yep, she's definitely one of them, and I don't mind one fucking bit.

"Come with me, we're leaving early," I say in Ivy's ear when dinner is done and she's thanked Nash for about the tenth time for what he did to help her mother.

"I have to help clean up."

"No, you don't. I played the pregnancy card, you're tired, it's been a long day."

Ivy grins, hand on her hip, defiant. "I have no intention of playing a pregnancy card. I'd be happy to clean up."

"I know you would, but I have a surprise for you and I need to make sure I have time to make you come at least twice before you send me into the kitchen to slave over whatever kind of ice cream sundae you and little bean feel like tonight."

She grins and it lights up my fucking soul.

"You're not lying," she admits as she shrugs, giving in.

I know I've piqued her curiosity—Ivy's eyes gleam with excitement.

"Do I have to change before this surprise?" She looks down at her tights and hoodie and I shake my head.

"No, we're not going far." I chuckle.

"Wade Ashby, what are you up to?" she asks as I set her shoes in front of her.

"Just walk with me, Trouble," I say, then I lead her out the door, hoping she'll always follow.

CHAPTER SIXTY-THREE

Ivy

I have no idea what we're doing, but the smug look Wade is wearing both scares me and excites me. The air is warm when we step outside, like spring is threatening to break through, and Wade holds my hand and pulls me down the gravel road toward his cabin. I've been moving what small amount of things I have into it over the last week, but we aren't going to get married right now, I told him one thing at a time.

First, I'm going to get used to becoming a mama and get these boys moving on prepping Angel for her juvenile season, then I'll think about becoming a wife.

I expect the surprise is at *our* house, and that is where we're going until he stops in front of Spirit cabin's steps.

He gestures a hand to the front door and I blink, not a clue in the world what he has to show me here. I know the contractors just finished working on it yesterday because Wade talked about paying them.

"Why don't you go in, take a look around," he says, and as his wide jaw flexes his dimples appear on full display, and I know something is up.

I narrow my eyes at him and creep up the old steps. An old

wicker sofa has been redone and sits on the covered porch with new outdoor cushions looking out to Sugarland Mountain. There's the soft sound of wind chimes in the cool, late winter breeze.

The old wood door has been redone and has a new black handle that I turn. I push through it to enter the tiny foyer. The scent of citrus and vanilla hits me, mixed with a hint of fresh paint.

Spirit is the smallest cabin on the property: the kitchen and living room is one open space with a small eating area in between. An old leather sofa and loveseat sits in front of the stone fireplace, throw pillows are perfectly placed and cozy blankets hang over each end. The coffee table is empty save for a large tray that holds the remotes for the TV and copies of *Magnolia Journal*. The windows are large and like in every other cabin at Silver Pines, the interior boasts warm log walls. New stainless steel appliances grace the tiny kitchen.

I make my way to the back of the house to the bedroom and attached bathroom, and find they've both been redone too. What looks to be a freshly made bed and old antique dresser grace the tiny bedroom. The bathroom is clean and efficient, not unlike Wade's, with a wide subway-tiled shower and new vanity. It's beautiful, but . . .

"Wade, I don't . . . understand why we're here."

He moves to stand in front of me and places a hand on each of my shoulders.

"I thought this would be a good place for your mama when she's done her treatment. What better chance does she have for success than right here on the ranch with us."

A large hand slides down to my low belly, almost covering the tiny bump completely that you'd never see with the naked eye.

I stand in front of him, shocked. Shocked as I quickly realize that he started working on this the day my mother went into the hospital, like there was never a question in his mind. Shocked that he loves me so much he would accept my mother with open arms—her flaws, her struggles and all. But I shouldn't be shocked.

This is who Wade is; he doesn't show it to many people but he has the most beautiful heart.

"If she agrees, we can gather her things and bring them here for her, bring her home here right from treatment. Start completely new in a place with no demons."

"I love you so much, Wade. Are you sure?"

"Of course. I thought she could maybe even work here a bit when she's ready; you said she used to assist your father, and surely there are some courses she can take to brush up on her skills, but I don't want to get ahead of myself. And this way she can be with you and her grandbaby."

"It's just . . . so much. Mama Jo knows about this?"

Wade kisses me on my lips, softly, gently.

"It was her idea." He grins. "She knows her grief; she's hoping they can become friends."

He kisses me as I stand there before him, still at a loss for words because this, this, is above and beyond my wildest dreams.

"Look, I know you Spencers can take care of yourselves, but we Ashbys take care of each other. And one day, as soon as you'll let me, I'll make you an Ashby too, unless you've changed your mind? We could get married right now?" he asks me for the tenth time in two weeks.

I reach up on my tiptoes and kiss him.

"So greedy, Chief," I tell him as he kisses me back and looks down at me with all the love I could ever ask for.

"For you, always," he says as he pulls my face to his, kissing my lips.

Warmth floods my chest and I just know. Wade is the

epitome. He's everything I've ever wanted. Everything I never knew I needed.

My dad's words play through my mind. *Where there's a will, there's a way.* I can't wait to find my way through life with this gorgeous bossy rancher that sets my soul on fire.

I think I'll keep him.

CHAPTER SIXTY-FOUR
Wade

Fourteen months later—the first Saturday in May

"Motherfucking . . . *Christ*, Ivy," I grunt as I slide my cock into her mouth, gripping her hair tight under her fancy pale blue fascinator hat.

"There's something so poetic about you choking on my cock like a dirty little slut with a two-thousand-dollar dress pooled around your knees."

She moans around me as she looks up under her hat, and I almost spill down her throat at the sight.

In my defense, there wasn't a shot in hell she would make it through the day in her derby dress without me sneaking her off somewhere to fuck her, especially when it was a baby-free drive and all she did was listen to her fucking book porn for almost the entire two hours. It's not my thing, but fuck, it's not like I can ignore it. It just so happens I couldn't even make it to the start of the race before pulling her into the bathroom and locking the door behind us.

"Fuck, Trouble, you're desperate for it, aren't you?" My hand moves in the back of her hair as I set my pace, sliding it further down to hold her jaw while she takes me deep.

She pulls her lips back and grins at me.

"Yes, baby, but only because you ask me so nicely."

My head tips back in a groan as my cock hits the back of her throat, and she's sputtering around me, deeper and deeper as she pulls me in.

"*Fuck,* Ivy." I see her fingers meet her clit as her other hand grips my ass, nails gnashing against my skin. I groan, a rumble from my chest that sounds like a growl, as I forget we need to be quiet so no one hears us. I pull her up by her arms, so goddamn desperate to fuck.

My lips meld to hers in a scorching kiss as my fingers find her pebbled nipples. Somehow her body drives me even more wild now than it did before she was pregnant—she's curvier and softer and I can't fucking get enough of her.

Ivy moans and her head falls back as my mouth finds each of her breasts and my thick middle finger finds her swollen clit.

I slide her arousal all over her, circling her with it, then pull my fingers to my mouth, sucking them clean. "So fucking sweet," I tell her before returning two to her pussy as she whimpers around me. I take my sweet time to drive her fucking crazy, even though the last thing we have in this shiny bathroom is time.

Fuck it, I'm taking it anyway.

"Wade, please?" she begs, and I grin, looking down at her from my full height. I fucking love it when she begs, I live for it.

"Look at you, Ivy, so pretty begging for my cock. You couldn't even make it one afternoon. But you know what?"

I grab her hand and wrap her fingers around my shaft. She moans when she feels how fucking hard I am.

"I can't make it either, so put my cock into that pretty pussy before I lose my fucking mind."

Her lips trail my shoulder and she moves them up to my ear as she whispers, "Don't you know, Wade? Acting this desperate for you, it's just my war tactic."

The little smirk she's wearing is enough to break me. I thrust into her so fucking deep her head falls back and rests against the mirror and her eyes flutter closed.

I drag myself almost all the way back out as I grip her thigh, before I push into her slowly, holding the friction she so desperately begs me for hostage while I continue fucking into her almost all the way, but never quite giving her what she needs. Her heels dig into my ass as I move, and it only makes me want to torture her more.

"Wade . . . I need . . . fuck . . ."

"What's that, baby? You finished acting like a little brat?"

"Please . . ."

"Use your words, Ivy. Tell me *exactly* what you want and maybe I'll give it to you."

Of course I know what she needs, but I want her words, they drive me mad.

"Fuck me harder, Wade . . . deeper."

"Say please, Ivy."

Her violet eyes flash to mine, glassy, spent and a little defiant, full of fire. These are the moments that she wants me so badly she'll do anything I ask, and I crave them like the ocean craves the shore. Her painted lips turn up in a tiny smile before she says, "Please, Wade, fuck my desperate pussy harder, *sir*."

Her sentence ends in a moan, and I'm done for. Who am I fucking kidding? Every ounce of power and control I think I hold belongs to her. It has for the last eighteen months.

I pull out of her and drop her to the ground. Spinning her around, I press her up against the sink, using my knee to spread her legs apart, and when she grips the countertop and looks at me in the mirror, her beauty stuns me.

"Was that nice enough for you, Chief?"

Fucking Christ, this woman.

I growl as I bite her neck and flip her dress up over her plump ass, using my thumbs to spread it apart before I sheath myself in her in one profound thrust, and she moans and falls back against my chest. I use my hand to pull her head up, gripping her by her throat as I hold her tight and whisper into her ear.

"Don't close your eyes, you'll miss my favorite show. The one where you fall apart on my cock." I squeeze her throat tighter; she whimpers as I feel her hot pussy clamping down around me, but she does what I ask and keeps her eyes on us in the mirror.

So she'll never forget who owns her, my hand around her throat and the glaring word *mine* reminds her. My other hand comes down to allow my middle finger to find her clit, and I give it a pinch and she cries out.

"Good girl, such a pretty sight."

"I am your good girl, Wade . . ." she whines as I piston into her, dropping my lips to her sweat-slick upper back, feeling my own high closing in with her acceptance of my praise; it barrels up my spine. Her pussy tightens even more around me as I give her needy clit the attention it craves.

"When you come, I come, Ivy," I say to her. I dip my head down to kiss her shoulder, her neck.

"Well, this may take a *long* time then." She gives me the look that tells me she's about to fuck with me. So I push her the only way I can, with my words and my fingers strumming against her clit.

"Nah, I think you're ready now. Tell me, Ivy. Tell *me* when *I* can come," I say, giving her the spark of control she loves.

Ivy reaches her arms back around my neck and pulls my head closer, looking right at me in the mirror. Her direct eye contact when she moans frenzies my movements in a way that reminds me I can't fucking get enough of her and I'm never in control around her.

"You can come now, Wade," she says with her eyes on mine, and I come, just like this. I spill into her as I pinch her clit and she comes with me, biting her bottom lip to keep from alerting everyone in the hallway to what we're doing in here.

The music that plays in the bathroom suddenly seems a lot louder as we still for a moment, coming down.

Ivy leans into the mirror while I'm still inside her and runs her ring finger over her still perfectly painted bottom lip.

"Fucking book porn," I whisper as I kiss her shoulder, chuckling.

"Got me what I wanted though." She winks, as she straightens the tulle on her hat. "And I didn't even mess up my makeup."

God, I fucking love her.

Ten minutes later, we're put back together and in the winner's circle suites where our entire family is, each of them passing around and vying for the attention of our little violet-eyed, blonde-haired baby girl, Billi Grace. Billi is already a handful at eight months old, crawling everywhere and pushing her mama to her limits.

Ivy takes it all in stride; nothing ruffles her. Hell, she trained Angel, and attended most of her prep races with me for five months, with Billi either on her hip or close by somewhere with Mama Jo or Glenda. Nothing slows Ivy down, and watching her blossom into motherhood has been the greatest gift of my lifetime so far.

"She miss her daddy?" I ask CeCe, who was minding Billi while Ivy and I went downstairs "to check on our documentation." They all know what we were up to, I'm sure, but I don't give one flying fuck, new parents have to take what they can get.

CeCe nods. "Seems so. Mama Jo says she slept in the back with Mabel all the way here."

Mabel drove up with my mama and they just had to bring Billi with them, because where Billi is, Mabel is. CeCe holds the second love of my life out to me and I bring my sweet baby to my chest, breathing in her perfect scent atop her wispy blonde curls.

CeCe shifts in her seat, her face contorting just a little. She is very uncomfortable in the May heat, seven months pregnant with her and Nash's first baby. If I thought Nash was her puppy before, it doesn't even come close to comparing how he is now.

I kiss Billi's chubby cheek as she pats a small hand to my face and mutters, "Da da da da da."

My heart fills with so much love, I feel like I can't take it. There are times I may even be more of a goner for this little girl than I am for her mama. I'm a total girl dad and I'm not afraid to say it to whoever will listen, which makes Cole and Nash utter snide little comments about how soft I've gone more often than not, but I couldn't give one flying fuck.

The crowd gets a little more animated as the horses and their jockeys start to load into the starting gates. Ivy comes to me where I'm holding Billi in the quietest area in our suite as the horses load. All the work we've gone through over the last year and a half to train Angel is coming to a head, and it's so surreal that this is all happening.

I look down at my beautiful girls and smile, pulling Ivy into me closer. I can feel my dad's pride from wherever he is in the universe now. Ivy takes Billi from me, and we wait not so patiently for the horses to be ready. I kiss both of them in the final seconds before the bell. Every single thing that Ivy and I have gone through, the people who've betrayed us, the people who let us down, the people we've lost and every choice we've made, have all brought us to this moment. To the kind of love I never would've dared to hope for before Ivy.

I tip my head down to her and whisper, "It doesn't matter

what happens today. It isn't about the finish line, it's about the journey, and fuck, we're nailing the journey, Trouble."

She smiles up at me and kisses me.

"We sure are, Chief."

As the bell rings and the horses fly out of the gates, I'm not even thinking about winning a race because I've already won.

Ivy Spencer is mine, and I'm the luckiest man alive because she landed on my doorstep.

And you know what?

Finders keepers.

EPILOGUE

Ivy

Nine years later

"And don't be afraid to straighten Scarlett up on the approach. You're the boss, Bean, and make sure your helmet is tight. Have Mama check it."

"I know, Dad. I've got this," Billi says as I finish braiding her long bronze-colored hair down her back.

"You know the course, don't be nervous," he tells her, sounding a little nervous himself.

I smile and suppress a little giggle. Wade's probably told her this at least ten times today alone, but she keeps letting him tell her like it's the first because she's a complete daddy's girl, and his only girl at that.

"What are you laughing at over there, Trouble?" he asks as I secure Billi's hair with a band.

"Go get your helmet so Daddy can watch us check it," I tell Billi. "And grab a couple diapers on your way down."

I stand before him and wrap my arms up around his shoulders, letting my fingers rest at the nape of his neck.

"I'm just sayin' is all, anyone ever tell you you're bossy, Wade Ashby?"

"I can think of a few times I've been told I'm bossy." He leans forward. "And a few times you haven't minded."

The heat of the blush he gives me even after ten years and three kids creeps up my cheeks. He kisses my forehead, then bends down to grab our eleven-month-old son River out of his high chair.

"Stop talking like that, Mr. Ashby, we can't be late today. A girl's first jumping competition is important."

Wade grunts. "Wish she'd chosen something a little less dangerous."

I laugh as I pack up River's diaper bag and toss some toys and snacks in for our five-year-old son, Wyatt. Lord knows it takes a lot to keep that boy entertained. He doesn't sit still for more than thirty seconds most days, which makes chasing him around the ranch Wade's full-time job.

Twenty minutes later, we're rushing because when are you not when you have three kids?

"Let's go, y'all, we're already running late to pick up Grammie from her cabin," I tell them as I usher them to the door to get their shoes on.

My mother has been sober ten years this fall and still lives on the ranch. She even met a nice man who owns the hardware store in town, and she started crocheting again, selling custom blankets as a little side business.

Getting my mother back has been the most incredible gift. She and Mama Jo are the best grandmothers we could ever ask to have for our babies, and they have become the closest of friends.

We head out the door of the home we built the summer Billi turned four. Finding out we were pregnant with Wyatt meant Bluegrass cabin would no longer do the trick, so we carved out an acre near the river and built a modest four-bedroom house on it, then we finally got married in front of all the people we love at the river when Wyatt was two. The other end of the river on

Silver Pine's property now houses the guest cabins that Wade added five years ago, to allow for retreats and team-building camps. I don't know how we've managed to do it and stay sane half the time.

After Angel's Wings came in fifth in the derby, we made one more go of it the following year with a direct descendant of Wyatt Sr.'s late horse Rising River and placed second.

Derby dreams gave way to Wade's dreams of adding a hospitality division to Silver Pines, and I spent some years working with the women's abuse shelter in town, hoping I could make a difference in someone's life with my story. There are moments I feel overwhelmed, but mostly I feel abundantly blessed, especially today as Billi heads to her first U-10 competition of the season. Of course, the entire Ashby clan will be there with bells on to support.

The drive from Silver Pines to Almost Heaven Farms in Midway, Kentucky, takes us about an hour, as my mama reads books to the younger two kids in the back of our SUV. When we get there and manage to exit the vehicle, I see CeCe first, holding the hands of two of the three Carter kids and wearing the third. Ruby and Billi instantly pair up when they see each other, being only one year apart; they've always been close. They start heading to go find Scarlett. Quiet, curious three-year-old little Rex wanders behind CeCe picking grass in the beautiful Kentucky sunshine.

"How'd that go, getting the whole crew out the door this early?" CeCe asks, smiling as I approach her and rub little six-month-old Rourie's blonde head. She's nestled right up to her mama, oblivious to the outside world, just snoozing the morning away.

"Probably the same as it went for you." I grin.

"Shitshow," we both say at the same time and laugh.

We maneuver slowly, with Rex toddling in front of us to the

seating area by the rails, where the whole family is waiting to take in the competition.

"It is hot enough to fry an egg on the sidewalk," Papa Dean says as we take our seats. I pass him River. River is his little buddy, and for some reason the bond between an eighty-seven-year-old and our almost one-year-old is strong. He bounces River on his lap as River reaches his chubby arms up and smiles at his Great-Pop. I'll never understand how this old man stays so strong. Wade is convinced he'll outlive us all.

"Great-Pop, you can't fry an egg on the sidewalk," Wyatt challenges him, like it's the craziest thing he's ever heard.

"Don't test him, he'll show you. You'll be left cleaning egg off the driveway, trust me," Cole says to Wyatt, grinning.

"Uncle Cole, are you telling the truth?"

"It's true, I've seen it," Nash adds, as he picks up Rex.

"One year when it was real hot, the power went out and we took a cast iron pan right out to the driveway, cooked us up some breakfast," Wade says to Wyatt.

I smile up at him as the tiniest threads of salt in his pepper hair shine in the summer sun. Somehow, ten years later and he's even hotter, however the hell that makes sense.

"Cool! Can we do it tomorrow?" Wyatt asks.

Jo looks up from her conversation with my mama and Olivia to scold them all and tell them, "*she ain't cleaning up their mess.*"

Mabel's boyfriend stops paying attention to her for all of three seconds to pipe up from beside her and say that he'll bring some bacon. Cole grunts, not taking Mabel's decision to start dating her high school's quarterback very well.

I roll my eyes as all four men look at each other, shrug and say, "Sure!" at almost the same time.

Mama Jo and I lock eyes over their heads and she mouths to me, "Men."

I smile back. Yes, men. Particularly *Ashby men*, always getting into mischief.

The show begins and we watch as best we can while we all wrangle our respective kids. Passing them off to each other and chatting until, finally, Billi's name is called.

"Let's go, darlin', you got the boots, wear 'em well," Ginger calls out to Billi, who grins back from her place atop of her horse Scarlett.

Ginger taps her ivory boots and in the ring Billi taps the matching riding ones Ginger bought her, then gives her a thumbs up.

I stand beside Wade as we watch our daughter start her round, her pretty little face furrowed in concentration as she rides, completing her jumps with perfect precision.

"Yes, baby! That's my girl!" Wade mutters under his breath when Billi clears the hardest jump like it was no trouble at all. As she rides out of the ring after her round she smiles up at us, and my heart swells in my chest.

"She's fiery like her mama," Wade says in my ear when he leans down.

I look up and smile at the love of my life. "And stubborn like her daddy," I add.

He kisses me a little too long for a family event.

"Mmm, you smell so fucking good. How many more hours till we're alone, baby?" he whispers.

"Too many, but you know, I thought I saw a closet in the main hall somewhere," I offer, gesturing to the farm's main building as his lips meet my cheek.

"Don't fucking tempt me, Trouble," he growls low in my ear.

"It really doesn't take much to convince me, you know. All you have to do if you can't wait one more second is beg." I look up at him and smile sweetly.

He chuckles, as if he'll never give in, but I don't miss the need in his hands as he grips my waist tight.

As my heart begins to accelerate under his touch, he dips his lips down, and just before they meet mine I hear it: "Mercy."

the end ... sort of.

Did you really think I'd hint at it and not give it to you?
WADE TAKES ALL, BONUS CHAPTER

Turn the page to read . . .

Wade

I glance up at Ivy across the table in the ballroom of the Grayburg Autograph Hotel.

Red strapless dress that hugs every ample curve she offers; her dewy, silky skin is glowing under the dim lights, reminding me how fucking soft she is from her head right down to her heel-clad feet.

Her raven hair cascades down her shoulders in waves, but the kicker? Crimson fucking lips. The kind of color that gives me the urge to smear it across her face as I'm driving into her tight little pussy from behind.

I clear my throat and force myself to listen to the chatter between Ivy and Stacy Atkins, the wife of Timothy Atkins, a Breeders' Cup horse owner and the proud owner of a derby horse racing alongside Angel in a month.

Ivy's in her element. This is where she thrives. She'll talk to everyone all night long. Not only will she talk to them, she'll charm the hell out of them.

Me? This is the last thing I wanted to do tonight. This night is unprecedented. A night where we are alone. For the last seven and a half months since Billi was born, we've never left her.

We've always brought my or Ivy's mother to help, and brought Billi along with us. This is the first night I have Ivy all to myself, and I wanted every spare second we weren't at Angel's last pre-derby race to be alone.

Preferably holed up in the hotel room fucking her brains out, but this dinner isn't one we could get out of. This is the owners' dinner at Keeneland, and although Angel technically secured enough points to enter the derby almost two months ago, this was the last race. The race that officially solidified her entry. So in turn, it's the last official dinner, and Ivy was adamant Silver Pines shouldn't miss it.

So I made Ivy a deal.

I would go to her dinner, with fucking bells on, but then I'll fuck her any way I want afterwards. So, right before she slipped that silky red dress over her head, I slipped the last plug into her ass for her. I've been readying her all day, changing them out to a bigger size every few hours. Just the vision of the little round, jewel-tipped end was almost enough to make me take her all three times we changed them today.

What I wasn't prepared for was how this would affect *me*.

Something about watching her talk to the room like the prim and proper head trainer of Silver Pines Ranch, just knowing the largest-size plug is buried in her ass has been keeping me rock hard all fucking night, and desperate for her to the point of no return.

I'm one sassy look from her away from taking her into the nearest closet and driving my cock home.

I reach into my jacket and slide my finger over the smooth remote button in my pocket. I see her flinch in her seat and her eyes snap to mine instantly, then to my hand in my pocket, then back to my eyes, understanding.

Didn't know that it vibrated, did you, baby?

I lean back in my chair and take a sip of my bourbon,

smirking at her, keeping her gaze when I know her pussy is growing wetter with every passing second.

The thing about my girl is, she never gives in. She's a fucking champ, so she just averts her eyes from mine and continues her conversation like the plug isn't pulsating a slow torture in her under that fancy dress.

It takes everything in me to make it through the next two hours, switching between turning her on and off as I see fit and conversing with a mixed bag of elite horse owners, trainers and industry suppliers.

Through it all, Ivy keeps her composure. Only staring at me once—okay, maybe twice—with the heated look that says, *I'm really fucking pissed at you but I still want to fuck you* all at the same time.

"Ready to get out of here?" I whisper at her side during a break in conversation. We've drifted to a standing table near a wall of windows overlooking downtown. "I know you must be fucking soaking wet by now, and I'm willing to bet you're even downright desperate for my cock."

Ivy's violet eyes flash in defiance. Yep, she's still pissed at me for toying with her, literally, all through dinner.

"I don't know, Wade. I'm feeling really social tonight. I think I could stay here for at least another hour," she says as she pats my chest. "So . . . patience, baby."

Fuck me.

And then she saunters off to chat with two women I've never even seen before, and for some reason, the amount of fucking people that Ivy needs to talk to after that is astronomical.

Of course, everyone and their brother wants to tell her how well Angel's Wings did today and how they look forward to seeing her race the derby.

All I can do is stand just behind her, loosening my tie because fuck, is it hot in here?

I watch her like a fool as the soft fabric of her dress clings to her perfect ass. I imagine hiking it up later and burying myself there, or running my hand up the tiny slit up her leg that every now and then reveals her silky thigh.

One hour and twenty-eight fucking minutes and another shot of bourbon later, I'm leaning against the bar, *still* waiting.

Ivy's eyes lift to mine from across the room, where she's baiting me by twirling her long waves around her fingers as she talks to yet another person I've never met.

She's full of that cocky sass that sets my body on fire when she comes over to me, casually running a finger down the center of her dress between her breasts.

"I feel like I've been waiting on you all night. Are you finally ready?" she asks me as a low growl erupts from my chest.

I grab her hand the moment she's close enough.

"We're leaving. Now."

"Who's desperate now, Chief?" She giggles.

I lean down to whisper my next words in her ear, but be sure to say them in a tone that tells her I'm dead serious.

"Ivy, if I don't get you out of here right this second, I'm going to end up lifting you onto this bar and fucking you ten ways from Sunday in front of the AQTA president and this entire fucking room."

She whimpers. I fucking love it.

I drop my empty bourbon glass to the bartop and usher her out of the ballroom to the hallway, pinning her up against the wall, pressing the up button for the elevator that will take us to our room with one hand, while I grip the side of her face with the other. My mouth comes crashing down on hers as she lets the tiniest moan escape her lips. It's quiet here. Not another soul in the hallway, thank Christ. Although I don't know that if someone were here it would've stopped me anyway.

We're only fourteen floors away from me taking what's mine.

"You should know by now, testing my limits isn't a smart thing to do, Trouble."

Ivy grins into my lips.

"Payback is a bitch, and there's just something about seeing my big rugged man so desperate and needy that makes me so wet, Wade," Ivy whispers as she trails a finger down my jaw, just to drive me wild.

I grip her by the waist and pull her even tighter, and a moan leaves her lips when I press my hardened cock into her.

"That so?" I ask as her eyes threaten to flutter closed and a soft blush covers her cheeks.

"Well . . . slide your hand up my dress and find out," she retorts.

Fucking hell.

The elevator bell dings and I push her into it, pressing the button for our floor before pinning her against the wall as the doors close. I do just what she tells me to, sliding my hand to the apex of her thighs, taking her silky dress with it. Any hope I had of making it up to our room before I slide my fingers into her dies as I find her soaked and wearing no fucking panties. I stand in front of her to block her from any camera in the elevator.

"Fucking bratty little tease," I growl as she reaches into my coat pocket and turns the vibrator on.

"Who's the tease? You didn't tell me it vibrated. You've been holding out on me?" She moans as her head tips back with her words.

Christ. Didn't fucking expect that.

I absorb her whimpers while I kiss her. I can't fucking get enough of her. My tongue trails the column of her exposed throat. I bite down on her sugar-scented skin and feel her swallow, and it turns me instantly into a man crazed. My middle finger slides into her soaking pussy as I spread her thighs apart with my knee, anchoring her against the elevator wall.

"Four more floors," she moans breathlessly, I assume watching the numbers behind me.

Fuck, I made her wear that plug so I could drive *her* fucking mad, and the damn thing had the opposite effect.

It drove *me* mad.

She slides my hands down her sides as the elevator stops at our floor, panting, soaked, waiting. And I'm about to blow in my fucking three-piece suit like a teenager after prom with absolutely zero self-control.

The second we make it into the room, I'm picking her up, crushing my lips to hers as I plunder her mouth in a searing kiss. I squeeze her ass in my hands and take her bottom lip between my teeth as the plug hums inside her. Her moans grow louder as she rocks into my hard-as-fuck cock, threatening to come already.

I continue to move toward the bed, no idea how I find it while never breaking the kiss, I just do. I drop her down on all fours and hike her ass up, sliding her dress up over it just like I wanted. I find the remote in my inside pocket and shut the vibration off for just a moment. My greedy girl whimpers when I do, which makes me grin. I thrust two fingers into her soaking pussy and she cries out. Whining my name and begging me to fill her.

"You're so fucking beautiful, Ivy, dripping down your thighs with my fingers in your cunt and this little jewel in your ass."

I pull my clothes from my body, then push each of her shoes off of her feet and slide my hands up the backs of her thighs as I kiss her from the inside of her ankles up. I turn the vibrator to its lowest setting, not enough to make her come, just enough to torture her, and she deserves every damn second.

"You thought it would be a good idea to tease me? Now I'm going to tease you. You can come, but I'm going to sink my cock into every hole you have," I tell her as I bury my face in her dripping cunt, kneading the head of the purple jewel in her ass as I do, and she goes fucking ballistic, pressing her pussy into my face, begging to come on my tongue in a matter of moments, but I'm a depraved motherfucker so I don't let her, not yet.

I tease her, flicking my tongue over her clit and massaging the jewel in her as she cries out. I smirk against her pussy and just as her legs begin to shake and she's about to fall apart, I gently kiss her clit and move away. She lets out a frustrated little grunt as I flip her over so she's sitting on the edge of the bed, practically riding it as the vibration torments her even further. Her head falls back and her lips pop open slightly.

"You're so fucking beautiful when you're desperate, Ivy," I tell her as I slide my thumb across her jaw.

"Wade," she moans as her fingers move to her clit and I just take in the fucking work of art in front of me. I stroke my cock as she thrusts a finger into her tight little pussy.

Using my thumb, I smear her crimson lipstick across her cheek, then I pop her mouth open and drop my cock on her tongue.

I groan at the sight. *Fucking beautiful.*

"Now, you can play with your pussy, Ivy, and come while I fuck your mouth."

I thrust between her lips as she whimpers.

Her fiery eyes stay on mine as she takes me deep in one fluid movement, my cock hitting the back of her throat. She gags but doesn't stop.

Fuck.

Every time I think I have the goddamn upper hand she does something like this. She looks up at me through those lashes as she comes apart all over her fingers. Her moans vibrate down my shaft and I threaten to spill down her throat on the spot. She's a fucking beautiful enigma. *My* beautiful enigma.

She pulls my cock out of her mouth and swirls her tongue on the underside, running it upward and licking precum from my tip.

"I have nothing but time. How about you, Wade, how long can you hold out before you need to come?" she asks.

Stubborn little fucking—

"I mean, here I am waiting so patiently for you to fill my ass with your cock, so how much longer can you wait to take it, baby?"

Heat licks up my spine with just her words, and my head lolls back as her tongue works its magic against me.

"Wade, you can come right now if you want. Come all over my pretty red dress, or right here." She points to her collarbone. "You know I'm always up for new jewelry," she taunts.

"Jesus, woman," I bite out.

Fuck, it takes superhuman strength to stop myself from coming all over her. I pull this little minx up by her arms and drop my mouth to hers.

"On your knees. Now," I command into her lips as I tear at the zipper to free her from her dress. I want to see all of her.

"Thought you'd never ask, baby," she purrs as she crawls naked across the bed, looking over her shoulder at me, and that's it, it's all I can take and this little brat fucking knows it. This sight is enough to make any man snap.

Hell, it's enough to make any man that isn't desensitized to Ivy spill all over this hotel room floor. It hits me as I feast my eyes on her. She just got exactly what she wanted from me without even really trying.

I hit the button to turn up the vibration and drive my cock into her pussy with a force that makes her pretty little mouth pop open but no sound leaves it, I can feel the faint hum of the vibrator against my cock and holy fuck, it takes everything I have to keep it together.

"Fuck, Ivy, this pussy, so wet for me, so fucking tight. So fucking mine," I tell her as I drive into her, giving her no gentle ease; I'm on a mission to take, to claim everything she has.

Moments pass like this, with me teasing her clit every time I thrust deeply into her, and she begins to clamp down around my cock.

I grip her hips tight, stopping my movement, preventing her from coming again.

She tries to rock against me but I don't let her. Another adorable frustrated little grunt makes me smirk. I use my free hand to turn the little jewel, pulling it slightly out and pushing it back in before loosening it free from her and tossing it aside.

I want more.

I need more.

Now.

"Thought you had all kinds of time, sweetheart? What happened to that?" I ask her, as I reach around and pinch her clit. She yelps as I pull myself free of her pussy.

I kiss her shoulder and chuckle as she whimpers at the loss of me. Her tiny, needy sounds electrify me.

"I was so close, Wade," she whines.

"Aww, baby, I know, but this is a teaching moment, and I know you love your lessons long and suffering," I tell her as I hike her body up on the bed even more and her shoulders slump into the mattress. She molds just the way I want, so pliable under my hands, so soft.

"Such a good fucking girl, Ivy," I tell her as I run my hands over the vines on her skin.

Her soaking cunt provides me with almost all the lube I need as I spread a generous amount from her pussy up to the cleft of her ass, then I slide my cock all over her arousal. She shudders, and I spit just above her ass for good measure. As it drips over her, just that sight alone sends me into a tailspin.

Knowing I'm finally taking the last virgin hole she has and making her completely mine.

I use one hand to strum her clit, the other to toy with the place I'm about to claim.

"Beg," I tell her.

She whimpers as I lose the tip of my thumb to her little rose-bud, slow enough to make it feel good for her.

"I need you. I don't think I can wait one more second," she breathes out in a desperate sort of moan that sends a carnal thrill throughout my body.

"More," I tell her as I kiss her spine and her upper back.

"Wade, please . . . mercy," she begs again as she exhales a shaky breath.

A growl rips from my chest. She knows with that word, I've lost it, she instantly wins and my fight to maintain control is over.

I see a hint of a smirk on her lips. Again, I'm giving her what she wants, everything she does is by design.

I spread her ass wider and slide my cock against her entrance there, sinking just the tip into her.

Fucking hell.

I continue to fuck her pussy with my fingers as she rocks back into me, getting into a rhythm that leaves me desperate to fill her like she's never been filled as her ass takes me deeper whenever she rocks back. She wants my control as much as I want hers—it's a game of give-and-take. Pushing the power back and forth, and it's a fucking high I'm addicted to. *She's* a high I'm addicted to.

She *moans* and my cock pulses with the sound. I've never been so fucking hard.

"Atta girl," I praise as I push into her deeper. "Tell me how much you love the feeling of my cock buried deep in your ass."

"I fucking love it," she moans.

My head lolls back and I groan, a raw sound that comes

from such a dark place in me as I strive to control myself with this feeling. All of her.

Ivy is panting, ready to come. I use her desire to sink further into her.

"Please, Wade, let me come. I want to so badly," she whines.

Don't I fucking know it.

"Deep breath," I tell her.

She shudders around me as I finally lose the last few inches of my cock to her. I'm not gentle about it but we both groan. I'm straddling the line of caring for her and fucking consuming her. I slide both my hands up and grip her hips.

"This is . . . *fuck, I have no words*," I breathe out.

She whines and quivers in a way that tells me she's just as desperate for me as I am her.

"Look at you, my good girl . . . listening so well while your ass welcomes my cock home."

She lets out a garbled moan as I pull out slightly and drive back into her, and she begs me again, for nothing and everything all at once.

"So full, Wade . . . it's so much," she moans as I thrust two fingers into her tight pussy and bury myself in her ass to the hilt.

Fuck me, I've never, ever felt anything like her before.

"Wade?" she asks.

"Yes, baby?" I grit out.

"Don't hold back."

"*Never . . .*" I growl.

Her words fuel me to claim her and she fucking knows it. I begin to move in and out of her, knowing this isn't going to last, it's a part of her where only I've been and that thought sends heat rippling through my body like wildfire as she drips down my hand. I feel her pussy clamp down around my fingers while she chases her high.

I wind my hand in her hair for leverage as she takes over for me at her pussy. The sounds of her fingers moving in and out of her and her moans fill the space around us as I close my eyes and revel in her, dragging myself out of her almost all the way. I look down to where we are connected and almost lose it.

"This feeling you have right now, Ivy?" I query as I push back into her so slowly, almost too goddamn slowly, but I want to savor this.

"Yes . . ." she trails off as her fingers work her pussy.

"This is the feeling of your ass taking me so fucking well. Just a perfect little slut for my cock," I bite out, nearly driving myself insane with the torturous pace as I fuck her.

She whines as my control slips, and I pull out and thrust back into her, not holding back this time. She cries out in broken moans.

"Fuuuck . . ." I groan and draw the word out.

I'm unable to go slow any longer. I pull her up by her hair, burying my lips against her slick upper back. I fuck her ass like it isn't her first time, because I know that's what she wants.

If she wanted a man that went easy on her, she wouldn't be with me.

I slide my hand to her throat and feel it work in a moan as my balls tighten. I feel it everywhere the moment she comes with my cock deep in her ass just like I wanted. The sounds she makes are strangled, desperate, almost animalistic, and holy fuck it sends me over the edge. I'm coming with a beastlike growl. Every part of me tightens and releases repeatedly as I spill into her, the force causing a type of static to cloud my vision. I come for what seems like forever, muttering her name, and tell her how pretty she is taking my cock as the still of her breath brings me back to the moment.

I stay just like that for a beat as I try to calm my racing heart before I know I'll be picking her up to carry her tired body to the bath. When I pull myself from her, I smile down at her and kiss her sweaty forehead.

"Every part of you is mine now, Ivy. I knew you'd love it," I tell her.

She kisses my chin.

"And I knew I'd break you faster than you'd break me." She smiles sweetly up at me and I chuckle.

"Fucking always, Trouble," I admit. "Fucking *always*."

the end ... really.

Acknowledgments

To my amazing husband for accepting his place as number two, always taking care of me as I write endlessly, as well as accepting Wade Ashby into our family because my mind has been filled day in and day out with him for months.

To my own amazing Not Angels, most especially Tabitha, my gifted Alpha reader – I could not have made this book (or any books) what they are without you, your mind (which is my mind) and your sparkle. To Ada, Wren, Katie and Rose. We talk about it all, no matter the time of day, and the laughter keeps me sane. Thank you for being with me through this process. You're stuck with me now, through every dirty-talking moment from here on out (early morning great butt debates and all). All the incredible suggestions, laughs and "ah-ha" moments that made this book the absolute best it could be. Cathryn and Caroline, thank you for making my book into an actual beautiful book and not just a really long, confusing word document.

Thank you to Jess Muscio with Penguin Random House UK as well as Shauna and Alicia at Dell New York for reading and believing in *Holding the Reins* and the entire Silver Pines series. All this greatness, the joy of bringing Silver Pines to a wider audience, is happening because you both decided to pick up my book. There are no words to express my gratitude.

To you, my ARC readers and all readers alike, thank you. I may not do it better than anyone else, but I pour my whole soul into these stories and every comment, like, share, edit and mention is noticed and loved wholeheartedly.

To my only Papa, who is no longer earthside but lives on through Papa Dean and Wyatt. You will always be the best grandfather a girl could ask for. Great advice giver, euchre player extraordinaire, Howdy-spewing, duct-tape-wielding, inappropriate-joke-telling, hand-holding, bear of a man. I love you with my whole heart and miss your mind daily. I am honoured you chose me to be with you for your last breath. I will forever tap my bourbon on the table for you and utter your sayings.

To Sasha for consulting on this book and being so open and poignant with her fertility struggles, I hope I did the rollercoaster of emotions justice; and to my very dear friend Carrie for sharing the turmoil that is emotional abuse. Both of your journeys are inspiring, empowering, and need to be heard. I love you both. Ivy's story is for you. To celebrate everything you've both overcome, learned and taken control of. Always remember I love you.

Thank you to (in no particular order):
Ashley Bell Harris – Springway Farms, Montana
Elise Noble – Danshire Ranch, NS, Canada
Peter R Smith – Rightway Farms, NM
Harris Ranch, Coalinga, CA

IMAGE CREDITS